The Shadow Blades
The Chosen Blood

By
Ryan Foley

An
RMF Enterprises
Production

For **Jeremy**
Because there were times when you believed
in me more than I believed in myself,

For **Alex, Jason, & Lauren**
Still the three most important characters I ever created,

...and, once again, for
Katy Perry
because obviously.

Chapter 1

The dark hull of the *Castella Mare* sliced through the crystal blue waters of the southern ocean. The magnificent sailing ship featured three masts, a narrow frame, an elevated forecastle, and an even taller stern palace. Positioned under the bow spirit was the ship's figurehead – a beautifully carved wooden representation of a hippocampus. The magical beast featured the upper body of a horse and the lower body of a fish. The great seahorse looked as if it were rearing from its position under the bow spirit. The ship's triangular lateen sails were unfurled, secured in position, and billowed by the stiff wind filling her canvas.

Yet, as the ship cut her swath through the ocean, the waves were relatively calm. The storm of wind pushing the vessel along dispersed and flittered away to nothingness once the ship passed.

The slightest hints of land could be seen on the western horizon. The grand peninsula of the southern kingdoms dipped in and out of view. But the *Castella Mare* had the ocean to herself on the bright and shining day.

Two weeks prior, the crew had been hastily assembled under orders from the ship's owner for an emergency run to the southern lands from the wizarding kingdom of Incanterra. Food and other supplies were gathered quickly. The stevedores running the docks in Highstone Harbor had their palms greased to get the boat moved to the top of the loading queue. Dockworkers were smoothly tipped to ensure the cargo was given priority and a little extra care. And while none of the manual laborers discussed it openly, there were enough whispers amongst them. They knew who owned the *Castella Mare*. It was uncertain if the crew worked harder to gain her favor or avoid her wrath.

Regardless of the reason, the quickly assembled crew – sixteen strong – had their ship ready to sail in record time. And yet, given the speed of the journey and the relative quietness of the sail, the crew agreed this was one of the easiest and fastest runs they had ever made.

The boat was staffed. The captain ran a tight ship, along with his first mate who doubled as his navigator. The ship utilized two helmsmen who alternated shifts. In addition to his regular duties managing the ship, the quartermaster served as the doctor and the barber. There were two boatswains, four windlasses to run the sails, and four mariners for the rigging. The crew was rounded out by the cook who doubled as the ship's mother.

There were no pages, no apprentices, and no cabin boys. Sailors were staffing double duties in some positions. The *Castella Mare* was running light. Ordinarily, such a skeleton crew would have drawn grumbles of discontent.

However, the run had been quiet and easy, improving morale. Then things were even more joyous when they learned wages for a full ship's complement were being distributed amongst the hands. Jokes were made, asking what would happen to their share of the wages if certain mariners or other crewies went missing.

Their speed was bolstered by a magical contraption brought on board by the ship's passengers. None of the sailors understood how it worked but every twelve hours one of the passengers would insert gold coins into the glyph-covered metal box to power its magical energy. And that magical energy filled the boat's sails with a consistent wind. It was one of the great advantages of sailing with a wizard.

So when any of the five passengers were topside or if they were passed on the lower decks, they were met with gestures of respect and even admiration. Every member of the well-paid crew was happy to have them on board.

On the boat's stern palace stood one of these infamous passengers. Cinder Fireborne sat under a light canopy to shield her from the high sun. Her long, flame-fire-dyed red hair trailed behind her in the wind. The rogue had exchanged her Incanterran fashions for flowing, billowy attire to keep her cool and comfortable in the heat of the southern kingdoms. Yet, she still wore her leather belts and carried her signature black dagger in a black sheath. Those in the know understood the importance of the sigil as the black weapon represented her allegiance to the Incanterran crime family known as the Shadow Blades.

Staying out of the way to let the crewmembers work, Cinder glanced west in the direction of the distant landmass threatening to emerge from beyond the horizon. Her thoughts were cut short as a fellow passenger made his way up onto the stern palace.

The same as Cinder, Valos Ironblade was also dressed in lighter, flowing attire to help fend off the heat. And also the same as Cinder, Valos kept his black dagger clearly on display. Tall and lean, Valos was undeniably handsome. He looked permanently cursed with afternoon shadow and more than a sprinkling of both gray and stark white was starting to creep through his dark hair, concentrating on his temples and streaking across his light beard.

With a slight wobble to his walk, Valos clutched the rail and made his way under the canopy and to the plush seating along the *Mare*'s aft railing. He looked over at Cinder with frustration etching his handsome features. "This is the absolute wrong way to introduce me to the natives of Malinsula. It is not fair. It is not just. And it is absolutely heinous how the gods are torturing me."

"Afraid seasickness doesn't look good on you?" Cinder asked with a smile.

"How is a man supposed to be smooth and appealing when he can't hold down a meal?" Valos asked. "I caught a glimpse of myself in my cabin mirror. I think my skin is permanently stained green. And my cheeks look sunken in! How did I get roped into this again? I could have stayed back, overseen the reconstruction of the Shadow's Edge."

"But then you are dodging the coppers. Hiding out in attics. But even more importantly, you would have missed out on the bronze-skinned natives and their ivory hair."

"They better be trotting up three at a time to remotely balance this ledger," he grumbled. "And they better have nipples that taste like butterscotch or something."

Cinder did her best to stifle a laugh. "We all agreed to an even split of the profits from this little venture. So that means we are all in this together. Would it be fair for me to travel all this way by my lonesome only to open a portal when I arrived? You would deny me the pleasure of your company for these last two weeks along with your witty banter? Although, I would have censored the comments about the butterscotch. We all have different standards I suppose."

"I am not completely boorish. I suppose I could have mentioned my other favorite parts of the womanly playground," Valos said as he leaned his head back against the ship's wood railing.

"Thank Niverana for those small favors."

"Still, I suppose I can *stomach* this – see what I did there?"

"Yes, very droll," Cinder rolled her eyes.

"What is one more day?" Valos continued. "If the navigator's charting is accurate – and I am told he always is – we should arrive on the shores of Malinsula by midmeal tomorrow."

"Excellent."

Valos leaned up and noted the helmsman standing by the large spoked steering wheel for the ship. The wheel had been tied off with smooth, silken lines to hold the vessel's course and the sailor had his nose buried in a small tome. "Ho, Sailor," Valos called. "Your navigator. He any good?"

The sailor looked up from his reading. "The best, sire."

"He knows all his numbers and his calculations? If he says we are going to be there, we will be there?"

"You could bet parts of your anatomy on it."

"Pretty stellar praise," Cinder said.

"Okay, so high sun tomorrow, I will be back on solid ground for a good spell," Valos said with a determined tone. "Good spell. That's two for two."

Cinder shook her head as Valos proceeded to lightly jab his elbow into her ribs. "How much longer am I cooped up on this boat with you?" she asked.

"Have you not been paying attention? The navigator said midmeal tomorrow."

"Yeah, if you keep these jokes up, that meal won't come fast enough."

The rumbling of thunder suddenly echoed across the water despite barely a cloud in the sky. The helmsman looked up from his reading and glanced to the west and the dotting of the landmass peeking over the horizon. "That gods-forsaken land," the sailor grumbled. "The farther we stay away from that cursed kingdom the better."

Getting to his feet and using the rigging to steady himself, Valos gazed out towards the western horizon. "That's Ignaterra?"

"Aye," the helmsman replied. "Those rumbles you hear are echoes of the Thunderfire Mountains. Tall black peaks spew molten rock into the air. Ash chokes the land. Nothing grows there. That place is cursed. We have to skirt it. We round the eastern horn to get to Malinsula but the captain will give her a wide berth. If you sail too close, starving beasts on leathery wings will swoop in. Some say they look like living gargoyles the artists put on temples. But they are big and strong enough to carry off a full-sized man."

Valos turned to look back at Cinder. "I know you set up your tracking stones along the coasts. Maybe we skip this one? Better safe than sorry."

Cinder surveyed the landscape with a critical eye. "It would be a shame to be right there and not bury a stone on the coast. Maybe we wait for the night. See how it looks. Use the cover of darkness so we don't endanger the crew."

The two looked out on the cursed land, listening to the rumbles of faraway thunder.

Chapter 2

Tall and broad-shouldered compared to most young ladies of her age, the young, blonde woman named Kynna moved carefully through the paved streets of the capital city of Incanterra. She was dressed in suitable summer fashions for the Northeast District within the grand city.

While a definite step down from the haughty, affluent Northwest District with its manses and grand estates, the Northeast District was filled with working-class citizens who had elevated their stature enough to afford accommodations north of the Queen's High Way bisecting the city.

Kynna was dressed in a black skirt, a blouse cinched at the waist by a corset, and a pair of scuffed shoes. With the sun high in the sky, the summer heat had started to bake the streets and the wide, cement sidewalks, so the young lady had removed her traveling cloak, opting to drape it over her arm.

She was fashionable enough to look as if she belonged in the district but not so elaborate to stand out. A tall, healthy, comely woman with flowing blonde hair would often warrant a second glance or a nod of approval from a male pedestrian but Kynna wanted to be seen and then quickly forgotten. Her goal was to blend in amongst the populace and she was succeeding.

If she was asked, she would introduce herself as Kynna Summerwind. The surname certainly sounded like one of the countless floating around in the grand metropolis. Few would have given it a second thought. She used her fictitious name and her commoner appearance to hide the truth. She had long discarded her grass green and copper-trimmed wizardly robes that would have connected her to the Lu'Scion magicians.

Kynna's real name was Kynna'Fyir Lu'Scion of the Lu'Scion dynasty.

Having broken into her twenties, the young woman was elevated above the status of the novices but not quite ready to join the ranks known as the adepts. She had established her magic enough to serve the Lu'Scion dynasty's interests down in the city proper. Kynna'Fyir was one of the many Lu'Scion magicians who provided the wealthy with illusory trips inside the mind. The thrilling experience was how the famed illusionists secured a significant portion of their earnings. As such, she was working down in the city when the echoing rumbles of the earthquake washed across the capital.

Like so many Incanterran citizens and the wizards trapped down below when the calamity occurred, Kynna could only look up in horror as the great wizarding isle of Sorceria – suspended one thousand feet above the city – shook, trembled, and then ultimately split in two.

The only saving grace for the city was that the broken and shattered foundations of the isle remained trapped within the magical well that reversed the pull of gravity. It was the only thing that kept massive boulders and hunks of the broken isle from raining down on the helpless population below. Splintered and shattered, the isle hung above the great city as a message. During the initial burst of the cataclysm, none of the population knew how or why it had occurred.

Communication from the isle was completely cut off. The enchanted floating ferries shipping those back and forth between the city and the island were suspended. In a panic, many citizens sought to flee.

Incanterra was a prized location to live because of her high perimeter walls that squared off the entire city and protected the citizens from the hideous monsters that prowled the wildlands. Since the city's founding three centuries past, no marching army had ever breached the high walls. Those defenses to keep the people safe had become their undoing.

Kynna noted this as she looked over at one of the few gates allowing movement in and out of the city. The gateway in her line of sight was sealed off with a dark magical wall that rippled with a swirling of red and black energy. The field was transparent and yet could not be seen through. The energy obfuscated the world beyond. With the city's entire population trapped inside, any reasonable observer would ask why efforts had not been made to break down the energy field.

But the answer to that question was why Kynna carried a bag of sundries. It was a convincing enough ruse to justify her moving about the streets. She had the whole scenario rehearsed to an art form. It involved a sick grandfather. A debilitating case of gout. Necessities. And even a small cheesecloth sachet of herbs for a special tea to help ease the pain. It would be enough if she was stopped and questioned. She had even practiced her pleading in the mirror. "Please, sire. He is in so much pain. Just let me take this to him. I beg you."

The forces that would question her were the same that kept insurgents from breaking down the barriers sealing off the city. There were three different regiments to be avoided.

First were the Knights of the Imperial Circle. They wore white vestments almost resembling those of the priests of Tadorin the All-Father. They also wore conical hoods and white, featureless alabaster masks. Yet their attitudes and demeanors were anything but holy. They were drunk on the power of knowing their side had "won." Thankfully, they were often easily avoided.

The second was the feared Necromangians. A new wizard faction, separate from the elitist houses on the famed floating isle of Sorceria, this new house had seemingly taken over the entire city in one fell swoop. They were also easily identified, as they stood out in their blood-red wizard robes trimmed with black silk. Yet their numbers were small. The Necromangians were not nearly as feared as their army was.

The army had emerged from beneath the city, circumventing the high walls. And it was this army that was feared the most by every Incanterran citizen. The Necromangian army consisted of the living dead. Animated skeletons marched in the city streets. Some were armored. Others were simply animated bones. Stripped of all flesh and organs, they were fearsome to behold.

As a large contingent of rank-and-files skeletons made their way down the city avenue, Kynna stepped up onto the sidewalk and tried to squeeze as tightly as she could against the towering building.

The skeletons were outfitted in field plate armor and each carried a longsword in hand. They marched with surgical precision and in perfect unison, the hard soles of their leather boots echoing down the avenue.

Kynna found herself standing next to another Incanterran citizen. The young woman had dark, black hair and naturally tanned skin. Kynna guessed she had to have ancestors from the kingdom of Selvaterra to the south. Many of those with Selvaterran heritage had come to Incanterra in search of a better life. Huddled together, the two women watched the skeletons march past, hoping none of them would turn and look in their direction with their perpetual grins and the twin pinpricks of red light floating where their eyeballs had once been.

"I can't stand those things," the Selvaterran said. "Mindless monsters. They are so… unnerving."

"I don't know if 'mindless' is the right description," Kynna said. "The way they follow their master's orders, I think they understand plenty."

"Soulless then."

"Soulless. Yes. That is the better descriptor."

"In more ways than one," the Selvaterran lass spat. "I saw them clearing out one of the apartment buildings yesterday. You are right. They follow their orders. I mean to the letter. Women were begging and pleading. The children were crying. Those things have been stripped of their souls. There was no bargaining. They were immune to pleading and tears."

"There has to be a reason why they drape them in armor," Kynna questioned with her eyes narrowing and an edge to her voice. "I bet a well-placed hammer strike knocks a skull off a stack of neckbones."

The click-clack of wheels began echoing down the street, drawing the attention of pedestrians, passersby, and other citizens. The feared Necromangians had not limited their magic to only human forms. A pair of skeletal horses pulled a great wagon behind them. The wagon was piloted by two Knights of the Imperial Circle. Situated atop the flatbed with its solid wheels and heavy axles were the iron lattices of a great iron cage.

Inside were Incanterran citizens. Unlike during the early stages of the occupation, these were not the infirmed, the sick, the elderly, or those needing isolation in the city's sanitariums. These citizens looked positively normal. Those housed within the cages could easily have been swapped out with the citizens walking the streets, a fact not lost on those who still held their precious freedom.

Kynna and the Selvaterran woman looked at each other nervously, neither knowing what to say. The Selvaterran glanced at the bundle of sundries Kynna was carrying. "Supplies?"

"For my grandfather," Kynna said, melting into her well-practiced lie. "He is sick. His foot is swollen and he has difficulty walking. I am bringing these foodstuffs to him."

"Perhaps, I could walk with you? Where are you headed?"

"Away from those marching skeletons and away from anything that will put me in one of those wagon cages."

"Then we should head south," the Selvaterran said as she looked about the streets to gain her bearings. "If we avoid Trader's Cross and get to the southern part of the district, the dark presence is not as prominent."

Despite the late-day heat, Kynna slipped her traveling cloak over her shoulders and pulled up the hood to help her thwart off attention. The secret Lu'Scion hefted the weight of the sundries and gave her new companion a nod.

"Kynna Summerwind," the hidden magician said, smartly avoiding the use of her true surname.

"Sabella Shorewater," the Selvaterran replied.

"Well, Sabella Shorewater," Kynna said, "let us head south then."

Chapter 3

Thade Skystone watched intently as Mema Honeygold went about her work. The brigand stood almost six and a half feet in height and often had to duck to avoid the support beams in the *Castella Mare*'s galley. With his mass and muscles, working in the cramped kitchen was difficult yet it would have taken a team of hippogriffs to haul him away from Lady Honeygold's side.

While the aching in her fingers acted up more often than not and the weariness of her age was starting to grind on her, the grandmotherly dame was still a master at her craft. She pulled the last tray of the oat and walnut muffins from the galley's oven. The aroma alone made Thade's head swoon.

"This will tide them over until dinner time," Lady Honeygold said confidently. "Mariners love their bellies full above anything else."

"Then why do I hear so many stories about rum and fermented drinks?" Thade asked.

"Safer to store on long journeys," the ship's mother replied. "Well, it *was* until you and your group came along with those fancy wizard water chalices. Don't fool yourself, my good lad. An army marches on its stomach. A navy is no different. Crews will tolerate long hours, squalls, and cramped quarters... but if you feed them well, they work hard. Sailors are a hearty bunch but they are happiest when they are fed. I have yet to find a group of people who aren't happier if their bellies are full. You would be wise to remember that in your line of work."

"What line of work is that?" Thade asked.

Mema waved a hand haphazardly. "You can deny it all you want, you big lubber. I know who owns this ship. I see how the crew hops to when she bats her eyelashes and snaps her fingers. And I have heard the stories of certain 'pleasure cruises' where say twenty-five people go out and twenty-four come back."

Thade shrugged his shoulders. "I wouldn't know anything about that. I am just a simple hotelier trying to make his way in the kingdom by offering an intriguing menu."

"Of course you are," Mema said with a roll of her eyes. "Nevertheless, always remember that cooks run the kingdom. They can say it is the castellan or the king or whatever title the ruler wants to give himself. But I know the truth. That's why I am so excited to get my hands on those Malinsuli goats I hear so much about. I bet they cook up real nice."

The mother pulled a woven basket from her many cubbies and proceeded to fill it up with her freshly baked goods. "Now, since you were so helpful, I will let you earn the favor of the crew. Take these up topside and hand them out to the boys on duty."

Thade accepted his task and made his way topside. The big man happily made the rounds, passing off treats to the boatswains, the windlasses, and the mariners tending to their tasks on deck. With the crew fed a quick snack, Thade noted Swayna Snowsong standing with the captain amidships, looking down into the water. Sway caught sight of him and quickly waved him over.

"Captain," Thade said politely as he approached.

Captain Hendrix Twinriver turned and acknowledged one of his patrons paying for the Malinsuli run. He was a tall and lanky man who sported a braided beard and kept his long hair pulled back out of his face with a leather loop, revealing his array of ear piercings. "Master Skystone," he nodded in acknowledgment. "I just got word from our navigator. We are farther ahead than we realized."

"That is good to hear," Thade said while nodding towards the small magical contraption Cinder had brought on board to keep the sails full of wind. "Lady Fireborne and her magical trinkets are earning their keep."

"I will admit I was unnerved when we left Highstone without our full slate of provisions," the captain said. "I was particularly alarmed about the lack of water aboard. I was even more unnerved when Lady Fireborne's course did not let us port in Selvaterra to stock up on fermented drinks but time has proven all of you wise."

"I can't imagine the crew is grateful to have *less* rum on board," Sway countered.

The captain laughed. "True enough. Still, a man needs at least half a gallon of water a day. Sixteen crew on board, five passengers. Eight pounds per gallon. We have shaved half a ton off of our weight and you can feel it. The ship sits higher in the water. That means less drag and that means more speed. We don't have to stay tethered to the coast to resupply so we can head out into the deep water. Couple that with you keeping the wind in our sails... I have never made a run this fast. And my first mate has confirmed it."

"How fast is fast?" Sway asked.

"Well, let me put it like this. Keep in mind you are a slave to your wind speeds. But if the current was right and the winds were favorable, on a good day, I could maybe get three leagues an hour out of my sweet darling here," Captain Twinriver said while rubbing the oiled railing affectionately. "But the wind is fickle. So I would say an average was a little more than a league an hour. Call it thirty leagues a day for easy math."

"What is our speed now?" Thade asked.

"With your wizard wind, running light, and the hull as shallow as she is, we are consistently maintaining our top speed. Faranor charts us a little more than three leagues an hour. Three leagues an hour consistently? Incanterra to Malinsula in two weeks? It just isn't done."

Sway shook her head. "So why aren't all the ships set up with magical utilities like us?"

"The wizzers are not exactly known to just hand out their magic on a whim. Most ships can't afford it," Twinriver said with a laugh. "Do you know how much them wizzers charge for their services? Private vessels can't cough up that kind of coin. You gotta be one of those guild vessels owned by the commerce consortiums."

Sway cast her gaze up to the fully unfurled sails and the crewman manning the crow's nest. The large canvas billowed with a consistent wind filling all of the sails. "In her defense, I know that her magical contraption doesn't just function on its own. I have seen her feeding a gold coin into that thing every twelve hours and it is not exactly spitting back silver and copper coins in change."

"I don't pretend to know how all of their magic works," Twinriver said. "I hear stories all the time of the various factions all looking for the next big way to power their magical spells. Devouring gold or precious gems to fuel their magic doesn't seem like the craziest of things. But, we are making great time and the crew is happy. That's all that matters to me."

As the captain broke away to advise the windlasses, Thade and Sway admired the bright blue of the water, the fluffy clouds, and the tranquil surroundings. Thade gave a grumble. "Not for nothing but if this portal network is such a good idea, why hasn't the Corvalonn dynasty done it already?"

"You got me. It sounds like they are seriously letting coins slip through their fingers. Then again, those wizzers seem less apt to open a portal unless the people are paying a premium. Greedy tossers."

Thade chuckled. "That makes me appreciate Cinder that much more."

"Aye. I have to admit, without us getting paired with her in a crew, I don't think we would have done as well for ourselves as we have."

"You are thinking of a promotion?"

"I don't know," Sway admitted. "Shaded Light is acceptable but the goal is to get a room in the Moonshine Gloom, right? Get up to Gamble's level. Could you imagine if each of us were running a crew?"

Thade remained silent, drawing Sway's attention. She looked over at him curiously when she noted a sad expression creeping onto his face. "Was it something I said?"

"I know Gamble is managing more than just us. He probably keeps an eye on a few crews. He has his responsibilities within the family. I am all for moving up the ladder. But I don't want us splitting up. If they gave Valos Nestorian Heights to run, we wouldn't be working as closely as we do now."

Sway reached over and rubbed her hand lovingly on Thade's broad and muscled back. "With the number of coins we bring to the family, I think we would be able to dictate our terms. And if this 'trade agreement' stunt works out, we are going to be swimming in it."

Thade looked over as Sway shook him by the shoulders. "Swimming in it? See? I made a sea reference because we are on a boat!"

"You are close to creeping into Valos's thing."

Cinder's brow furrowed. "Wait. Is it a boat or a ship? Is there a difference?"

As the captain returned to amidships, one of the mariners approached the trio with a smile on his face. "Begging your pardon, Captain. Neshan's spotted some visitors approaching the starboard. I thought our benefactors might be interested in seeing a pod of dolphins."

"Dolphins?" Sway said hopefully.

"They like to race the ship. You will see them breaking at the front of the bow. Rezan, take Masters Sway and Thade to the bow to give them a look at how the Mother is blessing our journey."

As the mariner escorted the two towards the bow, he looked back at them hopefully. "It's true. Sailors consider dolphins a sign of good luck. They even fend off hungry sharks. What you don't want to see are mermaids."

Thade's eyes grew wide. "That's an old wives' tale."

The mariner shrugged his shoulders.

"That *is* an old wives' tale. Right? Right?"

Chapter 4

Members of the Incanterran populace gave way and scattered as best they could. Down one of the city's large sidewalks, two members of the Knights of the Imperial Circle were marching in lockstep with an Incanterran citizen between them. The man of meager means – dressed in a stained jerkin and threadbare breeches – was looking about nervously. His wrists were bound by hemp rope. He looked to the general populace, silently pleading and praying for some form of mercy.

But no mercy was to be found considering the two knights were backed up by half a dozen undead skeletons. The animated bones were suited in field plate armor and brandished longswords. With no weapons of their own, none of the citizens looked to challenge either the knights or the undead.

Racing up from behind the trio, the local baker was shouting loud enough to draw the attention of pedestrians and others walking past. "All this over a loaf of bread? This is insane!" the baker yelled.

Having reached the intersection, the Imperial Knights in their alabaster vestments halted on the corner. One of them was using an enchanted ring of communication while the other knight held his prisoner fast. The undead skeletons had formed a protective ring around their charges. "You cannot do this!" the baker protested. "Where will you take him? What is his punishment for trying to steal a loaf of bread?"

One of the two Imperial Knights turned and looked at the baker, his featureless alabaster mask concealing all emotions. "For his crimes, the tribunals will decide his fate," the muffled voice called back, loud enough for everyone around him to hear.

The baker's jaw shifted back and forth as he ground his teeth. "Fine. I don't want to press charges. I give him the bread. It is my gift to him. There is no crime to charge him with."

"He stole from *society*," the knight replied. "He knowingly and willingly engaged in a crime against the society of Incanterra. Such abhorrent disregard for the law cannot go unpunished. We have our orders."

The crowd forming around the commotion began to audibly grumble and their numbers started to close ranks around the two knights and their half-a-dozen skeletal protectors. From around the corner, one of the ubiquitous wagons with a latticework cage turned onto the street and began to make its way toward the intersection. It was accompanied by a small cohort of even more undead skeletons. The air began to deflate out of the crowd's bellows as more and more of the dead army arrived on the scene.

"I suggest you let him go," a voice called from the crowd. "I will not grant you another warning."

The knights turned in the direction of the voice. The crowd parted as the pedestrian shed his brown traveling cloak, revealing black robes trimmed with gray and accented with yellow. The young man – possibly fresh from his first shave – stepped out of the crowd and brandished a bronze, ornamental scepter.

The warlock stared down the knights from underneath his eyebrows. Seeing his allegiance to the Ce'Mondere dynasty, people scampered away as quickly as they could. "Let him go," Idorius Ce'Mondere repeated. "You will not get another warning."

Though emotionless through his mask, the knight cocked his head in such a way that an outside observer might imagine a sly smile curling up one side of his lip. "Oh, I heard you the first time. But – technically speaking – you just issued a second warning when you said we would only get one. Is this your first time brandishing your weapon in combat?"

"If you don't let him go, this will be the last time you get to brandish yours."

"I have an army of skeletons, boy."

"And I have a death angel."

The frame of the young warlock should not have been able to conceal the summoned demon as well as he did. And yet, the knights were surprised when the slaughterath death angel leaped over Idorius's shoulders and into the fray.

The creature was twisted lengths of multijointed limbs ending in scythe-like blades. Pointed fangs lined its gaping maw and the beast's howling scream echoed through the city streets. The first skeleton to meet the scythe hands of the demon was able to form a modest defense to start. The armor plating held firm and the flat of its longsword blunted the first few attacks.

But the savage demon was relentless in its assault and eventually, its superior weight and strength brought the bony adversary down. While the people of Incanterra were frightened and screamed at the sight of the summoned devil, the skeletons held no such fear. They charged directly at the demon with a forward lean one would confuse with eagerness.

As the marching columns engaged the demon, they were joined by the skeletons protecting the prisoner wagon. Like army ants attacking a larger predator in coordination, the skeletons swarmed the demon. They viciously stabbed gray flesh with their swords or scraped with bony fingers if they had to.

While the demon was able to smash apart the bodies of a few of the swarming skeletons, eventually there became too many blades to defend against. Slices and stabbings did their work. The slaughterath eventually fell under the weight of the skeleton horde.

Once one of the skeletons found the perfect position, it plunged its blade into the front of the demon's neck. There was a scream of frustration and anger. As its death was imminent, the demon's physical form began to disintegrate into wafting ashy dust.

Now alone on the street and with the Incanterran people keeping their distance, Idorius Ce'Mondere quickly found himself surrounded by skeletal guards. One of the two knights calmly approached. Standing face to face with the young warlock, he held a sword in one hand and extended an open palm to the wizard.

Knowing he was beaten, Idorius handed over his bronze scepter.

From the prisoner wagon, another knight brought forth a unique set of metal manacles. Once in place, the bindings would keep the wizard from properly contorting his fingers and lash his hands down by his waist, keeping him from properly casting any spells. "A valiant effort," the knight whispered respectfully as he locked the manacles in place, "but futile."

Idorius looked over the knight's shoulder and saw the thief being loaded into the prisoner wagon along with other apprehended Incanterran citizens. "Where will you take us?"

The faceless knight looked back at the wagon. "They will be taken before the tribunals and tried for their crimes," he said, locking the elaborate manacles. "But you won't be going with them."

A great shadow fell over the intersection and the Incanterrans scattered quickly. From above, one of the enchanted sloops used to travel from the floating wizard isle down to the city proper landed on the street. Touching down effortlessly in the intersection, the gangplank descended.

Walking onto the street was Nikkala Whitesnow. A statuesque woman with classical beauty and long, blonde hair, she was dressed in blood-red wizard robes signifying her as a Necromangian, a member of the newly returned Catabaysi dynasty.

Approaching the pair of Imperial Knights, Nikkala halted in front of their captive and glanced him up and down. Referencing a small palm-sized leather tome, Nikkala scanned through one ear-marked page. "You must be… let's see here… ah, yes… You must be Idorius Ce'Mondere. We've been looking for you."

Snapping the book shut, Nikkala reached into her wizard robes and produced a sack full of jangling coins. She passed it to the knight. "Let this be a reminder," Nikkala called loudly to the assembled crowd. "Wizards are still here, hiding amongst the general population. They hide amongst you. We are not asking you to apprehend them yourselves. That is far too dangerous. But if you provide information that leads to the capture of these wayward wizards, you will be handsomely rewarded. Not only will you receive gold, but Master Nalazar Catabaysi has also decreed that those earnings will not be taxed."

The crowd stood by silently watching as the Necromangian proceeded to fit the warlock with a restraining collar and placed a bit in his mouth in case he pondered casting a spell utilizing only verbal components.

Whitesnow then marched Idorius Ce'Mondere up the gangplank to the waiting sloop. Once aboard, the boat began to thrum with magical energy and lifted off the ground to begin its ascent up to the broken hunks of the shattered wizard isle.

The assembled crowd began to meander away and go back to what could barely be described as their normal lives. The grand capital of Incanterra was under occupation by the vast undead horde, the army's sergeant knights, the commanding Necromangians, and their supreme leader Nalazar Catabaysi. Even during the bright summer, darkness had fallen on the great capital and no one could predict if or when the light would shine once more. Citizens tried to survive under the controlling thumb of the Necromangians. Few knew how the story would unfold or how their rolled dice would land. But every citizen knew for certain the last place they wanted to end up.

And that last place rolled past Kynna'Fyir Lu'Scion. The magician watched the cage wagon with the bread thief and other Incanterran citizens inside. The hidden illusionist glanced over at her Selvaterran traveling companion, Sabella Shorewater. The young woman could only shake her head.

Kynna craned her gaze upward and watched the sloop sail toward the broken isle. She could only imagine what horrors waited for Idorius Ce'Mondere. She had spoken to the lad a few times at social functions. She often saw him up on the isle sketching charcoal renderings of the various statues dotting the landscape. He was as talented with art as he was with summoning his infernal servants.

But Kynna knew if she had tried a rescue, she would be on board the floating sloop with him. With a resentful sigh, she and her traveling companion continued south.

Chapter 5

From the ramparts of the Baelannor tower, Nalazar Catabaysi watched as the sailing sloop docked at the main landing for the floating wizardly isle of Sorceria. He watched as Nikkala Whitesnow disembarked from the boat with a new prisoner in tow. The wizard did not recognize the young lad but he knew the black robes of the Ce'Mondere dynasty. Having another of the demon-summoning warlocks in custody meant another threat to his Necromangians was neutralized.

The thought made Nalazar smile if one could consider the twisted visage capable of smiling. Through a daring and difficult spell – with success purchased through the sacrifice of the Ce'Mondere dynasty's matron – Nalazar had transferred his soul to an enchanted phylactery and reanimated his undead body into something terrible.

It had been centuries since a wizard had attempted to transform himself into a hideous lich. But Nalazar's success left him lording over the famed wizard isle. After unleashing terrible magic to fracture the wizarding home, the lich and his superior magical talents took control.

Hearing the sound of rustling and moans of anguish behind him, the undead horror turned. He casually drifted back into the private chambers of Asaric Baelannor. The leader of the dynasty was splayed out and lashed to a large table, his wrists and ankles bound by leather straps.

The elderly wizard would have been described as frail even on his best days. Now, his weakness was on full display. His cheeks were sunken in. His eyes looked hollow. His skin had the thinness of paper. Slowly and with disorientation, Asaric Baelannor finally started to regain consciousness. As he began to come around, he was quickly reminded of the wracking pain that shot through his body. Wincing and moaning, he struggled for breath.

Asaric gasped in horror as Nalazar moved close. The lich's transformation had happened almost two weeks prior and his undead body continued to slowly desiccate. With each day, he became more skeletal and his features withered as if all fluids were being slowly siphoned by the will of a dark entity.

The lich approached. "Good afternoon," he said, the voice scratchy and grating.

"Please," the elderly patron pleaded weakly. "No more."

"No more? How can you say such a thing, Asaric? You disappoint me," the lich said as he came closer. His tone was soft and his demeanor was almost alluring. "You were so desperate to cling to life, you were willing to siphon the essence of your loyal Incanterrans. You were willing to risk outlawed magic –

magic outlawed by your dynasty. You broke the law. You murdered to live. To cling to these last vestiges of your life. And now, after a few short weeks of... What should we call it? Discomfort? After a few weeks of discomfort, you would throw it all away?"

The lich shifted, glaring at the patron with his horrible yellow eyes wreathed with red. "Was it all for nothing?" he suddenly screamed, his voice echoing off the chamber walls.

With purpose and frustration, Nalazar floated to a box of sundries left on a nearby table. He rifled angrily through the contents, finding the vial he wanted. He thumbed the cork, letting it drop to the floor. The monster stalked towards Asaric. With his free hand, he gripped the old man's jaw, forcing his head back and his chin high. He angrily dumped the contents of the vial down the patron's throat.

"If you spit this out, it will be much worse for you," the lich seethed. "You drink it! All of it!"

The thick, pink liquid slid down Baelannor's throat and into his gullet. Nalazar threw the empty vial at the nearest wall, shattering it into pieces and making it match so much of the chamber's furniture that had also experienced the lich's rage. Turning back to glare at the wizard, the lich watched.

Slowly, Baelannor's color began to return. His flesh gained more of its pinkish hue. Smaller nicks, scratches, and scrapes began knitting themselves back together and then vanished entirely. Through the healing potion, Baelannor felt his vitality return but he knew this would only extend his torture.

"When will enough be enough, Nalazar? How many times will you usher me to Zaneger's doorstep before you finally let me walk through?"

"This is the second time I have to remind you. Before all of this, you were so afraid of your final walk. Were you afraid of your judgment? Were you afraid that you would not walk with your ancestors? Were you afraid of your soul being condemned to the Dark Destroyer? Why were you so afraid of death?"

"It was not fear of death," the wizard admitted. "It was the love of life."

Nalazar swooned melodramatically and clutched his bony hands to his chest. "How romantic of you." The lich spun to look around the room curiously. He glanced up and down. He overturned one of the shattered couches, searching for something. "Tell me. Since the Dinaciouns and the Lu'Scions are so chummy with one another, do the magicians gift invisibility potions to the journalists in the city's paper? Is there someone in here taking notes that I cannot see?"

Baelannor shook his head. "What do you mean?"

"Are you playing to some crowd I am not aware of?" the lich roared. "Tell me the truth! Why was my dynasty wiped from the kingdom but it was acceptable for *you* to use the outlawed magic? Why was it acceptable for *you*?!"

Baelannor held his tongue, unwilling to speak.

Nalazar stormed forward. "Tell me, conjurer! Why are *you* so special?"

"Because I deserve it!" the wizard spat back. "Look at the *people* we targeted to extend my life. The insane. The addicted. People living in the gutters. People no one would miss. Yet, I am a master wizard. Do not forget that, Nalazar. Despite your self-aggrandizing sense of superiority, I am a wizard and the leader of a house, the same as you. It is our magic that makes this city thrive. Without us, these animals would descend into savagery. We keep order. We keep the peace. And because of us, countless lives thrive. Because of Baelannor, these people eat. Without us, they starve. So, yes, every single person I siphoned for their essence? I did it because I was better than them!"

The lich took a step back. He gazed at his fellow patron with a different look in his horrible eyes. "Now... was that *so* hard?"

"So have I earned my noble death now?" Asaric asked.

Nalazar paced back and forth and clucked his tongue. "Oh, my friend. You see so much but you still fail to comprehend. Death is an escape. A release. For oh so many, death is something to fear. But look at me. Look at me now. I have conquered death. I no longer fear it any more than I fear the judgment of the Pantheon. Instead, now, I am one of them. And from my godly position, I see it as my place to judge you. And judge you I shall."

Nalazar continued his pacing. "I acknowledge your position and the superiority of those blessed with magical gifts. It is difficult to argue against it. But murder is still murder. It is an unforgivable sin. And what you did was no accident. This was not a sin of omission. This wasn't where you got drunk and gave into temptation or a crime of passion where a man murders his wife's lover. This was *intentional*. And you went to the well multiple times. I would ask you if you are sorry—"

"I am not," Asaric interjected.

"Exactly. No matter how much I torture you... No matter how much pain is inflicted... How can you apologize for something you do not feel sorry for? If allowed, would you do it again? I hope you can see my conundrum."

"You said you acknowledge my claim to superiority. You don't care that I siphoned off souls to feed my energy. You are just mad I used your dynasty's magic to do it."

Nalazar spun on his heel to face his captive. He spread his arms out wide and smiled. "Indeed."

"So this is not penancing for my sins or retribution for the people," Asaric surmised.

Nalazar walked over to one of the few still intact tables and lovingly rubbed his bony fingers on his house's spellbook that had been reappropriated from the Cellarium Vaults. "No, this is retribution for the eradication of my house. This is revenge for the fall of House Catabaysi."

"And yet your revenge is spilling out down into the city below. How can you justify your attack on the Incanterran people? The Great Expulsion was a wizardly affair. Their kind had nothing to do with it. They are innocent."

Nalazar turned sharply. "No one is innocent. Those below fed your coffers. They afforded you your lifestyle. They were collaborators to your atrocity. They stoked the fires of your egos and turned you into what you have become."

"If I am so hated, then why not kill me and be done with it?" Asaric asked.

"Because at this very moment, my friend, you are worth more alive than dead to me. The executioner's blade hovers over the back of your neck. Your house and all those within it know this. And as long as I keep the blade suspended, they continue to conjure food for the people below. As you said, the Baelannors keep order maintained. A fed populace is a compliant populace. A starving populace... not so much."

Nalazar stalked closer and hovered his face a few inches away from Asaric. "But rest assured, when I no longer need you as leverage, I will give you the relief you crave. I will end your life."

Asaric tried his best to hide his relief.

But Nalazar noted the tell and smiled even wider. "And just as you are set to embrace the Never, I will pull your soul back to your broken body. I wonder how many times I can resurrect you through my necromancy before I truly drive you insane..."

Nalazar's laughter wafted from the Baelannor tower and out into the shattered isle of Sorceria, mingled with Asaric's roars of anguish and the screams of pain as the maestro continued to weave a symphony of sorrow.

Chapter 6

The sound of jangling chain mail, the weight of sheathed weapons, and the heavy footfalls of hard-soled boots echoed down the ship's hallway, up the stairs, and out onto the main deck of the *Castella Mare*. The infamous undead slayer Cavin Jurare emerged from below decks and scanned the horizon. The purple and pink painted sky was dotted with candy floss clouds. Looking to the west, the sun was long past the horizon and the seemingly eternal storm clouds that roiled over the cursed land of Ignaterra flashed with wicked forks of lightning. The shoreline of the plagued kingdom was a safe enough distance away and yet still loomed too closely.

The easterly peninsula of land that was home to the dead kingdom of Ignaterra was the last mass the *Castella Mare* had to skirt and then they could make a direct sail towards the island paradise of Malinsula. The famed "Isle of the Shark" was known for its indigenous population of bronze-skinned people with their white hair and swirling tribal tattoos. But first, they had to sail around the dangerous land of Ignaterra – the aptly named "Land of Fire." And much to Captain Twinriver's chagrin, Cinder Fireborne had asked the ship to sail a little too close to the coast for the seafarer's liking.

The mood was tense and quiet amongst the crew. The mariners and windlasses walked the deck while armed with longbows and quivers full of black-shafted arrows. On the forecastle of the ship, three sailors were manning the ship's ballista – a giant deck-mounted crossbow armed with cold-rolled metal quarrels. Every man had an eye on the west.

There were too many stories of razor-beaked lizards with enormous leathery wings. It was said they were reptilian versions of the pelican birds that dotted the coastlines. With the cursed lands not providing enough meat, they would hunt in the oceans. Stories had their wingspan as wide as the beam of the *Castella Mare* and they could easily carry off armored men. Plucking a sailor off the deck of a ship was as easy as pulling fish from the water. So the crew stood ready with barbed arrows and longbows.

Emerging onto the deck in his armor and carrying his death-dealing long blade, Cavin was quickly envied. The slayer saw the collected foursome he had traveled with. Valos Ironblade, Swayna Snowsong, and Thade Skystone were dressed in their summer fashions. Despite the sun long past the horizon, the heat of the equatorial region hung heavy in the air. And as the three shifted, Cavin smiled when he looked into Cinder Fireborne's eyes. The young woman stepped up to meet him as he approached.

"Magic hour," the undead slayer said. "I would prefer a decent rainstorm for cover. I would even take some fog."

"We will have to settle for dim light," Cinder replied. "If we went in darkness, I am afraid the portal would be too prevalent."

"Do you have your stone?"

Cinder produced a rough-hewed rectangle the size of her palm. The dark gray stone was dotted with flecks of white and chips of lighter gray. "Basalt," she said, passing over the hunk of rock. "With all of the volcanos and such, it felt like an appropriate attenuating marker."

"Daylight's burning," Valos called. "Captain is going to want to snuff the lanterns."

The two nodded. Brandishing her wand, Cinder Fireborne began to summon the proper magical energy. Starting as a pinprick, a ring of light resembling angry blue glowflies began to radiate outward. Locking in place at the height of a grown man, inside the swirling ring, reality rippled and then washed away. Looking through the ring, the view of the deck of the ship was replaced by the Ignaterran coastline.

Wasting no time, Cavin stepped through the ring with his slayer sword drawn and at the ready. Walking from the ship to the faraway shore was as easy as walking through a doorway. Thade turned and looked off the starboard side of the ship. There in the distance, he could see the faint light of the blue magical companion ring. And while little more than a stick figure, he could see Cavin Jurare step through from the boat to the shore.

All had heard the rumors of the dangerous, twisted, and horrible monsters stalking the cursed land. Thankfully, all was silent. Cavin waved Cinder through. Maintaining her concentration, Cinder stepped through the glowfly ring as well, setting foot on Ignaterran soil.

Stealthily crossing the beach, Cavin found a suitable outcropping of rock and fixed Cinder's basalt stone into place. He glanced about nervously, looking for any sign of movement. Thankfully, the coastline was deserted. Hustling back to Cinder's side, the two took in the terrible coast for as long as they dared. Cinder could feel the vibrations and the energy of the basalt left behind.

With their mission complete, the duo stepped back through the swirling glowfly ring and back onto the deck of the *Castella Mare*. Releasing the spell energy, the portal collapsed in on itself and vanished into the wind.

Satisfied all was correct, Cinder turned to the trio of the captain, helmsman, and his navigating first mate on the sterncastle. "We are done, Captain," she said proudly.

"Stealth running, gents," the captain called out.

With stunning coordination, the crew went to work. Topside lanterns were doused. Any mage-light stones were promptly covered. Even down below decks, lights were either extinguished or the heaviest of curtains were drawn across portholes. The ship had successfully transitioned into its dark running, so a rogue light out on the ocean would not draw the curiosity of the winged lizards.

Safely back on board, Sway was quick to check on both Cavin and Cinder. "No issues?" she asked.

"Smooth as silk," Cinder replied.

"When you ported in, did the land feel strange like people say?"

Cavin shook his head. "No different than any other land I've been on."

Sway breathed a sigh of relief. "I've heard that people who go into that land... being there too long turns their insides to mush. Or they sprout these terrible growths under their skin."

"If the land is cursed in such a fashion, I don't think we were there long enough for any such hex to take hold."

Sway nodded. "The crew members were whispering earlier. They said it was the last revenge of the great red dragon. A final curse spewed upon the world at his death. They say all that lightning above the land never stops. Day, night, all seasons. It is just a permanent storm. I wouldn't want to go traipsing across the Ignaterran plains wearing metal armor."

Sway pounded the bottom of her fist against Cavin's chest, issuing a rustle of his chain mail links. "Sounds like you got lucky. Eh, Slayer?"

"Well, hopefully, Cinder never has to use her attenuation stone to bring us back to that gods-forsaken land," Cavin said with optimism in his voice.

"Aye," one of the mariners said as he walked past, bow still in hand and his wickedly barbed arrow still knocked. "That land? That land is death incarnate, mate. I thought you two were mental for just kissing the shore. You go in there... You ain't coming out."

Thankfully, the *Castella Mare* had rounded the horn of the peninsula and each league took her farther south and back to the west as she sailed towards Malinsula. As the infamous land of Incanterra continued to recede into the northern horizon, everyone allowed themselves to breathe a little easier.

As twilight faded to true darkness and the sky became littered with stars, the crew began to turn their thoughts to the tropical paradise of Malinsula. Now down below decks, in her stateroom, Cinder sorted through her box of various attenuation stones. She placed the companion basalt stone in its place amongst the others. She had stones for the coastlines of Incanterra, the eastern coast of Selvaterra, the isle of Agavinsula, and now the horn of Ignaterra. Once she could place an attenuating stone on the shore of Malinsula, the Shadow Blades would have a unique trading network to begin importing goods to the city itself.

The plan was certainly working.

She looked up at the steel mirror hanging on the back of her stateroom's door. Gazing at her reflection, Cinder almost had difficulty recognizing herself. It was far beyond just the unnatural shade of red she had dyed her hair. It was beyond the physical transformation she had gone through as well. The pronounced hair color and the addition of muscle to her frame were hard to deny. But there was something different in the eyes that glared back at her. Somewhere deep within those hazel pools was a newfound strength and confidence she never remembered having when she was dressed in the blue and black-trimmed wizard robes of the Vocazion dynasty.

Her reverie was broken by a polite rapping at the door, heralding Cavin's entry. The slayer smiled seeing Cinder at the chest of drawers bolted to the deck and against the bulkhead. "So that was a thing," he said with a grin.

"I am happy that it all went according to plan."

"You and me both."

"And now we have a portal destination on the offhand chance we need it," Cinder said as she filed away the basalt stone.

"I think we both can agree that accursed land is the exception. The less time spent there the better but the amount of time we spent on Agavinsula was criminal. I didn't get to try any of their spices, their food, or that volcan drink the isle is famous for."

Cinder smiled as she started helping Cavin take off his slayer weapons and his armor. "This was never really intended to be a sightseeing cruise," she said as she unbuckled his leather bracers.

"We couldn't have stopped for *one* meal?"

"Time is money. Ask any Blade. I am surprised Gamble doesn't have that expression tattooed on his ass." Cinder paused and looked far away curiously. "Or for all I know he *does*."

"Well, I say once you get this whole network of yours tied in and all the magical strings connected, we need to make an excursion."

"That might be a trip we have to take just the two of us."

"Even better," Cavin quipped as she pulled off his chain mail shirt.

"I am sure the rest of my crew is looking forward to getting back to Incanterra. I wonder how construction on the inn is going."

Cavin waved off her concern. "Bah, I bet everything is just fine. What could go wrong in two weeks?"

Chapter 7

Masquerading as a commoner citizen, Kynna'Fyir Lu'Scion continued her journey south through Incanterra's Northeast District, following her newest acquaintance, one Sabella Shorewater. The magician had seen the shield placed over the city's gates. She had seen ordinary citizens rounded up by the undead horde. The sun was starting to get low in the sky and the last thing either of the young women wanted to do was be caught out after the mandated curfew.

Many of the businesses in the district were starting to lock up for the evening if they hadn't closed already. For the last two weeks, movement in and out of the city had been completely curtailed. There was no way to get inventory in or exports out.

Some services simply refused to open. The alleyway shop providing tattoos and piercings felt wholly unnecessary. The portrait painters were not patronized. Some shopkeepers did their best to attract customers with whatever stock remained but with no new imports and travel between districts becoming snarled, inventory was growing sparse. Social parlors closed their doors after one raid accused patrons of conspiring. Kynna could only shake her head as she noted so many shuttered businesses.

Pausing at one of the intersections, Sabella surveyed her surroundings and gauged which avenues would be the least populated. But she was also keeping a sharp eye out for more conical hoods or skeletal patrols. "This is just sad," the Selvaterran grumbled. "I mean... look at all this."

She gestured towards an almost vacant mercantile shop. "Those wizzers were a bunch o' haughty pricks but they knew how to keep coins flowing. They were greedy as sin and had their fingers in every pie but these new wizzers, they are choking the life out of this city like a thicket of eboneedle creeper vines."

"At least they still deliver food and water," Kynna noted.

"Once that gets choked off, then the real riots start."

Kynna noted an apothecary shop on one of the street corners. The windows were lined with candles and there was a strange assortment of items that were typically only valuable to the wizarding class. Xanthorr plants, powdered gemstones, various minerals, rare herbs, and the lot. After the founding of the great capital, so many suppliers flocked within the walls of Incanterra looking to cater to the wizard clientele through stocking the material components necessary for their magic spells.

Commoners rarely needed what the shop offered so the business was sorely lacking customers. Despite her material component bag running shallow, Lu'Scion knew better than to enter such an establishment. Whispers had spread quickly. The apothecaries were game trails for the Knights of the Imperial Circle.

During the opening skirmishes of the occupation, before the truth spread through the people, more than a few wizards and wizardesses down in the city found themselves surrounded, clapped in irons, and loaded onto one of the floating sloops the same as Idorius Ce'Mondere.

Kynna noted the shop but made it a point not to let her gaze linger too long. She then glanced nervously at Sabella Shorewater. Her attire was certainly not ratty. She wore fashions for north of the High Way. Still, she was sure the woman would sell her out to the nearest Imperial Knight if she learned her surname was not Summerwind. Kynna had heard the jangling of coins and noted the heft of the purse passed over to the knight by the Necromangian. It would be a bounty too high for any citizen to ignore.

In the distance, the district's clocktower rang out its bells to signify the top of the hour. Shorewater glanced back to the center of the district nervously. "Curfew will be in effect soon," she said. "Do you have a place to stay?"

"I've been moving from place to place," Kynna said.

"I've got someone that I stay with," Sabella admitted. "But I don't know. You might not like the price he charges for haven."

"I have some coin."

"No, sweetie. His type? They don't want coppers and silvers."

"You mean...?"

"Look, he is a mush-head. Slumber is his spice of choice. If he is deep in its thrall, sometimes his little worm won't even get rigid. And even if he does, he just kind of ruts on top of me like the sow that he is."

"That... does not sound appealing."

Sabella shrugged. "It's three minutes out of my day. Sometimes less. But it gives me a place to sleep. And if he mounts me from behind, I don't have to look at him. He's got the space. And his mattresses are comfy. Well, comfier than an alleyway."

"That's just blatant exploitation."

Sabella gestured around at the city. "The wizards, the Way, the Blades, the consortiums... when is this city not? Right now, it's a seller's market and he knows what he's got. If I won't let him hump away or tug him happy, someone else will. And look at your alternative."

In the distance, a column of skeletons marched past led by a pair of their white-cloaked knights. "There has to be a better way," Kynna insisted.

"Unless you can find it in the next hour, you are going to leave yourself exposed. I am going to head over to Mennot's place. If you change your mind, come over to Fourth Street and Iron Avenue. Northwest corner. Look for the tall apartment building with all the carvings of ravens on the top floor. Or if you stick on this road and head south, you are going to run into Nestorian Heights, Brickyard, and Shaded Light. Don't go east of Brickyard. The Way owns that territory and you will get your throat cut. The good news is with so many people getting snatched up by the skellers, there should be some vacant rooms for you to squat in... even if only for a night."

"Thank you," Kynna said honestly.

"Best of luck," Sabella whispered before heading east.

Kynna grimaced at the path before her. Still, there was logic to the Selvaterran's thinking. There had to be a vacant room to hide in. Kynna pushed south down Gold Avenue, although the buildings this far south and west in the ward did not look lustrous enough to match the name of the street.

The Queen's High Way, running perpendicular to Gold Avenue loomed large in the distance. On the west was Shaded Light and on the east was Brickyard. She contemplated which ward might be the best to find shelter in. As she was trying to decide, a voice from the east called out. "Youse lost, honey?"

The grating, gravel tone was anything but welcoming. Kynna turned towards the voice and saw a man standing in the entranceway of one of the taller buildings lined with small, kiln-fired bricks that the ward was named for.

Kynna swallowed hard. He dripped with intimidation and there was an aura about him of menace. She was trying to calculate how quickly she could dig into her side pouch for the material components needed to obfuscate the man's senses if he tried to rush her. "Youse don't want to get caught out in the open after curfew there, little bird," he said ominously. "Lucky for youse, I've got a place youse can hold up in for the night. Come over here."

Kynna knew she was not going to approach the man but in a strange ward, she was not certain which direction to move in or how quickly she should hasten her steps. Judging by the sparse populace and how they were concerned with getting themselves home, no one was paying her attention. Kynna doubted if she ran down the street screaming that anyone would give her a second glance, much less help.

Thankfully, a voice called out. "There you are!"

A young woman with ginger hair and a warm disposition hastily approached Kynna from across the street. She wore a light tunic for the summer weather, a flowing skirt, and an apron tied around her waist. "I told you. Shaded Light is *west* of Gold Avenue. Not east, silly."

"I can never keep directions square in my head," Kynna said with a smile.

As the young woman approached, she looked past Kynna to the creeper on the apartment stoop. "What have I told you about lurking about, Hestor?"

"Gold Avenue is the boundary, girlie," the man called back. "Maybe youse needs to get yourself one of them city maps or something."

The woman pulled back a section of her apron revealing a black dagger in a black sheath. "This is not the day to test me, Hestor."

The man smiled, revealing his yellow teeth. "Look at whose they're giving daggers to these days. Or maybe youse is just fronting. Pretending to be a Blade when you ain't one is a long stay at the bottom of Highstone Harbor."

"You think I am not? Do you want me to take this up with Valos?"

The man sauntered off of the stoop and began toward the center of the street. "The word's out, Mira. Valos ain't running the show no more."

"Are you sure about that? That's an awfully big gamble if you're wrong."

The big man laughed and scratched his protruding paunch. "I would say something quippy like 'that group must be desperate to hand a sheath to the likes of youse.' O' course, what can you expect when youse got an axe wound running the family?"

"Types like me?" the woman asked. "Do you mean the types of people who can add two columns of digits without a quill and ink? Quick, what's seventy-eight plus fifty-four?"

The predator's eyes narrowed. He turned lazily and started making his way back to the stoop. Once he was out of earshot, the woman looked at Kynna. She kept her voice low. "Actually, without quill and parchment, I have no idea what that totals but he doesn't know that."

"One hundred thirty-two," Kynna whispered back.

"Let's get you somewhere safe," she smiled.

As they passed into the Shaded Light ward, Kynna swore she detected the odd, out-of-place, syrupy smell of sunflowers. The hour was getting late and she wanted to stay close to the scullery maid.

"Don't worry. You are safe with me," the young woman said. "I am going to take you to the second safest place in Shaded Light. It used to be the Shadow's Edge Inn. I worked there 'til a wizard burned it down last spring."

Kynna tried to keep her eyes from growing as wide as saucers.

"Don't worry. This place is just as safe. Don't you worry one bit," she assured her new sister. "I'm Mirawen Autumnlight. It's a pleasure to meet you."

Chapter 8

Darkness.

It was dark as far as the eye could see. The sky was scattered with twinkling stars and with both of the planet's twin moons in their hiding phase, without even a sliver of illumination, the pinpricks of light had never been brighter. The sky was so dark that the red line of celestial dust clouds was even visible in its streak across the firmament.

From his position on the forecastle, Valos Ironblade looked out on the vast sea under the night sky. It was a curious sensation as the ocean resembled more of a sheet of glass than the rising and falling hills of water he was accustomed to. On this night, there was not a breath of wind to be found. For so many other crews, such tranquility would have left them stranded and at the mercy of the pantheon. Yet, the *Castella Mare* sailed on.

Powered by the magical contraption Cinder Fireborne had brought along with them, the ship's sails were unfurled and filled with a propelling wind. The magical evocation pushed the ship on, letting her knife-like hull slice through the water, sending her further and further south.

Most of the light crew manning the caravel were tucked away in their staterooms, private quarters, or in their hammocks below decks. Only the helmsman and the mariner who drew the short straw were up on deck, making sure the vessel stayed on course and each kept the other awake. Occasionally, the mariner would look up for a glance around, see nothing but open water, and then he and the helmsman would go back to their strategy game of Scachi.

The lantern's open flames had all been replaced by Cinder's mage-light stones. While the stones could have cast the ship in as much light as a noonday sun, the hoods had been closed narrow and the light had been softened for the night's journey. Everything was muted and as tranquil as the surrounding ocean.

Valos looked out on the vast water in wonderment. He was so lost in thought that he did not even notice when Cinder Fireborne joined him on the forecastle. "It is tough to feel significant," she said, giving Valos a slight startle.

"You are lucky my reflexes didn't take over," Valos warned. "You would have at least two daggers in you right now."

"Are you even armed?"

"That's not the point," Valos waggled his finger. "When these heightened battle skills take over, I can't be held responsible."

Joining him at the railing, Cinder shared Valos's view of the vast expanse of ocean, stars, and the enveloping cosmos. "How are you dealing with all this?" she asked earnestly.

"You are right. You look out on all this... The sun rises and sets. The moons wax and wane. The ocean does its whole wavy thing. And look around. Right now, it is like we are the only people in existence. Tough to feel significant."

"Still missing the sights and sounds of the big city?"

Valos laughed. "Always. But I've got my eye on the target, even if it is far downrange. What we are doing here... is going to change a lot. And make us a lot of coins. Two weeks now for coined-filled coffers later? No issues at all."

"No issues at all?"

Valos eyed her curiously. "Should there be?"

"I do have a... concern," she admitted. "Thade and Sway have their brother and sister thing going on. They confide in each other and they have their bond. And it feels like since last spring and up through this summer here, you and I formed a strong bond."

"I agree."

"And now, Cavin is part of the equation. I feel like you could be in the position to be the fifth wheel on the carriage."

Cavin gave a little scoff. "I am doing just fine."

"I am just saying that we need to find you one of those island girls."

"I appreciate your concern," he laughed. "If anything, the bigger issue is not me being the odd man. The bigger issue is *you* losing focus."

"Me?"

"Don't give me that surprised little girl look. I've seen what happens when you get all enthralled with someone. Your mind trails to them. Any spare moment and your thoughts drift and linger. It can happen so much that you can lose sight of the important things or miss key details. We can't afford slip-ups. Not now. Not when we are so close to the goal. We are close to launching our boat into the lazy river. I firmly believe that the more money we make, the more money we will make. No more hustling. No more grinding. And that opens up more avenues."

Cinder thought of the impossible wealth of the wizarding dynasties. "I have seen that before."

The two looked out on the vast ocean for a bit.

"So why didn't you ever find someone?" Cinder asked.

"A lady? Who has the time?"

Cinder looked around to confirm they were the only ones in earshot. The helmsman and the mariner were too far away to hear and too involved in their strategy game to pay the pair any attention.

"It is just you and me," Cinder said. "You don't have to play the role."

Valos winced and scrunched his face. "On a long enough timeline, a relationship with anyone has an inevitable conclusion. And I am not much of the fatherly type. I have yet to meet a woman that doesn't want children. And when that conversation finally rolls around and you admit that you never want to have any, it sours the milk."

Cinder looked out at the distant horizon where the stars met the water. "I think you would be a good father."

"Ain't a question of 'good' or 'bad.' My father was in this life. I was secondary. It wasn't like he and my mother were betrothed or anything. But he was married to the life. And I want to be better than my father in this thing of ours. I mean... look at where we are now. My father wasn't even close to where I was. And if a kid was in the picture, they would always come in second. I can't do that to him. Or her. So, nah. I'm not looking for anything."

Cinder smiled. "You think I was? It has been my experience that once you stop looking for it, love has a habit of knocking on your door."

Valos scoffed. "You make it sound like one of Niverana's little servants or something. Sneaking about all invisible, making poor saps stare at each other with big doe eyes. I doubt even those Mutaccio wizzers with all their potions have ones that can make people fall in love."

Cinder just smiled and looked away wistfully.

"Did you ever come close?" she asked after a stretch.

Valos was silent for a time. For too long a time.

"Once," he whispered.

Cinder remained silent.

"There was one girl. She was special. Beautiful. She was beautiful to me. She was one of those girls – you know the type – she was pretty to me but she didn't believe it. She didn't think she was pretty. And not in that way where the girls try to play it down so they get more attention. But she was. It wasn't just her face or those spectacular breasts."

"There's the Valos I know."

"I mean those were the icing on the tart but it was her spirit. It was her soul. I loved her soul.

"One night, she ran afoul of this man. Actually, she ran afoul of several men. It was a gang of them. Things... things went bad. After she healed up, I tried to convince her that she was still pretty. But she was like a scared kitten after that. I couldn't touch her. And I don't mean just that way. Even a soft hand on the shoulder. Nothing.

"Those scumbags took someone beautiful and hollowed out her soul. She never recovered. She was a seraphfly and they broke her spirit. I tried to help her but I couldn't. I tried to keep an eye on her. Help. But about six months after that, I got busted with a wagonload of hooch and went for my stretch up in Irongate."

Cinder stayed silent for a long time.

"What happened to her?"

"I heard she got real bad. Friend found her. Noose around her neck."

The two stood in silence.

"So when I hear a story about a man forcing himself on a woman – like that pair of lasses last spring? – well, it all comes oozing back to the surface. And all I want to do is make them pay. Because they took my seraphfly and they broke something beautiful. I never want anyone to go through that again. That's why I didn't feel one ounce of remorse when I watched that scumbag slice his tooleywag off. Better that than any woman forced to endure something like that at his hands."

Another long stretch of silence occurred between the two as they watched the night waters sail past.

"You think you know a person," Cinder mused. "You are impressed by their courage and their determination. And then they find a way to impress you even more by revealing part of their character to you."

The wizard turned to look at her rogue friend. Admiration swam in her eyes. "You are a good man, Valos Ironblade."

"Bah," he grumbled. "I'm on a mission to a tropical island to illegally smuggle hooch into a city. How good a guy can I be?"

"Hey, we are not just going to smuggle up spirits," Cinder said. "A good portion of this whole thing can be legit. We could import barrels of live fish from this island and sell them to those highfalutin chefs in the Northwest District... and we can overcharge the shit out of them."

Valos laughed. "I wouldn't have it any other way. After all, it's immoral to let a sucker keep his money. Those rich pricks have so much coin. They won't even realize they are being overcharged. And since it is all legit, the Crown can't come after us for toeing into their territory."

"Trust me, Val. This is the mission that is going to make us all legends amongst the Blades."

Chapter 9

"So this is Shaded Light?" Kynna Lu'Scion asked.

"The hidden gem of the Northeast District," Mirawen Autumnlight replied.

Shaded Light was tucked in against the King's High Way and Bronze Avenue on her western border and against the Queen's High Way and First Street to her south. She then ran north up to Third Street and east over to Gold Avenue giving her twice the size of most wards within the district. But Shaded Light was also considered the poorest and the farthest down on the social ladder. Yet, over the past two seasons, dramatic changes happened within her borders. As Kynna glanced about, despite the late hour, there was a wholesomeness to the area.

Fresh coats of paint were on the plaster. Businesses and homes felt kept up. There were flower boxes outside of windows with their beautiful flora in bloom. Things felt closer together and yet in a cozy way rather than a claustrophobic feel. And it was all too obvious her guide knew her way around. Mirawen moved with a purpose. Rather than the major streets and avenues, the young lass navigated the side streets and even the alleyways as they were making their way to the southwest corner of the ward.

Emerging from one of the alleys, Mirawen stopped short and kept Kynna from stepping out onto the street. Hustling back into the safe confines, Mirawen peered out from around the corner.

"Death wagon," she whispered.

From the shadows, Kynna took a cautious glance. In the street was an ominous, black, horse-drawn wagon of the *domici dauthis*. It was a wagon no Incanterran wanted to see. It meant a family member had passed away and their body was being retrieved by the acolytes of Zaneger. The members of the house of the dead would prepare the body for its final resting place either in the capital's graveyard positioned out in the northern hills or by engulfing the body in Zaneger's Breath. However, those milling about in front of the tall tenement were not the black tabard and ebony-cloaked servants of the death god.

Instead, there was a pair of Imperial Knights in their white hoods and a small collection of undead skeletal servants. On a stretcher, the skeletons were marching out a body covered in a black sheet. Mirawen could not hide her sneer. "Freaking tosspots," she hissed. "See them there?"

Kynna nodded.

"They have commandeered those wagons from the house of the dead. When the *dauthis* torch a body, it uses these big ovens that burn hot. I mean all the way hot. Turns the bodies to ash and the chimneys belch out this white smoke. There is a house of the dead over in Brickyard. I haven't seen that chimney smoke since the undead army showed up. And now look at them. Hauling away another body using the wagons of the *domici dauthis.*"

"You think they will add the body to their forces?"

Mirawen nodded. "Aye. The longer they stay here, the bigger their army gets. How long before we are all a part of it?"

"I saw a prison wagon earlier today with citizens loaded in it. Do you think that is where they end up?"

Mirawen could only shrug. "With everything all in lockdown, so much of everything now is rumors. A bunch of old hens on a stoop clucking. But what the whispers say is that the jails are empty. The sannies where they keep all the crazies who foam at the mouth are supposedly empty too. The sick. The invalids. I hear they all up and vanished.

"It is like them sharks that swim out beyond the Highstone. What kind of seals do those big sharks go after first? They want the easiest meals. So they go after the old, the lame, or the dumb. In these walls, I bet a sicky addicted to spice still has good bones. That's probably why the Under Roads are empty now. I bet the mush-heads, the crazies, and the dying were the first rounded up."

"Probably put up less of a fight," the secret wizard reasoned.

"Aye."

"If they are transforming the bodies into their skeleton warriors, it would be the perfect cover-up," Kynna said. "It is pretty difficult to identify someone based on their bones."

The clip-clop of horse hooves on the stone street began to echo toward them. The duo retreated into the safety of the shadows as the wagon and her protective column of marching skeletons made their way down the major street.

"Are we in danger?" Kynna asked.

"Once they are gone, we should be alright," Mirawen whispered. "My place is close. Shaded Light is too far out of the way for constable patrols. The boners were probably only here to pick up the body. And here a bit ago, some of those whities came to the ward looking for trouble. It did not go well."

Mirawen crept forward to look out of the alley but the wagon and the columns had not ventured far enough away yet. The duo remained patient. "I heard the Necros are offering bounties on the members of The Eight that might be hiding down here," Kynna said. "Is that true?"

Mirawen scoffed but then looked at Kynna with a smile. "That was not directed at you. That's for those Necro freaks. Look, I hate those greedy wizzers as much as the next person but even I know that sometimes you gotta fight dragons with dragons. Any person that rats out a wizzer to deliver them to another wizzer? That is just a short-sighted coin grab. People gotta start thinking about the big picture."

Still hiding in the shadows, Mirawen chanced another look. The wagon was gone and it was safe for the two to be on their way. "Mirawen, what do you do?"

"I'm a scullery maid over at the Shadow's Edge Inn," she replied. "Or at least I *was* before the fire."

"Right, the fire you mentioned."

"The owners are getting it rebuilt. Well, they *were* in the process of getting it rebuilt. After all this, who knows? The city being thrown under siege tends to snarl up those long-term plans."

"You are excessively knowledgeable for a scullery maid."

"Oh, well once we get the joint back open they promised to make me the manager."

"Quite a career advancement."

"After the fire... we had an opening," she replied, trying to hide the sadness in her tone. "Hopefully I can do a good job for the owners."

"But you're always in the interest of earning extra coin on the side?"

"Who isn't?"

Mirawen considered the line of questions and despite the curfew and the danger, she paused on the sidewalk and sidled close to one of the multi-floor tenement buildings.

Kynna glanced around nervously as Mirawen stepped close. "Look," Mirawen said sternly, "if this is your roundabout way of asking for an introduction, I can't. They aren't out there. It's all a big rumor. And even if they were, this? This is not how it's done. You have to have a family member introduce you to them. And you seem nice and all but I don't know you. If I vouch for you, it's on me."

"I don't understand," the secret wizard said honestly. "What are you talking about?"

"What are *you* talking about?"

"I was just saying that *if*... and let me stress *if*... I had a line on a wizard and where they were hiding... what would you do with that information?"

Mirawen's eyes narrowed. "I got some friends. They have an expression. Do you know how the fish gets caught?"

Kynna pondered the question. "Bait?"

Mirawen stepped closer, an air of menace about her. "By its open mouth. If you know about a wizzer, you keep your mouth shut. It's how you don't end up on the end of a hook and keep your guts in your belly. You hear me?"

"I do," the wizard-in-hiding said, managing to suppress her smile.

If anything, the scullery maid had just proven that the Lu'Scion wizard had found the perfect person to help her stay safe. The young woman took a deep breath to steady her nerves and looked her rescuer right in the eyes. "You are a very interesting woman, Mirawen Autumnlight. I am very happy to have made your acquaintance."

On the stoop of the tenement, the main door opened a crack and a grandmotherly woman poked her head out. "Mirawen, is that you?"

"Good evening, Lady Blackstone."

"Girl, what are you doing out here? You know the clocktower chimes have rung. Don't give those creepers a reason to snatch you up," the elder said adamantly. "You get up in here, quick like now."

"My place is not too far, my lady. We are headed there now."

The two ladies prepared to take their leave when Lady Blackstone hushed a whisper toward the maid. "Have you heard from Ironblade? Or that fire hair lass?"

"They were gone out of the city before the curtain dropped," Mirawen replied.

"A shame. We could use them. Now more than ever. Wishes and dreams for another time. Now you two get off the street!"

Mirawen and Kynna hustled to the west to follow their elder's orders.

Chapter 10

Accursio Twotrees looked out from his elevated position amongst the walkways within the warehouse's rafters. Like his father before him, the tall, blonde man of Monterran descent was a taxidermist who worked in the Southwest District. His public profession – dealing with animal innards, gore, and other viscera – did not cause a single citizen to turn heads or inspect him too closely. None wanted to dig into the oaken barrels hauled from his warehouse weekly. He worked for years providing animal bones for dagger handles, tanning exotic hides, and he even stuffed a Northwest resident's faithful hound after an untimely passing. Death was his business.

Skillfully, he had masked his allegiance to the secret Catabaysi dynasty and no one knew he was a Necromangian wizard. Only members of his cabal knew that Accursio used his shop in the Northwest District to strip absconded human bodies of their flesh and organs. No one had an inkling the Necromangian wizard animated those skeletons to serve in the undead horde.

After the great shattering of Sorceria and the grand reveal, the loyalists to the Catabaysi dynasty – the Necromangian wizards – were finally able to pull their robes from the backs of their closets and step from the shadows. And Twotrees's master was clear. He wanted the taxidermist's operation moved out into the open. Nalazar Catabaysi also wanted it to progress on a massive scale. Within the Southwest District, the Mutaccio wizards were quickly overwhelmed by the Necromangian's undead forces.

So shocked by the shattering of Sorceria, the majority of the population was looking up in horror. It kept them from looking down and seeing the skeletal horde emerging from the city's vast sewer system. Few even realized the city was under siege until bony hands were holding swords to their throats.

The Mutaccio potion brewing facilities were conquered with nary a shot from a crossbow, a slash of a sword, or a blast from a wand. The alchemists practiced transmutation and profited by bottling their spell effects into drinkable potions. Enhanced strength, speed, immunity to damage, and other effects were a swig of a potion away thanks to the Mutaccios. But for such a massive operation, the dynasty needed brewing stations and those stations were scattered across the poorest sections of the Southwest District.

It was these stations that were quickly commandeered by the Necromangian forces. It was one of these stations that Accursio Twotrees was overseeing. The massive, oversized cauldrons were perfect for his acidic solution to prepare bodies for their transformation.

Walking down the stairway and onto the warehouse's work floor, Twotrees observed his labor force. Most looked at his blood-red robes with silken black trim and were afraid to make eye contact with him. The facility's manager – a broad-shouldered man from Mnama'tellus named Hammad – approached Accursio as he made his way down to the floor. Hammad was scribbling on his workboard and the scrolls he kept pinched in place to keep track of his inventory. "Milord," Hammad said.

Twotrees waved off the formality that the big man always wanted to bring to any conversation.

"Production?"

"We continue to maintain our quotas," Hammad assured. "But there have been some questions amongst the workers. And some problems."

"What problems?"

"Many are complaining. Quietly, mind you. But they are complaining. Headaches, bouts of nausea. Some have been commenting about a wet, hacking cough. It was not uncommon for workers to have issues with the fumes from the Mutaccio potions. Healers sometimes had to be consulted, especially amongst those who had worked the longest for the dynasty. But this is more... intense."

Accursio glanced about the warehouse particularly up into the rafters. "The Vocazions," he grumbled in contemplation. "I believe that dynasty has magical spells to conjure wind. Perhaps they can arrange some sort of contraption to keep the air circulating. Something to pull the air out so the fumes are less concentrated. I will look into it. Anything else?"

"There seems to be no end to this supply of bodies."

"Incanterra is a big city. People die here every day without any sort of sinister undertones. Few people saw it because of the *domici dauthis*," Accursio said as he gazed around at the facility. "Every one of these bodies is a tragedy. But it is also part of the grand play we call life. The story ends. Everyone's curtain has to fall eventually. And the audience gets up and leaves the auditorium. But now, thanks to us, their remains are given purpose."

Accursio paused his walk. He turned sharply, a look of genuine concern on his face. "Do the workers understand that? Do they understand what we are doing here?"

Hammad stammered, glancing between his master and the scrolls clipped to his workboard. Accursio turned again. He snapped his fingers at the nearest worker, a young woman hauling a bundle of herbs. She wore a mask of cloth over the bottom half of her face.

"You!" Accursio said. "You there, girl. Come here. Come here, please."

The girl approached delicately but not so slowly as to appear disobeying.

"What is your name, girl?"

"Morowen," she replied, a tremble in her voice.

"Tell me, Morowen, what are we doing here? What is the grand purpose of this laboratory?"

"We make the skeletons, sire."

"Yes, yes. We make skeletons but *why*? Why are we making them?"

The young lady shook her head nervously, afraid to give the wrong answer. "Because you told us to."

Accursio hung his head in defeat and sighed heavily. He called out, his voice echoing across the warehouse. "Does anyone know why we are making all of these skeletons?"

The warehouse grew silent as the workers paused, waiting for the inevitable rampage and anger from their wizard master. Instead, Accursio threw up his hands in defeat. "We are making soldiers, my friends. We are making *soldiers* who follow orders without fear or question. My master – Master Nalazar Catabaysi – is making an army to fight so *you* don't have to. He wants to put the army of the dead on the battlefield so that you, your sons, and your brothers don't have to take up arms.

"The dead are gone. Their time in this world is over. But we can use their bones to defend the innocent. They can march forth into war to *save* lives. They can serve a purpose. So which is better? You all tell me. Which is better? Putting their corpses in the ground or setting them on fire with Zaneger's Breath or dumping them in the ocean... *orrrrr*... using their bodies as fodder in the great war so you don't have to fight?"

The warehouse remained silent.

"Very well," Accursio said. "Since these bodies are valuable and what we are doing here is valuable, you all should be adequately compensated. There is a price for what you are doing here. So, effective today, everyone's wages will increase by twenty-five percent."

Finally, there was a ripple of excitement amongst the workers.

"Okay, back to work," Accursio said.

The warehouse workers did as they were told. They went back to preparing the solution in the oversized cauldrons that resembled a viscous pea soup. Bodies would be dunked in and slowly their flesh and organs would be separated and sloughed away from their bones. Pristinely preserved skeletons would emerge which would later be animated by Necromangian bone wands.

Accursio turned to Hammad and gave him a nod of approval. "I am going to do some arranging. I will bring foodstuffs here for the workers. I want everyone under our banners to be fed. None of these fine people should be working on an empty stomach. And I will make sure it is not just the standard, bland rations that are being mass distributed around the city."

"If you will do that and with the increased wages, you will easily surpass the Mutaccio masters that ran this operation before," Hammad replied.

"This mission is too important for us to fail. Master Catabaysi needs this for the greater good of us all. Without this army, we will be doomed."

In the large doorway of the warehouse, a flash of red and black caught the Necromangian's eye. The wizard let his foreman get back to work and he approached Demina Summerstone with a wide smile.

The young woman with her flame-kissed hair was the same as her colleague. Once an investigator for *The Heraldry*, the young woman was now able to wear her wizard robes openly. "A pleasure to see you," Accursio said. "I have to say. Your robes look fantastic in the light of day."

The young lady smiled and nodded her appreciation. "New orders," she said, passing over a leather-bound ledger.

"And what changes does Master Duskwood have in store for us?"

"That's not from Dragan," she replied. "It's from Nalazar himself."

Accursio opened the ledger and gave the contents a cursory scan. "Wait... is this... possible?"

"With the master gaining access to the lost grimoire, there are all sorts of untapped potential that he wants to harness. This is his newest fascination."

As Accursio continued to read, he grew more and more agitated. He started to walk outside into the sunlight and politely ushered Demina to join him. "Have you read this?"

"On the flight down. The recipe is convoluted so he wanted it hand-delivered."

"I can't sell this," he hissed quietly. "I just gave a whole speech about how we are using the bones for a greater good."

"Sorry I missed it."

"It was quite stirring. But *this*? This is going to be..."

Demina nodded solemnly. "Monstrous. But are you going to tell him no?"

Chapter 11

The dawn of a new day had brought with it a ceiling of dark gray clouds and the wind was all but stagnant. Thankfully, the *Castella Mare*'s magical winds continued to push her along. Rain fell in fat drops, splattering on the wood deck of the ship and peppering the ocean waves with concentric ripples.

With the consistency of the magical winds and the proper calculations, the ship's navigator had been true to his word. If the crew could have found the sun behind the veil of clouds, they would have known it was at its zenith. And within that hour, the caravel was making her final approach to the tropical island kingdom of Malinsula.

The southernmost free kingdom, the isle was described by many foreigners as a paradise. Unfortunately, Aurorean refused to smile on the Incanterran sailing party. They were greeted with rain and clouds, spoiling their arrival to paradise. Approaching from the east after rounding the horn of Ignaterra, the ship approached the island's northeast side.

The port city of Searock was the ship's destination as the sailors knew the Malinsuli had long ocean piers to accommodate trading vessels. But as she made her final approach to the island, the call from the crow's nest brought the crew to the ship's railing.

Along the isle's magnificent pink sand beach, there were humanoids emerging from the water and a host of Malinsuli hunters were rushing to engage them and push them back into the ocean.

Captain Twinriver surveyed the scene through his spyglass and let out an audible curse. "Kai'kamina."

He handed the spyglass to Cinder Fireborne who was standing beside him.

"What are Kai'kamina?" Swayna Snowsong asked.

The captain stammered his words for a bit as he tried to translate the Malinsuli title. "Rough translation would be… uh… like a… a… a sea folk? Like a cross between a human and a… sea lizard?"

"We have to help them," Cinder said, looking through the spyglass.

"Can you coax more wind into the sails?" the captain asked.

"We don't need to," Cavin said. "Cinder can see the beach."

Cinder nodded as she began to prepare her dimensional gate.

Cavin looked at the crew. "We want to leave enough crew for you to port the boat but anyone you could spare," he told the captain.

"Battle positions! Spears and halberds!" Captain Twinriver called out. "All ashore who's going ashore."

As the *Castella Mare* continued to sail towards the island, the force of mariners, rogues, and a lone undead slayer quickly scrambled to don armor and gather weapons. Intermingled with the splashes of rain, the sound of fighting began to echo across the water and reach the ship as she continued her approach.

With the force assembled, Cinder produced her magic wand and began creating a new portal in the center of the ship. As reality warped and warbled within the swirling ring of glowfly sparks, the Malinsuli beach appeared on the other side of the gateway.

Wasting no time, Thade Skystone banged the hafts of his twin handaxes together, flaring the magical energy infused into the weapon's steel heads. He roared defiance and dashed from the deck of the *Castella Mare* and onto the pink sand beach.

Charging behind him, Valos, Sway, Cinder, Cavin, and a host of *Mare* mariners poured out onto the beach, brandishing their long halberds and spears. Shoring up the Malinsuli fishermen, the warriors moved to match the Kai'kamina hunters.

Incanterran steel clashed against chitin armor shields. Coral spearheads sought to stab Malinsuli flesh. Island arrows whistled through the air, fired by singing bowstrings. Woven bullwhip kelp nets anchored with heavy shells were tossed in hopes of entangling opponents. The battle for the shoreline raged fiercely.

The Malinsuli knew better to engage the Kai'kamina in the surf. It was too great a risk to be overpowered and then drug beneath the waves. And while the merfolk were stronger, their long, webbed toes did not make them overly graceful on the sand. Each side did its best to break the other's lines, battling back and forth.

Valos fought side by side with the Malinsuli fishermen. His heavy sword and his accurate strikes began sending splashes of the Kai'kamina's purple blood across the pink sand. He was funneling two weeks' worth of pent-up frustration into his sword strikes.

Stalking the battle line, Swayna kept her crossbow at the ready. The ensorcelled quarrels were charged with electrical energy waiting to be released upon impact. The young rogue did not have to rely on brute strength to end a foe. She just needed her arrows to make contact. As the mer-hunters broke the surface of the water, Sway tried her best to put a quarrel in close, hoping the electrical bolt would spread through the water and hit multiple targets.

Thade was one of the few humans that could match the Kai'kamina's strength. His axe heads clanged heavily against the carapace shields that resembled segmented plates from oversized lobster tails. While the enchanted blades did not break or penetrate the shields, more than a few mer-warriors found themselves spilling backward onto the sand under the crushing weight of his heavy blows.

As Thade found himself fighting beside Cavin Jurare, the two were able to drive back the line. While the undead slayer typically wrestled wights, gashed ghouls, and sliced up zombies, his battle tactics against the Kai'kamina proved equally effective. With his sword in one hand and his wizarding battle staff in the other, his abjuration shields presented defenses that the merfolk could not chop, slash, or bash their way through.

And the true tide turner was Cinder Fireborne. While her nimble rapier was ineffective against the heavy shields and had difficulty puncturing the Kai'kamina's rubbery flesh, the wood wand she carried in her left hand was the real difference-maker. Streaming jets of flame were highly effective in wounding the water dwellers and the sight of the flame flashes quickly robbed them of their courage.

The mariners spared from the *Castella Mare* used their halberds and their spears to fight the corseque pole weapons and tridents. The crew silently hoped their sailing ship would be in range soon. Her ballista could fire its massive bolts into the Kai'kamina lines.

But even with the best defenses, more than a few of the Malinsuli found themselves overwhelmed by the Kai'kamina offensive. While sprays of purple blood stained the sands, eventually, more than a few splashes of red mixed onto the horrible canvas of war. But while the Malinsuli fishermen, the *Castella Mare* mariners, and the rogue forces could be counted, there was no way to tell how many more of the Kai'kamina forces were approaching the beach from under the surf. So for every Kai'mer warrior felled, one was ready to emerge from the waves and take his place.

While the opposing forces battled for every inch of sand, as the Kai'kamina continued to rise from the waves, the landwalkers found themselves being slowly pushed off the beach. As more and more of the merfolk stacked in, the air breathers were forced to retreat a step at a time.

Cinder's fire blasts could only do so much. Cavin's magical shielding could only span so far. Sway's quarrel quiver was running shallow. As strong as both Valos and Thade were, eventually exhaustion would take them both. And while the mariners and the fishermen were skilled with their spear strikes, they started to see forces that had landed farther down the beach begin to close in on their flanks.

"Tighten ranks!" Cavin bellowed.

The proud force stepped backward, giving ground, but their retreat allowed them to shore up their defenses as they moved into tighter ranks. Fear began to radiate through the group as they saw Kai'kamina breaking from the ranks and beginning to stream up into the nearby village. They did not have a wide enough defensive line to keep the Kai'kamina from diverting around them and going after the women and children.

Unsure of what to do, Cinder looked about frantically. But then the whole beach reacted as a tremor rippled across the sand. A shallow quake rippled from somewhere deep within the island and then radiated out across the beach and toward the surf. The concentric wave disturbed and swelled the sand from underneath before settling still. The disturbance gave both sides pause. The Kai'kamina looked about nervously and the fishermen's forces were happy for the brief respite, allowing them to catch their breath.

The Kai'kamina returned their gaze towards the direct adversary and brought their tridents and their corseque polearms back to bear. But then...

In the space between the defensive line of fishermen warriors and the vegetation of the island, within the sand itself, a massive hulking brute began to emerge. It was not rising from underneath the sand. Instead, it was pulling more and more sand into itself to create its hulking form.

It was a large beast with a barrel chest, shoulders the size of boulders, and distinct, stumpy arms that were thicker than they were long. It reared its featureless dome-shaped head. The only thing that vaguely resembled features were a pair of angrily glowing flairs of light that could be considered eyes.

The summoned sand elemental brought its oversized fists with pudgy, rock fingers to bear and began pounding what would be considered a fist against what would be considered its open palm.

Chapter 12

The sun crept from its slumber and began to rise in the east, bathing the kingdom of Incanterra in her warm light. From her river border to the east to the mountain borders to the west, the kingdom soaked up the life-giving light. For the rich farmland nestling up in the northern valleys, the summer air was warm. The amber waves of wheat swayed in the breeze. Herds of farm animals went about their grazing. Along the southern border of the kingdom, the coastline was treated to a lovely, lightly salted breeze. Cottony tufts of clouds hung in the air. It should have been a day that elevated moods and made people smile.

It should have been.

But the kingdom's grand capital had been walled off from the rest of the realm. Her citizens were trapped within. Dark plumes of black and green-tinted smoke rose from the Southwest District and those plumes traveled up to the floating, magical isle of Sorceria.

Once the gem of the capital, the wizarding isle was a place where a commoner expected the streets to be paved with gold. Unfortunately, the land of milk and honey had been shattered by Nalazar Catabaysi. Its broken pieces managed to cling together through the magical energy keeping the isle suspended above the city.

Trapped on the isle, many wizards chose to remain within the confines of their house towers. Few dared to walk out in the open and when they did, it was to serve the wishes of their new Necromangian masters. As such, the isle was quiet.

However, in the morning hours, Marius Vocazion and Aldor Mutaccio – patrons of their respective dynasties – were out for their morning stroll. The two wizards were dressed in finery worthy of their station. Vocazion was in his regal blue with black silk trim and Mutaccio wore scarlet and silver.

Marius Vocazion was tall and distinguished, clean-shaven, and well-kept. While his hair was thinning too quickly and his skin sagged more than he desired, Vocazion was still handsome and virile.

Aldor Mutaccio was a squat, barrel-shaped man. Stocky and strong, Mutaccio was one of the few wizards in Sorceria that opted for facial hair. He sported a neatly trimmed salt-and-pepper mustache. But while Vocazion was more distinguished in his increasing age, Mutaccio wore every year in the form of a wrinkle. Time and stress had not been kind to the old man and he carried his tension in a perpetual scowl.

The duo walked through the central plaza, silently condemning the rampant devastation wrought by the sundering. Cracks formed on walkways.

Priceless statues had toppled. The soil had been ripped away to reveal bedrock. In some sections, boulders taller than hill giants hung in the air, slowly spinning on their axis.

"...and the biggest issue is my lack of material components," Aldor Mutaccio lamented. "I don't keep a doomsday level of supplies in my tower. Why would I? The skill to brew powerful potions is easily neutralized when you cut me off from my ingredients. It is like asking a chef to make cuisine with galley rations. And I never felt a need to stockpile our brewed potions. They are all down in the city where they can earn me coins. The Catabaysi have neutralized me without a single wand blast."

"So striking back?" Marius Vocazion asked.

"Not unless you are going to put a sword in my hand and no one wants to see me in armor and wielding a weapon. How many material components do you have? How much magical energy can you summon internally to cast your fireballs and lightning bolts? Enough to destroy that undead horror? If not, it is best to not even try. We saw what happens to those that fight back."

Together, the two patrons cast their gaze to the northwest corner of their wizard isle. Where the grand tower of the Jurare wardens once stood, there was now only smoldering rubble. Large chunks of land were torn asunder where the tower once stood. It was a grim reminder for the population of the isle and a testament to the power that Nalazar Catabaysi now held.

No longer fearing the physiological damage of the *pherein*, the lich was able to summon impossible levels of magic that no single wizard – even a patron – could rival.

"So what are we going to do?" Marius asked.

"I could answer that question better if I knew what their plan was. Fortunately or unfortunately – depending on how you look at it – I have a meeting with the Necromangian hierarchy later today. Perhaps that will provide some insight."

"So we are just to sit by and do nothing?"

"Marius, you were there. You were there during the initial salvo. When you surrendered, Nalazar ceased his aggression. But you know Jurare. Asking a former military general to surrender? He was never going to do that. And look at the punishment for his hubris," Aldor motioned towards the shattered remains of the Jurare tower.

"You think they need us for something?"

"I think there is a reason Catabaysi didn't just unleash wholesale slaughter. I think he does want something. So I believe our task now is to survive. Live to fight another day."

"Some would brand that as cowardice," the mage postulated.

Aldor tittered. "And they can have that philosophy etched on their tombstones or into the urns that hold their ashes. I know it is not a popular opinion. Bards don't sing about retreating. The playwrights who write the operas and the performances by the actors don't use it as a story point. But there are the heroic tales and then there is this real world.

"Fighting to the death is stupid. Instead, surrender. Let yourself be conquered. Some call that cowardice. I call it strategy. You survive. Then you irritate from within. Jurare didn't heed this lesson and where are he and his matron now? He would have been better served to play lickspittle to Nalazar, gain his trust, get close, and then assassinate him."

"Grim," Marius said.

"These are grim times. Don't fault me for being practical."

"And what if we are just lambs being fattened for the slaughter? What if this is all just a game for Nalazar?"

The two patrons looked at the massive tower of Baelannor. The grand tower's main gaits had been twisted and wrenched from their hinges like they had been a titan's playthings. The whole of the island had heard Asaric Baelannor's cries at the hands of the merciless lich.

"How long until each of us is on Nalazar's slab, screaming the way Asaric does?" the mage asked.

Aldor broke wizardly protocol and reached over to squeeze Marius's shoulder. "I can hear it in your voice, my friend. I know you think you failed us. You did not. Jurare failed Sorceria. He failed us by dying and now he is no longer here to help us carry on."

Marius gave a shallow nod and took a breath to steady his nerves. "I thank you for saying that. But we still have to oust these Necromangians. How are we to do this?"

The two continued their stroll. Finally, Aldor gave a little smile. "I bet you play fast and loose with your empress and sovereign pieces in Scachi."

"I don't see what that has to do with—"

"And if I played the game with Canarr, I bet his defenses were impenetrable. I wonder if that is a coincidence. With him being an abjuration warden and you being an evocation mage. So it's just in his nature to evoke a defensive strategy while all you want to do is go on the attack with your fireballs and lightning bolts?"

"Canarr's defensiveness didn't secure his victory," Marius stated.

"And I doubt your wand blazing will secure you one either," Aldor quipped. "So I am afraid we are going to have to meet somewhere in the middle. It will mean setting up a fluid response to whatever the Necromangians are planning. Adaptation is going to be the key here."

As the two patrons continued their stroll, they noted a small handful of the Necromangian wizards going to and fro along the aisle. The same as any wizard dynasty, there were apprentices. There were the adepts – mid-level wizards who had not quite attained the responsibilities of leadership. Then there was the handful of select masters.

Marius's eyes narrowed as he saw one of the wizards tending to various duties. He was a handsome man with a lantern jaw and a gray-brown head of hair who was often seen with a younger apprentice, most notable for her ginger hair. "I've seen that one about," Marius said.

"Aye, Dragan Duskwood," Aldor replied. "If I have their house hierarchy figured out, I believe he is their second-in-command."

"Have I seen him before?"

"Possibly if you spent time down in the Academia ward. He was posing as a professor. I mean… a fraud professor would be easy enough to sus out. I suppose they all were who they said they were."

"So, he was a history professor who was *also* part of the death magic cult," Marius said.

"Scary, isn't it? All this time, this magic house was spread throughout, hiding down in the city. You never had any idea that members of the populace had those red robes hanging in the backs of their closets."

"Hiding in plain sight," the mage mused. "Perhaps it is why we never knew. And who would have thought to even look for them?"

"And now here we are, trapped on our own island," Aldor said. "Honestly, if I wasn't the one imprisoned, I would want to admire them. If they used this technique to besiege Castratellus or usurp the throne from the boy king over in Arvaterra, I would have applauded them."

"You might not want to praise them too strongly," Marius warned. "They might have all of us entombed before it is all said and done."

Chapter 13

The Incanterran sailors and the band of rogues were taken aback when the hulking sand elemental emerged from the beach and loomed over the battlefield.

Easily rising to eight feet, the colossal creation of sand was as wide as it was tall. The elemental's torso rose in and out of the sand as if it were swimming amongst the granules. It slid and slithered sidewise along the sands as if bound by an invisible tether. It strained against its constraints, eager to be set free. It turned to look back at the island and her thicker vegetation. That was when those on the shore realized the sand elemental was not tethered. It was waiting.

Heavy footfalls heralded the partner's arrival. From out of the tropical foliage was a mass of stone, dirt, and Malinsuli soil far more coherent and solid than its sand elemental counterpart. The earth elemental stomped forward on squat legs that were too short and swung arms that were too long. While its feet were similar to an elephant's, the rest of its rock body appeared simian-like. And from its posture and aggressive, purposeful gait, everyone on the beach could tell the earth elemental was not happy.

The beach trembled and shook under the weight of its thick, flat feet. If the sand elemental was tall, her rock counterpart was taller. The sand elemental slithered about but the earth elemental stomped. While the sand elemental's hiss sounded like grit being poured from an hourglass, the earth elemental's guttural growl was granite grating and grinding in a tumbler.

As the earth elemental stomped forward, the first Kai'mer warrior that it encountered could only look up in horror at the massive form. It stood slackjawed until the elemental delivered a heavy uppercut with its thick arm and flat fist. The Kai'kamina warrior went airborne, sailed completely off the beach, and splashed down back in the surf of the ocean.

While the rogues, the mariners, and the invading Kai'kamina were amazed at the elementals before them, the Malinsuli fishermen were energized and gave forth a rallying cheer. With such a threat now in their midst, the Kai'kamina trained their weapons toward the elementals.

Their tridents and spears either plinked off hard stone or easily sank into the soil skin of the earth elemental. Some of the stab wounds leaked loose mud which could have been confused for lifeblood. Strikes against the sand elemental were even harder to distinguish because the creature's body was constantly shifting and reforming back into a vaguely humanoid form. It was impossible to tell if their strikes were even causing damage. But it was quite obvious if the elementals were.

Kai'kamina were tossed through the air, pinwheeling and tumbling head over webbed feet. Some were reduced to what one might call chunky jelly if caught underfoot or on the receiving end of the earth elemental's double-fisted ground pounds. The sand elemental shot blasts of itself from its outstretched hands, knocking Kai'kamina off their webbed feet, filling their lungs, or driving them back to the water.

As the elementals disrupted the Kai'kamina, the Malinsuli fishermen were quick to exploit the chaos. Bringing their spears back to bear, they did their best to break the Kai'kamina lines and drive them back into the surf.

Despite the battle raging around her, Cinder Fireborne looked upon the elementals with admiration. The wizard in hiding had studied Malinsula as part of her cover story that allowed her to disappear from Sorceria and down into the capital of Incanterra. In another life, her story had been real and a version of her had traveled to the island paradise to study how to tame such elementals.

From out of the village, Cinder spied a pair of the renowned Malinsuli shamans storming down onto the sands. The duo was dressed in island fashions of sarong wraps and strange, flowing tops that resembled a blend between a wide-sleeved tunic and a billowing cloak. The male and female duo wore masculine and feminine versions of their island's fashions. They were also adorned with shell necklaces and other ornamentation derived from the sea.

Like all Malinsuli, their skin was a rich bronze color and their long hair was naturally snow white. The female shaman's hair was pulled back and braided in elaborate plaits. But the man's long, shaggy hair hung past his shoulders. Both of the shamans wore hammered bronze cuffs on their wrists and they flared with angry magical energy that perfectly matched the glow in the earth elemental's and sand elemental's eyes.

The rogues and mariners had new allies amongst them and the arrival of the shamans bolstered the warrior fishermen even more.

From outside of the conflict, the Kai'kamina that had circumvented the battle were quickly snatching up stringers of freshly caught fish, traps filled with scuttling crustaceans, and any other foodstuffs that could be quickly acquired.

The scavengers were looking to grab and dash. Some of the Kai'mer warriors brandished their spears menacingly as their Kai'mia mates grabbed whatever food they could get their webbed fingers on.

The skirmishes were more threatening jabs and angry posturing as long as the Malinsuli did not try to keep the Kai'kamina from taking the spoils of invasion. Slinging the stringers of fish over their shoulders, many of the Kai'mia raced quickly for safety beneath the surf. The Malinsuli were happy to let them go. Most villagers were more concerned with snatching their children up and ushering them away from the battle.

As more villagers rallied to the threat, targets of opportunity started to evaporate and the Kai'kamina looked reluctant to venture too deep into the tents and palapas. The scavaging Kai'mia were quick to retreat beneath the waves, absconding with whatever foodstuff they could carry.

The Kai'mer began to pull back from the line of fishermen warriors. The Malinsuli inched forward to reinforce their command of the beach. They did not chase after the retreating forces.

The line of the Kai'kamina warriors halted where the surf met the sand and the Malinsuli fishermen gifted them an even wider berth. None of the land-walking fishermen were foolish enough to be lured into the surf with the water swimmers.

But there amongst the retreating Kai'kamina stood a tall and proud merman. He was adorned in an assortment of decorative seashells and he wore a kelp-woven loincloth and raiments that might have resembled priestly robes. He even wore an almost miter-shaped crown fashioned from coral. While the Kai'kamina looked ready to retreat into the surf, the holy merman was not ready to give up his position just yet.

There was an odd call amongst the Kai'kamina. It resembled frogs croaking while blended with unique clicks and warbles. At the surf's edge and in the presence of their holy man, the Kai'kamina suddenly became emboldened and the Kai'mer warriors closed ranks and snapped their pole weapons back to offensive positions. The Kai'kamina priest then held a long curling shell up to its lips and proceeded to blow it as a horn. The long, warbling, and eerily haunting sound rang out across the beach and the nearby water.

The Malinsuli fishermen halted any creeping advance, content to let the mer-warriors close the gap and come to them for the next round of fighting. Everyone remained locked in their stalemate, looking about nervously and struggling to catch their breath.

"What in the hells...?" Valos Ironblade whispered from amongst the ranks.

Out in the blue and green ocean, under the surface, a distinctive shadow was moving towards the beach from down in the depths. As it drew closer, it pushed a displaced rogue wave of water ahead of it.

Amongst the Malinsuli, one of the fishermen managed to squeak out a single word. "Ula'Kanaka."

The man's spear clanged against the pink sand of the beach. He turned to flee as fast as his legs could carry him. Others looked around nervously, uncertain of what to do. Amongst the group, the male shaman stormed down into the ranks. "Hold your ground!" the shaman barked.

Tall and broad-shouldered, the shaman pushed beyond the lines to form the center of the new phalanx. His metal bracers still flared with magic and he brought his trident to bear.

One of the fishermen called out. "Amman, is it an Ula'kanaka?"

The shaman glared at the dark shadow as it was close to breaking the surface. He brought his gaze back behind him and his earth elemental approached to stand at the ready. "This will not be easy, my friend," the shaman said.

The earth elemental looked down and nodded its comprehension. It raised a flat palm and pounded his fist into it several times. "You honor our people with your service," the shaman replied.

A noise came from the earth elemental that sounded like a bag of rocks being shaken against one another in a burlap sack. The shaman nodded. "We will be with you," he replied. "And looks like we have some outlanders that can help."

The shaman turned to acknowledge the rogues and their mariner companions. "We are indebted to you," he said with a heartfelt inflection.

Before anyone could respond, there was a noise from the Kai'kamina that might have been a cheer of ribbits along with a violent splash of water. If the Kai'mer in the strange priestly attire was indeed a holy man, his chants and songs had summoned forth the equivalent of whatever a Kai'kamina might describe as either an angel or a demon.

Whatever the nomenclature, the servant of the deep had arisen.

Chapter 14

Wincing in pain, Tanairs Corvalonn took a seat on a bench within one of Sorceria's communal greenhouses. The glassed-in building was home to a variety of unique flora imported from a variety of the free kingdoms. Seraphflies flittered about, although their enchanting bioluminescent glow was dampened in the daylight.

The patron of the Corvalonn dynasty, Tanairs was an elder no matter who was asked. His natural blonde hair with his widow's peak was stubbornly fighting off the march of gray but losing the battle against his encroaching forehead. He was tall, long, and lean. The master wore his crimson and cream robes handsomely and with regal elegance. Yet his walk into the greenhouse was slower than usual.

His steps were tender and careful, measured and precise, using an economy of movement. He utilized this same slow progress as he took a seat to admire the ambiance of the forum. With his labored lungs finally returning to normal, he took a deep breath in through his nostrils to appreciate the swirls of aromas from the various flowers. Amongst the various patches, plots, and pots, one could find almost any color in the rainbow if one looked long enough. There were tall blooming blossoms, wide-faced florals, teacup shapes, spiraling swirls, and all kinds of flowers in between. The greenhouse was truly a sight to behold.

From his seat, he gingerly touched his chest over his heart and winced in pain. Through both his outer and under robes and then underneath his salve-soaked bandages, the wizard could still feel the wounds where the lich had sunk his fingers into his chest. The healing potions had certainly helped but the pain remained. He was uncertain if it was all in his head or stubborn remainders and reminders of the lich's long and razor-sharp nails.

Behind him, the door to the greenhouse opened. He glanced back to see a flash of black and gray purposefully coming around the bench where he was seated. Accents of yellow jutted out against the stark, deep blacks of her wizardly robes. Cedalia Ce'Mondere swept into the garden with a purpose.

Corvalonn was almost twenty-five years her senior. He was the ruler of his house and an authority on the wizarding council. Cedalia was at a lesser adept level. Despite their difference in status, the two had formed an unlikely bond. No poet or playwright would designate them as "friends." Few wizards would ever utilize such a term when describing a member from a rival Sorcerian house. It was a mutually beneficial association.

And yet, the beautiful young woman's comely features were etched with genuine concern.

Before the upheaval, Cedalia had sought to continue her fallen patron's legacy. While she was a talented warlock in her own right, the Ce'Mondere wizardess needed a patron to understand the highest levels of magic. So a rare partnership between two dynasties was formed.

All immediate plans were cast aside when the grand isle cracked in two.

Cedalia swept around the bench and took a seat. The young woman was not standing on ceremony. She did not ask permission and an outside observer might have accused her of sitting too close to the patron.

"I thought that was you," she whispered, hooking the stray lock of her dark, almost black hair behind her ear. "Are you alright?"

"I will be," the patron replied honestly. "Nalazar Catabaysi is thoroughly convincing when he needs to be."

Cedalia wanted to comfort the man. She even reached out hesitantly for a heartbeat and then decided against it.

"I wanted to come and see you but arriving at your tower…" she stammered.

"I am well. I just need time to regain my strength after Master Catabaysi's… questioning."

"He has the power formula?"

"And the amorina. During the siege, the vyrkolka was banished but he used a member of your order to summon him a new one."

Cedalia sighed in defeat. "I knew I recognized the energy signature sealing the city. He has it reinforced with our energy?"

"He does."

Cedalia shook her head in defeat.

"However, my 'agreeing' to hand over the magic power source did result in a cessation of hostilities," Corvalonn said, trying to find some silver lining. "If I hadn't, we might have all ended up like the Jurare."

Cedalia ran her hand through her thick, raven hair and let out a long sigh. "Jurare gone. I mean… at least my dynasty isn't theirs."

"I am afraid the only saving grace any of us have right now is that Nalazar still needs our magical resources. I am told he wants to unlock the secrets of the *pherein*. He needs us…"

"For now," Cedalia sighed. "What happens when he doesn't or if we refuse to cooperate?"

"Then I am afraid we all end up like the Jurare dynasty."

"Unless we can find a way to escape," Cedalia said hopefully.

"Working with you for a short while now, I can tell when you are leading me. I assume you already have a plan?"

"It is more like a… a theory," she replied.

"Enlighten me."

Cedalia shifted back and forth in her seat uncomfortably. "We summon our demon servants from the infernal realms. The pool we pull them from is not tremendously different from the dimensional gateways you all create."

"I don't know if I approve of where this is going."

Cedalia waved a hand. "Now, now. Yes, some of the summoned demons are savage. Monsters. Brute killers. But not all. The infernixies are surprisingly intelligent. And I have worked with Libydiss on multiple occasions."

"The sultry one with the wings and the tail that you used over in Governance Ward?"

"That is the one. I might even go so far as to say she likes me."

"Cedalia..."

"I have never been cruel to her. She is an excellent enforcer. Jumping through the sphere surrounding Sorceria, through the gates, or the membrane tenting the city is impossible. We know that. And all of your gateways are blocked. But you said yourself, Nalazar had a new vyrkolka summoned. Those little imps are easy. Any of the warlock novices could have pulled one from the infernal realms. But if they summoned a demon, it means we have a gateway they don't know about!"

"So you are suggesting you summon forth your Libydiss, dismiss her back to her infernal plane of existence where she takes you with her, and then from inside the infernal realm, you open a second portal to bring you back to the Prime Material plane of existence but now outside of the city?"

"Yes."

"Two things. You are putting tremendous trust in a *demon*. And you are assuming your mind won't collapse in on itself by witnessing whichever of the infernal planes Libydiss resides in."

The two wizards stared at each other for the space of several breaths, neither willing to give in and speak first.

Cedalia threw up her hands. "Well, we have to do *something*. Jurare is a smoking pile of ash. Dinacioun is leaderless. Even if the Lu'Scions had not vanished, they were useless from the start. My patron and matron are dead. With Qaava gone and so few aunts and uncles in place, many are looking to *me* for help. How desperate is that?"

"I think you are not giving yourself enough credit."

Cedalia wanted to continue her rant but the words of praise from the patron gave her pause. She took just a moment to bask in the glow and she had to look away at the multitude of flowers, afraid she would look at him as a childish schoolgirl would.

"The problem is we don't have a way to coordinate our resources. I don't know who is alive and who is dead. I know Idorius was captured down in the city and returned to the isle," Cedalia said. "He has been sentenced to tower arrest. I don't know if the Necromangians will seek justice against him for his crimes."

"If he is like the others, they will commute his sentence if he promises to assist the lich in whatever his grand master plan is."

"And what is this grand master plan?" Cedalia asked.

"I do not know," Corvalonn admitted. "But in his current state, Nalazar Catabaysi is the single most dangerous entity in the free kingdoms. He is someone that can now tap directly into the *pherein* with no consequences. My fear is he will now use all of Sorceria's resources to cast all the magic that has either been too dangerous or we have been too fearful to cast."

"So why seal off the city?"

"I think he doesn't want his test subjects going anywhere."

The patron's statement hung ominously between them.

"I've heard the screams coming from the Baelannor tower," Cedalia said quietly, despite them being the only two within the greenhouse. "A quick death might be preferred to what Nalazar is doing to the old man in his tower. The portal plan with Libydiss might mean death but if I have to choose between *possibly* dying with her or *definitely* dying at that monster's hands... only being resurrected to die again? I'll take my chances in the infernal realms."

Tanairs Corvalonn folded his arms across his chest, careful to avoid the wounds left by the lich. His impressive mind continued to whirl as the inklings of a plan began to formulate. "Asaric will be dead as soon as Nalazar is tired of playing with him. With Baelannor providing food for the city, they might be too closely scrutinized. The Jurare are gone. As you said, the Dinaciouns are leaderless and I don't know how much they could help even if Gaviel was still alive. The Lu'Scions conveniently vanished. So we will have to recruit the Vocazions and the Mutaccios for our mission. It will be up to the four of us to take down the shield walls. We have to escape the city."

"How are we going to do that?" Cedalia asked breathlessly.

Tanairs Corvalonn narrowed his gaze. "We are going to take away his power source. We are going to kill the amorina."

Chapter 15

In the Northwest District, the Governance Ward was the beating heart of the capital's leadership. The halls were populated by representatives of the local magistrates for the frontier territories and provinces within the kingdom but it was also home to the office of the castellan who ran the capital itself. With the city of Incanterra housing more people inside its walls than the population living outside of them, many felt that as the capital went, so went the rest of the kingdom.

Throughout the day, the halls of governance were usually filled with a dull roar. People were talking in various parlors and voting halls. Representatives of the trading consortiums often had business with the archons. And all those voices mingled together to form a muted cacophony.

Today, the halls were uncharacteristically quiet. Doors were shut. Whispers were used more than voices. And several offices were suspiciously empty. As such, there was an audible echo as a signature pair of hard heels clicked and clacked against the marble floors.

The swish of her red and black-trimmed robes caught the attention of many and prompted more than a few closing of doors as she passed. Her long blonde hair was tightly braided in a dangling plait that reached the small of her back. But what people feared most was the magic wand crafted from bone, dangling from the silken sash around her waist.

As she entered the reception hall for the castellan, the only thing that changed about Nikkala Whitesnow was her robes. Yet now, because of her robes and her wand in plain sight, the receptionist was barely able to summon up enough courage to look the Necromangian wizard in the eye. She was far too nervous to engage in any sort of polite conversation. Not wanting the wizard in the reception hall for a heartbeat longer than necessary, she gestured for the guild advocate to enter the castellan's office.

Castellan Mahon Tallhill was looking out the window and down in the public square as Whitesnow entered. A scant two weeks earlier, he was lamenting the angry shouts and rhyming slogans of the Unbound – a group protesting wizardly spells and influence within the city. Now, the square was deserted.

Whitesnow cleared her throat as she stood in the doorway. Tallhill turned and welcomed her half-heartedly, returning his gaze to the square below. "Still wearing the red, I see," he harumphed. "I preferred you in ivory."

"I am sure you did. But I am enjoying the freedom of being my authentic self," the wizard replied.

"How can I help you this day... Lady..." Tallhill was confused. "Is it still Whitesnow or am I to call you Catabaysi?"

"Which would make you more comfortable?"

"How can I help you this day, Lady Whitesnow?"

"My master is requesting the evening curfew be adjusted to six bells as opposed to sundown," she said flatly.

The castellan turned sharply but the Necromangian was not going to relent. "You cannot..."

"We *cannot*?" Whitesnow asked with an aggressive emphasis in her tone.

"This is not governmental defiance. This is simple logic. You are going to ask parents to lock their children behind their doors while the sun is still shining? Do you think there is pushback with the curfew now? Lock parents in a house with three whelps or a pair of punks suffering their way through puberty. You would rather face a cohort of Agavinsula pirates over parents wrangling toddlers behind closed doors."

Whitesnow sighed. "I will tell Master Catabaysi that we tabled the discussion. Perhaps I can convince him to keep the curfew at sundown."

"Thank you," the castellan said. "Or at the very least, if we could negotiate to seven bells, it would certainly be easier to swallow if such a decree came with extra rations. You have kept the water flowing as well as certain services. For that, we are appreciative but if people are going to be locked in their houses, extra food can be a soothing balm."

"I will negotiate it with my master."

Castellan Tallhill nodded somberly.

"I know you see us as the villains in this tale," she said. "I hope that soon the population will understand that we are serving the greater good."

"How so?"

"I study history," Nikkala said proudly. "Fifty years ago, there was a dispute over territory between Monterra and Arvaterra. It was a territorial dispute over a patch of islands. When the Arvateri navy sieged the Monterran island, the king declared that one Arvateri coin was the equivalent of twenty Monterran ones. So an Arvateri sailor could walk into a cheese shop or a winery and buy mountains of things on a meager salary. They could buy out entire shops and leave nothing for the people. Our skeleton forces do not eat. They do not drink. We are not absconding away with your resources and leaving nothing for the people."

"I have studied history too, Whitesnow. Maybe we studied different eras. Maybe you have forgotten the stories of when the Blue Death gripped this city."

"All Incanterrans know that tale."

"Truly? Because your master might need to be reminded. But you certainly cannot label these bland foodstuffs delivered by the Baelannor dynasty as sufficient. You have cut off the harbor. We cannot import food from other kingdoms. We cannot even bring in food from our northern farmlands. Eventually, the cupboards are going to go bare.

"You have seen the riots perpetrated by the Unbound. Those were riots perpetrated out of principle when people had the luxury of being mad over trivial things. I have read the journals of civil servants during the Blue Death. When the plague gripped this city, it almost tore itself apart.

"Xizzen Avernden knew the truth. You have to keep the public sated. You have to keep food in their bellies. His lineage forgot that. And if the royal family had not fled to Castratellus, I am willing to bet their shoulders would have been alleviated from the weight of their heads.

"The Unbound Riots were nothing compared to what a riot will be when it is executed by starving people. And then, your skeletal forces better be damn strong or a riot will not be the only thing executed."

Tallhill let his threat hang in the air. Whitesnow paused and took a deep breath.

"Between you and me?" she asked.

"I've longed for many things to be kept just between you and me."

Nikkala cocked her head to the side. "Even now? Even with everything going on, you would attempt to lure me into your bed?"

"Now who is being naive? How do you think most of the adults in this city are handling your little coup after the sun goes down and your lockdowns are in place?"

"Nevertheless," the woman quietly seethed. "Look at your population. Look at who Master Catabaysi has recruited into the ranks. Prisoners, the mentally deranged, the dregs, the addicted. They brought nothing to your streets but misery. There was a reason the Under Roads were so feared. But now, not only do their disappearances alleviate the strain on your resources. In their death, they are being called upon to serve a greater purpose, far greater than anything they have done in life. Once we have our army – our strong army – we will march forth to fulfill our destiny. That fact is what you need to be selling your people."

"But am I selling them an authentic bill of goods?" the castellan asked. "When you have your force, you will leave? Because as the population of the city thins out – all the more reason to issue more food – it feels like those remaining still have a noose tightening around their necks."

"I will discuss things with Master Catabaysi. Unlike the previous patrons and their endless greed, my master is generous. Our dynasty is not looking to rule and keep the people subjugated. It will be a matter of how much more food can be squeezed from the existing resources. I believe in the mission that my master is laying down. I believe in it with all my heart. Otherwise, I would not be part of his house."

Tallhill's eyes narrowed as he considered the situation. "So you truly believe this? You believe that your master is on some sort of holy crusade?"

"He is."

"Well, a significant portion of the population agrees with you. They are content to ride this out because they believe this will not be a protracted siege. It is why they are respecting the curfew."

"See to it that they continue to do so," Nikkala warned. "Otherwise, they may find themselves within Master Catabaysi's legions."

With the threat hanging ominously, Nikkala swept from the castellan's office. The workers in the reception hall avoided all eye contact as the Necromangian left.

Nikkala smiled. Despite his lascivious ways and his buffoonery, Mahon Tallhill was an excellent politician. She had come intent on imposing more sanctions and instead walked out promising more food.

Down staircases, hallways, and finally out of the entrance of the grand building, Nikkala could feel fearful eyes upon her.

Before, she could always sense the lecherous glares of the male bureaucrats who saw her only as a conquest. She had used that to her advantage as a guild advocate. But now, her whole aura and her wizardly robes had changed the attitude of these so-called men of power.

It was a fact not lost on the wizardess.

Chapter 16

Hoisting their spears and tridents high above their heads, the Kai'kamina raiders cheered as the dark shadow from the deep broke from the surf with authority.

The great beast was enormous. Its lower half resembled a lobster with eight chitin-covered walking legs, a thorax, a segmented abdomen, and a fanning tail. The lobster anatomy was covered in thick, rigid armor that was coal black with red striping and splotches. But where the lobster's head should have been there was an upright torso resembling the Kai'kamina. Its thick, muscled arms ended in chitin blades resembling lobster claws more than hands. The massive beast was so tall it could look the towering earth elemental in the glowing energy pools serving as its eyes.

As the monster arrived on the beach, it was cheered on by the Kai'kamina lining the waterline, eager to let their summoned champion turn the tide back in their favor.

"Ula'Kanaka," one of the defending fishermen said while doing his best to keep his shaking hands from dropping his spear. All around them, ripples of fear and uncertainty washed over the land-walking forces.

Amongst the line of defenders, Cinder Fireborne and Thade Skystone found themselves standing shoulder to shoulder on either side of the shaman woman who was controlling the sand elemental.

Thade glanced over at the beautiful islander. "I am told your island doesn't have many cows."

"*This* is your concern?" the shaman asked. "Right now? You want to worry about our lack of cows?"

"Not your lack of cows. I am more concerned with your lack of butter. I know you all have a variety of goats. How is their milk production?"

The shaman looked at the foreigner with a confused expression and gestured toward the beach. "We have *literally* much bigger problems."

"The only problem I see is not having enough butter or a big enough pot to put that big ass tail in when this is over," Thade said confidently. "Cinder, feel like bringing the heat?"

"Sure," the rogue wizard said with a smile. "Although we would greatly appreciate it if your elementals could maybe tenderize the meat a tad before we begin?"

Breaking from the ranks of the fishermen's lines, the five adventurers started making their way down the beach with their magical weapons at the ready. The lumbering earth elemental quickly joined the rogues as well. The sand elemental closed ranks, slithering and sliding within and amongst the pink sand.

While the Ula'Kanaka was certainly colossal and its mass was intimidating, with the Kai'kamina taking a step back and allowing the champion to storm forward, their forces had made a critical error. They now allowed the land-walkers to concentrate their attacks on a single target.

The Malinsuli shaman sent her sand elemental in first. Its amorphous form sank amongst the pink sand and proceeded to slither underneath the many legs of the mighty Ula'Kanaka. The unstable footing of the beast robbed it of its ability to generate real power.

Her companion shaman also sent his big, lumbering earth elemental in to challenge the Ula'Kanaka directly. The full-frontal assault was impossible to ignore as the creature's large rock hands delivered staggering punches that the Ula'Kanaka was forced to counter and parry.

Doing so left its flanks vulnerable. If it wasn't Swayna peppering the monster with crackling bolts from her crossbow, it was Valos slicing at the joints of the monster's exoskeleton. Thade's vicious hand axes cracked and splintered the Ula'Kanaka's carapace. Cavin's silver sword, typically used on the undead, was no less sharp and slicing against the sea creature. And all the while, Cinder continued to whip lashes of lightning down on the monster's thorax.

With every strike against their summoned champion, enthusiasm and hope continued to drain from the assembled Kai'kamina forces. The raw power of the Ula'Kanaka began to slowly wane as its strikes became fewer and fewer. The hits against the earth elemental chipped stone. Claw slices spilled loose earth and mud from the creature's center. But the emotionless features of the elemental showcased no sign of fatigue.

The Ula'Kanaka swung one of its oversized great claws forward but the elemental shifted and dodged backward. The missing strike left the Ula'Kanaka overextended, off-balance, and open for the staggering, heavy-handed counterpunch from the elemental. After receiving more than a few counterpunches, the beast finally staggered.

It attempted to desperately land a hit with a wild haymaker but the stone elemental simply blocked the strike with its stubby arm, shoving its forearm into the crook of the Ula'Kanaka's elbow. It then delivered a silencing uppercut that connected squarely under the monster's jaw.

There was a sickening crack. The monster froze, hanging in the air for a heartbeat, and then collapsed lifeless onto the pink sands of the Malinsuli beach. The monster's equally massive death rattle echoed out over the waves and across the island.

Then... silence reigned.

The only sound was the lapping of the waves against the shore.

The Kai'kamina that had not retreated beneath the waves stood silently. The assembled Malinsuli fishermen allowed their speartips to droop. Valos Ironblade looked back and forth at the Malinsuli and the Kai'kamina. He lowered his weapon and the rest of his cadre did the same.

The Kai'kamina could only stand and look on with shock etched across their green faces. Finally, with a slowness spurred by disbelief and surprise, the Kai'kamina high priest brought the large seashell horn back to its rubbery lips. The sound produced was far different from the boisterous blasts heard earlier. Now, it was a melancholy tone. Reluctantly, the Kai'kamina began to retreat into the water. Some were unable to take their eyes off the fallen Ula'kanaka and had to be pulled back into the ocean by the members of their tribe who kept their sensibilities.

The Malinsuli fishermen were not chasing after them. They were not hurling spears or arrows during the retreat. They were content to let the water breathers leave their island.

Slowly, the merfolk disappeared beneath the waves. Swimming with grace and speed, their dark shadows melded with the deepwater as they completed their retreat.

On the beach, there was a brief rousing of cheers but the celebration did not last long. There were wounded to tend to and the security of the children needed to be addressed.

Valos kept a sharp eye on the water. He had seen feints and false retreats before. Several of the Malinsuli shared his paranoia as they formed loose lines along the beach. But as they stood their watch against the waves, an elder began a chant in their native tongue. Several of the warriors joined in.

The shore guardians then proceeded to slap rhythmically on their thighs, their chests, their abdomens, and the meat of their arms. As Valos watched, he saw this was not just random or haphazard. The men worked together in a unified war dance. The men pushed against an invisible wall as if projecting out a shield to keep their island safe. But their war chants were also directed at the fallen body of the Ula'Kanaka as if honoring the great creature for its noble effort despite being on the opposite side of the conflict.

The sound of rumbling stones drew Valos's attention. He turned and saw the tall, wild-haired shaman interacting with his earth elemental. He had seen such connections before but with men petting large dogs. The big elemental was down on one knee and leaning over to look the human in the eye. The shamanic master was showering his summoned elemental with honor and he wore a wide smile.

Finally, the earth elemental nodded and stuck out his stony hand with his palm facing toward the sky. The shaman smiled, raised his hand high into the air, and then slapped his palm against the elemental.

The shaman then extended his hand and held his palm face up. With surprising gentleness, the earth elemental returned the gesture. There was a nod of respect between the two and then the pools of energy serving as the elemental's eyes blinked and winked out. The massive pile of stone and soil inanimated and disintegrated, collapsing back onto the rich earth.

The shaman caught sight of Valos and quickly moved to approach. He waved warmly and carried the same smile as he did when dealing with his elemental ally. "I cannot thank you enough," the shaman said.

Valos offered an open palm and an exposed wrist. The shaman returned the gesture, grasping the rogue's wrist in greeting. "Valos Ironblade of Incanterra."

"Amman, shaman of Malinsula," he replied with a smile. "Incanterra? You and your crew have made quite a journey."

"I'm just happy we showed up today instead of tomorrow."

"I've got a village full of children thinking the same thing. You all pack a wallop. I think the Kai'kamina would not have been as easily rousted if not for you all. You spared a lot of lives today."

"Is this a regular thing?"

"Hardly," the shaman replied. "Sure, we fish and do some clamming but we never enter their deep waters. Conversely, they don't invade our shores. Occasionally some divers will stumble across some scouts. They share the water with us with an unspoken agreement. We don't go too deep into their territory and they don't come into ours. There has always been an... an *uneasy* peace."

"I got some relationships like that with some girls back home. Most of 'em are mad I didn't come by and see them the next day," Valos said with a grin. "So why the sudden change?"

The shaman looked out on the waves and the water. "I wish I knew."

Chapter 17

In the light of the new day, Mirawen Autumnlight and Kynna Summerwind made their way through the streets of Shaded Light. From Mirawen's quaint apartment, the duo was heading towards the center of the ward. "While I am waiting for the inn to get rebuilt, I have been supplementing my employment," Mirawen explained. "I think I can get you some papers drawn up that can keep you out of the fire if snouts start poking in."

"What do you do?"

"I work with the Necromangians," she replied flatly.

Kynna paused her pace. When Mirawen noted, she stopped short and came back to offer a whisper. "It is not as bad as it sounds. I help distribute rations."

"That work has to put you right up next to the wizards though."

"It does," Mirawen replied.

Kynna stood as still as a statue and was just as difficult to read. She tumbled her options over in her head. After taking too long, Mirawen relented. "We don't want to be late."

Not knowing what else to do, Kynna fell back into step with her guide through the Northeast District. As the two continued, Mirawen noted a friend from across the way and waved her over. Dressed in her modest summer fashions, the young lady had to stand on her tiptoes to break five feet tall and she defied the laws of gravity by her bodice not pulling her forward onto her face. Mirawen reached down to give the girl a warm embrace.

"Amber, this is my friend Kynna," Mirawen said. "Kynna, this is Amber. She's a servant for those fancy Goldcrests over in the Northwest District."

"Was," Amber said flatly.

Mirawen turned. "What?"

"Three years I have been working over there. I never once missed a shift. I often worked over and extra. But it is that way with almost all the servant staff for those wealthy types."

"They fired you?"

"Technically, we are all 'on leave.' None of us are getting paid but we haven't lost our employment status. Which I suppose is our saving grace when the tax collectors come around or when we have to declare our work status. But for most of those fancies, they sent everyone home but the barest of the staff. Their gates are all closed and they are living off their larders until the boners move on."

"So how are you set for coins?" Mirawen asked.

"I've got a bit for a bit but if this whole siege drags on, things are going to get bad real quick," the young woman replied. "It is part of the reason I was glad I ran into you. You got any openings?"

Being in the center of the ward, the trio was near the wooden bones of the Shadow's Edge Inn and its halted construction. "If I had the inn up and running, I would bring you over in a snap. You put those assets even just a little on display and extra coins for your service would be plentiful."

Amber's green eyes shifted nervously at the unknown Kynna. "I got out of that," she whispered. "I'm not looking to go back. Things aren't *that* desperate."

"Everything is above board at the inn. I'm talking extra coins for men happy you keep their tankards full. Nothing else," Mirawen smiled, placing her hand on the pommel of the black dagger on her belt. "But until the boners move on and the curfews get lifted, no one is working. You have to assume the Goldcrests will recall you before I can put you to work."

"I heard that over in the Northwest, there is a family offering security to the richers," Amber said. "Any chance you have heard of anything like that here in the Northeast?"

Mirawen gave a smile. "I have no doubt you filled out that scullery maid's outfit much to old man Goldcrest's liking but I don't see you dressed in chain armor and swinging a sword."

"Definitely not but if you are providing security, it might mean you are offering other services. Opportunities."

"I can keep my ears open," Mirawen replied.

Amber nodded. "Well, I am back in the ward. I'll be staying until the Northwest opens back up. Anything you could throw my way would be appreciated. Plus, it would make me feel better. The last thing I want is to get rounded up by the boners for not being able to produce a job card."

"I promise you, you will be on the top of my list. And if things work out, we might be involved in something where I can match your pay. Maybe we can keep you out of the estate permanently."

"I would be indebted to you," Amber said.

The two shared an embrace. Mirawen whispered, "Whatever you need."

Back to a duo, Kynna noted Mistweave Mercantile. While the business was open, through the windows, she could see how empty the shelves were. Important staples had long been snatched up. The only things left were less than useful items in a city under siege. And with the gates sealed off by magical barriers, there was no new inventory to restock the shelves.

As they were waiting, a fellow Shader – a big man with a wicked scar on his cheek and eyes that did not quite line up correctly – jutted his strong jaw in the woman's direction. "Ho, Mirawen," he grunted. "When is the high and mighty Ironblade going to grace the ward with his presence?"

"You don't need to worry about Valos, Hendrick."

"We pay his crew to keep the ward safe. Any of this look safe to you?"

The young woman stepped close to keep her voice low. "Look around you. This is an act of the gods. And I don't mean that in a pantheon way, you dumb lummox. What happens when a hurricane bears down on the city? Do you expect them to go down to the docks and stand at Highstone Harbor to ward off the storm?"

The big man squinted. "Lots o' talk. Lots o' promises. And when the going got tough, they tucked tails and ran. Tell your little bosser that he ain't getting another copper out of me."

"Tough talk now," Mirawen replied. "I'll let Thade know your feelings."

The man blanched slightly and then disappeared into the crowd.

A dark shadow passed over the ward. Looking up, right on schedule, Mirawen saw one of the ensorcelled sloops that belonged to the wizards. With her hull crackling with energy, the floating ship descended into the intersection of Second Street and Gold Avenue, which served as the center of the ward.

A Necromangian dressed in his blood-red and black-trimmed robes helmed the boat. There was a female representative of the Baelannor dynasty in her purple and gold-trimmed robes. And then there were a collection of animated corpses. Unlike the skeletal warriors that patrolled the streets, the corpses were still utilizing their reanimated muscles. Although, they wore concealing cloaks and leather masks to hide their graying flesh. Ironically, the ghouls did not reek of death as one might have expected.

The animated ghouls moved with commanded purpose, following the instructions of their Necromangian masters. They used their unnatural strength and their immunity to fatigue to offload the Baelannor-conjured foodstuffs to the waiting Shaders in the intersection.

Helping accept the large bags of summoned supplies, Kynna made it a point to keep her backside to the boat and the wizards on board. It was purposeful and did not escape Mirawen's detection.

The same as every other day, the food was offloaded. The ghouls returned to the boat without a sound. The Baelannor wizard offered the smallest of salutations and the boat lifted off into the sky. It would float over the Queen's High Way and back to the industrial workrooms in the southern districts where the conjurors created more life-sustaining food for the population.

Mirawen and her collection of workers set to breaking the shipment down into manageable piles and began filling bags. They would then be distributed to the citizens of the ward. As Mirawen was putting yet another bag of supplies together from the pallets of the foodstuff, she made it a point to get close to Kynna to keep the conversation between the two of them.

"I could try to use some elaborate ruses and draw it out of you," Mirawen said flatly. "But that has never been my style. And I hope we can both agree that if I wanted to turn you in for some sort of reward, that was my opportunity. I could have clapped you in irons and delivered you to them wrapped in a satin bow."

"What are you talking about?" Kynna asked.

"Yeah, you are going to fit right in here in Shaded Light. I knew... No, I *know* someone that was just like you. And you are sticking with the rules. Deny, deny, deny. But when you have seen it before, you know what to look for. The rest of the Shaders don't but I do. So I will just say your secret is safe with me."

Kynna continued to work silently, stuffing another bag with supplies.

"So, did you lose your wand? Is that it? So now you can't cast? Or is it one of those things that you got caught when the curtain came down? So you have been dodging and ducking from ward to ward for the last two weeks and now you find yourself in Shaded Light."

Kynna sighed deeply and turned to face Mirawen.

"I'm a Lu'Scion."

Mirawen's eyebrows raised and she smiled. "A magician? Look at you. Although, why am I looking at you? You obviously didn't want the wizzers to recognize you. Why not use all your illusion magic to change your appearance? Wait, you're not secretly a man are you?"

Kynna managed a laugh. "Probably more than any other dynasty, my magic is component intensive. And my stores are running low. Besides, my illusions are only effective if there is a mind to deceive."

"One of those 'if a dragon roars and no one is around to hear it' riddles?"

"More or less. And the undead don't have living minds to see my illusions. So as powerful as I can be, against them, I am useless."

"Well, I am happy to keep your secret as long as you..."

Mirawen trailed off as she looked over Kynna's shoulder. She grumbled. And then hissed out an unflattering curse.

Very softly, Kynna followed Mirawen's lead and went back to work with the bags. Setting the next one to the side, she used the movement to look behind her. That was when she saw several Knights of the Imperial Circle sauntering towards the intersection.

Chapter 18

The mer-forces of the Kai'kamina had retreated beneath the waves and left the isle of Malinsula to her land-walking natives. Scores of bodies littered the pink sand beaches both human and Kai'kamina alike. There was also the corpse of the massive Ula'Kanaka left behind. The island had returned to her peaceful temperament with the two most prominent sounds being the soft howl of the wind and the crashing rumbles of the everpresent tide.

Walking the beach, the Malinsuli shaman Sario was inspecting the battlefield. Navigating the carnage, the young woman shook her head at the rampant loss of life on both sides of the battle lines. Splashes of red and gouts of purple stained the perfect pink sands of the beach. Thankfully, the hints of the coming tide began to lap against the minuscule grains and had already begun the slow and steady cleansing process. With the storm from under the sea and also in the sky above having receded, life had started its quick march to normalcy.

From out of the village of Searock, women and children were streaming out from between the tents and other structures, bearing medicine and bandages for the wounded. The fastest was dispatched to summon the healers while others would run the cobblestone paths to the center of the island and inform the king of the attack on his people. King Muera and his coterie of elders would no doubt arrive with provisions and resources to help the village.

The women were quickly tending to the injured. Salves and unguent were being applied to cuts and slashes. Wounds were being wrapped in liniment-soaked bandages. Once triaged, the wounded would be taken to the tents for rest and care. For those that could not be moved easily, a second wave of helpers was making their way onto the beach with litters fashioned from bamboo poles and their fishing nets. The more severely wounded would be treated by the healers. Sario knew others would come soon to collect the bodies of their sacred dead so they could be prepared for their final journey to join their ancestors.

But as Sario walked the sands, her eye was drawn to the fallen Kai'kamina. Squatting down beside one of the fallen foes, she noted certain emaciation along with swollen and distended bellies. Their merfolk features included sunken eyes and a gauntness she rarely recognized amongst the tribe. The long tendrils that dangled from their chins – almost resembling braided beards – were positively brittle for an aquatic species. Looking back at the village, Sario noted several of the fishmongers and harvesters scampering about. Many of them were in tizzies and fretting over the stringers of fish snatched from their stores by the fleeing Kai'kamina.

The shaman returned to her feet. Looking about, she found the five foreigners beginning to regroup into a cluster along with Amman further down the shoreline. What was more, a great sailing vessel was drifting in to make port along their piers. The shaman had seen such arcane spells in the past. While vastly different from their elementalist magic, she knew the dimensionation art.

Pulling the long braids of her white hair back out of her face and lashing them together, she adjusted her sarong and moved to join her cousin for a proper introduction.

Amman was already standing beside the handsome man with salt-and-pepper hair and the beginnings of a beard. As the other two men approached – the big one with all the muscles and the long-legged one that fought with the silver sword – Amman gave them the custom greeting. He clutched the backs of their necks while placing his forehead against theirs. To the two women, he placed both his hands in an **X** over his chest and bowed submissively.

Amman saw Sario approaching and motioned warmly for her to join them. "Incanterrans, allow me to introduce my cousin, Sario. You will be hard-pressed to find another shaman on the island with a deeper connection to the elements than her. Her skills make mine look amateurish by comparison."

"Incanterra?" Sario asked with a curious smile. "You all are a long way from home."

She approached the big man first. He nodded and began to stoop down to press his forehead against hers but then halted awkwardly. "Do we do the forehead thing?"

Sario smiled and instead put her palm against his chest. "The *mai'here* is performed by men to men. You touch the forehead and nose to honor the ancestors and continue the line of breath. It is a way for us to say you are no longer visitors. You saved lives today. Because of your actions, men will go on to make children and those children will make children. You allow our greatest resource to continue. In honor of your actions, you are now family. Forever."

Amman smiled. "She explains it more poetically than I can."

Sario kept her hand on the big man's chest. She closed her eyes as she felt his energy. "You have a mighty heart," she said with a smile. "We feel your heart to know your spirit. Men show honor to women by crossing their hands at the wrists as a shield and offering a bow."

The handsome man with the salt and pepper beard threw his hands up. "So we can't feel their spirit? That's not fair."

The shorter woman smacked the man's shoulder in aggravation. If they had been sitting at a table, she no doubt would have kicked him in the shin.

The muscled man brought his hands up to cross his forearms. "Is it right over left or left over right?"

"The fact that you care enough to ask honors me," Sario replied. "It is whatever feels natural; the most comfortable."

The shaman felt each of the men's hearts and moved to warmly embrace both women as if they were long-lost sisters.

All of the proper names and titles were shared amongst the assembled. Sario smiled warmly in her greeting. "Welcome to Malinsula. Your help with the Kai'kamina and the defeat of the great Ula'Kanaka eternally binds you to the people of Searock and with all the people of our island."

"Searock is the village?" Swayna asked, nodding towards the collection of tents.

Unlike the tall stone and wooden structures within the great city of the Incanterran capital, the homes of the Malinsuli looked almost collapsible as if they could be taken down and moved if needed. The frames of the tents were literal bones of great sea creatures. Rather than canvas, their tents were made from cured hides, sewn together, stretched tautly over the bones, and lashed to stakes.

As the group talked, Thade noted several of the villagers beginning to gather up the corpses of the felled Kai'kamina. He cleared his throat and gestured toward the workers. "What will they do with the bodies? You all don't... eat them. Do you?"

"Have you never had frog legs?" Amman asked.

Sario turned and waved off her cousin. "Stop it," she hissed. "No, Thade Skystone. They will not be eaten.

"And that has nothing to do with the fact they taste terrible," Amman quipped.

Sario offered another smile. "Desperate times call for desperate measures. It sometimes works out well. I doubt only the most starving of men would crack open one of our passion eggs, see what was inside it, and consider eating it."

"It is true," Amman added. "Inside this purple plant egg, it looks like someone blew their nose into it."

"Charming," Cavin quipped.

"But the taste is phenomenal."

"So we can all rest assured we will not be eating the legs and buttocks of the frogmen," Cavin said, trying to sound positive. "So where are they taking them?"

"Just burying them would serve no purpose," Amman said. "Bones can be harvested for tools and weapons. Organs and meat can be used for bait. The Kai'kamina tastes terrible to us but not necessarily to the sharks that swim on the eastern side of the island. And while the skin is too small to be stretched and cured for the homes, it does make amazing leather. Dried merfolk skin can make for a strong and lightweight shield if you can stretch it far enough. But northerners pay good coin for a genuine Kai'kamina belt or boots."

"If you like that hideous green color," Valos said with a curled nose.

"Oh, I don't know," Sway said. "They might make for some stylish bracers. Or a nice pair of shoes. You get a crate of these up to the Northwest District and tell all the snoots that this is all the fashion rage, I bet they sell out in a week."

Sario smiled. "We try not to let anything go to waste."

As the group was discussing the high fashion of the Kai'kamina skin, Cinder and Valos found each other. They exchanged certain looks. An understated raise of an eyebrow. A subtle shrug. The faintest of nods. Both were thinking the same thing and while Valos was silently asking for permission to move forward, Cinder gave him the slightest of "not yet" gestures. Valos nodded in agreement and moved to pivot.

"I assume that our captain and his vessel will need to meet with your dockmaster. I hope our ship can purchase supplies."

"Of course, although after your assistance, I would be surprised if they would be willing to accept your gold coins," Amman said.

"We'll see about that," the rogue said with a grin.

Chapter 19

The Knights of the Imperial Circle – for all of their pomp and pageantry – possessed an incredible gift of intimidation, especially up close. If not for their rhetoric entwined with the belief of wizardly superiority, those of a nonmagical class could have found their vestments charming. The quality of the material, the stitching, and the embroidery were not too different from the holy regalia of the All-Father's priests. And yet, most felt their alabaster masks and their conical hoods were wholly unnerving. The masks resembled porcelain dolls. There were very few defined features and no ornamentation. The expressionless faces staring back at the accused were enough to unsettle even the most stalwart under scrutiny and questioning.

As the Knights of the Imperial Circle entered the ward of Shaded Light, those milling about gave them plenty of space. Shortly after the chaos of the initial undead siege settled, the Knights were publically proclaimed the city's marshals by order of Nalazar Catabaysi. They were his hand and their authority was absolute. They could detain any citizen for any reason.

At first, there were vocal protests when people saw their fellow citizens clapped in irons and drug away. Once days passed and those taken failed to return to their apartments, people learned not to give the Knights any excuse.

The quartet of knights commandeered the center of the intersection where Shaders were putting together sundry bags for the people. One of the four knights began ringing a brass handbell to garner attention. Producing a rolled scroll, another of the four proceeded to announce the formal proclamation. His voice was magically enhanced and echoed down the streets of the ward.

"Hear ye! Hear ye! Let it be known to all citizens of Incanterra. The Knights of the Imperial Circle are offering rewards leading to the apprehension of any renegade wizard hiding amongst the populace. Note that these wizards are far too dangerous to be apprehended by citizens but our organization will pay coin rewards for information leading to the arrest of these fugitives."

Kynna Lu'Scion looked nervously at Mirawen Autumnlight. The young woman was a natural beauty that would often draw many curious eyes to her. Yet, she was dressed in the modest fashions of an Incanterran commoner. Any wizardly tokens had long been shed. The knights would have had to have been inspectors of the finest order or known the magician personally before the siege to recognize her. Unfortunately, Kynna did not know who was behind the alabaster masks.

Mirawen abolished Kynna's fears with the slightest shake of her head. The young woman stood at rapt attention, like so many of her fellow citizens, but she was intent on keeping Kynna safe.

"Let it be known. Aiding and abetting a wizard fugitive is a crime. Knowing the location of a wizard, helping hide them, and not reporting them to the proper authorities will also be considered a crime. Harsh punishments will be meted out by those charged with endangering the safety and security of the kingdom. This formal announcement is considered due notice for all citizens who have heard these words either directly or indirectly. Ignorance of the law is not a defensible justification. It is so decreed."

With their proclamation proclaimed, the Knights began moving east, no doubt intent on delivering the same message to the citizens of Brickyard in the next ward over. The Shaders were happy to let them go and those in the intersection went back to compiling the sundries.

"This makes no sense," Mirawen huffed. "Last month, these guys were kissing the ass of wizarding dynasties. The wizzers were the saviors of the kingdom and sunlight streamed from their orifices. Now the Knights are rounding them up like criminals?"

Kynna looked up and down the streets of the ward. "Everything has a ranking within this city. This district is better than that district. This ward is better than that ward. Even the lowest ward in the Northeast is better than the best ward in the Southwest. And round and round it goes. The wizards are no different. Up there on the isle, before everything cracked in half, all the dynasties were jockeying for position. It was all part of the game that was happening without anyone admitting it was happening."

"And then this new dynasty comes along?" Mirawen asked.

"The Knights are just backing the biggest dog in the fight," the secret wizard explained. "But it still doesn't explain why you didn't turn me in. If one of those men behind the masks had recognized me for who I was, your neck would be in the noose too."

"I hate the wizards for their greed, not because of their magic. Yeah, they are selfish, arrogant, and high and mighty but they were essential for the kingdom. These death magic users? They ain't. Any wizards that end up in their hands are going to be in for a world of hurt. I'm not contributing to that."

"How long do you think that loyalty will last?"

"As long as Baelannor keeps delivering food and water, we won't get too desperate."

Mirawen and Kynna went back to work preparing the bags of foodstuffs for their dispensing to the community. While they were working, Mirawen spotted another of the ward's staples. She smiled and gave a wave to Zavala, son of Dulgallah.

The constable's heritage was from the southern kingdoms. Tall and handsome, the peace officer kept his long braided hair lashed out of his face. He moved with a smooth but less than purposeful gait, keeping an eye on the surroundings. Without making a direct line, Zavala continued his wandering, bringing himself closer and closer to Mirawen without appearing too obvious.

"Citizen," he said with a nod. "You are doing good work getting this food ready to be distributed."

Mirawen nodded and smiled. "Thank you, constable. This is one of our newest helpers. Kynna Summerwind. I am working on getting her employment papers drawn up."

Zavala gave a nod. "You are serving a good cause, milady."

"It feels more like I am contributing to the house arrest of citizens," Kynna said quietly.

The constable handed one of the flour bundles from the table to Kynna for her to place it in the sundry bag. "Too many businesses have been shuttered. People can't work. Which means they can't earn coins to buy food. These rations are feeding people. So I am thankful for women like you and Mirawen. You are helping me keep the peace."

"Been arresting a lot?" Mirawen asked quietly.

"Thank the ancestors, no. But those hood knights have no problem rounding up people. I want you to be aware. Catabaysi has granted them special powers. If you are going to get arrested, make sure it is a constable doing it. You will end up in a holding cell. If the Knights grab you, you just disappear."

"Citizens want to complain but they don't know who to complain to," Mirawen said.

"And if they do, chances are they will disappear," Zavala warned. "So don't end up on the wrong side of them. Don't give them any excuse."

"Where do you think all the rabble-rousers end up?" Kynna asked.

"I cannot say for certain. Moving between districts is pretty difficult right now but there are always rumors. I have heard terrible things are happening in the Southwest District. I heard sections like the tanneries and all of Mutaccio's potion brewing operations have been appropriated. The rumor is fresh skeletons are being marched out of those warehouses. I don't think you have to be a genius to put that puzzle together.

"The Imperial Knights are looking for any excuse to add to the army of living skeletons. Their death squads are looking to round up any conspirators. So, keep your nose clean."

"We will," Mirawen said. "But still why all the pretend?"

Zavala shook his head. "I don't know."

Kynna looked out at the scattered groups of citizens in Shaded Light. "It provides the lie. It provides some semblance of order for the masses. It is no different than providing this food. It keeps all of us docile so we all don't band together. Let them come for the old, as long as they aren't coming for me."

"Real ray of sunshine, this one," Zavala said to Mirawen while nodding at Kynna.

"Yeah but she is still a friend of *mine*," Mirawen said.

Zavala picked up on the subtle cant.

"And I can't say that she is wrong," she continued. "That basic instinct of self-preservation is hard to deny."

"Well, all the more reason for you to be careful," the constable replied. "Getting picked up by one of mine is one thing. Getting snatched up by those hoods, I don't think even people in high places could save you before judgment and sentencing were passed."

The constable sidled closer. "Speaking of people in high places... have you heard from...?"

Mirawen shook her head. "I don't know if any of them know what is going on. And even if they did, how would they even get back into the city? If none of us can get out, I don't see breaking in being any easier."

"If anyone could get in, it is those four."

Chapter 20

Impressing a wizard with magical power was not an easy feat. The inducted of the arcane class understood spellcasting better than those who lived outside of the sphere. As such, wizards from the free kingdoms who were not Incanterran natives would often marvel at the sheer logistics behind the creation of the isle of Sorceria. Generations ago, after the combined magic of The Eight floated Sorceria above the grand capital, wizards came from far and wide to admire the achievement. Those who lived upon the utopian isle – from patron to adept to apprentices – understood the legacy created by wizardly cooperation.

All those living upon the isle understood the significance of one wizard sundering Sorceria. The attack from Nalazar Catabaysi had conjured colossal cracks along the natural faultlines of the floating island. Foul fissures formed from the terrible magic unleashed by the undead lich. Thankfully, the undead horror had not compromised the crystals containing the magical energy keeping the island floating above Incanterra. What was left was a testament to the great wizard's power. The undead wizard wanted to send a message and that message had been both received and heeded.

Nalazar Catabaysi's commands were to be followed.

The entire fleet of magical floating sloops that ferried people from Sorceria to the capital city were sent below. When they returned, they were filled with wizards in blood-red robes trimmed with black silk. They came from all walks of life, shedding their vocational masks and no longer pretending to be simple butchers, bakers, and candlestick makers.

Their red robes emblazoned with their hourglass symbols no longer needed to be hidden in the backs of wardrobes, in the bottom of trunks, or stashed under beds. They were finally able to be worn in the light of day. And these loyalists to the undead wizard carried their wands crafted from bone to deliver their outlawed magic. For generations, the Necromangians had been forced to hide in the shadows. Now was their moment in the sun. That newfound freedom combined with the fear of their magic made for a dangerous concoction that even Mutaccio apprentices would recognize as volatile.

This haughtiness was exemplified in one Raptum Shadecrest. A young man just having broken into his second decade, he would still be considered a high-level apprentice within most dynasties. Down below, Raptum worked at the city's kennels. An unglamorous position by most standards, his tax-funded office was charged with rounding up stray canines and other animals to keep their population in check. It was also his job to put those animals down. Few citizens would want to accept such a position. But the profession gave him access to a litany of corpses. As such, his necromantic skills were incredibly honed and rivaled some adepts twice his age.   ·

His best friend was Ravok Greenvale. A Necromangian who had survived the initiation into the order, Ravok worked for a curio dealer. While his duties included dusting and sweeping the shop, the importer had regular access to a variety of strange oddities serving as material components for the wizard spells. It made Ravok a valuable supplier for Raptum.

The two worked together to reanimate the corpses of particularly vicious breeds of dogs. Under their complete control, it was quite a sight to see Raptum strolling the ground of Sorceria with a pair of Rotte butcher dogs.

Named for the southern Monterra region of Rotte, the butcher dogs were used to herd livestock and the larger of the breeds even pulled small carts filled with butchered meat to the market. Tall, broad-shouldered, wide-headed, and known for their signature black coat with a tan underbelly and feet, the butcher dogs were considered noble at their best and terrifying at their worst. There was a reason why statues of Zaneger the Death God were often portrayed accompanied by the dog breed. Seeing one reanimated from death was the perfect encapsulation of the meaning of "hellhound."

On this bright, sunny day, Raptum and Ravok were strolling the shattered isle, enjoying the stiff breeze and the summer warmth. They strolled with a pair of their butcher dogs. And as the two came around the bend, they found a trio of wizards – a Mutaccio wizardess and a pair of Dinaciouns – talking next to a broken fountain that had been damaged during the sundering. The trio was close in age and house rank as the Necromangians.

"What do we have here?" Raptum asked with a drawl. "A potion brewer and a pair of seers. How goes the prognosticating, you cute little prognosticators?"

Before they could hasten a leave, one of the butcher dogs followed a mental order from their master and cut off the pathway. "Butling off in such a hurry?" Raptum asked. "It is so rare that I get to be in the presence of such beautiful ladies. A lesser wizard might take that affront personally."

The trio of apprentices remained silent, afraid to say the wrong thing. Raptum's eyes darted between the Dinacioun wizard and the two wizardesses. "So what would a pair of houses be discussing?" Raptum asked. "I thought your houses all despised working together. Isn't that right, Ravok?"

"That's what I hear," the companion replied.

"Working out some sort of arrangement so a Mutaccio potion might enhance your magical spying? That is what your dynast is known for, right? Spying?"

"Scrying," the Dinacioun wizard said, clearly irritated. "It's pronounced scrying."

"Your magic allows you to see things far away. Hear things at a great distance. Even remote seeing. Looking through the eyes of a bird overhead," Raptum said. "Sounds an awful lot like spying to me."

"We also find things that are lost," the Dinacioun wizardess said. "We ply our magic for learning and greater understanding."

"I don't think you have to be a Dinacioun to know how powerful we are," Raptum said, motioning a finger between himself, Ravok, and their butcher dogs. "Powerful wizards make powerful allies. Wouldn't you ladies agree?"

The Dinacioun wizard put his hands on his hips and cocked his head to the side. "And I don't have to be a top-tier magus to know where you are driving this conversation. For your information, it is not going to happen."

Raptum looked at the seer curiously and gave a little laugh. "For my information... Ravok, was that a joke?"

"Play on words maybe."

"Right because they practice divination... It's clever."

With blinding speed, Raptum's bone wand materialized in his hand and was pointed at the Dinacioun wizard. Before anyone could react, dark tendrils wreathed in red light snapped out. Squid-like in their movements, the tentacles latched onto the magus's torso. The two ladies attempted to move to help but the butcher dogs and Ravok's extended wand kept them in their place.

The Dinacioun wizard struggled to remain on his feet as his life essence was being drained from him. The tips of his brown hair were starting to turn gray. His green robes suddenly looked a size too large. His eyes began to sink in and his cheeks went hollow. Uncontrollably, he collapsed to his knees.

Raptum snapped the spell off with a flourish and the tendrils retreated into his wand. The Necromangian lorded over the wizard. "You see a lot, seer. Here I was looking for a playful tussle with one of your lady friends. But given that look in your eye and the way you carry yourself, something tells me you would be more skilled and knowledgeable when it comes to pleasing a man. You tell me. How are my divining skills?"

The wizard stayed on his knees, breathing hard, and tried to regain his composure as his life essence started to return to his reserves. He could not bring himself to look up into the eyes of the Necromangian. So, Raptum squatted down to look the Dinacioun in his eyes.

"At least, now you know," Raptum whispered. "That was but a taste. Try to subvert our rule again and I will not take it out on you. I am going to take it out on your Dinacioun sister. I will defile her in physical ways you cannot possibly imagine. My depravity runs deep, you pansy flower. Do you know one of my favorite things to do? I like to take women to the brink by strangling them while I mount them from behind. It is amazing the way they kick and fight when it is too much. But the thing about necromancy is... if she dies because I go too far, I can just bring her back. And then do it all over again. I might even make you watch."

Raptum returned to his feet. He stared at the pair of wizardesses. "Of course, it doesn't *have* to be this way. I find such pleasures are more enjoyable when the participants are... nice."

Raptum stepped to the Dinacioun wizardess. He took a lock of her long auburn hair between his fingers and held it to his nostrils. "You know what I mean by being nice, don't you? Nice. Willing. Not just willing. Eager. Would you be willing to be nice to me?"

The Dinacioun swallowed hard as she weighed her options. Raptum smiled at her. "What do you say we take a stroll over to that villa?"

Raptum reached out and took the Dinacioun wizard by the hand. As they turned to leave, they found their path cut off by a man in similar blood-red robes as the ones they wore. But this was no apprentice or even an adept.

Dragan Duskwood – the right hand of Nalazar Catabaysi – stood in their midst. And by the look on his face, the second of their dynasty was not pleased. "Raptum. Ravok."

"Master Duskwood," the duo said in unison.

"I want you to report to Twotrees down in the Southwest District. He needs help preparing the army. You are on his detail until I release you. And you are not to step foot on Sorceria without my permission. Assist in creating Twotree's assembly... or become part of it. Go. Now."

The master Necromangian turned to the trio of wizards and gestured with an open palm for them to take their leave. As he watched the trio depart, Dragan believed he noted the flittering aroma of sunflowers. He dismissed the smell as a lingering enchantment within the isle and went to continue his business, satisfied that the hooligans would be too tired after working with Twotrees to cause more problems.

"Power," he grumbled with a shake of his head.

Chapter 21

With permission from the Searock harbormaster, the *Castella Mare* made port alongside one of the large piers stretching out from the island into the ocean. The large ship with its three masts dwarfed the local vessels.

The Malinsuli were known for their canoe boats. Some vessels were two canoes of equal size set apart and parallel but tied together by long bamboo poles. The double-hulled boats offered great stability in the water as well as a shallow draft so a single sail was all that was needed. Tightly woven nets were often lashed between the double hulls. But the boats were built for speed and they rarely let the island of Malinsula drop below the horizon.

A few of the large versions of the canoe vessels featured small huts built on the frames between the two hulls. While these vessels were rare, they could make the crossing from the isle to the main continent. Still, they could not match the long-distance capability of the caravel-class *Castella Mare* or the galleons of the Arvateri navy.

Bronze-colored hands were happy to accept the mooring lines tossed down from the Incanterran ship. Others were quick to bring immediate freshwater stores aboard. Children scampered and clamored about the docks. Some precocious few even wanted to climb up the mooring lines to risk a look over the deck railings at the peculiar foreigners with their pale skin, strange clothes, and odd trappings. Several sarong-wearing youngsters laughed at the sleeves the sailors wore on their legs and their funny sandals that sheathed their feet and toes for some reason.

Down on the docks and nowhere near ready to step foot back on the *Castella Mare*, Valos was happy to coordinate with the locals. Back on the beach, Cinder watched him curiously. Valos was trying desperately to hand pouches of coins to the harbormaster but the Malinsuli kept refusing the gesture and pushing the coin purse away. Even at a distance, Cinder could understand the entire exchange. The Incanterran rogue could not believe the Malinsuli were generously just handing supplies over to the ship. The harbormaster's sarong did not even have pockets for Valos to pull an "Ombraterran goodbye" and secretly slip coins into.

Cinder laughed as Valos's visible frustration continued to grow as he looked around for someone to pay off. She thought she might have to step in until a phalanx of Malinsuli women arrived bearing gourds. Cinder knew. She had heard the stories. Those corked and stoppered gourds would be filled with a potent drink blending red wine, freshly squeezed juices, sugar, and slices of the local citrus fruits. If anything was going to temper Valos it was attractive women and tasty booze.

She looked about with satisfaction. The *Castella Mare* was in port and receiving supplies. The rain had broken up and moved on. Now, the sun was out and bright. The waves lapped gently against the bright pink sand along the shore. Within the ring of the sands lining the island, there was bright and dense green foliage where entire swaths were undisturbed by human hands. Tufts of candy floss clouds hung lazily in the sky. Everything was kissed with a salty breeze. And if Valos would get some of that sangria down his gullet, everything would be perfect. Cinder smiled. The island truly was a paradise.

"It is not the first time they have seen deepwater sailing vessels but it is always a treat," a voice called from behind Cinder.

She pivoted and saw the shaman Amman approaching. "Why aren't there any deep-sea vessels?" she asked.

"We have a few," the shaman replied. "But they take a lot of resources to create and truthfully, we don't need them. The elders have an expression we use often. 'The island provides.'"

"That is part of the reason why we are here. Tell me. Would you speak with a woman about business and coin?"

"Why would I not?" the shaman replied, skepticism in his voice.

Cinder cocked her head to the side and clucked her tongue. "You might be surprised. More than a few of the kingdoms in the north believe that a woman should know her place."

"And what place is that?"

"In the kitchen. Silent. Her stomach swollen with babes."

Amman gave a harrumph. "These are probably the same women that scream at the sight of a mouse. The Malinsuli are not this way. Our women are warriors. Equals."

Cinder gave a light laugh. "Tell me, Amman, do you believe in fate?"

The shaman offered a sly grin that curled up one side of his mouth. "I believe in the ancestors. I have often asked them for help. I feel like from beyond the great veil they often... *nudge* things the way they are supposed to be. But I believe that if you want something in life, there are better ways to get there than sending up prayers to the pantheon."

Cinder nodded. "Perhaps fate is the wrong word in this particular circumstance. What if I changed it to... let's say... fortuitous timing? A sudden squall or an adverse weather event could have hit the ship on our way here from Incanterra. That stopover in Agavinsula could have been a day."

"I've always wanted to go there. How is it?"

"Honestly? Hot. Here you have the wind and the breeze. You would think being an archipelago as they are it wouldn't be that way but the place is a furnace. I think it puts people in a bad mood. And their men are not as progressive as the Malinsuli with the role of women."

"I wonder if all that heat is why the peppers they grow there are so spicy?"

"I don't know enough about nature to say."

"I am sorry. I have skewed us from your path of thought. You were saying?"

"I think this is a perfect example. You have used their peppers to spice up your dishes?"

"It adds such flavor and heat!" the shaman said. "When you pair that with the right fish, it is amazing."

"And what if I could get you some of those peppers here? Now. Tonight for your evening meal. What would you pay? What would your islander brethren pay?"

"Is this why you and your cohort of travelers are here on Malinsula? Do you have a collection of peppers in the hold of your great ship you are looking to unload?"

"Not exactly," Cinder said with a shrug. "If I had been smarter in this negotiation, I would have learned in advance that was what you wanted and had them at the ready. But knowing what I know now…"

With practiced ease, Cinder withdrew her wizardly wand. With a sprinkling of material components, keywords whispered, and a dramatic flourish with her wand, she opened one of the same magical gateways that the crew had used to jump from the deck of the *Castella Mare* to the island's beach. When Amman looked through the portal, he saw the main island of the Agavinsula archipelago. Cinder had focused on the keystone left behind on the main island. "I could send Thade and Sway on a run to their market. I could get a whole host of those peppers – the red ones, those milder green ones, or even those bright orange ones flecked with white that are hotter than lava. How would that do?"

With a wave of her wand, the swirling glowfly ring collapsed in on itself and disappeared. "So you are one of them," the shaman said.

"Yes and no," Cinder replied confidently. "Yes, I am a wizard. But not like the other Incanterran wizards you might have dealt with in the past."

Amman eyed her skeptically. "They come here for their holidays. Some of them use the magical gateways the same as you… although theirs looks different. More red-colored with all these black spots."

"The Corvalonn dynasty," Cinder nodded. "I know their kind."

"They wear all their fancy robes. Or they bring with them the types who throw coins about. They occasionally grace the villages but rarely. They are here to play in the surf. They lay in the sun hoping to mimic our bronze skin. And then they eat as guests in King Muera's palace. They are..."

"Elitists," Cinder was more than happy to finish Amman's pensive thought.

He smiled at the wizard's admission and bounced his eyebrows.

"Which again brings me back to the fortuitous nature of our chance meeting," she continued. "I am not concerned with the wealthy like the king of yours who lives on his hill. I want to bring wealth to the common man. Not just to the people of my kingdom but to the people of your island. I need an envoy here for this plan to work. Fate has brought me to you. Or perhaps your ancestors have. Maybe it is a roll of the die; a stroke of the celestial author's quill. Or maybe it is all just dumb luck. Nevertheless, we are here."

Amman smiled and stroked the long hairs of his white beard as he contemplated Cinder's words.

"One day earlier or one day later and the *Castella Mare* does not arrive when she was needed most. And yet here we are," Cinder said. "I can tell about people. Call it a gift. But you? Your cousin Sario? You feel like good people. Authentic. And your magic is amazing. I don't want to be in business with an elitist. I want to be in business with people who want to help the people."

"So you want to develop a trade route between Malinsula and Incanterra?"

"An *instantaneous* trade route. But not just a trade route. A trade *network*."

"How do I know this is not some foothold for you to march an army onto our shores?" Amman asked.

Cinder turned and looked Amman right in his eyes. She even took his hand and placed his palm against her chest and over her heart.

"Taking your resources by force is for bullies and the small-minded. I am here to make money. Not just for us but for you all as well. So you tell me. Am I telling the truth?"

Chapter 22

The King's High Way and the Queen's High Way divided the grand capital of Incanterra into four distinct quarters. These districts were vastly different in their wealth and their prosperity and that disparity was all too abundantly on display when it came to the siege of the city.

Amidst the densely populated Southwest District, the citizens were known to possess a rougher edge. Constables were often called for crimes that ended with the offender locked away in Irongate Prison for a substantial time. Citizens were constantly dodging gang wars. Territory was claimed through muscle and steel. So it was no surprise when the skeletal oppressors found themselves on the brutal end of significant resistance to the occupation.

The Southeast District predominantly catered to commerce. But with no raw materials coming into the city and no goods being exported out by ship, boat, wagon, or buckboard, the district had ground mostly to a halt. Opposition to the occupation had to be handled harshly in the initial weeks. Salty sailors, strong soldiers, and even mad merchants fought fiercely against the undead. Death magic quickly took the wind out of their metaphorical sails.

The Northeast District was filled with more people who commuted to the Southeast to work rather than find her streets filled with such industry. There were more children, academies of learning, and families trying to live a quiet life. Staunch opposition was quickly quelled and the people retreated into their apartments to comply with the orders of lockdown.

In all three of the aforementioned districts, people lived stacked atop each other in impossibly tall buildings. Feats of architecture bolstered by magic grew the city upward. It was the only option when the capital was surrounded by defensible walls. However, the Northwest District was the least populated of the four and if one strolled about the wealthy quarter, one might be hard-pressed to see a difference before the arrival of the skeletal siege.

The Northwest was home to generational prosperity passed down through bloodlines. The wards were dominated by elaborate estates and magnificent manses. When the Necromangians declared the city theirs, most of the nonessential staff were sent home to their apartments in the other wards. Gates were closed. And much like with a rampaging hurricane, the wealthy were content to tuck up and ride out the storm.

The estates were shuttered. Those within were content not to draw an eye or ire toward them. The few businesses sporadically spaced around the district adhered to even stricter curfews than the Necromangians imposed. Cafes, restaurants, and other eateries would sometimes serve breakfast. Most opted only for lunch. Finding a spot for dinner was almost impossible. And with no goods moving in or out of the city, the boutiques and shops specializing in the unessential never warranted enough patrons to open their doors. The streets were empty and the quarter was quiet.

So it made a citizen stand out all the more when they walked down the avenues. It was a concept wholly foreign to Grayson Rathorrian who often used his skills to blend in amongst the population. In his line of work, he wanted to be forgotten by witnesses as much as possible.

When he rounded the corner with his bag of sundries, there was no cluster of citizens to hide behind. There were no day-trippers to conceal his movements. There were no people to pad his passing by. As such, he was easily and quickly spotted by the Knight of the Imperial Circle patrolling with a dozen of his armed and armored living skeletons.

Grayson Rathorrian knew better than to try to run or hide. Doing so would only increase the suspicion of the Imperial Knight. With just the hint of a stuttering step, Grayson continued on his path down the avenue. He watched the knight pivot and move to an intercept course.

Grayson muttered a curse under his breath but did his best to force a smile. He even gave a polite nod in the direction of the knight as the two moved closer together. "Citizen," the knight said, his voice slightly muffled behind the alabaster mask concealing his face.

Grayson's eyes narrowed. "I am not certain of the proper etiquette for addressing you. Lord? Sire? Is it just 'Knight'?"

"Knight is fine. Do you carry weapons?"

Grayson chuckled. "I'm an entrepreneur. I do not need blades."

Unwilling to take the man at his word, the knight quickly gave Grayson a pat-down to search for any concealed arms. "Where are you going?"

"I am headed back to my apartment."

"And where are you coming from?" the knight questioned.

Grayson hemmed and hawed, "It is a *tad* embarrassing."

The knight stared back silently. It was impossible to gauge the reaction concealed behind the mask.

"Look. Truth be told, I have a standing appointment with a certain lording lady. I cannot say who for... *reasons*. But we meet over at Saffron Springs. She says she is going there for their rejuvenating beauty treatments. Which is true... in a sense. We have a villa in the back that we meet in. I take her on a tour around the kingdom and she lets me explore her hidden valley."

The knight grumbled.

"With everyone behind the walls of their various estates, Saffron Springs has closed its doors. I was unaware. You can imagine my disappointment."

Grayson rustled his bag of sundries. "So it was not a total loss, I grabbed some stocks for my cupboards. But now I get to go home and rather than storming the pink castle, I will just have to honor the old king and his crown."

The knight was not amused by the playful euphemisms. The skeletons showed even less emotion. "I assume you have your employment certifications."

Grayson shuffled the bag of sundries and slipped a hand into one of his belt pouches. "Of course," he said. "I still want to call you constable for some reason. But you aren't sporting a copper badge, are you?"

The knight accepted the credentials and gave them a look-through. With the knight distracted with his reading and the skeletal soldiers looking rather mindless, none noted that Graver had shifted one of the rings on his bracer which then issued a vibrating warble that only he felt.

"I have heard of these consultants," the knight said, noting the certificate. "Is there a guild that you are a part of?"

"I am a private operator," Grayson replied with a smile.

"So how does it work?"

Grayson bobbed his head back and forth as he sought the right words. "The simplest way I can describe it... They don't talk about it but the wealthy have learned the hard way. There's big money in a kidnapping. Absconding with an heir and demanding payment for his safe return is a way to make serious coins. Coppers aren't much help if a 'napping does occur. So they pay me to secure their estates. Better to pay me before than to need my services after.

"But on more than one occasion, I have had to help broker deals to make sure the brats get returned home safe and sound. I deal with the kidnapping filth so the estates don't have to. The real money is a contract from the wizards."

"What do they contract you to do?"

"I find people they want found."

"And you are good at this task?"

Grayson gave a little smile. "I am like the grave. No one escapes me."

"You haven't met Nalazar Catabaysi yet," the Imperial Knight said as he handed back the credentials. "You know my organization has been looking for quite a few people who have escaped our detection. Perhaps the Necromangians could hire your services."

The Knight made a gesture and the skeletons moved to surround Grayson Rathorrian. "I don't know," he replied. "My services aren't cheap."

"Money is rarely an object for Master Catabaysi. What he is more concerned with is results."

Grayson managed a smile. "I am no stranger to Sorceria, friend. Something tells me that if I let you escort me up there, I might not set foot back on Incanterra again."

92   Ryan Foley

"And while your credentials are certainly in order," the knight replied, "you said you were an entrepreneur yet you also deal with a criminal element. In these dealings, do you ever carry a weapon?"

"If the situation calls for it."

"So you do carry weapons."

"Not unless I have to. I find weapons can complicate situations and people can get hurt."

"So you were not truthful when I asked you if you carry weapons."

"I am not carrying any now."

"But you still lied. I am curious. What else have you lied about? Maybe your whole story about your tryst with a lording lady is a lie... a cover. So we are going to talk about it up on the wizarding isle."

Grayson nodded. "Fine. Yes. You are right. I was lying."

"About the tryst?"

"Oh no. That fact is very real. I leave her quivering and gasping. My lie was about carrying weapons."

From the magic contained within his bracers, Grayson Rathorrian materialized a pair of short swords. His bundle of sundries dropped to the street. Before the Imperial Knight could react, the blades found purchase in and across the man's throat. Bright gouts of crimson sprayed down the white priestly vestment of the knight. The knight – caught completely unaware – quickly realized why Grayson Rathorrian had earned the sobriquet Graver.

Equally shocked by the sudden attack, the squad of skeletons hastily scrambled to remove the swords from their scabbards. Graver charged the skeleton within the ring closest to him. With no vital organs or throats to slash, Graver hit the skeleton in a bull rush before it could draw its sword. The plan was to run for the nearby alley which might negate their numbers advantage and give the assassin a fighting chance.

Still, as the skeletons gave chase, Graver could only curse. The odds were far too long. But then from the shadows of the nearby alleyway, bright bolts of blue-tinged and white-cored lightning shot past the assassin and into the ranks of the skeletal warriors.

Chapter 23

The assembly of seven slowly meandered through the village square. Curious eyes were trained on the foreigners of Valos Ironblade, Sway Snowsong, Thade Skystone, Cinder Fireborne, and Cavin Jurare. However, as they were being escorted by Amman and Sario, any grumbles or labels of interlopers were whispered at best. Word amongst the Searock villagers had spread quickly how the Incanterrans had helped ward off the Kai'kamina invasion.

Many of the villagers wanted to present their honored guests with gifts like seashell jewelry and native fashions. It became so much that Amman had to start politely turning people away. Sario gathered up a pair of teenage girls and whispered to them. The duo looked at the foreigners, giggled with their hands over their mouths, and then hustled away.

"Do I want to know?" Amman asked with a squinting eye.

"Our guests will need a place to stay tonight," Sario replied. She turned to the group. "Or were you intending to sleep on your ship?"

Valos held up his hands. "Speaking for myself. I would rather not be rocked to sleep by waves if that is acceptable."

"I figured as much," the shaman said. "So I had Erina and Natana make sure that a suitable tent could be made available to our guests. We will make sure you have all the bedding you need."

"You honor us," Cinder said with a bow.

"I hope you are not big fans of walls," Amman said.

Sario rolled her eyes. "He's not wrong. But his presentation leaves a little something to be desired. Malinsuli families sleep in tents together."

Sario gestured towards one of the large tents nearby that were inhabited by four generations of fishermen and harvesters. Valos looked inside, noting the tall ceilings, large monster bones, and the cured hide to keep out the weather. "How do moms and dads have privacy to... you know... make future generations of Malinsuli?"

"Such a beautiful act is not something to be ashamed of," Sario replied.

"Now whose presentation leaves a little something to be desired?" Amman groaned. "Sario is right but I don't want you to get the wrong idea. She makes it sound like we are humping each other in the streets in broad daylight. We aren't savages living in a forgotten era. It's 1355 here too."

"It's 1356," Sario whispered.

"Since when?"

"For like six months now."

"What month is this?" he asked.

"You will have to forgive him," Sario said to the group with a smile. "I will admit that for *some* of us, time can move a little differently down here. Still, others have come here from the north – some of them your kingdom men – and they are amazed at our fluency in the trader's tongue and our modern amenities. I think they expect us to make hand gestures and say things like *'Greet from islander, pale skin.'*"

The shaman walked with a pronounced waddle over towards Cinder and looked with wonder at her bright, unnaturally apple-red hair. She spoke with a slur and kept her tongue tucked low in her mouth. *"She must be demon with such... how you say... hair of red."*

Sario then almost pulled a muscle rolling her eyes so hard. The shaman then turned abruptly back to Cinder. "I do love your hair by the way. I cannot imagine how long a dye session it took to get it that way."

"Oh, thank you," Cinder blushed. "I love your natural white!"

A pack of laughing children suddenly came charging through, weaving amongst the adults with far more dexterity and speed than they deserved. Amman roared playfully and lumbered after them, swinging his arms wildly, trying to wrap them up in bear hugs that the youngsters ducked to avoid.

"What about the big storms?" Thade asked.

Sario gave a grim nod. "Hurricane season is coming soon. Did you hear that, Amman? It will be hurricane season soon! You might jot that down."

Her fellow shaman was too busy hoisting a pair of children up by his bulging arms so they could hang off his biceps. Others had plopped down to ride on his feet while clutching his calves. "Yeah, yeah. Big winds. Lots of rain. What do we do when the strong winds blow?"

"To the caves!" the children all said in unison with deflated energy having been told time and time again.

"The central part of the island is littered with an amazing cave structure. If we feel things are going to be too dangerous, we simply pack up and wait out the storm in their shelter. Most of the bones are dug too deep to be moved but the tent skins can be taken down quickly," Sario explained.

"Now, go tend to your chores," Amman called out to the children. "Tend to your chores or no swimming. And honor your mother. Tell her goodbye. And check on Gran'ma Kiriwhi. Make sure she laughs at you!"

The children all playfully called out to Sario, gave her quick hugs, or slapped her extended hands with theirs before running off down the path.

Valos looked around curiously as the children all scampered away. "Wait. Are these your kids?"

Sario smiled. "In a way. They have their mothers, yes. But we are all their mothers. We raise them together. There is no word for 'aunt' in the old Malinsuli tongue. It is the same as there are no words for 'marriage.'"

"How do relationships work?" Sway asked.

Sario looked around to consider the explanation. "Couples stay together long enough for the child to reach the age of accountability and then they move on to find new partners if they wish. Or they continue to make more children. But we all live… together."

"No word for marriage," Valos said with a little chuckle.

"Which also means no word for divorce," Sway pointed out.

"We raise the children as an island and we also care for our elders as an island," Sario said. "But it is also important to note… we don't own anything. We all have cherished possessions to be sure but it is based on sentimentality over value."

"Try to take a warrior's trident that he favors in battle and it is not pretty," Amman added.

"So I understand you want to set up a trading relationship. Exchanging things would be good for the island I am sure," Sario said. "But you will find the Malinsuli are not motivated by coins alone."

Valos, Sway, Thade, and Cinder all looked at each other. They exchanged glances, nods, and shrugs, as they all silently shared their concerns as a group. Finally, the four turned. Valos smiled. "We can work with that. So we will just make sure to bring you items based on usefulness over monetary value."

Sario leaned out to catch the attention of Cavin Jurare. "And what's your opinion, long strider?"

Cavin's eyes grew wide and he pointed at his chest. "Me? Oh, no. This is their deal. My time is spent hunting the undead. This is their thing. I am accompanying the demon with such… how you say… hair of red."

Amman grew quickly curious. "Like vampires and ghouls?"

"Or ghasts. The occasional wight. Living skeletons. Stuff like that."

"Fascinating," the shaman whispered.

Sario tapped a finger to her lips as she considered the possibilities. She spun on her heel to look at Amman with a broad smile. "Cattle."

Amman nodded with encouragement.

"Cattle?" Valos asked. "You want cows?"

Sario nodded. "Thade asked about our butter reserves on the beach earlier. If you want to get King Muera to agree to a trade deal, bring him cattle. Loading them up on a boat and sailing them here is an expensive venture. Mnama'tellus rarely lets their cattle be exported."

"They are also not the most hospitable of trading partners," Amman explained. "They ride their thunder lizards like you all ride horses and their mounts are not partial to eating grass. Keeping those things fed cannot be cheap. So they are rarely willing to export their livestock. And the Selvaterrans are notorious for inflating their prices."

"Getting a single cow to stay balanced in your little boats is probably hard as well," Thade said.

"By now, word will have reached the king. He will want to know about the strangers on his shore. He will come claiming to be honoring the hallowed fallen but he will want to know about you all as well," Sario said. "He'll conk two crabs with a single rock."

Valos looked expectantly at Cinder. She nodded in approval. He looked at his pair of new shaman friends and extended a smile as wide as his arms. "If you want cattle, we know a guy. I can have a couple of heads tonight if you want them. Fresh off the farm and not a dose of seasickness to spoil the taste."

Sario was finishing her calculations. "Your group arrived through the magical portal onto the beach to fight. I am guessing you arrived from the deck of your fancy ship."

"We did," Cinder nodded.

"And you can open up a portal... let me guess... to an Incanterran farm where cattle are plentiful."

"I've seen it," Amman said. "Well, it was Agavinsula but the principle is the same.

The collection of foreign visitors could not hide their smiles.

"How interesting," the shaman mused.

Chapter 24

Grayson Rathorrian pivoted on his heel after the first blast of white-cored and blue-haloed lightning shot from behind him and slammed into the chest of the nearest skeletal warrior advancing on him.

From out of the darkness of the alley, a second lightning bolt sailed directly at him but then abruptly forked with separate tines slamming into two more of the skeletal squad. A figure emerged from the darkness brandishing a magic wand.

Drennid Vocazion was not dressed in the typical robes of his wizarding dynasty. Instead, the mage was attired with expensive city fashions allowing him to blend in with the general population – if a general population could be found. Instead, he witnessed a Northwesterner wielding a wizardly wanded weapon.

Though armored and armed with longswords, the skeletal enforcers were no match for the mage. As lightning strike after lightning strike contacted sternums and coursed through their bodies, the connective energy bonding the bones together vanished and the skeletons collapsed to the street in heaps of renewed lifelessness. The rattling of their armor and clanging of their weapons served as a louder death rattle than the skeletons themselves.

As he closed the gap, Drennid Vocazion brought his wand up over his head as a length of lightning trailed behind it. Snapping the wand like a whip handle, the arcing lightning lashed forward, slashing one skeleton warrior across the waist, above the pelvis. Sliced in two, the skeleton collapsed to the smooth stone of the thoroughfare.

The sounds of battle echoed down the avenues and streets until they ceased as quickly as they had started. When it was all over, the Imperial Knight and the piles of skeletons lay scattered across the intersection. Before Grayson could issue his thanks, Drennid stormed forward and kicked over the torso of the skeleton he had whipped in two. While its lower half was lifeless, there was still a sinister essence flowing through the undead.

Drennid angrily pulled off the monster's helmet. It thrashed against Drennid and tried to grip his legs with its bony fingers. Grayson noted the red pinpricks glowing in the skeleton's eye sockets. All it took was a sharp strike of Drennid's bootheel to end that. As the skull caved in, the lights winked away into nothingness. The skeletal arms collapsed with a sudden lifelessness like a torch being plunged into a rain barrel.

Looking around for any potential witnesses, they saw none. Drennid tucked away his wand and turned abruptly. "Hello, Uncle."

"Nephew," Grayson replied. "You are not who I expected to see in this ward."

"The city is full of surprises. Still, this is best discussed away from the slaughtered knight and disassembled skeletal brigade."

Grayson walked past, careful to respect the wizard's personal space, and motioned for him to follow. Aside from the opulence and the inherited wealth, the general map of the Northwest District was not too different from the less affluent quarters within the city. Streets and avenues laid out a specific grid that brought much-needed order and organization to the city after past disasters threatened her existence.

But unlike in the Southwest District where streets and avenues were dominated by tall, scaling apartments, or in the Southeast District stuffed with her warehouses, the streets and avenues of the Northwest divided estates and their manses. Still, there were side roads and lesser-traveled alleys if one knew how to use them. Given the lack of people out and about in the wards, Grayson and Drennid used the side roads more for cover than speed. "I am surprised to find the infamous Graver so close to being apprehended, Uncle."

"I was crossing over into another ward when they chanced upon me," he grumbled. "Skulking about or abruptly reversing my direction would have only made them more suspicious."

"And what was so important to have you out roaming the streets? I am betting the false bag of sundries was just a prop in the event you were stopped and questioned. How am I doing?"

"An accurate assessment. I could ask the same thing of you. Why are you out and about risking exposure? Don't get me wrong. I am thankful for your timely intervention but…"

"You didn't answer my question."

"And I'm not going to."

Crossing another empty street, the duo arrived at one of the few apartment buildings within the ward. Rather than use the main entrance and risk the door sentinel recognizing Graver's guest, the two slipped in through the backway and used the rear staircases to get to Graver's apartment on the upper floors. Off the main living space was a floor-to-ceiling window. Drennid took a peek through the curtains. Grayson's apartment faced north and west so the compromised view from the King's High and the Queen's High Way was not an issue. "Nice view," he said with an approving nod.

"Your mother has a habit of disparaging it. She feels it is always inferior to the one afforded her through Sorceria."

"And look at what that hubris has earned them," Vocazion replied.

"You are still a part of that conclave, young master."

"Yes, I just happened to be on the wrong side of the curtain when it fell. For the last two weeks, I have been looking over my shoulder. With the city on lockdown, wizards are getting handed over left and right for rewards being offered by the Imperial Knights and the Necromangians. You do not know who you can trust... and more importantly who you can't. So I have been on the move. How are your coffers stocked, Uncle?"

Grayson smiled. "Admirably. And a betrayal would be a silly thing to do after you saved my life. Plus, your mother would be furious with me."

"How are they? Do you know?"

"Your guess is as good as mine. The red robes are not overly forthcoming with information regarding what is happening up there in Sorceria."

Drennid exhaled sharply as he pulled the curtain back closed. "Necromangians, I can hardly believe it."

Grayson moved to the adjacent kitchen to prepare a quick meal and something for the two of them to drink. "I still don't understand who they are," the procurer said. "I see them about. I first assumed they were from some foreign kingdom but they don't have the skin of the southern lands. And their accents are Incanterran."

"If I understand it all correctly, it is... complicated."

"Well, I am just a lowly city dweller. Try to make it as simple as you can," Grayson said as he took a knife to the vegetables.

"Necromancy is a magic art that takes energy from one source and places it in another. But doing so can create terrible abominations."

"The living skeletons, the ghouls, and the like?"

"That is what most people tend to focus on," the mage replied.

"And with good reason."

Drennid raised his eyebrows in agreement. "I can't say I know every wizard within every dynasty but I know most. I know those that matter. I don't know any of these red robers. And you are right. They are Incanterran. Generations upon generations ago, there was a dynasty that practiced this magic of the dead. But they grew too powerful. So the eight dynasties united to eliminate the ninth."

"And a crack job they did."

"Please, Uncle. It was centuries ago. Obviously, their teachings and spells have been passed down secretly from generation to generation. Now, for whatever reason, they have finally decided to reveal themselves.

"But the real issue is their raw power. The last time they posed a problem, it took the combined might of The Eight to take them down. And now we are scattered across who knows how far."

Grayson rubbed his chin. "And there is no secret way for us to infiltrate the isle?"

"I do have one way to get back in but it is not like a dimension door spell. It involves teleportation. The last time I used it I was in bed for… a while. And I fear that when my essence disassembles and then tries to reassemble within our tower, their defensive wards will leave me scattered across the swirling energy surrounding Sorceria."

"And I assume you have no word from your mother?"

Drennid shook his head. "I have no idea what is going on. People are still alive up there. I see the sloops still making runs from the isle to the city."

Grayson paced back and forth as he considered his options. He gave out a series of grumbles, hmmms, and herrmms until his pacing slowed and came to a stop.

"Uncle?"

"If we are going to oust these boners, it is going to take magic. Of that, I have no doubt. We need to gather forces to consolidate our power. That means rounding up any wizards still down here in the city."

"How do we do that given all the betrayals as of late?"

"You need an organization that specializes in secrecy. You need skulkers who work in the alleyways and behind closed doors. You need people who work… in the shadows."

The color drained out of Drennid's face as he realized just exactly who Graver was talking about.

"No, no, no," the mage said, hostility creeping into his voice.

"Now is not the time for ego, Nephew. We have a kingdom to save. And you know who can help us the most…"

Chapter 25

Dragan Duskwood stood silently in the underbelly of the sundered isle of Sorceria. The second-in-command of the newly reestablished Catabaysi dynasty was still fuming from his interaction with the lesser acolytes. He was less focused on the magical marvel positioned in front of him.

The Cellarium Vaults was a treasure trove of magic deemed too powerful by the patrons of The Eight. Resembling the treasury vaults used in the banks in the city below, the strongroom featured a massive door with complicated locks but it also utilized shielding magic supplied by the wizarding dynasties. The grand vault was thought to be impenetrable until Dragan's master, Nalazar Catabaysi, tapped into the *pherein* to defeat her safeguarding wards.

Ripping open the vault had given Nalazar access to the feared Necronomicon with the spell notes necessary for the wizard to transform himself into the terrifying lich he had become. The Cellarium Vaults came through the sundering of Sorceria almost unscathed and one of the first orders issued was the vault door's repair. Then, it would only be accessible by senior members of Catabaysi's command.

The order gave Dragan a sigh of relief. There was magic within he wished could be undiscovered. In the wrong hands, kingdoms could fall. It was magic Nalazar was too eager to dive into.

The sound of slippers echoed from one of the adjoining passageways. Dragan turned as Demina Summerstone walked into the mage-light of the Cellarium foyer.

A young lady with a shock of natural red hair, Demina was a vision. Before the great reveal, the lass served as a journaler for *The Heraldry*. Her position allowed her to stay interconnected with the web of information within the city. But Dragan knew she was also very talented when it came to waving her wand. At twice her age, the seasoned wizard considered her almost a daughter he never had. With Dragan hiding in Incanterra as a professor of history and she hiding as a journaler, the two had convincing excuses to find themselves in each other's orbits, none the wiser that they were bonded through their necromancy.

"Admiring his handiwork?" Demina asked as she sauntered into the foyer.

Dragan turned back to admire the great circular door and its massive hinges. "It is very impressive. It is what you get when the disincentive of the *pherein* is taken off the table."

"Master Catabaysi was pretty adamant about getting the vault repaired and then resealed so only our order could access it."

"Did he say why?"

Demina shook her head. "He wasn't particularly forthcoming and I wasn't going to ask."

The two stood silently. Putting in a deep focus, Dragan could feel the hum and the thrum embedded within the vault door. Demina looked around and despite the two of them being alone in the Sorceria underbelly, she still whispered. "Can I tell you something?"

Dragan looked over at the young adept and offered the smallest of smiles. "When have I ever told you no?"

"And it stays between us?"

Again, Dragan smiled. "Out of everyone in our house, I trust you the most. I would trust you with my life. Of course, it stays between us."

Demina took a moment to summon her courage.

"Nalazar scares me."

Dragan took a deep breath through his nostrils.

"When you first started teaching me our discipline, I understood it. I could see the role it played. I see the importance of it. I still do. And I also see why people can be afraid of it."

"A bunch of animated corpses tend to do that," Dragan kidded.

"But we are no more fearsome than the warlocks of Ce'Mondere and they use demons. Even with all the skeletons and the death and the bones... I have never once feared our magic."

Dragan nodded. "I remember my mother used to talk about magic. She believed it was no different than a sword or an arrow. They could not be inherently good or evil. What mattered was the intent with which it was used. I agree with her. I do not fear our magic and I do not consider it evil."

Demina took a breath of her own, almost afraid to force the next statement past her lips. "I think the transformation did something to him."

Dragan stood silently.

Demina continued her whispering. "He is... himself and yet he is not. I hear the screams coming from the Baelannor tower. Torture is hard to ignore. Our... emergence from the shadows... I didn't expect it to be like this."

Dragan continued to stand silently.

Demina let him absorb her statement.

"And you are worried about a repeat of history?" the master asked.

"We follow his orders. Have you been down below? All you have to do is head up topside and look to the south. A fog hangs over the city. A green haze permeates the Southwest District. The everyday people hate us. There is a reason why we walk with skeleton escorts when we are down amongst them."

Dragan's eyes narrowed and his brow furrowed. "Our mission remains—"

"Nalazar has lost sight of the mission!" Demina proclaimed with a sharp interruption. "Even if those brain-eaters arrive – 'if' being the keyword – there will be no living souls left in Incanterra for them to feed on! No living souls left to protect!"

Dragan walked forward and placed his hand on the large vault door. He could feel the vibrations of the magic. He took a breath to steady himself. From somewhere deep in the connecting passageways, he swore he detected another hint of the smell of sunflowers. It must have been a byproduct of the magic that kept the isle suspended above the capital. With everything sundered, there were erratic waves of magical energy flowing from the crystals. Odd, out-of-place smells were the least of his concerns.

"Our magic is not evil. You know it. I know it," Demina said adamantly. "But the people don't know this and the avatar of our house – the only face of our dynasty – is now an undead monster who is torturing Asaric Baelannor and transforming the dead into his skeletal army. It is no wonder that they hate us... and part of me thinks they have every right to.

"If things go on the way they are, there is going to be a repeat of the Great Expulsion. And when they hang him from the gallows, we will be strung up beside him. We will be guilty by association. Or they will be afraid we will take up his mantle if he is felled."

Dragan turned slowly. "Or he conquers the kingdom."

Demina stood silently, gauging her mentor's tone. She hesitated for a heartbeat and then threw up her hands in frustration. "Those up kingdom already know. Word will get out. And when it does, the kingdoms will mobilize. Arvaterra, Castratellus, Ombraterra, Mnama'tellus, Monterra, and even the island kingdoms will send their forces. They will have to."

"Unless..." Dragan mused.

Demina folded her arms across her chest and stood silently.

"You do realize the risk you have run speaking to me about this?" the former professor asked. "You are suggesting turning traitor against our master."

Demina stood silently. There was the slightest quiver in her lower lip and Dragan could see her pulse rampaging inside the veins in her neck.

"One word to Nalazar and his torture of you would be endless," he said coldly. "Not even death would be an escape. He would probably resurrect you, force you to drink healing potions to repair the damage he would inflict upon you, and then go at it all over again."

She nodded shallowly and tears were beginning to line the bottom of her stark green eyes.

"So we are going to have to be *very* careful with who we talk to about this," he said. "If we tell the wrong people – or even the wrong person – they could rat us out and that would be it."

Demina breathed a sigh of relief. "'Rat us out'? Look at you talking like the streets." The young woman took a moment to absorb the information. "Zegan. Zegan Goldheart. We should approach him first. I know before all this, he was using his 'skellies' to dig a secret tunnel from the city to the formal graveyard. If anyone in the group is going to align with this philosophy, it will be him. But beyond that?"

The wizard contemplated for a series of breaths and then gave an exasperated sigh. "A coup," he hissed.

Not wanting to linger too long, the duo began to take their leave. Once more, Dragan swore he caught the whiff of sunflowers. He started to comment but Demina cut him off before he could. "I know it seems impossible. We have seen his power. But there is an entire population down below that wants to see him hoisted from his throne," Demina stated.

"Aye," Dragan replied. "The trick is we have to recruit the right people to do the dethroning. And I have an idea of where to start."

Chapter 26

Sario guided Cinder Fireborne along a well-worn path on the island of Malinsula. The tall palm trees, the wide, leafy foliage, and the dense plant life had some of the most brilliant shades of green Cinder had ever laid her eyes on. Bright plumes of color spurted between the verdant greens. Exotic flowers dotted the jungle with their bursts of purples, yellows, pinks, and reds. The soil under their feet had been packed down hard and was free of roots or rocks that might have sent a walker for a tumble.

Cinder kept an eye on the vegetation, nervously listening for any stray sound that might indicate a less-than-friendly member of the local wildlife. But Sario strolled without a care in the world.

Very quickly, the vegetation and the path cutting its way through it disappeared. It was replaced by tightly tended grass, a rocky shoreline, and a frothing pool of clean, pure water fed by a trio of tall waterfalls.

The shaman wasted no time and happily waded into the water up to her ankles. "I will admit," Sario said, "I have always been fascinated by your arcane magic. It is very different from ours. Your magic is so precise with your spellbooks and your scrolls. The exact enunciation of words. The wavings of your wands or staves. It is beautiful in its own way. I don't want my words to come across as derogatory but it all feels so terribly... *academic*."

"I take the future generations of your shamans are not taught together in classrooms where a wizarding instructor raps your knuckles with his wand if you pronounce a verbal component incorrectly?"

"Is there often violent yelling involved as well?" the shaman asked.

Cinder Fireborne's mind drifted back to classes Lucinda Vocazion sat through as a young apprentice. "If the situation called for it," she admitted.

"Strange," Sario said. "You know how I mentioned earlier that there is no word for 'aunt' in our language?"

"I do. It must be strange having so many mothers. I cannot even imagine what that would be like. To be surrounded by such devotion and love."

The Malinsuli shaman let the moment hang silently to let the beautiful wizard sort through her various emotions. Slowly, Sario drifted towards Cinder until she could place a reassuring palm on the small of her back. "The men train the boys and girls how to fight. They teach them the sword, the spear, the trident, the net. They teach them the *melee'kaua* – our ritual war chant."

"I saw the men doing that after the fight with the merfolk was over. It is impressive."

"It is designed to be so. It is a very specific ritual to show any would-be invader that we are united. It is our way of deterring violence against us by showing great force."

Extending her hands and closing her eyes, Sario began to reach into an unseen energy. Cinder stood silently, watching intently. "We also have other methods of discouraging invaders."

Out within the pool of water, there was a rumbling from deep beneath the surface. Sario's fingers twisted and contorted. She could feel the essence within her reaching into the ethereal. Once there, her spirit found what she was searching for. An invisible tether connected to the being within the elemental plane. A request was made. An invite was acknowledged and accepted.

Cinder watched as the water began to defy gravity. A column of liquid began to rise out of the pool. Slowly, the water swirled and tumbled within that column. It resembled a translucent pillar of clay being formed by unseen titan hands. What started as raw shapes slowly began to taper and became more recognizable forms. A torso. Arms. Even fingers. Long, liquid tendrils of hair were formed. While the lower half of the creature continued to swirl and spiral like an inverted whirlpool, its upper half resembled something positively humanoid. And her eyes resembled glowing pools of magical light radiating with a soothing, pale blue glow.

With flowing grace and elegance, the water elemental began to move in the direction of Sario. There was an inherent enthusiasm Cinder had seen in the body language of pet dogs. "Undaqua," Sario said with a smile. "Thank you for accepting my summons."

Cinder watched as the elemental shivered, a visible line running up and down the creature, distorting the features. There was a vibration within the elemental that caused its core to ripple. "Yes, she is a friend of mine. She has traveled from far away and was curious about how you all help us."

The creature rippled again.

"Yes, she *is* very pretty," Sario said. The shaman turned to smile at Cinder. "She likes your hair."

Cinder laughed. "How do you know what she is saying? Is there a language I can't decipher or is it a translation thing?"

Sario stroked her chin. "It is difficult to describe," she admitted. "Imagine communicating with someone but you cannot hear them. But you can read their expressions. You can tell if they are angry or sad or happy. I cannot *hear* her words as you would perceive them... yet, I know what she is saying."

Cinder looked on. "So a blend of empathic communication and something telepathic?"

"If you must quantify it in academic terms, I suppose that would be an accurate description."

Undaqua shimmered and shook once more. Sario nodded. "She *is* smart. She is a wizard but she practices arcane magic."

If Cinder did not know any better, she swore the elemental wanted to recoil but Sario was quick to offer reassurance. The water elemental turned and peered sharply at Cinder as if looking into her soul. The elemental slithered forward with caution. Then, in a show of trust, it offered a tendril of water in the form of a four-fingered hand.

Cinder mimicked the gesture and offered her own. As the two touched palms, Cinder was surprised to feel a surface tension within the creature's hand. Unlike dipping her hand into a bucket of water, the water pushed back, wetting her hand but also holding it.

There was a shimmer, a shudder, and then a ripple. Cinder smiled and laughed at the curious sensation as her hand sunk into the watery appendage. Her hand was simultaneously submerged but she could also feel the waters flowing around her. Suddenly there was pressure on the inside of her wrist and the elemental held her in place. Trying to equate the sensation to a real-life experience, Cinder swore the water elemental was feeling her pulse. She believed the creature wanted to feel the way the liquid flowed within her veins. With her hand plunged into the elemental, Cinder closed her eyes.

Somewhere deep within, there was a rhythmic flow. The elemental was not a stagnant pool of water. It was not a hollow vessel filled with fluid. The very creature itself possessed a current of a river or the ebb and flow of the great ocean waves. The same as the elemental could feel Cinder's heartbeat, Cinder could feel the elemental's tide flow.

With the overwhelming sensation subsiding, Cinder managed to force her eyes back open. The elemental was close, looking deep into her eyes with her glowing magical orbs. If Cinder did not know any better, she would have sworn the elemental was smiling at her.

"Amazing," she whispered. Cinder turned to Sario. "So where does... *she*... come from?"

"The elemental plane of water. She resides there but elementals are curious about our prime material plane of existence. I think they see coming here as... playing," Sario said. "Some can be a little more temperamental. Most, if you ask nicely, will help."

"I have to ask this question otherwise Valos would chastise me and you should get exposed to things like this early. I assume the fire elementals are..." Cinder grumbled and rolled her eyes, "...hot-headed?"

Sario paused for a second and then burst into genuine laughter.

"I know. I know."

Sario continued to laugh.

"And they are boys so when it comes to air elementals they will be making jokes about breaking wind. So just get ready for that now."

The water elemental looked back and forth. Given her quizzical expression, one would assume she could not translate the words but she was happy at the mirth between the two ladies. Sario continued to laugh so Cinder turned her attention back to the water elemental. "Back home, there is a dynasty. They summon demons from an infernal plane of existence. You all pull from the elemental planes. I suppose somewhere down the history line of magic, you could find the branch on the family tree where you two diverged."

"They sound… interesting," the shaman said.

"I know it sounds bad when you say it out loud," Cinder laughed. "And the demons they summon are no laughing matter. But I believe many armies have refused to march on Incanterra because they know the threat they would be facing if they did."

Sario nodded while looking at the water elemental with genuine admiration. "I think without the aid of the elementals, Malinsula would not have flourished the way we have. The water elementals help us fish. The fire elementals are both protectors and givers of life. You heard Amman warn the children about what to do when hurricanes come. The earth and air elementals have helped us survive storms that would have been tragedies."

Cinder looked at the magnificent beauty and elegant fluidity of the elemental. "Magic," she said with a smile.

"Magic," Sario nodded in agreement. "It is an amazing thing."

Chapter 27

With the perimeter of the magical floating isle of Sorceria divided up among the eight wizarding dynasties, each of the respected houses cultivated its small parcels of land. Boundaries were clearly defined. One never saw bordering houses crowding in on one another. It was an unironic metaphor for how the dynasties treated each other.

Seeing each other as cold rivals and implied competition, wizarding houses rarely intermingled, especially in large numbers. Occasionally, hormonal teens would let their urges get the best of them. Tales of torrid, tangled trysts were whispered as the pubescent novices would often cross house boundaries to explore one another.

There were tales of adepts meeting in secret locations to partake in libations, enjoy the Lu'Scion's hallucinogenic mushrooms, or indulge in other euphorias deemed illegal down inside the city walls. Such interactions were always behind closed doors.

But when a patron of a dynasty crossed from one house over to another, the wizard citizenries took notice. Aldor Mutaccio was a recognizable man even out of his scarlet and silver-trimmed robes. While shorter than some and barrel squat, the potion patron carried a stern countenance. He wore his hair slicked back against his skull and he was the only patron to sport a mustache. He once would have been rivaled by Canarr Jurare who once sported a full beard.

The plot of Mutaccio land was located on the western compass point of the isle. Baelannor was on the northernmost cardinal point. Between them were the ruins of what was once the Jurare's tower. Thinking of Canarr, the alchemist reached up to stroke and smooth the hairs of his mustache.

Canarr and his defensive, military mindset responded to the emergence of Nalazar Catabaysi as any warden would. He brought his magical staff and his defensive shields to bear against the terrible lich. He, his matron, and his dynasty paid the ultimate cost for their defiance as evidenced by the still-smoldering remains that were once the dynast's grand tower.

Approaching the Baelannor tower, he was forced to walk past the Jurare wreckage. He steeled his resolve and hefted the small, handled satchel he was carrying. The massive gates to the Baelannor dynasty were still wrenched and pushed in from their hinges – evidence of Nalazar Catabaysi's forceful arrival.

The wizard patron made his way through the main gates of the dynasty where a Baelannor apprentice bid him welcome. Assured he did not require anything to drink or eat, the apprentice hustled off to inform their newest master of the patron's arrival.

Waiting patiently, Aldor turned when voices approached from one of the side antechambers. Dressed in her house's purple robes trimmed with gold, Devinaya Baelannor arrived with a pair of her apprentices hustling to match her determined pace.

Like so many wizards, Devinaya was well-maintained. She was tall and lithe with long curls of chestnut brown hair hanging down to the middle of her back. The wizard would not be considered old – especially when compared to the grandparently age of the patron and matron tiers – but she was a voice of authority amongst the adepts. Under the best of circumstances, Devinaya would have served as a matron and a potential steward for the Baelannor dynasty if the Catabaysi attack had not thrown the entire wizard class into chaos.

As she approached, Aldor Mutaccio could hear her issuing orders to her trailing apprentices. There was an authority in her tone and no would not be an acceptable answer. "...and we need to make sure that the kitchens are running at peak capacity but we cannot let the summoning cauldrons overheat. Losing even one of them will set back the food production."

The wizardess took a stuttering step seeing a rival patron within her foyer. "Master Mutaccio."

"Devinaya. It is a pleasure to see you as always."

"Can I help you, my lord?"

Mutaccio held up the squared-off, leather-bound satchel. "I have been summoned by Master Catabaysi."

"Indeed," she replied. "Can I get you anything or—"

Mutaccio waved a hand. "One of your apprentices has already butled off to inform the master of my arrival."

"Indeed," an echoing, otherworldly voice called from the top of the stairway off the foyer.

Both Mutaccio and Baelannor turned. Nalazar Catabaysi stood at the top of the stairway dressed in blood-red robes. The lich descended the stairs yet his feet never made contact with the steps. He floated down the staircase with the slightest hum of magical vibrations radiating out from his feet.

Reaching the bottom of the stairs, the necromancer issued what could have been a polite smile to his guest and then turned to address Devinaya. "You are headed down to the city?"

The wizardess nodded. "I am, my lord. There has been an issue with food being conjured."

"Then you should see to that right away," the lich replied. "Making sure the citizens are properly fed and gifted enough water should be our top priority."

"Yes, my lord," Devinaya said respectfully.

The wizardess bowed graciously and hustled out of the tower, leaving Mutaccio and Catabaysi alone. The lich turned and eyed the alchemist. The creature's gaunt features, sunken eyes, and flaking flesh were difficult to look at for any length of time. "You have my crowns?" the lich asked.

Mutaccio gestured toward his satchel.

The lich issued what some might have construed as a broader smile. He curled a finger in a gesture for the patron to follow him. Still, with his feet not touching the floor, the lich levitated across the Ombraterran marble and expensive, woven rugs lining the halls. In one of the Baelannor parlors, the lich gestured towards one of the tall, high-legged tables with a mirror-polished finish. Mutaccio complied, placing the satchel on the table.

From the bag, Mutaccio produced a series of half a dozen crowns resembling a cross between a princess's tiara and an open-top gladiator's helmet with protective shields for the wearer's nose and cheekbones. With the crowns on display, the lich threw up his emaciated hands and even curled his fingers in excitement. "So, Shae'ete's notes were helpful?" the lich asked.

"They were," Mutaccio nodded. "It is rare to be gifted the personal journals of a dynast founder. Her grasp of her discipline was... impressive."

"Yes," Nalazar hissed as he picked up one of the crowns to admire its craftsmanship and the inlaid gemstones. "Her knowledge of necromancy was unparalleled. And yet the patrons of your past were content to lock her knowledge away in a vault. Fools."

Mutaccio considered a reply but held his tongue.

Finishing his examination, the emaciated lich turned to look at his living colleague. "How soon can you have more created?"

Mutaccio cocked his head to the side and shrugged. "The crowns are no different from brewing potions. The first one is always the most difficult. Crafting more is not easy but easier."

"I will see the supplies you require delivered to your tower."

"Just don't skimp on the rubies. They are essential to the process," the patron said. "Still though, we had a deal."

With unnatural speed, the lich whipped his head around. In the fluttering of a glowfly's wings, the undead horror went from staring at the crown to boring a hole into Aldor's skull with his yellow eyes.

The patron refused to back down. "You said assisting you awards my dynasty safety."

"Your tower still stands. You still breathe life."

"Safety is not just immunity from the grave. It means a young apprentice being able to walk the grounds of Sorceria without fear of being accosted by members of your order."

"Boys will be boys," the lich laughed with a rattle and a wet gurgling.

"I still want the lasses of my dynasty to feel safe," Aldor harrumphed. "I will start to work on the next round of crowns. Will this be one of the last creations your order will need before you move on?"

The lich tickled his fingers over the collection of crowns laid out on the polished table. "Aldor, why would you say something so hurtful?"

The alchemist remained silent.

"As we speak, my forces are making your city stronger," the lich mused. "Look what we have done. We have taken the weak, the addicted, the sick, the old, the dying, and the infirmed. We have taken those whose minds were lost to madness. We have taken those who were criminals deserving of death. We have taken these... these dregs and we will use them to swell our ranks. Finally, they will provide a service for the greater good. We are *purifying* your city. And in the meantime, I am learning so much from your magical tomes. So, no, we cannot leave yet. Not when there is so much power to discover."

Aldor could only stand silently and grind his molars.

"Surely as a master, you must be curious?" the lich asked.

"I am not certain what you mean."

The undead wizard held up his skeletal hands. "I see how you look at me, Mutaccio. I see the contempt. You do not see what I see. This body I inhabit is the key. It is a key to unlocking the secrets denied to us by the infernal curses of magic. Surely you must see it? The magic the dragons and the gods didn't want us to have, I can obtain it now. We are so much more than just our bodies."

"Clearly, you haven't seen my matron."

"Temptations of the flesh," Nalazar hissed. "I am beyond that now."

"Seems like a cold life to me."

The lich managed a laugh. "I like you, Aldor. In another life, we could have been contemporaries. I have studied magic for two centuries. I am now immune to the *pherein*. But another mind and another pair of eyes are invaluable. Imagine the secrets we could unlock together.

"Dragan is a competent wizard to run the organization but he lacks ambition. You are more than just a potion maker, Aldor. You could easily become my apprentice."

Chapter 28

Valos Ironblade stood on the beach, watching the endless string of waves crash against the magnificent pink sands of the island of Malinsula. The wind was blowing on his face, licking the sweat from his body. The soft roar of the ocean was ever-present. He turned and offered a smile as the Malinsuli shaman Amman came to stand beside him. "I had to check on you," the big man said with a smile that creased his long beard. "The waves can charm a man's mind, lull you into a trance that you have to be shaken from."

"I think I was about halfway there," Valos laughed.

"Take a walk with me?"

"Of course."

The unlikely duo began a stroll down the beach, walking where the surf met the sand.

"Incanterra, the capital where I am from, the city sits on the ocean. Well... sort of. There is a deep water harbor that the ships use. But our beach is nothing like this."

"Something I have never understood," the shaman said. "The kingdom is Incanterra but the capital is also called Incanterra. Did the founders run out of names? There is a lot to choose from. They could have even just put 'city' at the end of the title. Foreigner mappers label it 'Searock' comma 'Malinsula'. Is your capital called 'Incanterra' comma 'Incanterra'?"

"We could write a strongly worded letter to the castellan."

"Is that the title of your chief? Your king?"

Valos considered his words. "Not really. He would be considered the king of the city but it is an elected position. No bloodlines. No birthrights."

"Hmmm. I have to imagine the guilds might be upset having to go back in and correct the writing on all their maps."

"But then the ships and fans of all things mapped would have to buy new maps to have the most accurate records," Valos said, rubbing his fingers together. "I am still waiting for a war between kingdoms like Arvaterra and Monterra. Let one annex sections from another. I just have to remember to invest in the local cartography business before the dust settles."

The shaman looked out on the water and smiled. "You are a curious one, Valos Ironblade. Is everything gold, silver, and copper to you?"

"I'm also a fan of gemstones," Valos quipped. "Or any resources that can earn me more of the same."

"I want you to remember that statement once we round this bend," Amman said.

"Noted. But speaking of resources, I do like your sangria. And I have been told you all ferment molasses?"

"Malinsuli rum. We are pretty famous for it."

"I hear it is fantastic. If I can get that in the bellies of the Incanterran women..." Valos gave a low whistle and shook his head.

"So it is not always *just* about coins?"

"I am a man after all," Valos replied as he noted several islander women walking along the beach, carrying baskets of fish and local fruit. Turning serious, he brought his gaze back to the shaman. "I do want to thank you for granting the crew of the *Castella Mare* some shore leave. I made sure to let all of them know that if there was any trouble, it would be reported directly to the ship's mother. They fear the wrath of Lady Honeygold's wooden spoons enough to walk the straight and narrow path. They won't be any trouble."

"She sounds like the mothers that raised me," Amman replied. "I never heard a single of them raise their voice to me or any child. They tell them if they are wrong but they never yell. Instead, they just give you that stare."

Amman tried his best to emulate the disapproving motherly glare he had been on the receiving end of so many times as a child, typically after notable foolishness.

"I wish I could say Ombraterran mothers are that way. They yell. All. The. Time. They yell at you when they punish you. They yell when they love you. I mean they love to yell."

"Ombraterran? I thought you were Incanterran?"

"I don't know if anyone is really Incanterran. The generations being born now might claim it as such. But almost everyone is from somewhere else. They come to the kingdom because of the promise of prosperity. But the way the city is divided, you can see the kingdom heritages change from ward to ward. It is rare to see you islanders though. But after seeing all this, I don't exactly blame you all. What do you do?"

"I'm a shaman. Did we not cover this?"

"What?"

"You asked me what I did."

Valos laughed. "Let's call that a cultural difference. 'What do you do?' It is like saying, uh, like saying, 'What do I know?' My father always used to say 'Ah, who needs 'em?' when talking about people he didn't like."

Rounding the bend Amman had mentioned, Valos saw a whole host of islanders working on a rocky peninsula outcropping. It was not just islander men and women. There was also a host of water elementals. The summoned elementals were wading up from the ocean onto the outcropping of stone and pouring their essence into stone vats. "What is all that about?" Valos asked.

"That is probably half of Malinsula's trade value right there," the shaman replied.

As the two drew closer and began making their way up to the flat plateau of the outcropping, Valos saw the large stone vats were filled with evaporating pools of water, leaving behind their precious valuables. "Salt?" Valos asked.

"Not just salt. Sea salt. The best in all the free kingdoms. You would be surprised how many coins people will plunk down to avoid unseasoned food. Malinsuli sea salt is our biggest export by far."

"You should have brought Thade up here," Valos laughed. "Not that I don't appreciate it but he is the cook in our group. You watch. He is going to be following your chefs around learning how they cook things. I guarantee it. And the man is obsessed with the proper spicing of food."

"Then you all have come to the right island." Amman gestured towards the living water. "It is a unique partnership we have fostered with the elementals. I think it is what makes our operation so efficient. You would also be amazed at how they help us fish."

Valos stood out of the way and watched the salt harvesters work. He then turned and looked at the coastal village further down the way. He noted the catamaran canoes sailing out in the crystal blue water. He even turned and looked at the highlands in the interior of the island and the city high on the hill where the king resided. Valos clucked his tongue and winced against the brightness of the sun. "It is a paradise you all have here, my friend."

"Thank you, Valos Ironblade."

"But I want to be clear. What my friends and I want to do… we want to open up a new trade route. But we don't want it to be between Incanterra and Malinsula. We want it to be between us and the Malinsuli people. We are not going to overrun your paradise with a bunch of people on tour. This ain't no invasion."

Amman laughed in response.

"But the problem is I don't understand how no one owns anything."

"The island provides."

Valos scratched the back of his neck and gave a wince. "The thing is… I don't want to negotiate a trade deal with a king. Look at me. Look at us. I'm not some dignitary. I'm just a businessman. The problem is I don't have another businessman to work with down here. I don't want to work with a king. That guy is a king. He's got enough already. I want to trade with the people. Those people go out. They buy things. I don't want some rich king throwing his wealth in his coffers to sit in a dusty old vault."

"Then the answer is simple," Amman said. "Don't buy our resources with gold."

"No gold?"

Amman waved a dismissive hand. "Gold is pretty. It is wonderful to adorn a woman with. Nothing looks prettier than a gold necklace on bronze skin. But it is soft. It is not practical. Instead of gold coins, trade us. Since you helped us stave off the Kai'kamina, the people will trust you not to bring us worthless trinkets. Bring us things that the whole island can utilize. Bring us something that the other traders can't on their fancy boats."

Valos's forehead wrinkled as he considered his options. "Like you all say. The island provides. What can I bring you that you want? We are Incanterran. You all want magic?"

Amman gestured towards the elementals. "We have magic," he smiled. "As I said earlier, bring us cattle. That is where you can distinguish yourself from the other traders. The island has goats. They grow strong and tasty. They eat the grasses close to the shore that get infused with salt from the winds. But beef is just... beef."

"Oh, no. I get it. So how about this? We get you the beef. You sea salt it up. And will throw in some Monterran potatoes and some Agavinsula peppers for even more seasoning."

From the look on Amman's face, Valos could tell the man's mouth was about to start watering.

"You do that and I will send you back casks of sangria and rum."

"And the sea salt?"

"And the sea salt."

Valos rubbed his hands together happily. "Brother, together, we are going to make stacks of coins!"

Amman shrugged his shoulders and did his best to emulate Valos's Incanterran accent. "What do you do?"

Valos threw his head back in excited laughter and genuine happiness.

Chapter 29

With the current instability within the confines of Sorceria, after dropping off the magical crowns, Master Aldor Mutaccio considered himself lucky to walk out of the Baelannor tower alive. The whole of the isle had heard the screaming coming from the tower in the late night hours when the kingdom was still. Few could guess what Nalazar Catabaysi was doing to the reclusive leader of the conjuring dynasty but, given the anguish within the screams, no one would ever consider taking Asaric Baelannor's place.

With the whispers of atrocities taking place down in the city, the wholesale destruction of the Jurare wizarding tower, and the deaths of Qaava Ce'Mondere and Gaviel Dinacioun – leaders of their respective dynasts – now public knowledge, it was all too apparent that anyone could become the next victim of the Necromangian horde. It was why Aldor had opted to work *with* the resurrected dynasty if only to keep his neck out of the proverbial noose.

Having looked into the yellow eyes of the power-mad lich, Aldor knew insanity when he saw it. The wizarding patron had no idea who Nalazar Catabaysi was before his transformation into the undead horror. He spoke with a clear Incanterran accent and he must have been hiding right under their noses. But whoever the lich was before, Aldor was certain the whole of Nalazar's mind had not made the transition along with him.

The wizard paused at the inner ring circling the isle. He considered a walk if only to clear his head. He could have turned to the east and made a circuit. He wanted to stop and talk with his closest confidant but he suspected there were unseen eyes upon him at that very moment. The last thing he wanted was for the enemy to see him talking with Marius Vocazion too much. Even with their visits staggered out, he was certain they had seen their strolling, morning conversations. He did not know how many eyes were currently on him, how he would navigate the fissures left by Nalazar's attack, or which of the Necromangian faithful feeling their oats would cause him issues.

Instead, the wizard crossed from the northernmost tower of the isle back to his tower at the westernmost point, all while trying not to look at the rubble of the Jurare tower between Baelannor and Mutaccio.

Walking through the main doors and into the foyer, the heat of the day was washed away by the cool, conditioned air within the tower itself. There was very little noise. Most of his apprentices and adepts had retreated into their private chambers, occasionally working on smaller projects while trying to manage their dwindling spell components.

Arriving in his private office, Mutaccio stood amongst his various tomes lining the floor-to-ceiling shelves. The Mutaccio spellbooks often read like complicated cookbooks from the fanciest of dining establishments with detailed instructions and hidden secrets to brew the perfect potions. The mage-light was dim and the room was perfumed with the scent of southern tropical fruit.

Before the alchemist could remove his outer robes and settle into the comfortable couch, the small teak box on his desk issued a telltale vibration. Mutaccio eyed the box curiously, surprised by its activation, and walked expectantly toward his desk. Taking a seat in the high-backed chair, the patron opened the hinged lid.

Inside was a rolled scroll tied off with a thin piece of scarlet ribbon. The barrier bubble keeping the lot of them imprisoned on the island was not adept at impeding the parcel scroll network Mutaccio had with his businesses down in the city. The only explanation could be that the scrolls were inorganic. Either way, the wizard was happy to finally get word from down below.

Sliding the ribbon off the scroll, he unfurled the parchment and hungrily devoured the words written inside. As he was reading, there was a delicate knock on his chamber door. He refused to look up from his reading and just called out, "Enter."

The tantalizing smell of her perfume arrived in the room before Acelendra Mutaccio did. The curvy beauty with her long black hair sauntered her way into the chamber. Her maquillage was elegant as always. Her wizardly robes of crimson and silver trim were impeccable despite the tower being under house arrest. "My lord," she said with a sultry tone.

"My matron," he replied. Mutaccio waved the scroll he was reading. "News from one of my brewmasters down in the city."

"What does it say?"

"The Necromangians have commandeered the whole of our potion brewing operations. They are using our facilities for their nefarious purposes. From the descriptions offered, they are using our cauldrons to create the animated skeletons they control, using the corpses of the people dying within the city walls."

"That sounds terrible," the matron said, covering her mouth with her fingers and her flawlessly manicured nails.

"Indeed," Aldor replied. "Every person lost to disease, imprisonment, or even just old age... every person that falls is added to the army of the dead. You can read the desperation in my foreman's words. He is afraid the Necromangians will not stop until the entire city is converted."

Acelendra walked over to the tall window to look out at the shattered isle of Sorceria. "Things are not going back to normal anytime soon. Are they?"

"I... don't know," the wizard sighed. "There are whispers. Some have been told that once Nalazar had what he needed, he and his undead horde would move on to fulfill some great destiny."

"And what is this *destiny*?"

"I cannot even be certain there is one. I have looked into his eyes, my matron. The creature he has become is no longer human. He is some monster immune to age, disease, and death," Aldor said with a shake of his head. "He wanted me to join him as an apprentice."

Acelendra turned sharply. "Are you going to?"

Aldor shook his head. "What he is doing is not wizardry. This is not what our role is supposed to be. I don't want to be part of a regime that rules over a scorched earth."

"So how does this end?" the matron asked. "How do we get things back to normal?"

"Is that all you care about? Sipping illegal spirits and going down to your spas for all your beauty treatments and massages?"

Acelendra glared at him. "And fine dining. And cotillions and operas. Yes! That is absolutely what I am thinking about! Why is it so wrong to miss the finer things in life?"

"Because people are dying! Or even worse, people are being killed! And their bodies are being added to Nalazar's legion."

Acelendra waved a dismissive hand. "Please," she grumbled. "If we gathered up the patrons of The Eight, all they would do is complain about how their coffers were not being filled. The patrons may play at being philanthropic but it is only after their needs are met first."

Aldor stood up from his chair. "I might remind you that three of those eight are dead. Asaric Baelannor's constitution will only last so long as Nalazar holds him under his thumb. And no one knows where Kerryn Lu'Scion has disappeared to. That leaves us, the Corvalonns, the Vocazions, and what is left of the patronless to wrest control from a dynasty more powerful than all of us combined! And how is your magic going to help the cause? How will coloring hair and nails, plumping up breasts, or making women's asses fatter help us against the undead army we are facing?"

Acelendra glared and squinted at her patron. "I do more than that," she hissed.

"Yes, you also drain my coffers you are so concerned about," the patron roared. "Maybe I should put you to work. Host a cotillion for some of Nalazar's acolytes. Maybe you can persuade them to join our cause with your only reasonable contribution to this dynasty and the only thing you are good for!"

The matron's face twisted in anger and she stormed for the chamber door. "Maybe you would be wise to remember how good I am at all of those carnal delights because memory is the only thing that will serve you. You will not be experiencing my delights for a *very* long time!"

The door slammed shut behind her. One might have expected the patron to sweep the collection of tomes, inkwells, scrolls, and notes off his desk in anger. Aldor Mutaccio was too reserved and organized to self-inflict chaos upon his tidy research pieces.

He did fume at her selfishness. Why such a superficial thing as a trip to a spa was so important to his matron was beyond his comprehension. They were dealing with greater threats than worrying about a mineral bath and a night at the theater.

Silently, Aldor Mutaccio wondered if the whole of the wizarding class truly understood the gravity of their situation. And he was afraid that by the time it was truly realized, it would be too late.

Chapter 30

Dragan Duskwood arrived at the Baelannor tower and began the ascent up the stairs. The wizard was always astonished at how the immaculate tower resembled a museum more than a home. He often wondered how the Baelannor children felt being raised in such a cold environment. But child-rearing was the least on his mind as he ascended the next level of stairs. Instead, his attention was drawn. He found it curious there were strewn pieces of broken marble from what resembled small statues and various objet d'art. The further up the stairs he went, the more prominent the broken pieces became.

On the top floor, Dragan realized it could have only been Nalazar who had thrown such a tantrum with force enough to mar the wooden doors and leave long gouges in the stone halls of the great dynast tower.

The wizard entered the narthex leading to the private chambers of the dynasty's patron which Nalazar had claimed for his own. Within were overturned tables, upended chairs, and a scattering of chaos and mayhem. Nalazar stood still as a statue looking out of the chamber window to the isle of Sorceria below. Rather than touching the floor, Nalazar floated half a hand's width above it.

"Your redecorating scheme has a few curious choices, Master," Dragan said as he entered the chamber.

The undead lich turned and eyed his second-in-command. Dragan did his best to stifle his reaction. The desiccation of Nalazar's facial features had amplified overnight. The second was happy his master was draped in his wizardly robes. He did not even want to imagine what the rest of his form looked like. But even with the sunken eyes, the pronounced cheekbones, and receding lips, Nalazar's displeasure was plain to see on what remained of his face.

 Dragan stood in the entryway, silent, not willing to offer another quip or snide comment. Nalazar had been tapping into a variety of magics, some of which were widely unknown to Dragan. For a brief moment, he feared the lich had been digging into the magic of telepathy. Could he be sifting through Dragan's memories and viewing his conversation with Demina Summerstone? Or would such magic allow him only to listen to the silent monologue within his subordinate's mind? And if that were so, had Dragan just outed himself by thinking about it?

Thankfully, Nalazar turned his frightening gaze from Dragan and gestured towards one of the few upended tables within the spacious chambers. Positioned upon the polished black finish of the table were the half a dozen tiara crowns delivered by Aldor Mutaccio. Dragan crossed the expanse to examine the magical items.

"What is this I hear of a company of our skeletons being set upon down in the city?" Nalazar asked.

His voice had a strange echo and an unnatural reverb. Before his transformation, Nalazar Morningflame had a soothing and grandfatherly tone with hints of being worn out from overuse as a lecturer in Academia. Nalazar Catabaysi's voice was shockingly different. If it continued to spiral at the same level as his physical form, in a few more weeks, the lich would no longer pass as human.

"Witnesses have not exactly been forthcoming," Dragan said as he gingerly tumbled one of the tiara crowns in his hands.

"You examined the bones?"

"Not directly. But the Necromangian who witnessed the scene concluded they were victims of lightning strikes."

"Lightning," Nalazar grumbled with a hint of amusement in his voice. "And there was not a storm cloud in the sky."

"We suspect a missing member of the Vocazion dynasty is down amongst the population of the city," Dragan said. "We are redoubling our efforts to have the missing wizards tracked down."

Nalazar eyed his second curiously. "Something is strange with you, Dragan. What is it?"

Dragan waved him off. "Ah, nothing. Every year about this time, some trees wake up and spread their pollen. It takes my body a heartbeat or three to remember how to fight it. It is nothing a good night's sleep wouldn't fix."

Nalazar gave a harrumph. "Sleep. I've almost forgotten what that is like."

"Lucky you," Dragan said. He held up one of the tiaras. "This is the joint venture between you and the Mutaccio dynasty?"

"It is. I am told that in the attack on our skeleton crew, a member of the Imperial Knights was slain as well."

Dragan tsked. "About those knights. I am not certain they are the best way to—"

"Such an open threat to our group is unacceptable," Nalazar interrupted, plowing through with his monologue. "Losing a score of knights makes no difference to me but I refuse to put our Necromangians in such peril. These crowns are the solution to our thankfully anticipated problem."

The undead wizard drifted across the chamber and halted at the black table. He levitated one of the crowns into his eyeline. "Wearing one of these will transport your consciousness into any undead soldier within our army. You will see what they see. You will hear what they hear. And with enough temerity, you will even be able to control their actions. It will be limited. I would not advise trying to command them in combat but you will be able to make them look in the direction you choose."

"Interesting," Dragan said while admiring the craftsmanship.

"Mutaccio warned about certain side effects."

"Such as?" Dragan asked with a slight pullback and a sudden desire to not want to touch the metal creation.

"When a person is wearing the tiara, the experience is tremendously immersive. You will not be able to perceive what is happening around you up here on the isle. Coming in and out of the realities can cause disorientation. I feel like Mutaccio was underestimating the constitution of my Necromangians but he warned of things like nausea. Possibly nosebleeds. And the effects can amplify the longer you wear the crown. So, lad, make sure that no one spends too long wearing them."

"You want me to manage this operation? Surely there is someone else within the ranks that can babysit—"

The lich waved his hand dismissively. "Delegate the responsibilities however you see fit. But I want someone utilizing these crowns regularly. Those wizards are down there hiding amongst the population. I want them found. The longer they are allowed to roam free, the greater chances they will have to wreak havoc. I do not want my plans disrupted, Dragan."

"Yes, Master."

And like that, the conversation was over. The lich swiveled and floated once more across the chamber, returning to a set of dusty tomes no doubt procured from the Cellarium Vaults. He did not even bother to dismiss his attentive second.

Gathering up the crowns, Dragan took his leave. He descended the stairs to the level below. The wizard was considering where the Necromangians would set up the station to monitor the city. He did not want to stray too far down to the lower levels where his people would be vulnerable.

Thankfully, just off the stairway, there was a parlor that would serve their purposes. There was already a pair of couches and a pair of sitting chairs. Dragan assumed the crown-bearers would want to be seated for their journey. Thanks to the tower's pockets of extra-dimensional space, the room was expansive but comfortable. It was elegant in its décor and design, the same as most rooms within the famed tower. Softly closing the door behind him, Dragan kept one of the crowns for himself and took a seat on the soft cushions of one of the couches.

He gingerly placed the red crown on his head and leaned back in his seat. He closed his eyes and his mind began to swim. He looked down on a shadowed vision of the Incanterran capital that had been drained of all color. Everything was washed in shades of black and white with all manners of gray in between. But scattered amongst the grays were pinpricks of glowing red light moving amongst the city streets.

It was only now, looking down amongst the plurality, that Dragan truly understood the sheer size of their undead forces, represented by the floating will o' the whisps glows.

Looking amongst the lights, Dragan could not even decide which one to choose. Finally, he settled on a single light at random, positioned in the Southwest District. From high above, Dragan sensed a tether being attached to his selection. His stomach lurched as he was pulled from a great height and his spirit plunged toward the city.

Dragan's vision whited out and when it returned, he found himself standing amongst the buildings of the Southwest District. It took substantial effort and it felt as if his body was centered inside a gelatinous cube. He managed to look down and bring his hand into his field of view. It was a skeletal hand clutching a longsword.

He looked around the city ward. Across the way, there was a darkened shop with tall windows. The shop should have sported all sorts of goods. But the business was closed and dark. However, within those windows' reflections, Dragan saw a living skeleton staring back at him.

Normally, the skeletons possessed glowing, floating pinpricks of light within their eye sockets that were always the color of blood. His eyes instead glowed with a cold, freezing blue hue.

"How interesting," Dragan said.

However, he did not only hear the voice inside his head. The skeleton had magically voiced his words as well.

The Mutaccios had created a unique magic item indeed...

Chapter 31

Following Sario, Cinder Fireborne and Cavin Jurare continued to marvel at the amazing foliage of the lush and tropical plants covering the island of Malinsula once they were far enough away from the surf and sand. "So, where are we going here?" Cavin asked as he dodged around another tree limb with wide, flat, green leaves.

"Arcane wizards are something of a rarity down here," Sario said as she continued to make her way down the path. "And those that have come to our shores wanting to experience paradise… well, their moral standing would be best described as… questionable."

In front of them, the vegetation gave way to reveal the tall walls of a sharp plateau. The exposed rock and soil jutted up from the landscape as if the walls had been crafted by the hands of the pantheon, chipped away with a giant celestial chisel.

Along the higher areas of the plateau and also along the landscape leading up to the wall, Cavin noted a series of strange cylindrical rock formations. At first, he thought they might have been anthills despite being as tall as he was. But their solid structures looked forged by nature. What was curious was the tops of what could be described as outdoor stalagmites had all been sheered off. That was when Cavin noted the faint whistling sounds. Looking at one of the smaller formations, he realized the faux stalagmite was hollow.

Cavin then noted Sario heading towards a cave entrance within the wall of the plateau. The opening was tall. He doubted he could have jumped and touched the top of the tunnel. Showing full trust, Cinder was happily walking behind her shaman escort. The undead slayer hustled to catch up.

"These are the caves you retreat to in the event of a hurricane?" Cinder asked.

"One of many," Sario replied. "The island is littered with them. No one ever has but I imagine if one were industrious enough, a proper mapping would discover that they are all part of one large cave system."

Before they entered, Cavin was already digging into one of his many belt pouches. He produced a trio of ornamental glass pieces infused with mage-light. He affixed one to his belt buckle and offered the two other stones to the ladies. Sario looked at the glowing glass and Cavin's buckle curiously.

"Vampires hide in caves," he shrugged. "I like to keep my hands free."

The warden gestured to the metal quarterstaff he carried and the silver longsword lashed to his hip. Sario nodded as she graciously accepted the mage-light glass. "Thankfully, you won't find any vampires in these caves."

The trio entered the winding underground structure, each of their mage-light casting the caverns in a soft but prominent glow. Cavin noted the variety of passages, tunnels, natural alcoves, and chambers stretching out in every direction. Looking up at the high ceiling, he noted pinpricks of sunlight from the hollow rock formations at the top of the plateau, allowing light in and the circulation of air. "Vampires are one thing and they would have a field day in here," Cavin said. "But are there any, you know, natural creepy crawlies that we need to worry about?"

"The magical light will send most things scampering in the other direction," Sario replied. "And nothing that would worry a renowned undead slayer."

"I don't know," Cavin replied while looking about. "I have an issue with things that have more than four feet."

"So no spiders?" Sario asked.

"I don't think anyone *likes* spiders. And not like they are on my list of favorite things. But more like the creepies. I hate bugs. Especially anything like those long centipedes. No way."

Cinder turned. "You have cleared ghouls out of graveyards but centipedes give you the willies?"

"The willies. The heebies. And the jeebies," the undead slayer said. "All those feet moving in unison. Blerg. No. They can piss off."

The trio continued their trek into the cave system. Among the naturally hewed chambers, there were elements of civilization. Many featured sleeping mats, chairs, tables, and other furniture to accommodate those seeking shelter from the dangerous storms. Cinder could imagine scores of villagers retreating up into the caves to wait for the hurricanes to blow themselves out. "Sario, what do you do for light in these caves when you seek shelter?"

"Fire elementals are invaluable during those times," Sario said. "We often summon small tufts of living flame. They help banish the darkness."

Cinder nodded, making mental notes on how her evocation magic might assist the islanders.

"We need to bring a few Mutaccio wizards down here or purchase some of their stone-shaping scrolls," Cavin said. "Smooth out some rough edges. Make some natural seating. Some tables. Turn it into a real garden spot."

Past a pair of antechambers, Sario approached a bamboo ladder. Its rungs were lashed together with tightly braided vines and led up into a second chamber that could not be reached without the ladder's aid. "This is what I wanted to show you."

One by one, the trio ascended the ladder into the private chamber above. The mage-light was more than enough to illuminate the space and there was a pair of small chimney vents that let dry air swirl through the room.

At first glance, Cinder thought the chamber was something of a treasure trove she imagined used by the Agavinsula pirates, stashing their ill-gotten gains looted from seafaring vessels. There were crates, chests with hinged lids, and an assortment of containers. "What is all of this?" Cinder asked as she looked around the room.

"Back during the Great Dragon Wars, before Ignaterra became the vast wasteland that it is today and the cartographers renamed the kingdom, there was a wizard," Sario said. "He was like you all. He practiced the scholarly arcane magic like you both do. And while he was Ignaterran, his heart belonged to a Malinsuli woman who he loved dearly."

Cavin cautiously opened one of the ancient crates, noting a variety of leather-bound tomes inside. Strangely, while the crates themselves were centuries old, the books looked as if they had been crafted yesterday, free from aging or even dust.

"The man had no heirs. There were no Malinsuli wizards to take advantage of his knowledge," Sario explained. "But my ancestors appreciated the man's genius. They recognized his talents for what they were. We felt that his legacy needed to be protected and preserved. So after he went to live with his ancestors in the great Never, we brought his collection of tomes and spellbooks here."

"I don't want to sound ungrateful," Cinder cautioned, "but why did you bring the two of us here?"

"This magic is different from ours," Sario said. "We cannot use it. Something tells me you can. Why would we not give this to you?"

Cavin smiled. "What you have done is very honorable, Sario. I thank you in advance for showing all of this to us. This is just one of those... cultural differences. Back home, the big wizarding dynasties consider each other to be... rivals. For someone to openly share power like this is unusual for us. Not bad. Just... unusual."

"I still don't see how your kind gets along," Sario said with a shake of her head, causing her white hair to wave about. "How is your kingdom not in absolute chaos every day?"

"Who says it isn't?" Cavin laughed.

"It's not easy," Cinder said simultaneously.

"I am assuming you all will want to poke around in here for a while?" the shaman asked as the two wizards were already curiously scanning the collection.

"Just don't get caught out in the jungle after dark. You remember your way back through the cave structures and the way back to the village?"

"I can open us a portal," Cinder replied.

"Those are handy," the shaman said. "Very well. Dinner will be special tonight. Don't be too long."

"Cinder's never accused me of that," Cavin cracked.

Sario started back down the ladder.

"I can open a portal to send you back to the village," Cinder offered.

From the hole below, Sario's voice called back. "I like walking through nature. Maybe I can find some centipedes or scorpions in the cave before I go."

"That's not funny," Cavin yelled down into the hole and at Sario's retreating light.

"A little funny," her fading voice echoed.

Cavin turned back to the collection of magical tomes. "I still do not see how a kingdom like Arvaterra has not conquered these people. If you had a strong navy, you could subjugate the island in a week."

Cinder kept flipping through the pages of a large, blue leather tome. Her features were growing more serious with each page she skimmed. "What is it?" Cavin asked.

"I can't believe it," Cinder said breathlessly. "I had always heard this magic existed. And I never understood why a dynasty didn't attempt to master it. But at the same time, I can see why no dynasty would even want to acknowledge its existence. I can see why they would want it whispered about. Obviously. It would be far too dangerous to let loose…"

"You are getting close to rambling," Cavin said with a smile as he stood to look over her shoulder. "What magic is it?"

Looking at the text, the diagrams, and the theoretical notes in the margins, Cavin squinted and cocked his head to the side. "Am I reading this right?" he asked. "Is that…?"

Cinder nodded her head as she risked saying the words.

"Anti-magic."

Chapter 32

Armelise Baelannor would have been well on her way to joining the ranks of the adept class of her dynast's wizards had the kingdom not been thrown into chaos. Now into her twenties, the young conjurer's talent exceeded most of those within the apprentice ranks – not only within her dynasty but amongst all of the other wizards within her age group. She was ready to become part of the class that would take apprentices under her wing. She would continue their education and transition them from a classroom style of teaching to more of a one-on-one mentorship. She would guide them to greater levels of magical understanding.

Instead, for the last two weeks, the young wizardess felt chained to the conjuring pools. While unable to be properly quantified as a kitchen, the Baelannors utilized several tall, open warehouses in Incanterra's Southwest District. Within these structures, Baelannor apprentices worked day and night to churn out their conjured foodstuffs for the population of the city. With the gates sealed and no replenishing food sources being imported – either from the kingdom's northern farms or via the sailing ships in Highstone Harbor – the Baelannors had become impossibly important in how the Catabaysi dynasty and their lich leader kept the population in check.

Still, such mundane conjurings from a wizardess of her skills felt wrong. Her talents were being wasted conjuring simple food. Under normal circumstances, the Baelannor dynasty would assign such tasks to their apprentices. They would cut their teeth learning these conjurings and then the business side of the dynasty would sell the literal fruits of their labor to the city government which would then distribute it amongst the poorer wards, notably places south of the Queen's High Way. It was a symbiotic relationship that had served the dynasty for generations.

Only now, to meet the incredible demands of the sealed city, every conjuror was needed. Having served a staggeringly long shift, the young wizardess was granted her return to the isle of Sorceria. Along with her contingent of other wizardly citizens, Armelise silently boarded the floating sloop that would take them to the floating isle. In amongst a collective of Incanterran natives, Armelise's Selvaterran heritage was on full display. She was set apart with her long, coal-black hair and skin that looked perpetually kissed by the sun.

Amongst the passengers, aside from the Necromangian chaperones, the wizardess noted a Mutaccio potion mixer and a Dinacioun seer. She had seen them both on the isle but had not learned their names. There was a small collection of house workers the wizardess barely acknowledged. However, she tried her best to conceal her emotions when she saw a pair of Vocazion wizards. She knew both Renarr and Kysanna Vocazion. They were younger than her but destined to join the adept class within their dynasty before too long.

Armelise was curious about what the mages were doing down in the city but she knew better than to ask... especially with the Necromangians close by. It would have been a pointless question. Of all the wizards on board, when asked what they were doing down in the city, they would all inevitably answer the same. "Whatever the Necromangians commanded."

The sloop lifted off and began its thousand feet ascent towards Sorceria. Unlike before when the sloops would take lazy spiraling ascents, now the boats wasted no time and ascended straight to the landing platform on the shattered isle's northmost point.

The crushed remains of the isle's sentinels – large animated suits of enchanted armor – remained silently laying where the lich had left them. It was a stark reminder for those coming and going of what the undead wizard was capable of. Disembarking from the sloop, Armelise gave a nod of acknowledgment to Renarr and Kysanna Vocazion before she broke right and they broke left to return to their respective towers. Through their eyes, the trio shared the same silent sentiment. "Stay alive."

Through the dynastic gates, Armelise approached the tower at a quick pace. She was happy to be home. She was looking forward to a quick bite of unconjured food from the tower's stores, a long showering of water to wash the day from her tan skin, and then collapsing in her bed where the infused mattress and the goose-down feather pillow would speed her to a healing sleep. Still, she was excited to see Devinaya Baelannor in the foyer as the young wizardess entered the tower.

Devinaya was one of the highest-ranking adepts within the order and the consensus amongst her peers was she would lead the dynasty through a matronly role one day. Armelise saw it as an honor when Devinaya made eye contact and gestured for the young adept to join her.

The two made it a point to stand to the side when Nikkala Whitesnow walked through the threshold. The statuesque woman with her classical beauty, pale white skin, and long, blonde hair strode with a purpose through the foyer and up the stairs. "They have been arriving all afternoon," Devinaya whispered. "Members of Nalazar's elite."

"Is something wrong?" Armelise asked.

"New magic. Mutaccio delivered half a dozen magical instruments earlier. The inner circle has been giving them a go."

Devinaya gestured for Armelise to follow. They ascended the staircase and walked past the parlor filled with assembled Necromangians. With a glance, Armelise noted several sitting in the parlor's comfortable chairs wearing the odd tiara crowns.

"What are they doing?" the young adept asked.

"You know how the Dinaciouns have their far-seeing spells? The one where they look through the eyes of an animal?"

"I thought that was how they predicted the future."

Devinaya shook her head. "That's foreseeing. Far-seeing is a spell where they look through the eyes of their familiars or some other animal. As far as I can tell, Nalazar is doing the same thing but with his undead servants. The Necromancers are seeing things through the eyes of their horde."

"Smart move if you don't want to expose your wizards to the people."

Devinaya nodded. "It also gives us an advantage. While their consciousness is looking through the eyes of the undead, their eyes are blind here. Their ability to hear is also dramatically compromised."

"If one of them were inside one of the crowns and left alone…" Armelise pantomimed slicing an invisible dagger across her throat.

"You would have to be very fast," Devinaya said. "And you would have to get rid of the body. Otherwise, Nalazar could bring them back from the dead to name their assailant."

The wind leaked out of Armelise's bellows.

"I wonder. Do the Necromangians speak to the departed spirits like the mediums who tell fortunes? Or is speaking with the dead more of a divination spell?"

"I am pretty certain those fortune tellers are all chicanery and theatrics," Devinaya replied. "But what I do know is that while they are distracted, we have a genuine opportunity to do things to tip the scales back in our favor."

"Like what?"

Devinaya produced two vials filled with a thick pink solution. "Healing potions?" the adept asked.

Devinaya passed over the vials. "I want you to get these to Master Asaric. Make sure he drinks them. Whatever damage Nalazar is doing to our patron, we have to ensure he is not taken to the Never. We cannot lose him. Just… don't get caught."

Armelise nodded and tucked the small vials into her wizard robes.

"I have been told Mutaccio is working on more crowns. That could play to our advantage. They are blind and almost deaf while using them. Nalazar is as well. He also only does remote viewing there in the parlor with his acolytes. Wait until Nalazar projects his consciousness down into the city. Then sneak into the patron's chambers."

The duo pulled back into the doorway of a nearby room at the arrival of yet another Necromangian. He said nothing as he went directly to the parlor. Then a shiver of cold swept through them as Nalazar Catabaysi arrived.

The lich floated across the floor and turned effortlessly to enter the parlor where his other Necromangians were assembled. "Give him a few minutes to settle in," Devinaya advised, "and then make your move."

Armelise nodded nervously. "For the dynasty."

"For the dynasty… and the kingdom."

Chapter 33

The illuminated cave was silent save for the occasional whistle of wind up through the natural chimneys and the fluttering turns of heavy vellum pages. The rogue mage Cinder Fireborne and the undead slaying warden Cavin Jurare sat pouring over the tomes of ancient knowledge stored within the recessed chamber of the cave network. "This wizard – this Sparax the Black – just might have been a genius," Cinder said, refusing to even hide the admiration in her tone. "He keeps referring to Aradisus. If I am pulling this out of the right context, could Aradisus be Ignaterra before it became Ignaterra?"

"I should have studied my history better," Cavin said. "But no, I had to spend my time learning how to use a sword and fight a graveyard full of ghouls. But you heard Sario. I bet Aradisus was a city in the kingdom that would later become Ignaterra – after the red dragon turned it to ash. So this wizard had a taste for the caramel skin and that white hair."

"You have never been more diplomatic than in this exact moment."

"But she loves the island too much to leave it. So he would bounce back and forth. And as Sario said, he is living life. Enjoying his time. Probably built himself a tower and all that. After he passed, the Malinsuli bring everything here."

"It makes sense," Cinder nodded. "Still, the way he crafts his spell formations. I've never read anything like it. He is so fluid and… poetic? Is that the right term?"

"If I am being honest, the more I read, the more irritated I am becoming," Cavin said as he clapped one of the large spellbooks shut.

Cinder looked up from her reading, a concerned expression etched on her face. Jurare picked up another tome and wanted to flip through it but he could not bring himself to concentrate on the spells scribed within. "This is a whole new tree of abjuration and I have never even heard whispers of this magic."

"So, why all the anger?"

"It is like your whole life you have been taught fifty-one divided by seventeen plus seven equals ten—"

"I will trust you on that one."

"—and here comes this Sparax the Black writing five plus five equals ten. It is the same result but his formula is simple. Cleaner. Easier. And you say, 'why have we made things so complicated?'"

Cinder remained silent for a few moments. "Is that so strange? Wasn't that the dream of Xizzen Avernden? Wasn't that why he founded Incanterra? So wizards of all the different kingdoms could come together, study, learn, and create new magic spells by pulling from all these different points of view and cultural histories?"

"So why have you and I never heard of anti-magic?" Cavin asked. "He has scrolls, books, tomes... Volumes! This whole aspect of abjuration was never even whispered. Why? Was Sparax the Black the only wizard in Aradisus?"

Cinder carefully turned another page in the tome. "It would not be the first time a magic spell was deemed too dangerous. That's what the Cellarium Vaults were built for."

"These are not magical theories or experimentations to create a more powerful magical effect," Cavin huffed. "This is an entire branch of abjuration magic lopped off like a diseased limb. And either my ancestors were too stupid to realize its potential... or... or... or... it was buried for a reason."

Still irritated, Cavin got to his feet to pace in the cramped space the chamber provided. "This isn't a cursed item or a magical potion that would spread disease. This isn't magic that turns the recipients into rampaging demons. These magical spells – this anti-magic – wouldn't be a threat to the people of Incanterra. The only people it would target are wizards. It is like they buried this magic only because it could be used *against* them."

Cinder casually turned another page. "I am not saying you are wrong. In truth, the more I think about it, I know you are right. But from what I'm reading here, this anti-magic has a downside. I mean a significant downside."

Cavin folded his arms across his chest, allowing Cinder to elaborate.

"In all of the initial reading – and I know we are scratching the surface – this magic does not rely heavily on material components. There are no shaved metals, no gemstone dust, no bat guano, no eyes of newts, or wings of bats in these material recipes. The verbal components are pretty simple. And even the somatic gestures aren't complicated. So to create these spells, the warden would have to pull from their inner reserves. That is a dangerous road to walk. You think the Lu'Scions are pulling from their inner reserves to power a spell?"

"That's where they use those glowing mushrooms that they grow in the bowel of Sorceria," Cavin said, finally relenting and taking a seat again. "And if that sentence doesn't make eating them sound twice as scrumptious, I just don't know what to tell you. I am hungry just thinking about Sorcerian bowels."

Cinder smiled as Cavin's usual boyish mirth was trying to return.

"I just keep thinking about that blight that terrorized the city here a while back," Cinder said.

Cavin wore a contemplative frown. His eyebrows raised and he bobbed his head back and forth as he considered Cinder's words. "So, you think if a wizard cast too much of their essence into these spells, that they could have an effect? Transform them into something like a blight?"

Cinder pondered the possibility for a moment.

"I suppose it depends on how you look at it," she mused. "So, look at Incanterra. It is all divided up into these factions. Wizards and nonwizards. All the different districts and wards within the districts. There is even a certain amount of kingdom segregation. And all of these different factions demand loyalty. When I pledged my allegiance to... a certain group, I had to swear a loyalty oath."

"What was that like? Was there like a ceremony or—"

"I can't tell you but I can tell you that this group demands loyalty above everything. They asked me if I was beside my mother's deathbed and they called, would I answer?"

"They obviously don't know your relationship with your mother."

"Well, they don't custom tailor the oath. They asked all of us the same question. But the meaning was there. The family comes first. And before you go casting judgments—"

"Magic pun. Nice."

"—wizards are no different. Which would be the greater scandal: the Jurare wizard partnering with a lowly commoner or a Jurare wizard partnering with a Vocazion?"

"You can practically sense the pearl-clutching all the way down here," Cavin said. "But you hear it all the time. Healthy competition between all the various dynasties is what propels us to greater magical achievements."

"Spoken like a loyal cult follower," Cinder grinned.

"Tell me again about this loyalty oath you had to swear? Was there a goat involved and maybe a cup to catch its spilled blood?"

"Exactly," Cinder replied. "And then between sessions of pleasuring our exalted leader, we feasted on the roasted flesh of infants."

"As any good cult does."

"I swear I was on my way to making a point," she muttered.

"Absent-mindedness," Cavin clucked his tongue. "One of the first signs that the mind is starting to go. Old age. It is a tragedy."

Cinder thumped the vellum page of the tome in her lap. "The point of concern I have is this magic requires an extremely strong wizard to master. I am afraid if this magic fell into the hands of someone inexperienced or didn't have the internal fortitude to cast it, they could be inadvertently transformed into something horrible."

The two sat quietly for a moment.

"It sounds great," Cavin said, breaking the silence. "And that is a possibility. Or..." Cavin drew his word out and let it hang ominously in the chamber. "Or it could be that these spells wouldn't affect the common citizens of Incanterra. If you cast—" Cavin flipped open the tome he was reading previously and ran his finger on the page, "—here. If you were to cast a 'wave of magic disbursement' on a crowd of rioters as we dealt with before, nothing would happen to them. These spells only target magic users. And maybe that is the reason why my dynasty was forbidden from mastering this entire magical line."

Cinder nodded but then gestured to the volume she was reading. "Well, if it makes you feel any better, this all looks to be an exercise in futility. In his writings here, old Sparax recommends only casting these anti-magic spells with a wand made from a very specific tree. A tree from a kingdom that is now a desert wasteland where no trees grow. The mariners on the *Castella Mare* called the land death incarnate. I am afraid that unless we find Sparax's magic wand in amongst these tomes, his theories of anti-magic died when the Great Red laid waste to what would become Ignaterra."

"Why can't you use your wand? Or why couldn't I use my staff?" Cavin asked.

"You would be casting anti-magic through an item infused with magic energy to channel magical energy. Plus all the magic residue infused into the item from all the casting. It would be like dropping a ball of lava on a frozen lake. Things don't work out well for that ice sheet."

The wind left Cavin's sails. "That's a shame," he grumbled. "It would have been a unique weapon to have in our arsenal."

Chapter 34

Cadwell Dinacioun sat on one of the many comfortable benches placed along the inner ring of Sorceria. The inner ring was a boundary between the individual estates of The Eight and the interior of the isle considered communal property. Normally, fountains would be trickling with water. The sun would be shining and bright. A cool breeze would keep the summer temperatures bearable. Instead, a depressive pall hung over the island.

As secretive and self-isolating as the wizards often were with their various magical research and games of superiority, the isle itself was often frequented with frequency. While not nearly the hustle and bustle of life down in the crowded city, wizards were often wandering to and fro. Conjurors, sorcerers, alchemists, warlocks, mages, wardens, seers, and magicians were always working on or moving toward their next big project, albeit with a lackadaisical gait. But now, students more resembled bunny rabbits or scurrying rodents. No one wanted to be caught out in the open by the raptor birds prowling the island.

Even now, Cadwell knew being out in the daylight left him a target for the Necromangians strutting about the isle, freely waggling their authority. But there were only so many hours out of the day one could spend couped up in a tower even if it was outfitted with interdimensional space and resplendent magic. In precedented times, Cadwell would have been working down in the city, overseeing the magical mass production of *The Heraldry* – the capital's daily newspaper. At the outset of the siege, the patron of the Catabaysi dynasty ordered the city's information source shuttered.

It left the wizard with nothing to do.

Sitting on the bench and looking directly south, Cadwell was observing between his own dynasty's plot of land and the one belonging to the Corvalonns. He could look out and see the lifeless waters of Highstone Harbor which were normally abuzz with ship traffic both importing and exporting goods from the kingdom. But now, the harbor was silent as the blockade kept the kingdom's ships in and the foreign kingdom ships out.

Sighing with contempt, the wizard ran his fingers through his thinning hair and took a moment to clean his spectacles with a silk kerchief.

"Adept Cadwell," a voice called from behind him.

Cadwell pivoted on his bench and turned to see a young Vocazion mage walking around the bend from a nearby collection of public villas. She was dressed in the traditional blue and black trimmed colors of her dynasty. Cadwell had noted the urgency in her voice and she approached with a reserved quickness – fast enough to announce her hurry but not so hastily as to draw a curious eye. He started to stand up from his seat but she waved him back down. The young mage took a seat beside him, setting a small stack of tomes in her lap.

"Kysanna, right?"

"Yes."

The Vocazion mage was one of the higher-ranked apprentices within her dynasty while Cadwell had been serving as an adept for years. The two were not close enough in age to be familiar but the isle was too small for Cadwell not to recognize his underclassman. The young woman adjusted her wizardly robes and did her best to look natural. "I just need a beard," she said with a whisper.

"A beard?"

"I need a distraction to ward off the attention of those Catabaysi stinkards," she hissed. "If they see me alone, it is not going to be pleasant. But if they see me with you, the worst it will be is some catcalls and empty threats. Just seeing someone of your status will deter them."

"Do you need an escort to your tower?"

"Please."

The magus and the mage got to their feet and started their counter-clockwise stroll around the inner ring. At the southeast corner, they noted the tall, black tower belonging to the Ce'Mondere – the dynasty of demon summoners. The façade of the tower was as intimidating as one would expect.

As they crossed to the eastern point, the next land parcel belonged to the Lu'Scions. The two paused. Belonging to the magicians, the Lu'Scions had a reputation for changing the entire theme and structure of their tower. The look would change depending on the season, upcoming events, or even just the whim of the patron. It was one of the joys of specializing in illusions.

Only now, the Lu'Scion tower was nothing more than a dark and lifeless obelisk of plain, gray stone. "It is hard to get used to, isn't it?" Kysanna asked.

Cadwell could only grumble.

"I remember being so excited," Kysanna said. "It was part of the reason I kept such a close eye on the calendar. As a child, I was obsessed with the first of the month. Going to bed on the last day, waking up in the morning, and seeing how the Lu'Scions had changed their home. I always found it fascinating."

Cadwell continued to look upon the ordinary stone.

"My matron said once the siege happened, the Lu'Scions must have run out of spell components," she continued. "I suppose there were bigger issues to deal with than making your tower resemble a giant fountain or putting living dragon statues on your parapets."

"I still want to know how they did it," Cadwell said. "How do you make an entire dynasty disappear?"

Marching through the open gates of the grounds, the magus was not met with any sort of deterrent – physical or magical. Not wanting to be left alone, Kysanna quickly gave chase. Cadwell tried not to fume. "I know that Master Kerryn was mourning the death of my patron. Master Gaviel and he were... friends. Not many people can say that especially amongst the patron ranks. But that doesn't give them the right to do what they did."

Walking the cobblestone pathway bisecting the lawn – which was quickly on its way to becoming unkempt – Cadwell Dinacioun strode up the estate steps and pulled open the twin oak doors. Hinges groaned in protest but gave way. Inside was an empty foyer leading into an even emptier tower. And once more, not a single deterrent stood in Cadwell's path. To allow such brazen entrance into any wizardly abode was unheard of.

And yet, there the two stood.

"The Jurares have been obliterated. The Ce'Monderes are decimated and leaderless. At night, we all hear the tortured screams of Asaric Baelannor," Cadwell said, trying to remain composed. "And at a time when the city needs them the most, the entire Lu'Scion dynasty absconds to the horizons."

Kysanna waited a moment, allowing Cadwell to silently seethe. "My matron always called their magic foolish," she offered. "One has to wonder... if the Lu'Scions based most of their magic on illusions and spells to affect the mind, would their magic even work on the undead hordes controlling the city?"

Cadwell scratched his temple and adjusted his spectacles. "It would be a valid point," he relented. "I suppose if any of us had the opportunity to escape, we would take it. But it still feels like they left the rest of us to hang from the gallows. And I have been deep in the tower. I was part of the crew that investigated with my matron. This wasn't a 'grab what you can' middle-of-the-night dash. Everything was systematically taken. All resources. All clothes. I want to know how they got out so cleanly."

"Do you really want to know?" Kysanna asked. "Or do you just want to know why they didn't take the rest of us with them?"

Cadwell stood silent and steadfast. For a moment, he almost crossed his arms over his chest but stopped himself. Kysanna nodded knowingly. "Do you think if the Baelannor dynasty was holding open a gate, they would pause for even a heartbeat to look back and make sure the rest of us were following them? The Eight are not exactly known for working together."

Cadwell wanted to offer a counterpoint but he knew the apprentice was correct. How was this young girl better versed in magical politics than he was? "Still, the Lu'Scions and the Dinaciouns were close allies. At least, I *thought* we were."

"Were you allies or was it more of the friendship between your patrons? Did you often hobnob with the Lu'Scion men? Were Lu'Scion magicians constantly pursuing Dinacioun seers? I only ask because my patron has a friendship with Aldor Mutaccio. But I have yet to find a Mutaccio that is not an elitist snob."

"They do like rubbing their coins in other's faces," Cadwell laughed.

"Still, I'd take that over what those Catabaysi necros want to rub in my face," the mage groaned.

"Everything is crumbling," Cadwell carped. "I don't even know which members of my dynasty are alive down in the city. No one knows anything."

"If only there was an organization that could spread the news around the city," she replied with a mocking tone.

Cadwell scoffed. "*The Heraldry* was one of the first institutions the Knights of the Imperial Circle targeted. Where do you think they plucked me from? Brought me back up here in chains."

"So why are you really mad?" Kysanna asked. "Are you mad that the Lu'Scions left or are you mad they didn't take you with them?"

"I am mad that they left us to our fate. They abandoned the city."

"So let me ask again, would they have helped repel the undead forces with illusions?"

"All wizarding dynasties serve their role. What if we needed one more push of magical power and that is the difference between life and death?"

"Then no one will be alive to remember their transgressions." Kysanna paused for a beat. "Unless you find a way to get *The Heraldry* back in print. Write an exposé."

"Well if that isn't a reason to stay alive, I don't know what is."

Kysanna nodded her head. "Outlast 'em. Prove 'em all wrong."

"Motivation indeed."

Chapter 35

Zodor Blackburn finally breathed a sigh of relief. Tucked away in the alley, the Knight of the Imperial Circle was happy to breathe unrestricted air. Having removed his alabaster mask and the conical hood concealing his identity, he was happy to breathe freely and let some of the sweat soaking his hair and his face evaporate.

Hamul Bronzebeller ducked inside the alley behind him but Zodor's fellow knight was reluctant to remove his hood. "You better not let anyone see you," Hamul whispered.

"Let them," Zodor said. "At this point, I don't care. I can't see properly. I can't breathe properly. And it is hotter than dragon's breath under there. No one ever warns you about that during the recruitment."

Hamul did his best to obstruct the view of the alleyway from any of the passersby. Thankfully, their squad of skeletons stationed on the street corner made sure people hustled past quickly. The last thing any pedestrian wanted was to dawdle and gawk down alleyways.

The knights shared pulls from an uncorked canteen and continued their respite in the cool shadows of the alleyway. Chancing a look out onto the street, Hamul saw the skeletal sentinels staying close, silently surveying the streets.

"Just between you and me?" Zodor asked.

"Always," Hamul nodded.

"I am starting to question things," the knight admitted. "I am loyal to the cause. You know that. I've been a knight since my father used to bounce me on his knee. You and I were raised right. But this? This whole thing? These necromancers? I don't know."

Hamul nodded and he looked out on the street. "Did you put the skull emblem above your door? And above the door of your parents?"

"Of course I did."

Hamul turned back sharply. "And have they been given the extra rations and security because of their loyalty?"

Zodor closed his eyes and nodded shallowly.

"You've seen it. I've seen it. We've all seen it. Those markings have kept our families safe. In the history of Incanterra, has an army ever marched on our soil? Has a navy ever tried to besiege Highstone Harbor?"

Zodor remained silent.

"They haven't because of The Eight. And then this undead wizard up and does the impossible. Not only does he attack the city but he attacks Sorceria. In his opening salvo, he cracked the island in half. His forces sealed off this city in a day. Like the Necromangians or hate them, they are going to win this war. And it is better to serve at the foot of the throne than be crushed under their boot. My father taught me to respect the magic same as yours. And these Necromangians are the most powerful of them all. It is our place to serve them."

"I am not saying you are wrong," Zodor said. "I am just saying it is odd we just flipped allegiances so quickly. We went from supporting The Eight to suddenly clapping them in irons. That doesn't seem... strange?"

"Lord Reeve Windwisher is our leader. He issued the order. We follow it. That is what good soldiers do. And again, your mother and father are safe because of it."

Across the city, the bells of the four towers located in the center of each district began to chime, signaling the top of the hour. "It's time. Get your face back on," Hamul said encouragingly.

Reluctantly, Zodor pulled his hood back on and affixed his featureless alabaster mask in place. The two exited the shadows of the alleyway and moved to join the skeletal brigade waiting for them. "I am just saying that some sort of chilling enchantment on the mask would help lift spirits," Zodor said.

"I'll mention that to Lord Windwisher the next time I have an audience," Hamul answered. "I am sure the general will make it his top priority."

With the skeletons in tow, the knights moved to the center of the ward's square where one of the Sorcerian sloops was prepared to make its arrival to distribute more of the conjured foodstuffs to the civilian population. From under his hood, Hamul nodded towards the descending sloop. "And say what you will about Nalazar Catabaysi and his Necromangians, they have worked hard to keep the population fed. Do you think if Arvaterra besieged the city, their boy king would provide the civilian population such treatment?"

"Are they doing that out of kindness or to keep the people from rioting?" Zodor hissed, careful to keep his voice low.

Looking out at the crowd beginning to assemble for the rations, the two knights slowly scanned faces, keeping their heads on a swivel. Seeing the emotionless knights behind their faceless masks, wearing their priestly vestments, and armed with long swords, the unarmed populace knew better than to attempt anything foolish.

Behind his faceless mask, the civilians could not know if the sweat pooling in the small of Zodor's back was a result of the high sun and the summer heat or the nervousness of being impossibly outnumbered. However, the steel swords and the shambling army of skeletons on their cracking and clacking joints were more than enough to keep the crowd in line.

As the citizens continued to gather, something odd caught Zodor's eye. While the fashions of Incanterra were mixed, there was always a representation of various colors. Topical tans, basic browns, and other earthy colors were mostly scattered amongst the citizens of the great city. Blue tunics, red cloaks, and green jerkins were easily spotted. But what was often missing from the palette was a healthy dose of shadowy blacks.

During his time living in the Northeast District, Zodor had learned to associate the color with one organization and particularly with the deity to which they had pledged their allegiance. At first, he thought it could have just been a trick of the light. It could have been that too many hungry citizens were packed too close together. The shadows could play tricks and the eyelets in his mask hindered his vision, especially in his periphery.

Because of the limitation, he heard the slice and the subsequent gurgling before he saw it. Pivoting on his heel, Zodor turned in time to see Hamul drop to his knees. His white, priestly vestment was quickly staining with a spreading pool of crimson. As his fellow knight dropped to the warm stone street, Zodor's eyes grew wide. Lording over Hamul's body was a tall and powerful warrior dressed in the blacks of Zaneger's acolytes.

Emerging from different points within the crowd were more and more adherents to the god of death. They moved with focused anger toward the skeletal sentries who were quickly moving to raise swords and defend themselves. These unholy abominations had slipped the grasp of their death god. Penance was to be paid. As they closed the gaps, the warriors of the *domici dauthis* brandished their short swords and single-handed representations of the reaper's scythes.

Amongst the crowd, there were no women's screams. The people did not panic. They fell back and let the acolytes fulfill their creed. One could only guess if they had been forewarned or had simply waited for this moment. There were no roars of rage or violent outbursts of emotion. The agents were as cold, methodical, and silent as their skeletal counterparts. Steel clashed against steel. Swords slashed skin. Blades banged bone.

The Necromangian overseeing the distribution of the Baelannor-conjured foodstuffs was the only one who panicked. Dumping the provisions out, the acolyte was quick to clamor over to the boat's wheel and rudder, triggering the magic to get the vessel back up in the air and off of the battlefield.

As the sloop began to rise, Zodor Blackburn made a last-ditch effort to make his way through the crowd, hoping the sloop might offer him sanctuary. No longer standing on ceremony, the knight ripped off his conical hood and the ivory mask restricting his breathing and his vision. The knight ran as fast as he could but there was too much congestion between him and the boat.

As the vessel continued to rise, the knight – fueled by adrenaline and fear – jumped on top of the crates of dumped foodstuffs. He knew that it would take all of his might. His grunt as he leaped off the crates transformed into a gasp of relief as his fingertips found purchase on the railing of the sloop.

But his armor was too heavy. The wood was too polished. And his grip could not hold.

At least he managed to land on his feet as he dropped back to the street. Crouched low from the impact, he looked upward and watched as the sloop continued its rapid ascent toward Sorceria. Watching his hopes sail away, the knight let his gaze drop.

Standing in front of him was Arator Dawnborne. The tall, handsome, and powerfully built agent of Zaneger stood emotionless. There were chips of shattered skeletons on the shoulders of his black cloak. Zodor began to raise his hands in surrender... but there was no quarter to be found.

There was a slash. There was a tumble. Zodor found himself looking straight up at the Sorceria underbelly and the ascending sloop.

At least he was out of that repressive hood.

The air felt cool on his sweat-slicked face.

He could finally breathe easily.

And then his eyes closed.

Chapter 36

Standing in the center of one of the large Malinsuli tents, Thade Skystone did his best to maintain his dignity as he stood with every bit of himself in full view. He was surrounded by women of the tribe who were busy scrubbing him down with coarse sea sponges harvested from a nearby lagoon and warm soapy water. The ladies gave him gentle pats to get him to raise his arms so they could scrub underneath. His eyes went wide as one of them proceeded to tend to his undercarriage and was not stingy with where she wedged the sea sponge to get him thoroughly clean.

"Everyone went through this?" he asked, his voice a pitch higher than usual.

Accompanied by laughter, the ladies continued their task, pouring buckets of warm water down his back to rinse off the suds.

"Your tall friend with the long stride looked positively embarrassed," one said as she took an amazingly soft towel and began aggressively wiping down Thade's thighs.

"Can't imagine why."

The army of women worked to towel him dry. With Thade's hair already short and his facial hair tended to daily, the villagers made quick work of his scruff with a straight razor. He was adorned with one of the larger sarongs available in the village and a comfortable pair of knitted sandals.

He stood with rapt attention as a trio of ladies came forward with hollowed-out coconut hulls filled with bright pigments. They carried stiff animal hair bristle brushes. As still and silent as a statue, Thade let the women turn his muscular body into a sculpted piece of art.

They ran the brushes loaded with pigment across his skin in the same swirling tribal patterns that so many of the Malinsuli warriors were adorned with. Thade only moved his head and his eyes slightly to watch the many artists create a masterpiece. Their steady hands painted with practiced ease, forming the complicated swirling patterns and tribal designs. Thade did not have to be told the importance of having this ritual bestowed upon him. He stood silently as the artists worked.

After his arms, legs, back, and face were adorned, the leader of the artists dipped her hands in the pigments. She approached Thade and placed the flat of her palms against his chest. She held them there to both mark his body and feel the beating of his heart. "You saved my mate on the beach," she said. "Because of you, your selfless heart, and your mighty arms, my children get to hug their father tonight. He will tell them stories and show them where their ancestors reside amongst the stars. Because of you."

The woman placed her painted hands on the sides of Thade's jaw, pulled him to her, and gently placed her lips upon his. "You are forever with us for your actions, Incanterran. From now and forever, you are also Malinsuli."

In response to her words, all of the assembled women closed in and placed a palm flat on Thade's skin. They then used their other arms to embrace each other. Thade stood in the middle of the circle, silent in his gratitude.

With his preparation complete, two of the women escorted him out of the large tent where his fellow countrymen were equally adorned with native sarongs and their unique body paint configurations. Each of the Incanterrans took a moment to admire each of their compatriot's unique paintings. But there was no time for conversation.

The villagers of Searock had already started their progression as they walked along a wide worn path leading them into the interior of the tropical island. Thade was happy as Sario took his arm and walked him amongst her fellow villagers. Up ahead, the big man could see the tribesmen carrying litters made of bamboo and woven rope. Even with the concealing white sheets, Thade knew they were carrying the bodies of the villagers lost in the Kai'kamina attack.

As the sun had dipped below the horizon and the shadows were growing long, many of the villagers carried flame-bearing torches. Others at the front of the procession lit stationary torches in bamboo brackets lining the path to guide the others. The villagers traveled deeper into the jungle, crossing over hill and dale. Some of the elders hummed and sang wordless songs that were simultaneously uplifting and somber.

Finally, the procession arrived at a gorge sliced from the landscape by the scythe of Zaneger. Carving through the verdant green foliage and ground cover, the walls of the gorge were made of hard stone and reflective black obsidian. However, the bottom was not lost in shadow. Instead, it was a roiling rise and fall of yellows, oranges, and reds.

Close enough to look down in, Thade saw the gorge was carved out not by water but by free-flowing molten rock. The yellow and orange magma was lazily making its way from the island's central mountain. It slithered under the earth along unseen, subterranean tunnels to make its way to the ocean. The gorge was a scar within the world allowing the villagers to look down on the underground river of molten rock.

On the other side of the narrow gorge, more villagers were filing in to take part in the sacred ritual. The fallen were placed near the fissure's edge as the procession gathered about. Thade looked out and saw a tall and broad-shouldered elder wearing a plumed headdress. His belly was swelled with age but his arms and hands still looked strong. Given his ornamental attire and his surrounding coterie, Thade could only assume this was the island chief.

While they waited for the rear of the procession to file in and take their places, Thade risked a whisper to Sario. He wanted to speak quietly so as not to disturb the solemnity. Thankfully, many of the islanders continued with their wordless melodies. "I thought you would have buried your dead out in the sea."

Sario rubbed the crook of Thade's arm and offered a smile. "If we were to bury them at sea, their bodies would be eaten by sharks, other fish, or the carrion crawlers that prowl the seafloor – crabs, lobsters, and such. Their spirits would then be transferred into those animals. These are honored dead. They deserve to rest. So, we will lower their bodies into the *wah'reinga*."

"Into the lava?"

"*Wah'reinga*. The ancestors would have called it... uh... mouth of the underworld? A gateway to the underworld? 'Gateway' is probably the more accurate translation. But what we are doing is granting their bodies back to the island. And this absolves the departed of any reason to linger here. With nothing to tether them, they can transition in peace. They will pass through the veil where their ancestors who went before are waiting. We have gathered here to say our final goodbyes and wish them a safe journey into the great beyond."

Thade nodded as he processed the legend. "So does Zaneger escort the souls?"

Sario considered the question for a moment. "If you want to believe he does... I am sure he does."

"So the pantheon of powers...?"

Sario smiled. "I think the pantheon has their hands full. If you are looking for help from the afterlife, wouldn't it be better to ask your family for a little celestial assistance? Soon, their names will be added to the leviathan bone pillars that every village keeps as a record of our people. Then, family members can go to the touchstone and talk to those beyond the veil to ask them for their guidance."

"It sounds nice," Thade said with his honesty on full display.

With the assembled surrounding the gorge, several of the islanders took their places to lower the deceased on vine ropes into the flowing lava at the bottom of the gorge. With so many hands, there was an ease and a gentleness. The litters and their drapings were lowered with reverence by hands honored to perform their tasks.

Amongst the men, the women, the warriors, the hunters, the fishermen, the gatherers, the gleaners, and even the children, the Malisuli began a solemn war chant that included slapping their thighs, forearms, chest, and stomach. There was a slow and deliberate rhythm to the chants but like a dance or beating on a massive set of drums, the Malinsuli knew when to strike each body part. It was simple yet foreign enough that Thade did not risk joining in, fearing he would hit his forearm when he should be hitting his chest. Instead, he stood still as a statue out of respect. Thankfully, Sario stayed close and kept a reassuring hand on him.

"We are sad," Sario explained. "We will miss them. But now, fathers will get to embrace daughters. Mothers will get to embrace sons. The pain of losing a parent is a terrible thing for a child. So, there is a reuniting. We will see them again when it is our time to cross the veil so how can we be sad for them?"

Thade looked down at Sario and smiled. "I love your kingdom," the big man said. "Malinsula is an amazing place and it is only made better because of your people."

Sario blushed and tilted her head to rest it gently against Thade's shoulder. "You honor us."

Chapter 37

As the sun plunged towards the horizon, the city streets of Incanterra quickly began to empty. None of the citizens wanted to be caught out after curfew and face the swift justice of the Knights of the Imperial Circle.

Unfortunately, for Slumbers, it hampered their business the most. Many of the local cafés served hot drinks made from imported *coffea* seeds and a unique variety of teas in the morning to provide the citizens with a jolt of energy. Slumbers had chosen a different route by brewing mellowing drinks to help people sleep. It was a quaint and simple shop with a small menu. Thankfully, the staff learned to close up quickly to make it home and avoid the roving undead patrols. Slumbers was one of the few shops remaining open during the occupation but the owner of the café and her small staff could only watch with dread as their remaining supply of imported tea sachets dwindled with each cup brewed. While the Baelannor dynasty was providing the wards with conjured food, such specialty items were not on their delivery manifests.

Even elevating their prices refused to level off the demand. It was when the owner truly understood the wealth of her clientele in the Northwest. Price was not a deterrent. As the resources continued to shrink and the occupation wore on, it was only a matter of time before the shop owner would not have a single tea leaf, bottle of Monterran spring water, or sachet left.

With so many of the other local restaurants already shuttered, the smaller kiosks that could still operate on their diminishing stockpiles were quickly becoming the only available options. Of course, that only depleted their reserves all the faster.

Still, even though the majority of the Northwest District resided in manors and manses, those eating from silver spoons wanted to get out of their estates and walk the streets. There was something enticing about having your food – or in Slumbers's case beverages – prepared for you. One of these moneyed merchants looking for something to take the edge off was Jeron Goldcrest.

Heir to one of the city's largest shipping guilds, the young man worked alongside his father and liege lord to run the family business. The young man's salary was impressive. Others within the guild knew to hold their tongues in reserve about the compensation packages for the owner's son. His wealth was impressive enough for the handsome man to not worry about the price of a drink having quadrupled since the undead occupation.

He passed over the requested coins with barely a second thought. After all, there was plenty more where that came from. The nightly curfews had cramped his social life and kept his coin purse heavy with no ladies to entertain, questionable wagers to place, or smuggled spirits or outlawed spices to buy. With his life now positively humdrum, getting out of the manor and walking the streets in the cool of the coming summer evening had become the high point of his day.

Or so he thought.

After paying for his cup of sleepy-time tea, he turned and saw a familiar face waiting for him. He recognized the man immediately despite the Sorcerian royalty not being dressed in his standard blue and black-trimmed wizardly robes. It was obvious why Drennid Vocazion had shed such attire and was instead adorned with modern fashions allowing the mage to blend within the population of the Northwest District.

"Dren," Jeron said, smartly refusing to use the man's full first name and smarter still not to utter his dynast surname.

"Jeron," he replied with a bow of his head.

Despite not being in wizardly robes, Jeron still respected Drennid's wizardly protocols. He did not offer an embrace or handshake. He maintained his respectful distance. Drennid returned the non-gesture.

"I was hoping to catch you out here. I did not want to make an appearance at your offices or your estate for... reasons."

Jeron's ice-blue eyes narrowed as he tried to gauge the implications. "Lucky for you my coin purse remains full," he said with a playful jangling. "The promise of rewards for the capture of any wayward wiz holds little intrigue for me. If those Necros were smart, they would be offering spice, spirits, or a taste of flesh. Then rocks are getting kicked over and lights are being shined into holes."

"So we can agree. The Necromangians are a shared enemy. We have to do something to oust their forces from the city."

Jeron cautiously moved forward. Having calculated the risks, he took Drennid by the arm and escorted him across the street. "You should mind your words in public," he hissed at the wizard. "You never know who is spying."

Safely away from the drink shop and other pedestrians, the mogul turned. "You are lucky you caught me out here at all," he said. "Father has ordered the lot of us to remain within the confines of the estate. Occasionally he grants sabbaticals like this... a little ambulating to keep us from going insane... But what are you trying to do? Recruit me into some sort of... resistance?"

"That is *exactly* what I am doing," Drennid said. "You are all here in the Northwest, hiding behind your estate walls. I have seen what is happening in the districts south of the Queen's High. I have seen the Under Roads. I know the jails are empty as well as the sanitariums."

"You are not selling this situation as bad if this is what you are bringing to the table, Dren. Good riddance to bad rubbish. This town needed a cleansing. Like a lightning strike starting a fire in the woods to purge the forest."

Drennid grumbled from deep within his chest. "And why do you think the Necromangian army of undead skeletons continues to grow and grow? How long before the Necromangians start kicking open your estate's gates to add one more skeleton to the army?"

Jeron waved a lackadaisical hand. "The Northwest District? Please, Drennid. They have said once they have their army, the wizard master and his ghoul crew will be moving on. They would have to chew through what? Eighty? Ninety percent of the city before they breach our ward's borders."

"You honestly think you could buy your way out of it?" Drennid scoffed.

Jeron had to strain to hold back his eye roll. "Dren. Any problem can be solved with enough coins. And until those skeletons are knocking on manor gates, the people of the Northwest aren't going to care. Oh sure, they will wring their hands and fret and fuss in a public display. But ask them to put something on the line and watch how quickly they retreat. I am just being honest."

"And what if they kill off eighty percent of the population?" Drennid inquired flatly. "It is difficult to make money selling things if there are no people left alive to sell to."

Jeron scoffed. "Plenty more where that came from. Do you think they won't fill back in? There are probably cargo holds of unwashed Ombraterran immigrants waiting for the harbor to open back up. Arvateri, Castratellans, and Monterrans will flood into the city once they learn what has happened. Hopefully, they beat all those from the southern lands. The city could use a lot less of their dark-skinned ilk."

Drennid silently fumed. While he hated what Jeron said, deep down, he knew the wealthy socialite was right. "They don't come here because of your wealth. They come here because of the wizards. And if we are all killed, this place is not special anymore."

Jeron recognized a last-ditch effort when he heard one. "Then I suggest you all don't get killed. Do whatever it is you have to do to broker peace. Go to this undead leader and pay him off to spare your lives. Everyone has a price."

"Saying it once, I could let it slide. This is twice now your answer has been bribery. You don't understand this wizard, Jeron. And I am afraid that by the time you do, he will have devoured this entire city."

"And what am I to do?" Jeron whispered with a hiss. "I am a businessman. We are importers."

"Then find a way to import an army or we are all going to die."

Drennid let his threat hang in the air behind him as he turned and stormed off. Leaving Jeron, the kiosk, and the smattering of wealthy citizens of the ward in his wake, the mage could only shake his head.

Turning a corner, Drennid ducked into a nearby alley. Assured he was alone, the wizard activated the magic of the enchanted cloak he had borrowed from his uncle. Given his line of work as a procurer of assets, it was not surprising that a man known by his sobriquet of "The Graver" would possess a cloak of invisibility.

The magic material gave him the ability to move freely down the city streets and with the hour of curfew speeding its way to the city, Drennid did not have to worry about bumping into citizens or dodging conveyances.

Suddenly, Drennid's attention was called to the skies as a shadow passed. He looked up and saw one of the Sorcerian sloops flying overhead and continuing on its path to land in a nearby square. As the single-mast vessel landed, Drennid spied the collection aboard.

He noted several of the grunt workers unloading the boat were tireless undead controlled by a Necromangian overseer. They were unloading large crates to Northwest District workers. Drennid recognized them as waitrons at one of the upscale restaurants.

Then amongst the crew of the sloop, he saw Devinaya Baelannor. The mage quickly started putting the pieces of the puzzle together. The delivery was probably foodstuffs. But the late night hour was curious. He bet these were not the bland rations with half flavor that were delivered to the lesser wards. He wagered they would be something more palatable for the wealthy around the ward.

Jeron Goldcrest was not going to be helpful in Drennid's attempt to oust the Necromangians. He needed someone with influence and an insider role... Someone like Devinaya Baelannor.

"How interesting," he mused to the winds.

Chapter 38

While the sun had set on the tropical island of Malinsula, the eastern seaside village of Searock was brightly illuminated by the dancing flames of torchlight. The entire village had come together to celebrate the transition of the brave souls that had defended the island from the Kai'kamina attack. And the same as with every Malinsuli fellowship, food was a central pillar.

For those who remained behind and missed out on the pilgrimage to the *wah'reinga*, they honored the memory of the fallen by crafting a grand meal to nourish the living members of the tribe. Upon the assembly's return, the ladies of the village wasted no time putting Thade Skystone, Valos Ironblade, and Cavin Jurare to work helping finish preparing the community feast. One of the older ladies – having never bothered to speak the trade tongue – instructed Valos in the traditional Malinsuli language. The rogue did his best to understand her instructions and she would admonish him with smacks on his backside when he made a mistake.

Cavin was smart enough to know how to stay out of the way and volunteered to stir the large cauldrons filled with boiling water and a vast assortment of freshly trapped shellfish. He used his ropy arms to stir the concoction with a long-handled spoon resembling more of a canoe paddle than a cooking utensil. He pretended to know what he was doing and the ladies were happy to let him help.

However, Thade was in his element. He was absorbing the cooking and preparation techniques like the sea sponges harvested from the island's western lagoons. He was amazed at how the ladies sprinkled the native sea salt with a technique of tossing it into the air and letting it fall over the meat. But they also used forceful throws that drove the salt into the meat as if the seasoning were pieces of ammunition.

The women ordered the trio of big, strong men about, making them lift heavy platters of food. They would send them scurrying and scampering back and forth to fetch their ingredients. And if Valos did not move fast enough for the elder's liking, she was quick with another smack on his rump.

On the perimeter of the cooking area, the youngsters would watch and laugh as the squat, round grandmothers half as tall as Thade would order him about. Thade followed every order with enthusiasm. Valos not as much.

On more than one occasion, the younglings would boldly point out and say various things. Amongst the prattling, Valos distinctly heard "white skin" or "pale man." One mischievous girl took to calling the Incanterran "night hair" and the moniker was starting to stick amongst the other children.

More than once, a precocious child would stray too far into the cooking area. The mothers would shoo them out, warning them that cauldrons were too hot and not safe to play near. The smarter children learned that the mothers would offer them bribes of food to leave them in peace, which was also a first crack at the piping hot food before the rest of the village. Toddlers would cry, just wanting to be held and one of the many mothers would hoist them up in one arm, bouncing them on a hip, while stirring or prepping with their free hand. If a task required more attention, another mother would happily take a turn holding a needy child and issuing soothing coos.

The countless eyes of youngsters ringed the perimeter of the cooking area, watching intently and listening to the many mothers give instructions to the Incanterrans and the Malinsuli cooking apprentices.

"So we are doing all the cooking over here," Valos called out to Thade and Cavin, "and Cinder and Sway get to go sightseeing? How is this fair?"

"Women grow life. They are sacred vessels," one of the Malinsuli cooks called back. "So our men treat them with reverence."

Valos looked around. "Unless you all utilize a technique I am not familiar with, last time I checked, men play a pretty significant role in that act too."

Another of the Malinsuli women came along and patted Valos on his shoulder. "Men plant the seed. Women are the garden in which the seed sprouts."

"Still feels like a fifty-fifty split to me," Valos replied. "But you don't see a bunch of women elders gifting me seashell necklaces, serving up goblets of your fruit wine, and taking me out to see the Thunder Cliffs. That was a hint if I was being too subtle." Valos looked at a trio of the elders tending to the large bowls of salad greens. He gave them a wink and smile. "How are you all, ladies?"

Almost on cue, the grand procession returned from the fabled Thunder Cliffs to the village square with Cinder and Sway each being escorted by a village grandfather and constantly circled by a swirling flock of children. The two Incanterran ladies wore wide smiles, still enamored with all their new finery.

With their countrymen's return, the house mother overseeing the cooking granted the three men their release from the preparations. While Cavin was quick to Cinder's side and Valos was prepared to mingle with the islanders, Thade was not so quick to abscond from the cookfires, the boiling pots, and all of the preparations.

Instead, he decided to lurk and watch the ladies, studying their techniques. He would interrupt only to ask questions or to help one of the elders move something essential from here to there. Thade was so wrapped up in the preparation he did not even notice the shaman Sario prowling the perimeter, keeping her gaze locked on him as he assisted in any way that he could.

From the west, a chorus of cheers erupted in the village as King Muera and his coterie of elders arrived to be the guests of honor at the feast. The king was quickly approached and greeted by Searock's leaders.

Thade watched at a distance as the island king was approached by members of the village. Thade was content to watch things from afar. There was a poke in his ribs and Sway sidled up beside him. Her arm found a way around his waist. "Look at you all prettied up and fancy," Thade laughed.

"So, I have to tell you this," Sway said. "Normally, a bunch of men taking you out into the jungle to look at some cliffs? No way I would have said yes to that. Are you kidding me? But these Malinsuli... I don't know how to describe it. It is like they fawned over me but with... respect?"

Thade smiled. "The women were talking about that when we were cooking. It is because they see you all as sacred vessels."

"I don't care what it is but a girl could get used to that kind of treatment. The rest of the free kingdoms need to take a scroll out of their cases. So what about you, meaty boy? Learning all sorts of new techniques?"

Thade threw his head back and his eyes wanted to roll back into his skull. "So much! These ladies are amazing. If we could convince two of them to come to Incanterra, our restaurant would be the talk of the town."

From outside the cooking tent, a trio of women began ringing the bells to announce the food was ready. The community became a whirlwind of excitement. Children were dashing back and forth. People began to file into the town square and formed orderly queues to get plates and bowls filled with the wonderful Malinsuli delicacies. Laughter peppered the pockets of people as they all came together to enjoy food, fellowship, and fun.

A ruler of the people, King Muera sat and ate alongside his tribesmen. He eschewed any sort of special seating arrangement and even stood in line with his fellow islanders, calmly waiting for his turn in the serving line, allowing any elders a place of honor in front of him. Naturally, the king was curious to meet the five strangers from Incanterra gracing his island home. But outside of the initial introductions and pleasantries, Thade was happy to fall back and let the more eloquent members of the crew ask for trade permissions.

Valos was skilled with such diplomacies and Cinder was a perfect second to help in the discussions. As Valos continued to give his speech – promising trade of valuable Incanterran resources – Thade was happy enough to slink away and let the business be conducted.

The big man dodged a flock of scampering children who went running past him, their laughter carrying on the wind. Aside from their flowing white hair, they were no different from the little gangs of Incanterran rapscallions running around Shaded Light.

Thade ended up back in the empty kitchen. The many mothers had taken their place amongst the rest of the community, happy to partake in their shared hard work that brought nourishment to the people. The cookfires had been doused. The clamor and the commotion had ceased. And the big man was content to lazily stroll up and down the aisles, past the various cooking stations, noting the collection of spices and herbs used by the mothers.

"You look so serious," a voice called behind him.

Thade turned and saw Sario standing. The big man laughed. He turned back to note a rack of spices. "I wanted to commit as much of this to memory as I could. But with the wizards, I have to change my thinking. Before, if I had a question about Malinsuli cuisine, it would have taken a month-long boat trip to get here to ask. Now, with Cinder and her magic, it is as easy as walking through a door. It takes some getting used to."

When he turned back, Sario had closed the distance between them. Thade looked down at her while she looked up at him intently. "The mothers said you were a great help. You have helped the mothers. You helped our hunters and our defenders. You are a unique man, Thade Skystone."

She stepped closer.

"You have an amazing island," he whispered. "Full of wonders."

Sario reached up and took Thade by his big, strong hand. She led him from the cook tent and down into the shadows of the empty village. With everyone so preoccupied with the feast, none even noticed their departure. Sario continued to pull him by the hand back to the small communal tent where the Incanterrans were lodging.

Slithering through the shadowed living area, Sario took Thade into the smaller alcove where his guest bed was illuminated by a single candle. She silently pulled the curtain door closed. The shaman turned back and began gently removing Thade's traditional sarong.

Thade was being treated to the most blissful paradise Malinsula had to offer. Soon, from behind the closed curtain, the sounds of exquisite ecstasy, meaningful moans, and playful passion whispered out into the night air. It wafted into the darkness until it was lost under the noise of the gently lapping surf and the chirps of crickets basking in the light of the two moons.

Chapter 39

Despite the hour of the night and the curfew in effect, young Kynna Lu'Scion was slinking her way through the inner alleyways of the Incanterran capital. She had learned to navigate the smaller side streets and the alleyways. They were faster to traverse and left her less exposed to the eyes of the undead skeletal patrols and the roving Knights of the Imperial Circle.

Like so many nights, the hot air rising away from the grand capital's coastline pulled in the cold and moist air from the bordering ocean. With it came the billowing and often thick fog the kingdom was known for. Lighthouses illuminated the entrance to Highstone Harbor, the large, deepwater bay where the ships could easily moor. The fog horns continued to sound and the lights continued to illuminate even though the harbor had been shut down since the Necromangian occupation had begun.

Adding to the haze were the beginning threats of rain. Wicked forks of lightning splayed across the sky. Looking up through the canyons of wood, mortar, and carved stone, Kynna could see only a sliver of the night sky painted by the wicked bolts of Aurorean's anger.

The young wizard knew better than to sightsee. Stacks of garbage and refuse had begun to clog the alleyways and were starting to become a real problem. Despite the dwindling population of the city and the curfews, the people still trapped within the walls of the capital continued to live. And each day, the trash piled up a little bit more. The last thing Kynna wanted to do was make an errant step or lose focus and upset a wobbly stack. The clamor would no doubt draw the attention of any nearby patrol – living or undead.

Suddenly, the sky opened up and rain began to fall, coating the walls and streets in a thick sheen of water. On the nearby building, Kynna looked quizzically as the sheets of water were running up the height of the wall.

Behind her, the methodical pace of footsteps began echoing down the alley. A looming figure came into view. He was tall and broad-shouldered but lost in the shadows. The reverberations of his footfalls felt like they should have belonged to a hill giant from the tales of yore.

He stomped forward, sending refuse scattering in his wake. Still, the figure remained in the shadows. Kynna noted the glint of steel in the flashes of Aurorean's lightning. He carried a terrible axe in each hand. Kynna screamed inside her head to run but her shoes felt filled with molten lead.

Ever closer the shadow stomped. Sheathing one axe, the looming, imposing figure closed the gap and reached out to grab Kynna. Her scream could voice no sound...

...and then she sat up abruptly in her bed.

The young wizardess took a moment to acclimate to her surroundings. The beginning rays of dawn were instead creeping through her open window. The curtains billowed in the breeze and the heat of the day would begin soon enough. There was no rain, no lightning, and certainly no mysterious figure. Trying to find her way out of the sheets, Kynna pressed her palm against her forehead to relieve the dull ache that resided within. "Just get up," she grumbled weakly to herself.

Finally up, around, and dressed, Kynna emerged from the unused bedroom to join Mirawen Autumnlight. "I am guessing you have had better nights," the mistress of the apartment stated.

"I usually go to bed to *relieve* headaches," Kynna replied. "Beginning the day with one is not my idea of a good start."

"Is this a regular thing for you?"

Kynna rubbed her temples. "Not... no... Not that I can think of. But these last couple of weeks, I swear it is getting worse. I wonder if I could find an herbalist to help."

Mirawen clucked her tongue as she was gathering up her things. "If we can find one open, the better question is what their stockpiles look like. But I know some people who might be able to help."

Wearing a light summer cloak to protect her from the sun and help keep her identity concealed, Kynna fell into helping Mirawen. Using a small hand-pulled wagon, the duo loaded up the dry ration supplies from one of the Necromangian-run supply depots and set to work distributing them to the people isolated in their various apartments.

It was bags of meager, magically conjured foodstuffs. Short on taste but long on nutrition, it was enough. There were glass stoppered bottles of water and whatever beverages the Baelannor conjurers had concocted. Most of the citizens were happy to accept what Mirawen brought them. Others eyed her nervously or warily. Some accepted their bundles angrily but were smart enough to know Mirawen was merely the messenger. It helped that those who were in the know knew. They knew whom Mirawen was connected to.

Emerging out of one of the tall tenements, Kynna continued her hushed whispers. "...but it was like I *wanted* him to catch me. Is that strange?"

"I don't even pretend to know what dreams mean if they mean anything at all. If you want, I can introduce you to a gypsy interpreter. It will cost you a silver. Keep in mind that she is a complete fraud and she knows it. But if her charlatan hocus pocus makes you feel better..."

Kynna laughed.

"For all I know, it means you should avoid cheese before going to bed."

Mirawen grabbed the handle of the wagon and prepared to move to the next tenement. "So how did you get this job?" Kynna asked. "How did you get appointed to the ward's food delivery service?"

"I was needing work anyway, what with the fire of my inn and all. Then the boners took over. This way, I am still helping the ward. I am from here. I grew up here. I figure me delivering the rations might help them taste better than if one of those spooky Necros or their boners were handing them over."

The two paused as Mirawen looked down the street at one of the ubiquitous patrols of the undead skeletons. Some just lingered on street corners. Still, they never needed water, food, sleep, or trips to the privy. From certain points of view, they would be considered the perfect sentinels.

Mirawen hefted one of the many food sacks. "It is weird. When this thing first started, I remember thinking there was never going to be enough food to go around. Somehow, they have made it work. But with the deaths or the roundups, I can feel the ward getting less populated."

"Is it like this in all the wards?"

Mirawen shrugged. "I hear things. I hear people talk. But I don't know how much of it is real. I mean before the boners put the clamps down, the Southeast was filled with warehouses of imports or things to be exported. So I heard that was part of the big initial ration push.

"Now, the Southwest? I don't know. That place is overly populated but it is not like the people are swimming in coins. You hear it all the time. Especially during the hurricane season. 'Why didn't the people flee the valley?' Do you think a person in the Southwest owns a wagon or a horse? Or has a palatial summer estate they can retreat to? Even when the boners took over, where would we go? Out into the wildlands? Outside of these tall walls that keep us safe from the monsters lurking out there? That district was almost lawless before. How they are holding up now? I can only imagine. Ration and survive; the best any of us can do."

As this was one of the most forceful and flustered Kynna had seen Mirawen, the young wizardess knew better than to speak up or offer a counter. The guilt of the decadent wizardly lifestyle hung heavy around her neck when she considered the poor living south of the Queen's High.

"And if we do die, with each member we lose, their army grows," Mirawen spat. "It is like playing that Castratellan strategy game, the one with the sovereign, the empress, the knights, and such."

"Scachi," Kynna said.

"Right, but it feels like for every piece – every soldier – that your opponent captures, instead of taking it off the board, they get to change its color and add it to their side. And if we fight back and we fall during the revolution, we just add to their forces. If we die from starvation, we add to their forces. We commit a crime, we get executed, and add to their forces. It is messed up. But with each person we lose, the less we have to fight back. Which means if we don't do something soon, whoever is left will have no chance of escaping their iron fist."

With another armload of rationing bags, Kynna and Mirawen continued on their appointed rounds. Reaching one of the tall tenements in the southeast corner of the ward, many of the occupants came down to pick up their bags rather than forcing the duo to come to them.

Kynna smiled as she noted several children happy to help carry the bags, especially for their elders. They were polite to the grandmothers. One of the teenagers even helped escort an elderly man whose back was hunched with age. Some of the older teenagers noted Mirawen and gave her nods of recognition. "You will let them know we are helping?" one of them asked.

Mirawen gave one of the strapping young lads a knowing nod and their eyes sparkled at the potential opportunity. Kynna wanted to know to whom the lads were referring until a wrinkled and withered hand clumsily took hold of her fingers.

Kynna looked down at the elderly woman whose head and shoulders were wrapped in a vintage cotton shawl. The old woman's pupils were covered in a milky sheen but she looked at her with a fiery purpose. The elderly grandmother looked at Kynna with stark recognition.

"I remember you. You used to run up and down these streets chasing after your brother. My, you have grown. And so pretty. But you can't be. I remember that blizzard and what happened. So sad. What is your name?"

She offered a smile. "My name is Kynna, Grandmother."

The old lady grumbled. "I swear you look like little Gwelin all grown up. And you are so pretty. What is your name?"

She offered a second, patient smile. "My name is Kynna, Grandmother."

Chapter 40

The scraping of Dragan Duskwood's shoes echoed within the softly illuminated subterranean caverns. The enchantments within Sorceria's underbelly were impossibly subtle but ingenious in their design. There was not a single light source to be seen and yet the caverns remained dimly illuminated with infused mage-light. Admittedly, cracks and shadows broke the radiant flow but that was more from the sundering of the isle than any failures of the wizards who transformed the underground tunnels.

Down a spiraling of hewn stairs and through another damaged tunnel, Dragan arrived at the foyer of the famed Cellarium Vaults. Only now, the massive steel door — repaired under direct orders — was wide open and the protective runes, defensive shields, and other magical fortifications were dormant. The complete collections of magic items and various volumes of forbidden texts were exposed to all.

On instinct, Dragan held his breath as he crossed the threshold of the grand vault, half expecting some magical barrier to fling him back into the foyer. But the aged wizard passed through without even a prickling across his skin. Inside the vault was a greater threat than all of the outlawed magic archived within her stone walls.

Nalazar Catabaysi stood in the center, floating a few scant parchment thicknesses above the vault's floor, flipping through yet another black-bound tome of arcana. Not wanting to interrupt his master's musings, the wizard casually strolled amongst the shelves, cupboards, and cubbies lining the walls of the vault.

He noted a collection of odd canopic jars with beautifully carved ivory tops fashioned into startlingly lifelike representations of various mythical beasts. He did not even want to imagine what organs — or whose — were kept inside the sacred containers.

There was an odd series of magic wands made of a unique wood he did not recognize. The identifying plaques labeled the wands from the kingdom that would eventually become the wasteland realm of Ignaterra.

There was a silver short sword perched on a stand. When Dragan looked at his reflection in the polished steel, he swore he heard a voice other than his conscience inside his head. The voice whispered for the wizard to pick the sword up and use it to spill blood and slake its thirst.

There were collections of books, tomes, and grimoires — all of various sizes and shades. Before he could read the titles inscribed upon the spines and covers, the sound of a tome being slapped shut echoed within the vault. Nalazar turned to eye his second-in-command. The lich looked at him with a curious undead eye. "My dear Dragan, you seem vexed."

"We stand amongst some of the most lethal magic ever conceived," Dragan replied, his voice almost a whisper. "I am willing to bet the originators of this magic wish they could un-invent their creations. And for that reason, I doubt anyone could feel comfortable amongst the accursed items sealed within this vault."

Nalazar turned, his head cocking to one side. It felt like the undead horror's gaze was boring straight into Dragan's soul. "And yet, here I stand. Granted, the fears of a mortal existence no longer apply to me."

"Well, they still apply to the rest of us, Master. It would do you well to remember that."

"You are standing in the courtyard, my friend. I am standing on the ramparts. I see the great beyond and the possibilities before me. I see the mysteries just waiting to be unlocked. And those secrets are almost within my grasp. What we are going to create will be magnificent. But I still sense your hesitation. And I don't think it is strictly the venue that has you so... flummoxed."

Dragan's lip twitched and he did his best to keep his hands tucked into the opposite sleeves of his red wizardly robes. Nalazar's head cocked to the other side. "Come now, lad," the lich said with what might be considered a smile. "You can tell me what is on your mind."

"The people are not happy."

Nalazar's cackle sounded like cat claws raking slate. "Of course, they are not happy. They fail to see the bigger picture, the grand plan of it all."

"They have reason to be angry. Sealing off the city. Representatives of our order throwing their weight around with the young ladies here on Sorceria. And what is this new strategy you are having Twotrees implement? Using the flesh stripped from the bodies to form some sort of unholy amalgam?"

"Waste not, want not," the lich hissed.

"I can't sell that to the people!" Dragan said, his voice just a little too loud. "Skeletons defending them from living threats, sparing them from marching forth into battle is still a stretch but we can spin that. The second that first flesh beast starts stomping down the streets, people are going to riot."

Nalazar turned and picked another tome off of the nearest shelf. He casually flipped through the vellum pages. "Yet the people stood by and let the Ce'Mondere summon demons from the infernal realms. Are we that different?"

"The Ce'Mondere might summon a demon to rescue a child from a burning building. It is hard to deny the benefit of their magic. If our skeletons were being used to fend off an invading force and kept citizens from being drafted to defend the walls, that crusade could be sold. But these flesh monsters? Or us rounding up the slightest petty criminal and condemning them to death? That I can't sell."

"The flesh was going to waste in those acid baths Twotrees uses," the lich argued. "This will be another powerful ally for us when the time comes and the threat arrives."

"You found the spell for this amalgamation within this vault?"

"I did," the lich hissed.

"Did you stop to ponder that there might be a reason the spell was entombed down here?"

Nalazar slapped the book shut and slammed it on the nearest bookshelf. The lich pivoted and floated across the vault with purpose, halting in front of his second. "Your words border on sedition, Dragan Duskwood. An outside observer might consider your motivations as... traitorous. Tell me. Whom do you serve?"

Others might have kneeled or averted their gaze in deference to their wizardly superior. Dragan held his gaze fast. "I serve at your pleasure, Master Catabaysi," the wizard responded proudly.

Before the lich could retort, the sound of clacking heels began to echo from the foyer. Dragan halted any further discussion. He turned and saw Nikkala Whitesnow emerging from one of the nearby tunnels, dressed in her red and black-trimmed robes emblazoned with their hourglass sigil. Dragging along behind her was a slivered disk of solid light adorned with a variety of food and various beverages. She halted at the threshold of the vault, afraid she had interrupted a privileged conversation and was now too nervous to enter.

"Lady Whitesnow," Dragan acknowledged her with a nod.

"I apologize for the interruption. I was on my way to feed the prisoners but we just received news from below," she replied. "I felt you would want to know."

Nalazar was too distracted with his reading but Dragan closed the distance to the vault's threshold. "One of our patrols was attacked. A dozen skeletons and a pair of the Imperial Knights were killed."

Nalazar picked up another tome. "The skeletons can be replaced. Have the knights' bodies brought here to the isle and we can either resurrect them or have them added to the skeletal forces."

"The Necromangian apprentice noted their deaths during their retreat. We don't have the bodies," Nikkala replied softly. "What is more concerning is *who* did them in."

"Yes?" Dragan said.

"The way the apprentice described it, I believe they were attacked by acolytes of Zaneger."

"There was a group of them?" Dragan asked.

"There was."

"That is… not good," he grumbled. "If the forces of the *domici dauthis* are attacking as a group, it could be the beginnings of a coordinated effort of a resistance against us."

The two wizards turned to see Nalazar uncomfortably close. "Then we will respond," the lich said. "They have foolishly placed their token on the game board. And we know where their operations are based. They have banners and statues that identify their targets. So, see them targeted."

The lich seethed and issued a wet hiss that could have been confused with a laugh. "Show the citizenry what happens when someone – or a group – stands against the Catabaysi."

Chapter 41

In the light of the morning, Sario and Cinder Fireborne walked the winding pathways stretching between the various communal tents of Searock village. The two stopped to look into the nearby lush and verdant valley where vegetation had been cleared out to make way for a collection of paddocks.

With Thade Skystone and Sway Snowsong lending their expertise honed and earned from their time spent on the Nightwater farm, the two were instructing many of the locals on how to set up the fencing, the weaning pens, milking barns, and other more slightly permanent structures. Once everything was completed, Cinder could open a gateway to the northern farmlands of Incanterra and bring through the first round of beef and dairy cattle.

Valos Ironblade had made sure to placate King Muera, promising him the finest heads of cattle raised on the alfalfa and long hay grasses of their kingdom. It was going to be the glorious beginning of a new trade agreement between the two kingdoms. However, few would have expected such a deal brokered by agents of an underground criminal family. Cinder smiled at the thought.

The famed Corvalonn dynasty had missed an opportunity. Now the secretive Shadow Blades would reap gold. Moreover, it would be open and legal trade to pad their ledgers. They would be able to return to their home with greater claims of being legitimate entrepreneurs as opposed to back-alley dealers working only in the dark markets.

As Cinder shook from her reverie, she noticed Sario's eyes drawn to Thade as he was hauling more pieces of hewed timber to extend out the corral. There was an unmistakable glint in her eye and an impulsive smile. "I have to ask," Cinder queried.

Sario turned.

Cinder threw her gaze back in Thade's direction. "A few nights ago at the feast to honor your people..."

"And every night since," Sario said proudly. "Twice last night. And once this morning."

"I know it is none of my business. And I am not asking because I *want* to know. I am not looking for a sampling. But I have to know."

"Surprisingly tender," Sario said, having anticipated the question. She did not bother holding back her smile. "Attentive. For a man of his size and strength, you wouldn't expect it. He is the most caring man I have been with."

"That is not a trait of all Incanterran men," Cinder warned. "Spare yourself an earful. Don't ask Sway about that. She has some real horror stories."

"I think you would be hard-pressed to find traits like Thade's in most men regardless of their kingdom. It took me some time but I might have found the reasoning behind it."

"Before I was just *curious* but now I am *interested*," Cinder said with a light laugh.

"You look at him. Most people see the brawn and the muscles. I know if he so desired he could do whatever he wanted with me. I couldn't fight him off if I wanted to."

Sario turned slightly to look at Cinder who wore an emotionless mask.

"He knows it too," Sario smiled. "He knows it and I think deep down, he is afraid of that. So he overcorrects. He gives me the illusion of control even though we both know he could do what he wanted."

"That is... surprisingly deep," Cinder smiled.

"So was he."

"Valos is becoming a bad influence on you..."

The two women laughed and shared a side embrace. Cinder continued to watch them work. "You can look at him and make a snap judgment. But if you spend a few moments with Thade, you see quickly that he is a big softy."

"Tell that to the Kai'kamina."

Cinder nodded. "Yeah, once his anger is unleashed, things go bad quickly. Nothing more dangerous than Thade defending his friends. It is one of the things I love about him."

"He is very fond of you all too. He talks about you all so much. He is proud of what you all are doing back in your homeland."

Cinder turned and offered a raised eyebrow.

Sario shrugged. "He's chatty afterward."

"So where does this leave the two of you?"

"I have no illusions," the shaman said. "I love my kingdom. He loves his. He will return soon to rejoin your operations. I will enjoy our time while it lasts."

"Now you sound like an Incanterran man!"

Sario laughed. "I know the northern customs and your traditional arrangements. It is tough to articulate. If Thade and I were to couple, I would be loyal to him. But we do not sign documents. We are just together. I would have his baby but then the village raises the child together. So if a Malinsuli man wants to create a child with someone else, he can.

"We all raise the children together so all the children are my children. Our women breastfeed children that aren't their own. We raise them together but we also let them run free. If a child needs to learn something, they need to know how to see and how to listen. They need to open their ears and their eyes. Then they can learn our songs, how to move in the jungles, listen to the sounds of the birds, and follow the tracks of the animals. They do this by engaging with the people. That is what makes the Malinsuli strong. A strong and loved child means a strong tribe."

Cinder let the Malinsuli traditions soak into her mind. "How do you deal with jealousy? Infidelity?"

Sario pondered the question for a bit. "Thade is not mine to claim. One could argue if he sires many children, the tribe grows stronger."

"But as you said, the coupling is more than just about making babies."

"That is why I take the herbs I take. It does not let the seed take root."

Cinder turned abruptly.

"You don't have those?" Sario asked.

"I know midwives make these concoctions. I never knew what was in them. But this is an interesting development. We may end up trading cows for more than just sea salt, delicacies, and fermented drinks."

With the last piece of the corral put in place and the hinged gate completed, Thade gave a mighty cheer and clapped his hands excitedly. Back slaps were handed out freely and the natives were proud of their accomplishment. All that remained was a portal and an influx of cattle with spare bags of feed. "To open a portal big enough to accommodate steers and sustain it for a suitable duration, I am going to need some material components," Cinder said. "Care to walk with me?"

"Of course," the shaman replied.

Sario took Cinder by the arm and walked her along the well-worn paths of the village. "One of these days, I will be able to wrap my head around how you summon forth your elemental helpers without using the arcane components," Cinder stated.

"Wait until I introduce you to the shaman who cast magic to control the weather. Their level of discipline and magical mastery is amazing."

The two reached the large hospitality tent Cinder and her fellow Incanterrans had been living in during their stay on the island. In the alcove where Cinder and Cavin were staying, the rogue mage began rummaging through the modest trunk she had brought with her from the *Castella Mare*.

The pine trunk held a collection of spell components, tomes of instruction, and other unique magical items that Cinder wanted to keep close but did not need unless she found herself in a pinch. She began searching through the stores of powdered gemstones, metal shavings, and other precious crystals and minerals to power so many of her magical castings. Finally, with the search exhausted, she allowed herself to grumble a quick curse.

"Is everything alright?" Sario called from the main living space.

"I use these dragon ash agates as a material component to stabilize my portal spell," Cinder said. "Otherwise, I have to pull from my internal reserves and that is not fun. I know I have a collection of these back in our vault. This is part of the reason why I love these portals. I will just open a small one, slide through, grab what I need, and be back in a blink. I bet I can even keep the gateway stabilized and keep it open the whole time."

With a circular wave of her wand, a whispered incantation of commands, and a consuming of material components, Cinder brought forth a portal that unveiled a swirling sparkle of blue-tinged embers. As the swirl grew to the size of a doorway, the far edges sparked angrily and Cinder had to concentrate to mentally muscle it into place. "Strange," she whispered.

Still, the swirling ring stabilized. Within the churning, reality rippled like water in a disturbed pond. The crew's undercroft came into view. It was lined with small kegs of their famous Nightwater brew and other stores of the ill-gotten gains they wanted to keep hidden from the world. Also within the vault was Cinder's private collection of spell components.

As Cinder approached the portal, she had to concentrate harder than usual to keep the magical ring from collapsing in on itself. Her brow furrowed and she began to doubt if she could keep the ring open as she gathered the necessary materials.

As she attempted to step through, tentacles composed of black darkness and wreathed with red flame materialized angrily. One of the tentacles collided with Cinder's midsection and sent her sailing across the hospitality tent. Thunder echoed. Sario turned as Cinder's limp body tore through the tent wall and she landed on one of the exterior pathways.

The magical portal did not dissolve or dissipate into nothingness. Instead, it was angrily snapped shut from the other end as if it were the jaws of the massive white sharks that patrolled the Malinsuli coasts.

Sario sprinted out through the hole in the tent left by Cinder's body, praying to her ancestors that the mage was still alive.

Chapter 42

Nikkala Whitesnow moved silently through the underbelly of Sorceria. Before the emergence, the tall and statuesque woman was often seen within the halls of power and on the streets of Governance Ward. She regularly dressed in the color of her surname, known for her white corsets and long, flowing snow-colored cloaks. Her long mane of hair glowed like spun gold.

It was easy to see why she charged guilds, associations, and unions premium coins for her advocating services. She was both silver-tongued and highly educated. Persuasive and deft at debating, she could convince archons and even the castellan himself to consider legislation changes for the city and the kingdom. None within the capital – save for her cabal – knew the truth of her allegiance. Many were stunned to see her standing side by side with the dread lich Nalazar wearing the red robes of the Catabaysi dynasty.

As she moved through the subterranean tunnels of the floating island, the wizardess halted outside a large alcove. Normally, the archway entrance to the chamber would be shielded with Lu'Scion magic barring entry. But the same as their now dormant and gray obelisk, the ensorcelling of the dynasty had faded.

As Nikkala walked into the alcove, muted mage-light came to life. It was just enough to banish the shadows but not enough to wash out the true light show within. The chamber was filled with a variety of composting boxes and long troughs filled with rich, black soil. Sprouting from that soil were all different species and varieties of mushrooms, lichen, and fungi glowing with their unique signature of bioluminescence.

The wizardess walked up and down the aisles between the troughs, looking for two very specific types of glowing mushrooms. She walked amongst the various versions, admiring their incandescence. Finally, she found the first one she was looking for. It featured a prominent conical cap with black flesh spotted with iridescent purple speckles.

The second mushroom had more of a spherical bloom and was the same color orange as the famous fiery peppers from Agavinsula. But she was told these had a more velvety texture and tasted something akin to a sharp mint.

Picking two of each, the wizardess returned to the hallways and placed the pilfered delicacies amongst the prepared dishes that she was dragging through the tunnel on a disc of hard light. With the light disc tethered to her, Nikkala made her way further into the isle's underbelly.

After a series of twists and turns, she arrived at a corridor whose abjuration magic was in full effect. The magical shield blocking the entrance to the chamber within was transparent but rippled with translucent sigils and abjuration geometry. The prison gate was ironic given the two individuals incarcerated within.

The chamber was outfitted with modest accommodations including a pair of pallets complete with full bedding. There was a subchamber offering some semblance of privacy that included an enchanted, metal pail and an oaken bucket that when commanded would fill with warm, soapy water. There were lamps of mage-light and upon Nalazar's command, a small library had been included. The occupants had also been given colored chalk and since Nikkala's last visit, a magnificent drawing of a blooming tree next to a large waterfall decorated the back wall.

Clearing her throat to announce her arrival, Nikkala Whitesnow offered a polite curtsey. "Patron and Matron Jurare."

Canarr and Jillayna Jurare stood up to meet the Catabaysi wizardess. With a wave of her magical wand, Nikkala opened a sliver within the abjuration shielding. She then slid through the conjured foodstuffs on silver trays, along with an assortment of beverages. She then passed through freshly laundered clothing and another assortment of historical tomes. "Master Nalazar thought you might find those particular editions interesting," she said, nodding toward the books. "I have presented you with everything that my master asked me to."

Jillayna eyed the wizardess curiously. "And are there things within these bundles that your master *didn't* ask you to bring?"

Nikkala stood silently.

Canarr went to put the gifted items away and noted the quartet of mushrooms. Such morels were oddly out of place. "The Lu'Scions have... had... they have an impressive subterranean garden nearby," Nikkala said. "I am told the sundown bloom is powerful. I know its essence is milked and added to a potion that renders its users almost catatonic. It is said someone who drinks the dew will lay perfectly still while a person could cut on them. They feel nothing."

Canarr placed the pair of black mushrooms in clear view. Nikkala pretended not to notice and said, "Conversely, the death's head shroom is said to offer a violent but quick death. Quite painful. One wonders how or even why such a thing was ever cultivated. However, if one took the sundown bloom and waited just before its dew took effect... one could eat the death's head and slip peacefully from this world. There would be no pain."

The two leaders of the Jurare dynasty stood silently, watching Nikkala through the abjuration walls of their prison cell. Nikkala swallowed hard and fluttered a series of furious blinks... perhaps wanting to banish any possible tears. "They say that on some nights the people down in the city can hear

Master Asaric Baelannor's screams. I would think if someone could avoid that fate, they would."

Canarr held up the black morel and inspected it curiously. "The magic of your dynasty has changed the game," the patron said gruffly. "Death is no longer an escape. What would stop a certain undead master from resurrecting someone who consumed these mushrooms?"

Nikkala winced, silently demeaning herself for not considering that option. "Not all resurrections are successful. Once some souls have crossed over into the Never, they cannot be called back."

"What happens to the bodies of those who cannot be resurrected?" Jillayna asked.

"Their bodies are then reanimated," the wizardess replied. "But the spark, the essence, whatever humanity that was part of the body will have long since dissipated into the great beyond. It would then simply be bones and meat. No trace of the soul."

"Another foot soldier added to the army," the former general stated flatly.

"Yes, Patron," Nikkala said respectfully. "Master Nalazar often says, 'Waste not, want not.' But your spirit would be free. Your soul would be free from his grasp."

Despite being the only three around, Nikkala stepped close to the abjuration shield, allowing her to keep her voice low. "I cannot facilitate your release," she pleaded, "but this is a way for me to show you mercy."

The pair of Jurare wizards stood stone-faced, looking through the shielding.

"I am an Incanterran citizen," Nikkala continued. "I know the legacy of the Jurare dynasty. Be it an escaped demon, a flight of dragons, or a marching army amassing on the borders, the Jurare were always willing to man the battlements and serve as the first line of defense for this great kingdom. But I have also seen the smoldering pile of ruins that Nalazar transformed your tower into. I know it was a warning to The Eight. Or... I guess technically the Seven. Either way, I respect you all immensely. This is my gift of mercy. Do with it what you will."

With the goods delivered, the hard light disc vanished in a sprinkle of spiraling glowfly lights. Nikkala offered another curtsy, turned sharply on her heel, and left the Jurare duo behind as she disappeared into the gloomy shadows of the tunnels beyond.

Canarr gave a sharp exhale from his nostrils and tried his best to smooth out his beard. The warden then smartly marched into the small, private alcove and returned with the enchanted metal pail. After setting it on the table, he scooped up the two pairs of mushrooms and unceremoniously dropped them into the bottom of the metal pail.

After a long enough time, the enchantment within the metal walls went to work and transmogrified the mushrooms into stone with a series of cracks and groans that sounded like granite gravel scraping together. Canarr then upended the pail and watched as the petrified mushrooms tumbled onto the table. An unknowing sculptor would have admired the lifelike artistry of the pieces. One could imagine the petrified mushrooms fitting in with a garden or in some sort of nature-themed statuary. Canarr returned the enchanted pail to their privy.

"It is not like we are stranded on some desert island," the dour warden grumbled. "They are still feeding us. There is no need to get desperate just yet."

"So how are we going to get out of here?" the matron asked.

"I am still working on that," her patron replied as he took a resigned seat on his bed.

"You still sound irritated."

"I think I have a right to! Necromangians living right under our noses. I heard the stories... the rumors... but you never take them seriously. It is like those myths of the cults worshipping Tu'Dagoth. People pledging their devotion to a dark god that wants to destroy creation? It makes no sense."

Jillayna took a seat beside her patron and affectionately rubbed his shoulders. She ran her fingers through his long, graying hair. "So this is the long-awaited revenge of the ninth dynasty?"

"After two centuries? They certainly took their sweet time."

Jillayna laughed as she ran her fingers along the back of his neck. "Why they chose now to reveal themselves is part of the mystery that we need to be uncovering. Maybe they sensed a weakness because of all the strife between The Eight as of late."

"It is hard to say," Canarr grumbled. "Either way, they are here now..."

Chapter 43

With all the subtlety of a rampaging ocher hulk, Cavin Jurare ran through the village and crashed through the flaps of the hospitality tent where the Incanterrans had been staying during their visit to Malinsula. The look of fear and panic on his face was genuine and this was a man who waded into graveyards to dispatch ghouls, ghasts, wights, and a host of other undead.

Thankfully, upon his arrival, Valos, Sway, Thade, and Sario turned to meet him. The shaman Amman was on Cavin's heels to enter the tent. In the western alcove, Cavin saw Cinder lying on their bed, surrounded by half a dozen islanders. The herbalist and healer mothers were utilizing all sorts of ritual remedies to keep the sleeping form of Cinder comfortable. Using the lightest of sheets to preserve her modesty, a pair of the mothers were busy sponging her clean with warm water.

Cavin's heart sank into his stomach at the sight and he gasped uncontrollably. Sway was quick to stand beside him. "Is she...?" he croaked.

"She's unconscious," Sway assured quickly.

"When I saw them bathing her, I thought for a moment that they were preparing her body," he gasped with relief.

"Well, apparently, whatever hit her was strong enough to make her lose all body control. The ladies said she made water," Sway said.

"'Soaked her sarong' were the words they used," Valos said. "So do you want to stake claim to making fun of her when she wakes up? Because if you don't, I am definitely going to."

Cavin looked at Valos and impulsively laughed. He even covered his mouth, embarrassed by his involuntary gaff. Valos wrapped up his friend in a brotherly embrace. "She is going to be fine," he assured the undead slayer.

Sway offered a comforting embrace after Valos. "Her heart's strong. She's breathing. The ladies believe her mind just needs to reconnect with her body after such a terrible jolt."

"What happened?"

Sario was quick to recount the events with the portal and Cinder's intent to gather more material spell components, the same as the shaman had done for the Blades when they arrived. Jurare considered Sario's words carefully. Being the most fluent in the magical arts, he pondered how such a thing could have occurred.

"We should let the mothers work," Thade said, placing a reassuring hand on Cavin's shoulder.

In agreement, the Incanterrans moved their small group outside the tent and down to the nearby pink sand beach where the cool, blue ocean lapped lazily against the blushing sands. Thade turned abruptly toward the group. "I know we need to project that positive aura for Cinder's healing but if she doesn't wake up, we are going to be trapped here for a long time. We've all seen the little canoes that the island has. Does anyone feel like paddling for a few months to get back home?"

"Thade is being pessimistic?" Valos scoffed. "We *are* in trouble."

"Wait, you all said Cinder is strong," Cavin stated.

"She is," Sway said swiftly. "She is strong. She is going to wake up and everything is going to be fine."

"If..." Valos said lightly, drawing out the word, "if, if, if she has some struggles, Cav, could you open up a portal to get us home? Even just a small one?"

Cavin shook his head. "I don't understand dimensionation. I wish I did. All my training is in abjuration. The shield walls, protective spells, and defensive energy. That's what I do. It is why Cind is so weird. Wizards shouldn't be able to jump disciplines as she does. She grew up mastering evocation but she is also casting dimensionation. It is just really strange. But even if I had the magic texts and tomes to teach me how to make a portal, it would be faster for Thade to paddle us in a rowboat back to Incanterra."

"Recalling the *Castella Mare*?" Sway asked.

Valos shook his head. "They've been gone, what? A week now?"

"Even if we called up Gamble on the magic mirror—" Valos stopped short. "Wait. Has anyone tried calling Gamble?"

Thade slumped his shoulders and Sway rolled her eyes.

"Give me a beat," Valos said as he spun on his heel.

The rogue headed back up the beach to sneak back into the tent and seek out the trunk Cinder had brought with her.

Thade turned to Cavin. "So, was it a Jurare shield that would have prevented Cinder from returning to Incanterra?"

Cavin rubbed his jaw. "Sario said it was like a black tentacle wreathed in red fire. All the wizarding dynasties have a... a signature."

Activating the platinum ring on his right hand, Cavin created a small magical shield. It was a swirl of geometric patterns, stark squares with hard angles, and glowing sigils. "This is the look of Jurare magic. What Sario described was something very different. Black shadows wreathed in red flame? My biggest concern is that none of The Eight have that as their signature. That is what worries me."

The group turned to acknowledge Valos as he returned to the pink beach and closed the final gap.

"So someone back home doesn't want us to get back in?" Sway asked the undead hunter.

"Us or anyone?" Cavin replied. "For a wizard dynasty to target you all directly? I don't think your group is a big enough stone to make that kind of splash."

Valos's sandals crunched against the sand as he closed the gap and returned to the group.

"That almost makes it worse," Thade said. "If we are not the target, does that mean the whole city is sealed off? How powerful do you have to be to seal off an entire city?"

Valos cocked an eyebrow. "Sealing off the city is not as hard as it sounds. Hells, the city walls do most of the work for you. What? You got the four cardinal gates. Seal them off. Seal off the half gates. So that's eight more. Then you just need a dome over the city. We saw them do it in the spring when those dragons flew over." Valos wagged a finger at Cavin. "And that *was* Jurare magic."

Cavin froze, lifting his hands in the air with his index fingers extended. His eyes were darting back and forth as the celestial alignment of his thoughts all clicked into place. "Why do you seal off a city to keep people from teleporting in or using dimension doors in the first place?" he asked. "They're doing it to ward off an attack."

The Blades considered Cavin's logic.

"It's the most plausible," the undead slayer reasoned. "If the Arvateri boy king sent his army to siege the city or if a naval force was besieging Highstone Harbor... Incanterra isn't the only kingdom with wizards. If a siege is happening... or if I was besieging the city, the first thing I would want to do is circumvent the walls. Open gates inside the city and then pour your soldiers through."

"Let's find out for sure," Valos said, holding up the silver hand mirror that was etched with runes and sigils.

It was a smaller version of the silver mirror Cinder kept in their living quarters back in the cadenta. Thankfully, the magic item was infused with energy so anyone – wizard or not – who knew how to activate it could utilize its enchanted properties. Valos triggered the magic mirror and sent out a call to its identical counterpart that was in the possession of Gamble Hallowhall. If anyone knew the inner workings of what was happening in the city, it would be their family captain.

Valos waited. Thade waited. Sway waited. Cavin waited.

Ordinarily, the mirror's reflection would darken, swirl with a flowing pattern, and then be replaced by the image of their captain. While their reflected features had darkened and the swirls had formed, Gamble's handsome features never materialized.

Dejected, Valos let the magic within the mirror dissolve away.

"What does this mean?" Thade asked.

"It don't mean nothin'," Valos said, his Ombraterran accent becoming more prominent with his frustration. "Gamble's a busy lord. He's got a lot of responsibilities. He's also big on his fashion so he is not carrying some big gaudy mirror on his person."

"He might just be out and about," Sway said.

"He's not sitting in his apartment," Thade nodded.

"He's making sure Shaded Light is taken care of in our absence and dealing with other issues that the family might have." Valos shook the mirror. "I will keep this on me in case he calls. And we can try again in a little bit. In the meantime, I suggest we keep the speculation to a minimum until we can get a proper accounting."

The crew all turned to look at the ocean waves lapping against the shore.

"In the meantime..." Thade said.

"In the meantime..." Cavin mimicked.

"In the meantime..." Sway said, "we should be there for Cinder. Help the healers out to get them whatever they need."

The group collectively nodded.

The group collectively watched the waves.

The group collectively stood in all of the uncomfortable silence.

Valos let a grumble slip. "Why isn't Gamble answering?" he whispered to the waves.

Chapter 44

The summons had been frenetic and urgent. After the Catabaysi dynasty had taken over the wizarding isle of Sorceria and the famed home of the Baelannor dynasty, Devinaya Baelannor had been studying the daily habits of the Necromangians and their undead leader. So when such a concentration of power was assembled on the top floors of the tower, with Nalazar Catabaysi included, she knew there was an opportunity.

Devinaya had heard the rumors the same as others on the isle. Nalazar was infuriated at the destruction of one of his squads of skeletal sentinels patrolling the streets of the capital. It was not an accident. It was not a coincidence. It had been a coordinated attack. The wizardess knew the sound of a counterstrike operation being planned when she heard it.

With so many of their controlling crowns having been delivered by the Mutaccios, Nalazar's anger echoing through the halls, and now a trusted collection of senior cabal members being assembled, Devinaya knew the Necromangians were about to make an excursion down to the city. Such a fortuitous event would keep them preoccupied.

And that gave the wizards trapped on the isle a window.

In one of the central villas housed in the common grounds of the isle, a secret meeting was set to begin. Tanairs Corvalonn, Aldor Mutaccio, Cedalia Ce'Mondere, Marius Vocazion, and the political novice Cadwell Dinacioun had answered Devinaya Baelannor's request for a meeting.

As Devinaya entered the lavish accommodations, Cadwell was finishing a spell that cast rippling, orange-hued, water-like reflections on the walls and ceiling of the villa. Snapping the last of the magic into place, he turned to the group and offered a shallow bow. "If anyone is attempting any sort of scrying magic, this will keep us shielded."

"Counter magic," Aldor said with an approving nod. "That is thinking ahead. Canarr Jurare would be proud of you, son."

"Thank you, Master Mutaccio," the magus replied.

"Our time is short," Devinaya Baelannor said. She quickly offered a summation of the enemy's recent activities and concluded by saying, "We have to come together to neutralize this threat. If not, we are all going to end up as part of their undead horde."

"So how do we stop them?" Marius Vocazion asked.

Slowly, the eyes were drawn to Tanairs Corvalonn. He was the senior member of the assembled and the patron of the second-ranked dynasty amongst The Eight. Without eyes being able to fall on Asaric Baelannor, it was only natural for the group to look to Corvalonn for his wisdom.

"I have given this considerable thought," the sorcerer said. "The lich's forces are legion. We cannot neutralize their threat fast enough on our own. The citizens would pay the price for our folly and every citizen felled is another soldier added to Nalazar's army. We cannot do this... alone."

"What are your thoughts?" Aldor Mutaccio asked.

"We need to send emissaries to Arvaterra to the east and Castratellus to the west. We need to convince the Arvateri boy king to send his troops to besiege the city. And we need Castratellus and their mighty war machines to come to our aid."

"We have to get out of the city to do that," Vocazion said. "And the gates are sealed."

"Specifically, I have to get out of the city," Corvalonn said flatly.

"Wait, why you?" Cedalia Ce'Mondere asked, with just slightly too much concern in her voice.

"Because once I am out of the city, I can be in the Arvateri capital in a moment," the sorcerer replied. "No one else's magic can match my speed. I can open negotiations with the Arvateri and then in the span of another heartbeat, I can be outside the moat of the Great Castle in Castratellus's capital."

Devinaya Baelannor shook her head. "How do you convince Castratellus to leave their high fortifications? The king will no doubt call for his people to seal off their mountain passes. Then he can claim it is not a threat to his people."

"Nalazar is a threat to *all* people," Marius Vocazion countered. "Castratellus can ignore it only at their peril. Nalazar is not some ill-tempered ruler. There was a series of terrible leaders in Monterran history. But rather than try to unseat them from the throne or commit regicide, the people just... waited it out. They knew a single mortal ruler would die eventually and then the kingdoms would be better."

"That doesn't... sound like... a great plan," Dinacioun said.

"Aye, but it is foolproof," Mutaccio added. "The sun sets on every empire... eventually."

"But not Nalazar Catabaysi," Vocazion said. "Not anymore. Time means nothing to him now."

Mutaccio nodded. "The one... flaw – if we want to call it that – is that right now, all of Nalazar's forces are concentrated into a single area. Once he has assimilated every dead body in the capital, he won't stop. His army will break out and begin to march. Right now is the easiest time to send forces against him, while they are all concentrated within our walls."

Baelannor finally offered a consenting nod. "And with every village, town, and city they consume, their numbers will grow. If not stopped now, his undead army will grow out of control."

"And how long before they spread beyond our borders?" Corvalonn asked. "That is how I sell it to Castratellus and Arvaterra."

Vocazion managed a weak laugh. "If ever there was a time we needed a *real* family of dragons to fly over the city."

Cadwell Dinacioun scrunched his face quizzically. "What do you mean *real* dragons?"

"So how do we get Corvalonn out of the city?" Vocazion asked quickly.

The sorcerer gave a heaving sigh and looked at the representative from the Ce'Mondere. He gave Cedalia his permissive nod.

"Dacadus Ce'Mondere succumbed to his injuries after his fight with a great demon," Cedalia said. "What we did not tell The Eight was that the demon broke through from the infernal realm because it was chasing a creature we had captured from the Elysium. We have been using the juxtaposition of the holy and unholy essences to create a new power source for magic."

Aldor Mutaccio folded his arms across his barrel chest. "That... is... fascinating."

"It was Dacadus's grand plan," the warlock explained. "And he paid for it with his life."

"Nalazar has this power source?" Vocazion asked.

"He has Dacadus's notes," Corvalonn confirmed. "He also has the summoned amorina and an infernixie. He is using the power source to fuel the spells that are sealing off the city."

"So if we were to kill the amorina..." Baelannor speculated, "...would that weaken the shields?"

"Not in the timeframe we need," Corvalonn said.

"Wait, kill the amorina?" Mutaccio argued.

"Technically, we wouldn't be *killing* it," Cedalia corrected. "If she sustains mortal damage, she just apparates back to the Elysium plane of existence."

"I don't care about the amorina's life. I care about her essence," the potion master said to the warlock. "Your patron is gone. His second is gone. That monster murdered your matron. If we lose that amorina, is there anyone within your stable that can summon a second one? We could be losing a power source that could change the very way that we power our magic."

"Our?" Corvalonn said with an arch of an eyebrow. "I don't remember seeing you at the testing of this magic or throwing gold into our coffers to bank our research."

Cadwell Dinacioun – despite being the least ranked amongst the wizards – held up a hand. "There is no time for this. And we certainly cannot be squabbling amongst ourselves about the allocation of resources. There will be no wizards left to harness the demon anti-demon energy if we are all undead slaves in Nalazar's horde."

Corvalonn nodded his agreement. Aldor reluctantly conceded as well but had to grumble, "I am just saying there could be an alternative. Capture it. Steal it. Hide it away. Something."

"We can cross that bridge *if* we come to it," Marius Vocazion said. "A plan to remove the amorina off the game board is pointless if we can't get Corvalonn out of the city. That has to be our priority."

"But if I could gain a vial of the amorina's essence, I might be able to lure out another vaedaemon, it could be a valuable ally in our plan," the warlock said.

"So how much time do we have to plan?" Dinacioun asked.

Corvalonn turned to Devinaya Baelannor. "How much time do we have?" the sorcerer asked.

"It is hard to say," the conjuror admitted.

"So, the Necromangians are all assembled up in your tower and they are projecting their consciousness down into the city with my crowns," Mutaccio said. "Why don't we just walk over there right now and slit all their throats?"

"They have defenses," Devinaya said.

"Nalazar is the only one I am worried about," Corvalonn warned. "Destroy him and the rest of his sheep fall. Destroying him has to be our top priority."

Dinacioun held a finger up to his ear as he heard a far distant whisper. Glancing out the window of their villa, the famed Baelannor tower loomed in the distance. "What are they doing up there?" the magus asked. "What is so important to have so many of them assembled?"

None of the wizards had an answer.

"Well, it must be huge," Dinacioun stated, "because whatever it is, it looks like Nalazar is going to take care of it himself..."

Chapter 45

Nalazar Catabaysi floated with impossible grace down the steps of the Baelannor tower. His long and flowing robes tented around him, concealing his legs. It was hard to tell if his lower limbs ambulated at all. Yet, his feet continued to hover just a scant inch above the ground. Wafting warbles of energy radiated out from the undead lich as he floated across the Baelannor grounds.

Without a word, he exited the walled estate of the dynasty, turned, and headed towards the northmost point of the floating wizarding isle. It was there that many of the larger floating transport ships would often dock. There was a crafted archway and pillars carved from magnificent Ombraterran marble. At one time, great animated sentinels served as guardians but had been quickly dispatched in Nalazar's initial attack.

Without the slightest hint of hesitancy, the Necromangian leader reached the edge of the landing platform and simply stepped off into the firmament. With his blood-red robes billowing about him, the lich proceeded to descend the one thousand feet to the city below.

However, with magical swirling energy radiating off of him, the lich fell at a rate of only half of what other objects would have fallen. More than a few pairs of eyes from down within the city watched his descent. As the identity of the lich revealed itself with more prominence and the closer Nalazar drew to the city streets, the more the panicked people sought refuge inside any available home or business.

Drifting intentionally on the winds, the Necromangian leader was looking for a ward within the Northeast District. Operations within the Northwest were too sparsely populated for his demonstration. The animals south of the Queen's High were far too small-minded to appreciate what was about to happen. So the Northeast was the lich's target.

Alighting on one of the ward's paved streets, the lich landed in a crouch and then rose to his full height, the gesture returning his feet to their floating position above the pavement.

On the city streets, the few people out and about resembled schools of fish parting in wide circles to accommodate an apex predator invading their waters. None of the pedestrians wanted to risk eye contact with the creature now floating amongst them.

The only Incanterrans willing to risk approaching the lich were loyalists draped in white priestly vestments and wearing conical hoods and featureless alabaster masks. Reaching a respectable distance, the Knights of the Imperial

Circle dropped to a crouch, genuflecting before their wizardly epitome. "I require ghouls. A half a dozen. And a host of skeletons as reinforcements."

The lich's voice was inhuman, projecting far louder than it should have with a frightening bass resembling two people speaking in harmony while a third offered a higher tone resembling cat claws on a slate.

The Knights practically jumped to their feet and rushed off to find whatever their master desired amongst the assembled forces patrolling the streets. There was no questioning. Nalazar could have commanded them to deliver their wives or firstborn sons. They would have dashed away with the same fervor.

It did not take long for the Knights to fulfill the master Necromangian's request. They returned with half a dozen of the requested ghouls. The undead monsters had risen from the dead, still possessing the majority of their organs, muscles, and flesh. There was a lifelessness in their eyes yet they appeared to cling to some form of consciousness. They were sturdier than the animated skeletons. But their reputation for consuming human flesh is what made them so impossibly feared.

Under the commands of the lich, the ghouls were each outfitted with weapons from the skeletal brigades. They were then adorned with various patchwork pieces of armor. This was not to protect the dead – as they felt no pain and did not even register damage – but it was more for efficiency. The lich did not want his senior subordinates to have to trouble themselves by jumping bodies once their plan was enacted.

With the ghouls assembled, the lich cast his gaze back up at the underbelly of Sorceria while he transmitted a telepathic command. The lich then turned and looked at the ghouls assembled before him. One by one, their eyes changed color and their pupils began to radiate an internal blue glow.

As each of the senior Necromangians up on Sorceria found their way down into one of the ghoul's bodies, the pupils winked with light, representing their show of control. Nalazar gave them a moment to adjust and stabilize their consciousnesses inside their new ghoul bodies. The lich then turned and pointed to the target.

Looming nearby was the cold stone walls of the ward's local *domici dauthis*. The house of the dead was adorned with black banners and featured an Ombraterran marble statue in its courtyard paying homage to Zaneger – the god of death.

With Nalazar leading the point of the echelon, the lich and his assemblage of ghouls, flanked and followed by an even larger contingent of animated skeletons began their long and purposeful march towards the dormant house of the dead.

Amongst the assembled Incanterrans, the people continued to scatter. They scurried to a safe distance so as not to draw the lich's direct eye but not so far that they would miss the coming spectacle. It was not a daily thing to see an echelon of undead marching through the streets with their lich leading the procession. Whatever was about to happen was going to be magnificently terrible and people – with all of their morbid curiosity – wanted to see it.

The echelon descended on the *domici dauthis*. With a raising of his hands and whispers of summoning through the *pherein* directly, Nalazar flung aside the wrought iron gates of the compound. The iron hinges crumpled and snapped like pieces of dried wood. The tines of the gates were torn asunder and flung aside with such force that they would have surely punctured clean through an abdomen or a carriage sidewall.

Floating up the paved path to the entryway of the great building, Nalazar brought his hands up once more. Tapping into his raw magical energy, the Monterran oak doors held fast for the slightest of heartbeats but then cracked, caved, and splintered into kindling.

The assembled citizens watched as the undead horde, led by the commandeered ghouls, stormed the open doorway and flooded into the facility like water. From within the structure, the echoes of combat began to ring out. There were roars of rage followed by screams of pain and agony. There was the sound of steel against steel. There was the chaos of doors being battered down and furniture being smashed. Splashes of red could be seen suddenly painting window panes. And slowly, stab by stab, the sounds of silent combat began to overtake the calls of pain and agony. Even if a ghoul was wounded or a skeleton was smashed, they did not cry out in pain or issue a death rattle.

Finally, the sounds of battle began to lessen until they started to resemble more of a trickle than a roar. From more than one window, belches of black smoke began to issue. Normally, calls would go out to the fire brigades. Instead, the Incanterran citizens stood fast.

Amidst the chaos and as the smoke started to become more prominent, most missed the form of Arator Dawnborne escaping the burning building out of the rear entrance where the herses and supply wagons were kept. The tall, muscular man was doing his best to carry a wounded pair of his fellow acolytes who were desperately clinging to life. He had one of his unconscious compatriots slung over his shoulder like a sack of potatoes and was doing his best to keep a young woman hoisted against his stomach while she kept her arms around his neck to help support her weight.

Undoubtedly, the reason no one noticed the escape attempt was that at that same moment, two of the controlled ghouls were dragging the senior leader of the *domici dauthis* out through the sundered front doors. The ghouls positioned him in front of Nalazar. Struck and dropped to his knees, the acolyte to the death god glared up into the lich's horrible visage.

"Surely, you had to know this response was coming," Nalazar seethed with a hint of pity in his voice.

"You and your kind are abominations," the vicar spat. "You have escaped Zaneger's sacred scythe. It is our responsibility to see your kind eradicated from the realms."

"And yet, in doing so – in obeying the command of your god – you have sealed your fate," the lich warned.

"You and your kind must be cleansed."

"And what is your reward in the Never for following Zaneger's commands?"

"We will assist him in ferrying the souls of the dead to their proper station in what lies beyond."

"And you look *forward* to this task?"

"It will be my honor."

The lich nodded with solemnity. "Let's not keep him waiting for such a loyal and faithful servant."

The lich summoned forth a deadly bolt of magical energy pulled straight from the *pherein*. The blast burrowed into the vicar's field of vision. It was over so fast that the man did not even have time to register the waves of pain about to ripple through his body.

All that was left was silence.

Darkness and the void.

Darkness.

Chapter 46

Darkness.

Darkness and the void.

But then at a distance, the warbling sounds of indecipherable voices. She could not tell what they were saying but through the echoing distortion, she recognized them. The firm and forceful bass. A smokey sultry sound. A distinct Ombraterran accent. And the cadence and inflection of a wizardly education.

She could not force her eyes open but she felt the warmth against her palm. She could feel the love seeping into her soul from the compassionate embrace. And there was an aroma in the air. Underneath the everpresent smell of salt on the wind and the syrupy sweet aroma of the native fruit, it was there. An odd anointing of his pleasant scent blended with the oil he used on his silver blade. He was there.

As she tried to open her eyes once more, she could feel the comfortable mat underneath her. There was a soft sheet covering her. And there was a pair of hands – no, two pairs of hands – massaging her feet, ankles, and her calves.

The warbling tones of their conversation started to echo less dramatically. She was finally able to make out more distinct words. Or at least parts of them. "...gonna sit there with a straight face and tell me... ...the Monterran mountains over this parad... ...people prefer the cold... ...ose types aren't to be trusted... ...with the snow, you have to be all bundled... ...golden skin from the sun... ...and then you get next to a warm fire? Nothing is bette... ...can go jump in that surf and cool... I can put another blanket on the be..."

"...once you get hot, there are only so many articles of clothing you can take off," Sway said.

"Now, we're talking," Valos quipped.

The sliver of light sliced through the darkness and slowly spread as Cinder opened her eyes. "Hey, hey, hey..." Cavin whispered, drawing the group's attention. "Look who's back."

Cinder Fireborne looked down at the foot of her bed. Two of the elderly islander grandmothers were massaging her feet. Crowding around were her crew members. Valos, Sway, and Thade were all smiles, sympathy, and relief. The shamans Amman and Sario were also present and equally concerned. And Cavin was sitting close to the head of her bed, holding her hand.

"You had us worried," Cavin said.

Looking out at the flap serving as the tent window, Cinder noted a plethora of islander children – all with their bronze skin and snowy white hair – looking in with curiosity. One of the grandmothers shooed them away with her native tongue but as the children scampered off, their voices and laughter echoed up and down the trails and between the tents. As they were making their announcements, distant cheers, applause, and praises to the ancestors rippled out amongst the village of Searock.

Cinder wanted to sit up but Cavin gently held her in place. "Easy. Easy. Go easy now," he implored.

"How long was I out?" she asked weakly.

"Two years," Sway said gravely.

Cinder looked at Sway nervously.

"Valos is married and has kids now. Of course, I haven't aged because of my natural beauty but look at what the ravages of time have done to Thade!"

Sway pivoted hard to look at Thade and then recoiled melodramatically in faux fright. "The horror," she whispered. "The tragedy."

Sario came close to Cinder, looking deep into her eyes, gently pulling up her eyelids, and examining her face. "Less than a day," she whispered. "I was afraid that if you didn't respond quickly to the massages and the aromas, someone was going to summon the local *taka'mattu*. You all would probably call him a 'witch doctor'?"

"Is there a big headdress involved?" Valos asked.

"Yes," Sario said flatly. "And he has concubines who all wear brassieres made of coconuts."

"I live here and I have never seen the coconut brassieres you speak of," Amman said.

Sario heaved a heavy sigh. "Be glad you woke up, Cind. The *taka'mattu* would have wanted to solve your ailment with leeches."

The group reacted harshly.

"I know," Sario replied. "They try to solve *all* ailments with leeches. That or maggots. But, thankfully, here you are. No blood-sucking will be required. Lucky for you, Searock has some of the best healers on the island. Everyone wanted to help. I had to start sending some of them away."

"Too many chefs spoil the soup," Cinder said. "Right, Thade?"

"Great. Now I'm hungry," Thade replied.

"When are you not?" Valos asked.

Once more, Cinder tried to sit up. She motioned for Cavin to give her a hand and the undead slayer was happy to provide. "Do you have any idea what happened?" Valos asked.

"I am not certain," Cinder said. "I was trying to open a portal to the vault. I walked through. Or at least, I *tried* to walk through. That was the last thing I remember."

"We've been trying to use the magic mirror to contact Gamble but there is no connection to the sister mirror," Sway stated. "I hate to be the person to state the obvious but one magic failing is strange. Two magics failing... I get the feeling something is very wrong back home."

"So we need to get back there as quickly as we can," Thade nodded.

Sario and Amman looked at each other, exchanging empathic communication. They both nodded. "So, you are going to open a portal to return to Incanterra?" Sario asked.

"If we can find a safe harbor," Cavin answered.

"We want to come with you," Amman said.

The crew all looked at each other but only Valos was unfiltered enough to voice what everyone was thinking. "Why?"

Sway pivoted and smacked Valos on the arm.

"I mean..." Valos stumbled. "That probably came out wrong. But we don't know what we are headed into. If you are worried about the cattle, we will make good on our word—"

Sario smiled and held up a reassuring palm. "Your kingdom is in danger. You saw our island being besieged and you threw yourself into the fray. Now, the tide is rolling out. If there is a way that we can assist you in your time of need, we are obligated to help you in any way that we can."

"It is what friends do," Amman said.

"If things go bad, we don't know if we can get you back," Cinder said earnestly.

Sario nodded. "It is a risk we are willing to take."

"Any chance you could open a portal to the *Castella Mare*?" Valos asked.

Cinder let her shoulders slump and she looked at Valos with a frustrated look on her features. "All this time, porting in and leaving touchstones in all these different ports of call. Why didn't we leave one on the boat? We are smarter than that."

"Well, I am," Valos said with a little grin. "I don't know about you fancy wizarding types with all your classical education. 'Street smarts' I believe they call it. But, yeah, we should put that on the list."

"But you know the *Castella Mare*," Thade said. "It has to be somewhere you have been before. Isn't that the... whatever you call it... the qualifications for the portal spell?"

"I know *what* the *Castella Mare* is but I don't know *where* she is," Cinder explained. "A Corvalonn could do that. Maybe. But I am not fluent enough in dimensionation to be *that* good. The bigger question is why the city is sealed off in the first place."

Valos jutted his chin at Cavin. "You want to tell her your theory?"

"What theory?" she asked.

"What if the Jurare sealed off the city... because it is under attack," Cavin explained.

"It wouldn't be the first time," Cinder theorized. "The Jurare put up those shields when the flight of dragons flew over the city. If Incanterra was under assault – from Arvaterra maybe? – the Jurare would have sealed off the city to prevent any sort of magical incursion."

Thade snapped his fingers and looked around. He had solved the problem with a solution staring him in the face. "Sealing off the city is one thing," he said. "Don't get me wrong. It is powerful magic. Not saying it's not. But sealing off an entire kingdom? No one is *that* powerful. So if we can't get to the city, where should we go?"

Sway smiled and nodded, picking up the big man's line of thinking. "I know *exactly* where to open a portal to."

The other two members of the crew suddenly all picked up their meaning. Cavin looked at the four with a quizzical expression. "Where?"

Thade Skystone smiled...

Chapter 47

To the unsuspecting, the private villas located within the interior of the isle of Sorceria were quiet and private respites from what little hustle and bustle were present on the isle. With the dweomers in place, those within the villa could look out the large windows but those walking the grounds could not see in. Even mage-light inside was undetectable. Magical enchantments muffled and in some cases outright muted the sounds coming from within.

While often a place for exclusive vendors to display their amazing wares to wealthy clientele, the villas were whispered to be secluded venues for scandalous trysts or hedonistic acts unable to be conducted within the regal and dignified confines of a dynast tower. The magic put in place was to secure secrecy and ensure discretion. Thankfully that magic was in place to conceal the continued private meeting between six representatives of The Eight.

"Any plans developed down in the city are worthless if we cannot find a way to get down off the isle," Aldor Mutaccio said, cutting off a string of ideas from the assembled six.

"I can get through the barrier," Devinaya Baelannor assured. "I have been taking rations and supplies down to the city so regularly that no one even questions me anymore."

"But we still have to get Tanairs down to the city," Marius Vocazion said. "How do we smuggle him out without being seen?"

"Invisibility?" Cadwell Dinacioun asked.

"That is an illusory spell," Tanairs Corvalonn said and then gestured towards the larger group. "We appear to be out of Lu'Scion magicians."

"The one time Kerryn could *actually* be useful..." Mutaccio grumbled.

"Could we smuggle him out with the rations?" Vocazion asked. "Aldor, do you have a spell to reduce his physical size?"

The alchemist was mentally sorting through his stockpile of various potions back in his private laboratory. "Even my most powerful magic would only reduce him so far. Granted a three-foot-tall Corvalonn would certainly be a sight but even being hidden amongst the rations doesn't guarantee the barrier doesn't hold. What if the boat drops down through the barrier and it leaves Tanairs behind?"

"That would be difficult to explain," Baelannor admitted.

As the group continued to bandy ideas back and forth, Cadwell Dinacioun rubbed his chin in contemplation. "What about a portable pocket?" the magus blurted before the idea had even truly formed.

The group turned to look at him in unison. "Surely we aren't the only dynasty to use them?" he bade the group. "It's a big kerchief. You unfold it, place it on the ground, and it becomes a pocket of extra-dimensional space. You put your stuff in it, fold it back up, and put it in your pocket. Don't tell me you all physically carry around all the spell components you need."

"Except there is no air within the pocket once it is closed," Corvalonn warned.

Cadwell wagged a finger. "Technically, there is the air that fills the volume of the space."

Cedalia Ce'Mondere shook her head, "But you are talking about smuggling three or four people down there. We would have breathable air for… minutes at the most?"

Aldor looked at Devinaya sternly. "You would have to be very fast."

The Baelannor conjurer nodded. "The timing would have to be spot on. If anything went wrong, whoever is inside the pocket would be in real jeopardy."

"We need four wizards," Vocazion said with an unusually confident tone.

Aldor Mutaccio arched an eyebrow at his fellow patron's proclamation. "Such a specific number, Marius. Care to tell us how you calculated that?"

"Devinaya acts as our smuggler. She will carry the portable pocket. Once she is down below, she will pass it over to either Drennid or our operative Graver. They are trapped down in the city right now. It depends on whomever I can contact first."

The conjuror nodded. "I know both of them."

"How will you contact Graver or Drennid?" Cadwell asked.

"I can send a note to my brewmaster who is down below," Mutaccio assured.

"As for the pocket, inside will be Corvalonn because of his portals. Cedalia will summon forth the demon to tear down the gates. The other two members will be me and my matron. We will use our evocation magic to help clear a path for the demon. The demon will smash through the gates and then Arania and Tanairs will fly through the broken gate on a pair of my crystalline drakes.

"Once I am captured — as I am sure I will be — if I am brought before Nalazar, I will tell him the truth… or at least a version of it. I wanted to spare my matron the fate that has befallen Jurare and Ce'Mondere. But I wasn't about to send my matron out into the wildlands alone so she is being accompanied by a bodyguard."

"A more convincing lie if we would have had the Lu'Scions at our disposal," Corvalonn grumbled. "I swear… if we survive this and Kerryn thinks he and his ilk will just be able to saunter back into our good graces—"

"We don't need magic for that kind of disguise," Cedalia said. "It works for the Knights of the Imperial Circle. We just need to put you in a hood and cover the lower half of your face with a cloth."

From one of the pockets of his blue and black-trimmed robes, Marius produced a silver coin of the realm and flicked it playfully at Corvalonn. The sorcerer snatched the coin out of the air. "Master Corvalonn, I want you to hire someone to serve as my dynast's man-at-arms. Do you accept?"

"I do," the sorcerer replied, understanding the playful ploy.

"There you have it," Vocazion said. "Now, if I am asked under duress or the undead bastard uses some sort of magic to detect if I am telling the truth, we punched a hole in the defenses so my matron and my newly hired man-at-arms can escape."

"And old skin-and-bones will know you are telling the truth," Mutaccio said.

"So where is our target?" Cedalia Ce'Mondere asked.

"The half gate on the east-northeast section of the city," Corvalonn replied. "The undead forces will be less concentrated and the magic is less likely to be as strong as attacking a cardinal gate. Plus, if Arania and I – that is… If Arania and her man-at-arms I hire are on flying drakes, once they cross the river, any pursuit will be futile."

Vocazion clucked his tongue. "You will also have to avoid the ballista mounted on the battlements. We have outfitted them with magical rounds that can fire wicked spells at you. I don't know if the skeletons know how to use those weapons but I would prefer we not find out."

Corvalonn nodded. "We will have to learn to zig and zag. But if we can get up into the hills and out of their eye lines, then we can portal out of the kingdom."

"And any tracking party will assume you vanished into thin air," Cedalia added.

"Can you track people flying on drakes?" Mutaccio asked.

"There is more than one way to track a person than footprints," Dinacioun warned. "Believe me, I would know."

"When is your next excursion down to the city?" Cedalia asked Devinaya.

"As soon as it needs to be," the Baelannor wizard replied.

"We will need to get things gathered and organized," Corvalonn said.

"Agreed," Vocazion answered. "But the quicker the better."

The six wizards agreed. The younger Dinacioun sage turned abruptly and cupped a hand to his ear. From off in the distance from somewhere on the isle, one of Cadwell's spotters had whispered in his direction a distant warning that only his fellow Dinacioun could hear.

The magus sent back a whisper of thanks that warbled strangely past his lips as it radiated out toward its intended recipient. He then turned his attention back to the collective. "Whatever Nalazar was doing down in the city, he has concluded his affair. He has been spotted returning to the isle."

A bristling of nervousness radiated through the group.

"At the very least, we have our plan," Corvalonn said confidently. "But we have all been here for too long anyway. We should disperse before some nosy Necromangian comes snooping about."

"We didn't resolve the situation with the amorina," Aldor Mutaccio argued.

"It will have to be a discussion for another time," the sorcerer said. Given his grave tone, no one was willing to challenge him.

The collection of wizards began to gather their things but was smartly prepared to stagger their exits so as not to attract attention. "Is this going to work?" Aldor asked Marius.

The mage shrugged. "The better question is how is Arania going to react when I give her the news?"

Aldor shook his head. "Better you telling her than me..."

Chapter 48

The swirling, blue, miniature glowfly signature of Cinder Fireborne's portal materialized just off the front porch of the Nightwater farm's main house. From inside the portal, the crew – still down in Malinsula – stood nervously. Cavin Jurare gingerly tested the boundaries with a trepid hand. But when there was no blowback and no forceful energy barrier, the group sighed in relief.

One by one the crew of the Shadow Blades, along with their undead slaying warden, and their two newest companions – the Malinsuli shamans – stepped out onto the Nightwater Farm. The same as in Malinsula, the sun was shining. Billowing clouds dotted the cerulean blue sky. The smell of concentrated crops filled the air along with the faint wafting odors of livestock in the distance.

Once everyone was through, Cinder collapsed the magical portal in on itself. Thade and Sway were already making their way up onto the wooden porch when the front door flung open with urgency.

Aunt Erayllia Nightwater charged through the threshold and scrambled to wrap Sway and Thade in a simultaneous embrace. Tears rimmed the bottom of her eyes and she frantically shifted back and forth over and over to kiss them both on their cheeks or – in Thade's case – his chin. "We thought for certain you were dead," she proclaimed. Shifting so only not to yell in their ears, Erayllia called out. "Roch! Roch!"

Uncle Adroch emerged quickly from the nearby barn. Seeing his collection of honored guests, even at a distance, the crew watched him sway. His shoulders drooped in visible relaxation. Smiling the whole time, he then hustled over to greet his guests.

Thade walked down the steps to meet his uncle, flinging his large arms wide for a welcome embrace. The two slapped each other on the back with appreciation. "We thought you were dead."

"That is just what Aunt Erayllia said," Thade replied. "So do you all know what is going on?"

"You mean you all don't?" Erayllia asked.

"We've been... traveling," Valos said as he made a gesture toward the newest pair in their menagerie. Greetings were exchanged between the Incanterran farmers and the Malinsuli shaman. "I love your hair," Erayllia said to Sario. She then gave a nod toward Sway. "I am curious what a few more weeks on that island would have done for you. I doubt you would go as white as her but the blonde hair certainly wears well on you."

Thade glanced down at Sway. "You did go blonde! When did that happen?"

"Your powers of deduction are just staggering," she replied.

"So what is happening down in the city?" Valos asked.

"We've been up here the entire time so everything we have heard is hearsay. Some rumors. Possibly fanciful stories," Adroch said.

"The kingdom was founded by a wizard and last spring a family of dragons flew over the city," Cavin smiled. "Incanterra's foundations were built on fanciful stories."

The grim look from the two farmers washed away any hope of mirth and merriment. "News started trickling up from the city because farmers couldn't get in to sell their crops or their livestock," Adroch began. "And you know the city is always needing food. Magical shields have the gates closed off. You can't get in or out. They say there is this magical dome over the city keeping everyone trapped. And the word is the floating magical island has been cracked in half."

"What?" Cinder asked aghast.

"And there are tales that the city is being patrolled by an army of living skeletons," Erayllia said glumly.

The group immediately turned to gauge the reaction of Cavin Jurare. His brow furrowed and his eyes narrowed. "What was that?"

"That is what the farmers are saying," Adroch said. "The shields went up, sealing off the city. The farmers approached the gates, the same as they always do, so they could go into the city and sell their wares. Skeleton guards. Not just skeletons. Armed. Armored. And not just a few. There was... a lot. *If* all of these stories are true, the capital is besieged by an undead horde."

The group stood quietly, processing the information they had been given. The Malinsuli remained respectfully silent. Finally, Valos relented. "What about the crew in the bunkhouse?"

"Your workers are exceptional," Adroch replied. "They learned something was wrong when the portal you all placed down into the city was no longer functioning. But even after, they just kept brewing. I think some of them have gotten a little squirrely trying to live the farm life. They sometimes head into Chanton. Throwing around coins in Two Swords the way they do has made them a favorite with the locals."

Thade issued a rumble from deep in his chest.

"No, no," Adroch said. "They are on their best behavior. They just like the chicken and they have caught the eyes of a few of the local girls. The stories over at Two Swords is where we have been hearing all the rumors."

"But the brewing?" Valos asked.

"Your kid, Damiano?" Adroch smiled. "He is a live one. He runs a tight crew. There was a small incident with one of his city workers and one of the hayseeds."

Valos tried not to smile. "Let me guess. Throwing around coins the way they do attracts attention. But there is only so much attention to go around. So if all the milkmaids are looking at your brewers, they ain't looking at the hayseeds. I am guessing they 'don't take too kindly to that in these here parts'?"

"Something like that," Adroch said.

"Damiano knows most problems can be solved with coins greased to the right palms," Erayllia added.

"Chip off the old block," Sway said while nudging Valos in the ribs.

"He is just following the Ombraterran Way," Cinder replied.

Valos wagged an approving finger at the mage.

"The boy is going to make you a good associate," Adroch said. "But he would make you even more coin as a soldier."

"Maybe after we figure out what in the hells is going on down in the capital," Valos replied.

"When did all this happen?" Cavin asked.

Adroch and Erayllia looked at each other. "Three weeks?" he speculated.

"Three and a half maybe?" she added.

Cinder groaned and ran her hands through her fire-red hair. "Two weeks travel on the open ocean. A week and a half down in Malinsula. When we were leaving port, I swear I saw a flash on the horizon from Sorceria. And the isle is cracked in half?"

"I haven't seen it myself," Adroch warned, "but that is the word floating down the road."

"We must have missed it by... hours," Thade said.

"Or we are lucky we left when we did," Sway added. "Otherwise, we would have been trapped inside with all the rest of them."

"We have to get down there," Cinder said.

"We saw what happened the last time you tried that," Cavin said.

"But we made it here," she retorted. "If these rumors are true, that shield over the city is designed to keep out people like me. They aren't using it to repel boulders thrown by hill giants or ballista bolts hurled from war machines. But it is enough to keep us from teleporting or using dimensional gates to get inside. So we just need to open a gate outside the city limits."

"No," Erayllia said flatly, drawing the eye of the collective. "I've just spent the last three weeks worrying if you all were alive or dead or transformed into one of those dreadful skeletons. Now, you get here. I know you all are alive. And you want to charge back into the dragon's den? No. No. You all are staying here!"

Adroch reached over to rub Erayllia's shoulders and comfort her.

"We have to," Thade said softly.

"Why you all? Isn't this some task for an army or something?" she asked.

The group stood silent for a moment. Finally, Valos cleared his throat. "We are going to do it but we are going to do it our way," he said confidently. "I am not just strolling up and knocking on the front gate. We're going to do it the Shadow's way." The rogue then looked up and found the sun's position high in the sky. "We are going to do it at night. So what do you say we all get cleaned up? I want to talk to the brew crew. And we can start making our plans to smuggle ourselves into the city."

Erayllia reluctantly agreed and turned to escort the group into the farmhouse. However, instead of following, Valos turned to Sario and Amman. "I knew we were walking into something. But I didn't know what. I think it is safe to say neither of you expected to hear the term 'undead horde.'"

Amman attempted his best Ombraterran accent. "What do you do?" he asked.

After a smile and a wag of his finger, Valos said, "I say we have Cinder open you all up a portal and send you both home. This threat is... too big."

"Isn't that all the more reason for us to help?" Sario asked.

"I appreciate it. I do. But as they said, if we can get into the city, getting back out is not something I will be able to guarantee," the rogue stated.

"I have seen maps," Sario said. "Your big capital is flanked on one side by a large river. Correct?"

"Yeah, the old sewer system dumps into the river that runs alongside the eastern part of the city. Then it flows out into the sea. Why?"

Sario nodded. "Maybe. Maybe. I might have a way in..."

Chapter 49

From the private villa within the isle of Sorceria, the various representatives of The Eight left at odd intervals and scattered back to their respective towers, hoping not to be noticed by the collective of Necromangians, any of the Knights of the Imperial Circle, or even the dreaded lich Nalazar Catabaysi. The last thing any of them wanted to be accused of was colluding.

Tanairs Corvalonn had used an inter-island portal to leave the meeting, making sure not to cross any of the entrapping Necromangian barriers woven around the isle. Cedalia Ce'Mondere broke east. Aldor Mutaccio went to the west. Devinaya Baelannor was the most suspect, having to return to the tower directly controlled by Nalazar. But, her reputation and her ability to move about the island left her untouchable by any but the most senior members of the lich's coterie.

The last two members to leave the villa were Marius Vocazion and Cadwell Dinacioun. With the Vocazion tower positioned in the northeast corner of the isle and the Dinacioun's ophidian spire in the southwest, the two should have been walking in opposite directions. And yet, the lad with his rail-thin physique, wire-framed spectacles, and thinning hair did not hasten from the villa while the Vocazion master was locking the door behind him.

"Was there something else, Cadwell?" Marius asked.

The academic was flustered as he attempted to summon his courage. It was not a daily occurrence to be in the presence of a dynast patron, especially in such an intimate setting with just the two of them. The young magus bunched his hands in the material of his grass-green and copper-trimmed robes to try to alleviate the dampness in his palms. "Master Vocazion, I wanted to say thank you for including me in... the... the session."

Marius nodded. "Of course, lad," he said with his signature baritone voice. "Lad. Such a curious term. I suppose it is just the nature of age. Anyone younger than me is a 'lad.' Yet, you are hardly a child."

"Almost forty," he said.

"Hmmm..." Marius uttered. "All of you. Cedalia. Devinaya. Even my two oldest – Lucinda and Drennid – are hardly children. Yet I still want to call you 'lad.' But I don't want to diminish your contributions. Your idea for using the interdimensional space was genius."

"You honor me, Master."

Marius smiled and did his best to wave off such formality. He took a deep breath and heaved a great sigh. "I will admit I did not like your patron very much," he said with forthright honesty. "But what Nalazar did to him... no one deserves such a final fate."

Cadwell gave a small nod. "He rarely spoke positively of you as well. He believed your magic was all flash and spectacle."

"Given that I trade in lightning and fire... he is not exactly wrong," the mage replied. "Still, our magic is like a painting or a sculpture. It is an art you can see. And while you wouldn't want to touch it, the Vocazion magic is tangible."

"The polar opposite of ours I am afraid."

Marius waggled a cautious finger. "Do not discount the importance of your art, my boy. Gathering information is critical. It has never been made more apparent than our current situation. All the sneaking and subterfuge is how the Necromangians caught us unaware."

"And what do you think of Master Corvalonn's grand design?"

Marius gave a resigned sigh. "It is a plan. It is the best plan that we have. That is not me saying it is a *good* plan but it is the best we have. The problem is there are so many factors and contingencies we cannot anticipate. We don't know how the Arvateri boy king will respond to Tanairs opening a portal in his throne room. The citizens of Castratellus may not join the cause and leave us to our fate."

"But that would be foolish of them," Cadwell argued.

"Show me a king that hasn't done something foolish or catered to their own self-interest and I will show you a man who has not sat on the throne for more than a month."

Cadwell sneaked a slight snicker.

"More than one ruler has 'kicked the can down the road' so to speak. Better to sit back and watch the situation develop so you can make a more informed decision... and therefore look like a strategic genius.

"I don't know what will come of Sorceria when this is all said and done. I am afraid we might not survive this... or if Sorceria does... I and my fellow elders will not. And then it will be up to your generation to take up the mantles of patron and matron."

Cadwell gave a grumble.

Marius nodded. "Believe me, I know. I have seen it within my dynasty. My progeny are ambitious but your generation has it easy. No one wants to step up and take the mantle. We can see that in how Ce'Mondere is falling apart."

Cadwell nodded. "But, in our defense, it is not like any of the upper echelons is freely handing over the keys to the kingdom. How long has Master Baelannor been in power?"

Marius arched an eyebrow and conceded. "Still, not all of you. I have seen you, Cadwell. You work very hard getting out *The Heraldry*. You put in the work. And it is easy for others to sit back and criticize. It is a whole other monster when yours are the shoulders bearing the responsibility of a dynasty. I fear your generation may find these mantles thrust upon you. And then the whole of the kingdom will have their eyes set upon you. Are you ready for that responsibility, son?"

"I hope so," Cadwell said after a hard swallow.

"I hope so too," the mage replied.

"And I hope there is still an isle left for us to rule from."

"You and me both, son. You and me both."

Marius could sense an odd feeling radiating off of the young sage. There was something there, just under the surface, wanting to emerge. Marius thought back to the harsh tones, scowls, and sinister ambiance that followed Master Gaviel Dinacioun around. Something told the wizard that the Dinacioun patron was not one to heap praise upon his adepts or apprentices. Before the master could say anything, Cadwell nodded towards the distance.

Marius turned to watch a pair of Necromangian wizards walking amongst the isle's paved pathways. The duo was going about their day. They had a handful of their skeleton slaves moving spell components and magical resources from one of the nearby dynasties to the grand tower of Baelannor. The plundering was relentless.

"Master Vocazion, I have a concern."

The two continued to watch the Necromangians. Marius got the sense Cadwell was more comfortable looking off in the distance as he spoke instead of eyeing the master directly.

"This plan we are concocting. I can see where your dynasty fits in, what with all the fireballs and the lightning bolts. The Ce'Mondere and their demons make sense. Better to send a beast from the infernal realms against the undead foot soldiers. It completely makes sense to have agents from those dynasties manning the front lines of this… strike force we are creating."

Marius nodded, seeing the path that the adept was starting down. "And you are concerned the Dinaciouns will not be contributing as much?"

"I am," he said honestly. "We ply in acquiring information. Offensively, I have a few cantrips at best. I cannot stand beside you or Drennid."

The mage gestured at the former magnificence that was the now sundered isle of Sorceria. "No single dynasty achieved all of this. Even everything down below. Lord Xizzen Avernden might have been gifted the land parcel to create Incanterra but he did not achieve it all on his own. He achieved his dynasty by working together. That is what we all need to do now."

"I do not doubt your wisdom," the seer replied. "I believe in what you are saying. But what I am asking is… *can* the dynasties work together?"

Marius issued a low grumble. "I know. There are a lot of very headstrong personalities we will be juggling. And we don't have the venue or time to set aside to practice. I understand your fears. If I were in less of a leadership position, I might even say I share them. But at this point, we have no choice. The enemies are no longer at the gates. They are inside them. So, we all *have* to work together."

Marius and Cadwell stood, watching the pair of Necromangians laugh and talk as they went about their broad daylight looting.

"We all will have a role to play and in that, do not discount the power of information, lad. Your seers and magus within your dynasty, you all could be the lynchpin within this conflict if we learn to apply your strengths."

Cadwell glanced back toward the ophidian spire that was the Dinacioun tower. "Master Vocazion, you wouldn't be interested in being a patron for our dynasty, would you? We do have an opening."

The mage issued a heartfelt laugh. "I am a Vocazion by blood. But I appreciate your vote of confidence. Let's force out Nalazar and his ilk first. Then we can figure out the grand destiny of Sorceria's future."

Chapter 50

The Baelannor Tower on Sorceria was the tallest structure on the isle. Resembling the Sovereign game piece from the Scachi game from Castratellus, there was barely a corner on the isle from which a person could not see the structure's capping crown. So one might have found it odd that a trio of prisoners from the city below would be taken to the top floor instead of imprisoned in the bowels of the island.

That is unless you wanted to make a statement.

The three men were dressed in attire to signify their service to the house of the dead and their allegiance to Zaneger – the god of death. Strong and muscular, all three men were warriors masquerading in almost priestly vestments. With their black hoods and long tabards, the acolytes of their order were feared across the city. It was not them as much as who they represented. None wanted to see the coal-black wagons, their ebony steeds, or the agents of Zaneger outside their apartment, home, or estate.

These men and women prepared the bodies of the lost for their final journey, be it interning them in mausoleums, placing them in the good green earth, or consuming their bodies with a terribly flammable concoction known as Zaneger's Breath which reduced flesh and bone to ashes.

After the attack on the *domici dauthis* down in the city, the captured acolytes were the few living survivors of the assault. Languishing in chains, the trio was brought to Sorceria under the watchful eyes of a quartet of Knights of the Imperial Circle where they were then paraded once around the floating isle for show and then escorted to the top battlements of the dynast tower. Initially struggling futilely against the steel chains, the three froze as still as statues when Nalazar Catabaysi exited the shadows of the stairway below and floated out onto the battlements.

It was one thing to see the living skeletons, the flesh-covered ghouls, and the other undead horrors walking amongst the city streets and avenues. But it was a more saturating fear to be in such proximity to the monster controlling the abysmal horde. "Acolytes of Zaneger," the undead lich hissed with a voice that sounded like the blending of three tones. "My followers were not exaggerating when they said they had captured... *unique*... prisoners."

Nalazar approached the first of the three – a southern warrior from Mnama'tellus named Kabaka – who glared at the lich as he came closer. "Look at you," the undead master said. "I can feel the hate radiating off of you like a furnace. Tell me, warrior, why do you despise me so?"

"Your very existence is a mockery of my god, monster," the man spat back with his thick southland accent.

"My existence infuriates the gods?" Nalazar asked as his receding lips formed what might have been a smile. "And yet you know nothing about me."

"You are perverse. Evil. An abomination," Kabaka spat. "You have escaped Zaneger's blade and denied your natural place in the world beyond."

"Then why doesn't Zaneger come forth from his grand celestial temple and smite me himself?"

Kabaka glared at the lich from under his eyebrows. "That is *our* mission."

"It is curious," the lich said as he wove his way between the three assembled prisoners. "I understood the mythology of it all. You have the Creator and the Destroyer. Fair enough. Then you have the Mother in the middle. Nature I suppose you could call her. The Creator bonds with the Mother and makes Life. Hence the temples to Niverana. The Destroyer bonds with the Mother and creates Death. Hence, your god Zaneger – to whom you have pledged your loyalty. But does this mean the pantheon is closed forever?"

The lich continued to circle his prisoners, drumming a single finger against his pursed lips. "There is another force within the universe. There is the power of magic. And maybe the pantheon is waiting for someone to run the gauntlet, comprehend the grand mysteries, and then ascend to become the sixth member within their supernal abode."

"You think you are some sort of god?" one of the other acolytes – an Incanterran native named Davan – asked.

Nalazar swiveled. It could have been described as spinning on his heel if his feet were touching the ground. Instead, it was more of a floating pirouette. The bottom half of his robes billowed and swirled about his legs. He then swooped forward to close the gap between him and Davan.

With effortless ease, the lich wrapped his bony fingers around the death hunter's neck and hoisted Davan off of the tower's stone. The man clutched Nalazar's wrist and struggled to find his breath. "You think that I am not?" Nalazar asked. "How do you know this is just not the first phase of my ascension to godhood?"

Nalazar released his grip and Davan crumpled onto the cold stone of the Baelannor tower, struggling to find his breath. "We have seen your work down in the city," Vazrig, another Incanterran native, said. "No one as cruel as you are worthy of godhood. Unless you wanted to be the god of cruelty."

Nalazar swooped over to the third man to stare him in the eye and gauge his resolve. "You make your little comment in jest and yet, have you looked at the world? Cruelty is the only everlasting thing. And now I am as eternal as cruelty. So maybe that *should* be my title. And yet, cruelty is not something exclusive to me. The mother sends hurricanes to decimate the shorelines. Earthquakes. Hurricanes. Volcanos. Wildfires. Would you call her cruel for unleashing the fury of nature on the very people that pray to her?"

The death hunter simply glared back in silence. The lich reached out and planted his palm on Vazrig's forehead, clutching at his head with his bony thumb and sharp pinky digging into the man's temples. Dark energy began to pulse out of the lich's palm and sank into the man's skull.

Vazrig resisted for a fluttering. He tried with all of his might. But the pain was too excruciating. The screams that ripped past his teeth were both guttural and piercing. The waves of sound echoed out from the top of the tower. The two watched as their brother-in-arms was drained of his vitality. His essence was pulled out and absorbed into Nalazar's undead form. The lich's gray flesh became less desiccated. His features strained to return to his state before his transformation.

Inversely, the death hunter's body shriveled, blackened, and collapsed onto the cold tower with a sound that resembled the smattering of fallen leaves tossed against stones.

"You have been loyal to your death god, mortal?" the lich asked the still corpse. "Yet he allows a noble servant to be tortured so? Your gods are cruel to allow such pain."

"And yet, you continue to perpetuate it," Kabaka stated. "Doesn't that make you crueler than them?"

The lich was about to storm toward the Mnama'tellus native until Davan spoke up proudly. "Our reward comes at the end," he said. "He will seat us beside him when we pass. Our job will be escorting the souls of the departed and rejoining them with those who have gone before. To witness that reuniting is our reward. And what a reward it will be. Tell me, monster, does anyone wait for you in the afterlife?"

"Given my newfound immortality, it is a pointless question."

Davan nodded solemnly. "Then I feel sorry for you. I look forward to seeing my father again. My mother again. I look forward to meeting my grandparents and their grandparents. I look forward to learning about my line before me. It is a joy you will never know."

"Then why wait?" the lich asked.

Once more, the lich's hand shot forward. Once more, screams echoed out across the isle for all to hear. And once more, the blackened corpse of the fallen acolyte of Zaneger collapsed to the stone.

"You are a monster," Kabaka said.

"If you think so, you should wait. Wait until you see what happens to your brothers-in-arms. I am sure you heard the stories of the frightful beast that terrorized the Feast of Nas Malador. Soon enough, your kinsmen will become just like the one that killed so many. But unlike the beast accidentally raised by the foolish Baelannor wizard, I will have control over the blights I have intentionally created. My only question now is... do I settle for two or do I make it a trio?"

Down below, on the grounds of the estate partitioned for the Baelannor dynasty, Dragan Duskwood looked up toward the top of the grand tower. A third set of screams echoed across the courtyard. These were the loudest and the longest yet. The second-in-command turned to look into the sorrowful eyes of Demina Summerstone.

"He is not torturing them for information," the young adept said to her master. "This is out of pleasure. This is pure pleasure for him."

Dragan nodded gravely.

"We are going to have to speed up our plans," the second said. "But we still cannot be reckless. Trying to recruit the wrong person could be disastrous."

"If Nalazar would torture the agents of Zaneger this way," Demina asked, "what would he do to members of his cabal?"

"You and I both know the answer to that," Dragan said glumly. "So we better have a damn good plan..."

Chapter 51

The sun had dipped below the horizon, below the jagged vampire smile that was the Pyrewind Peaks. Soon, the two moons would rise into the night sky. The distant ringed planet in the farthest reaches would become visible within a carpeting of stars and the far-flung red nebula swirling in her cosmic dance. But before that visual artistry could reveal itself, the last fingers of daylight dragging along the fields outside the capital of Incanterra had to loose their grasp. In the twilight hour, out amongst the waving summer wheat, a magical hole began to form just above the ground. It grew outward like a swirling whirlpool, ringed with sparks resembling angry glowflies.

With the portal solidified, the collection of seven jumped from the northern plains of Incanterra to gently sloping hills outside of the walled capital. Swayna Snowsong had to orient herself after jumping through a portal that opened perpendicular to the ground but exited parallel to it. She held her hands out wide and tried her best to steady herself as if she were poised on a high wire. "Explain the necessity of that again?" she asked through a wave of vertigo.

Valos Ironblade pointed to the walls of Incanterra that were closer than most expected. "Twilight hour. Cinder's portal would stick out like a sore thumb. You want the watchers on the walls to come snooping?"

With the four Blades, the undead slayer, and the pair of shamans through, Cinder Fireborne collapsed the magical portal in on itself and the fiery glowfly sparks dissipated into nothingness. The collection hunkered down amongst the flowing grasses, hoping their full-length black cloaks would conceal them amongst the deepening shadows.

Thade Skystone took the briefest of heartbeats to stand up and look around. "Perfect location, Cind," he said with approval. "Great job. We are right where we need to be."

With so much magic coursing through the veins of the city, for Incanterra, there was no such thing as true darkness. Mage-light illuminated the crenelated battlements patrolled by the army. Even the outer walls of the city were cast in illumination. Then there was the light on the various buildings illuminating the architecture, the glow from within the various apartments, and the halos from the street lamps concealed behind the high walls. Despite the twilight hour, Incanterra could very much be seen.

And the same could be said for the floating isle of Sorceria.

"Tadorin's stones," Cavin Jurare whispered. Despite the dangers, the undead slayer rose from his crouch, disbelief etched on his features, as he looked at the grand capital of the kingdom looming in the distance. One by one, the others turned to join his gaze.

Sorceria sagged sundered.

While the floating isle still hovered fast over the capital, her bedrock had been cracked open like an egg. The isle hung in splintered chunks, appearing to be held together only through wispy, spiderweb-like tendrils of magic.

"What in the hells?" Cinder whispered.

The Malinsuli shamans – Sario and Amman – glanced at each other and then looked at their native counterparts. "I am guessing it is *not* supposed to look like that?" Amman asked while pointing a digit at the sundered isle.

With the Sorcerian shock beginning to subside, Valos made it a point to get his squad crouched back in amongst the summer wheat. He produced a spyglass from underneath his black cloak and began scanning what he could of the city. "It's all true," the rogue muttered before passing the spyglass over to Cinder. "Look at the north gate."

As the spyglass was passed back and forth, each member of the group saw the same thing. Living skeleton guards were manning posts where the Incanterran army once stood. "They are in the corner towers and on the battlements too," Cavin sighed.

"Did you note the magical shield sealing off the gateways?" Sway asked.

The Jurare warden grimaced. "Yes. It looks like abjuration shielding but that's not our magic."

Holding the spyglass, Sway watched intently. "I wonder what happens if one of us tries to push through it."

"You wake up naked a day later with a pair of Malinsuli grandmothers rubbing your feet," Cinder said. "And a Malinsuli *toko'mattu* wanting to cover you in leeches."

"*Taka'mattu*," Sario corrected. "But your pronunciation was really close. You are getting better."

"I don't remember the walls and the battlements being so illuminated," Valos said with a grumble and then turned to Sario. "You had a plan?"

"Possibly," the shaman nodded.

"That can't be a good sign," Amman said. He nodded in the direction of a cohort of skeletons emerging from the ensorcelled gate and marching up the Mercari road, which would take them dangerously close to their position.

The group began to retreat down the gently sloping hill, hoping to gain cover. "Detected the magical signature from the portal?" Cavin asked.

Cinder could only shrug.

"Ambershore," Thade said.

He gestured to the small fishing hamlet north of the hills and just down the slopes on the western border of the Blue River. Far different from the stone, brick, and mortar construction of the Incanterran capital, the small hamlet was made up of wooden homes and huts with thatched roofs. There was also a collection of wooden piers and shallow-bottom fishing boats. However, in the late hour of twilight, it was odd that no lights were emanating from the village. "It is a place to hide," Thade said.

"You know the people?" Cavin inquired.

"I know their product more than their people. They bring river fish and freshwater eels to the markets."

Moving quickly but not without compromising their stealth, the group hustled down into the hamlet and through the open gateway of the wooden palisade surrounding the dormant structures. As they entered the hamlet, there were still no signs of the local inhabitants. The windows were dark and all of the various homes were closed tight.

In the shadows of the town square, illuminated by the light of the two moons, Cavin unleashed his silver sword from its sheath. "Skeletons are simple to kill..." he advised, "...although simple doesn't always mean easy. They don't have defenses like vampires and, unlike ghouls, you don't turn into one if you get killed by them. But you can't treat it like regular combat. Slice a person's arm or leg off and they are done. Hack a skeleton's arm off, the arm becomes lifeless but they are going to keep coming. Pulverize the skull or separate it from the body. Do that and they will clack to the ground. So target the neckbones."

As the others were busy drawing their weapons, Sario was rooting about in the leather satchel on her hip. The shaman produced a small sprig of bamboo that was hollow but capped on both ends with candle wax. Fine crimson dust with a texture of powdered sugar burst from the broken sprig and swirled in a halo about Sario's face and around her snow-white hair.

The shaman then turned to the closest member of the menagerie, which happened to be Valos. She placed her hand on his chest, looked deep into his eyes, and said, "I love you. I believe in you. *Hanau'tahi*."

"I am flattered. Maybe a little curious, sure. But I don't think now is the best tim—"

"Repeat it," she whispered. "I love you. I believe in you. *Hanau'tahi*."

Valos looked around skeptically. "I love you? I believe in you? *Hanau'tahi*?"

Sario reached up and gave him a loving but deliberate slap on his cheek. "Look who is suddenly an Ombraterran *nonna* over here," Valos laughed.

"Sands are flowing," Amman urged.

"I love you. I believe in you. *Hanau'tahi*," Sario said, clutching his chin. "Repeat it... and mean it."

Her words soaked into Valos's soul and he nodded knowingly. "I love you. I believe in you. *Hanau'tahi*."

To each member of the group, Sario walked over and repeated the same phrase, making each of them repeat it after her. All the while, the flowing crimson dust continued to swirl about her, with tendrils and currents wafting through the air to connect with the other members as they said the words. With the magic dispensed, Sario tucked away the bamboo sheath and drew out her hand club to defend herself.

Cinder had cast more than her fair share of magical spells. She had been on the receiving end of more of the same. She knew the sensation of incantations and enchantments when she felt them. But the shaman's magic was different. As the magical energy unspooled, Cinder swore she could feel a tether to each member of their group. It was not as if she could hear them louder or touch them with more sensation. Instead, it was an awareness. She could feel a connection to them.

It was bonding to their minds, their hearts, and even their souls. She could just *feel* them. Without needing to be told, Cinder knew Thade was heading to the gate to keep an eye out for the encroaching skeletons. He was afraid the skeletal squad would break the horizon and come down over the hilltop, not satisfied with the fruitless inspection of where their dimensional portal once was.

Cinder could also sense Sway's anxiety which was counterbalanced by Cavin's assuredness. She had seen Sway deal with rough customers back in the capital but living skeletons were admittedly an unnerving thing. Valos was calm enough and there was a silent discussion between Sario and Amman about summoning reinforcements.

But it all changed when Thade's fears were realized. Silent save for the clacking of bones and the clattering of armor, the skeletons crested the hilltops and began descending towards the abandoned hamlet of Ambershore.

Chapter 52

Of the eight wizarding dynasties, in a vote by the common people, the least inviting and welcoming tower would belong to one particular dynasty. Certain people with phobias regarding snakes might eschew the ophidian spire of the Dinaciouns. With all of their illusions dispersed, others would certainly find the now-defunct tower of the Lu'Scions lifeless and boring. Some might find the size of the Baelannor tower ostentatious and with good reason. But with its obsidian black stone, intimidating sigils, and the frightening gargoyles perching along her sides, the Ce'Mondere tower bordered on the description of frightening. And given the known reputation of the warlocks summoning demons to do their bidding, the tower was the epitome of intimidation.

Positioned in the southeast corner between the Lu'Scions and the Corvalonns, the Ce'Mondere had a view of both Highstone Harbor to the south and a view of the Blue River running along the city's eastern border and the delta where the two bodies of water intermingled.

Having broken from the clandestine meeting of the patrons, Cedalia Ce'Mondere left behind the villa and was making her way to the dynast tower. She had with her a satchel of items and a collection of tomes in case she was stopped by a Necromangian or one of those insufferable Knights of the Imperial Circle. Much like the wizarding patrons the knights admired so much, the men had little respect for women wizards. While Cedalia knew her worth, she did not have the same level of protection a patron had to walk the isle, especially with the sun now having disappeared behind the Pyrewind Peaks. Cedalia knew how the male adepts and the apprentices looked at her. It was the same way she wished Tanaris Corvalonn would look at her. And the last thing she wanted was to stumble across a knight, inflated with a sense of self-importance and deciding to approach her with lecherous intent in the waning hours.

Thankfully, most of the isle was quiet in the twilight. One might even describe the mood as melancholy as if a blanket of resignation had settled in over the wizards. She strode through the gates of their estate with intent. The pair of animated stone gargoyles positioned on either side of the coal-black gates recognized their Ce'Mondere master. They refused to come to life and impede her progress in any way.

Through the richly stained double doors of the tower's main entrance, Cedalia was met with a variety of sounds. From one of the main salons, she could hear the arguing of her uncles. It was the same as it had been since the passing of the dynasty's patron and matron. Only now, with the threat of the Necromangians and their undead horde, decorum was less of a concern. Each was more than ready to pick the bones of the corpse and take over the dynasty. Cedalia felt it best not to involve herself. After all, if their plan succeeded, Cedalia anticipated harsh reprisals from Nalazar Catabaysi. Maybe it was best to let an adept ascend to the role of patron – if only for now. Then, when the undead eye fell upon their tower, he would be the first targeted.

Ascending one of the staircases, Cedalia heard whispers behind doors. Tears were being shed behind others. From one door she even heard moans of passion and ecstasy. It was probably a wizard with a house attendant or a resident maid. She doubted a belowsie could be smuggled up from the city. Still, she did not blame them. For all they knew, they could be dead tomorrow and their animated bodies integrated into the horde.

Up another flight of stairs and then another and then another, Cedalia arrived at the tower floor that included her private chambers, tucked away in a pocket of extra-dimensional space. Such enchantments gave the tall but narrow tower a considerable increase in square footage to accommodate the many members of the dynasty.

Before she entered the pocket dimension containing her chambers, Cedalia halted in the central hub of the floor. Unhooking her scepter from her belt, Cedalia began enacting the precise verbal commands, the somatic gestures, and the sprinkling of her ever-dwindling material components necessary for her summoning spell. In the center of the floor hub, a sickly pool of bioluminescent green ooze began to form and swell outward. After it finished bubbling and congealed together, the portal opened a gateway to the infernal realms.

A trusted servant of Cedalia emerged. Libydiss was a beautiful and shapely female demon standing seven feet tall. She had purple-pink skin, goat legs ending in cloven hooves, a long devilish tail, and horns protruding from her forehead. Large, black bat-like wings sprouted from behind her shoulder blades. She was dressed in demonic, chitin-forged armor scantily cladding her sensual form.

Turning to look at Cedalia with her solid white eyes radiating white flames, a genuine smile revealed her fanged ivory teeth. "Cedalia..." she hissed happily. "How may I be of service?"

"I need information," the warlock said.

Cedalia dispelled the summoning pool and retreated into her private chambers. Libydiss followed her obediently through a series of glyphs and magical barriers ensuring their privacy. Once in her chambers, Libydiss took a deep breath through her nostrils. "Are you sure information is all you want?"

Cedalia brought out a large, black tome and placed it on her reading desk aglow with mage-light. She opened the tome to a specific section adorned with artistic renderings and classifying information about the infamous infernal vaedaemon. "Oh, mistress..." Libydiss hissed. "What would you ever need such a blunt instrument for?"

"One of these things killed Arynaud. Patron Dacadus gave up his mind to wound the creature," Cedalia said. "Can it be controlled? If I summon this thing forth, how do I keep it from turning against me?"

"Vaedaemons are hatred personified in physical form," Libydiss said. "The only way one could be lured in is either with the promise of rampant destruction or..."

"Yes?" the warlock asked.

Libydiss turned and smiled. "The infernal realm is not so different from this one. Demons have a society. It is not too dissimilar to yours and we do talk. Thug'xilvi'machtan said that he found an open gateway and beyond was something from the Elysium. An Elysium essence within your plane of existence? Of course, he risked coming through for that."

"The hatred is that hot?"

Libydiss smiled once more. "Hate? Oh no. Do you know what happens to a demon if they can absorb the holy essence of a creature from the divine planes? It is... exciting."

"They become even more powerful? How powerful?"

"It depends on the essence. Thug'xilvi'machtan said he smelled an amorina. Small. Far inferior to a Nas. Lesser than a seraph. Too small to rival an animal spirit. But still. It is why we hunt them so. Not out of some silly hatred or bitter rivalry. No... it is because of the power they hold."

Cedalia pondered the possibilities. "And if I could get this vaedaemon a vial of amorina essence, would he obey my commands?"

"I suppose it depends on the commands."

"Chaos. Bedlam. Mayhem."

"They do specialize in that," the demon whispered. "I suspect it would take little cajoling."

Cedalia let her mind drift back to the experiments conducted alongside Tanairs where they combined the essences of demonic and holy forces as a new magical energy source. It was something she could not explain. It was his power. It was his control. His skills in his magical casting made it all too obvious how he had ascended to the rank of a patron. His voice was domineering without needing additional volume to make his point. He was stern yet kind... in his own way. It was clear through his instructions that he wanted success but he also wanted Cedalia to succeed as well.

She thought about his hands gripping his wand and the way he summoned forth his magic. His mind was curious and not deadlocked in tradition like so many of the other elder patrons. Tanairs Corvalonn was... different.

From behind her, Cedalia felt Libydiss draw close. The demon had noted the elevation of her temperature, the quickness in her breath, and the increase in her heart rate. Her hands began to slither over Cedalia's form.

The warlock closed her eyes for the briefest of moments but then shrugged the demon's hands off her shoulders. This drew a stern pout from Libydiss. "You could even think of him if you like…" she whispered.

Cedalia turned on her smartly.

"That will be all," the warlock said sternly.

Libydiss's white smoldering eyes narrowed and her features turned threatening just before her material form began to melt away in a swirling, smoky haze. "This transgression won't be forgotten," she hissed.

Left alone in her private chambers, Cedalia Ce'Mondere took a deep breath and tried to keep from rolling her eyes when she whispered to the walls.

"Demons…"

Chapter 53

As the skeletal squadron marched towards the small fishing hamlet of Ambershore, the most disconcerting feature – save for the dead bones brought to a state of unlife – was their precision. After leaving the gates of the Incanterran capital and while traversing the worn dirt pathway to the nearby fishing hamlet, the skeletons marched in lockstep with one another.

But it was not just the gait or the striking of their booted feet against the dirt. The swing of their arms, the sway of their shoulders, and the swivel of their hips were all in perfect consort. In their matching arms and armor, the skeletons were faultless replicas of one another. There was an unnatural uniformity and synchronicity among the force.

It was no more evident than the sounds of their hard-soled boots stomping up the pathway to Ambershore. The clanging of their armor, metal pauldrons clacking against shoulder blades and clavicles. The rattle of metal helms on exposed skulls. The jangle of chain mail. The clatter of longswords in sheaths on belts. It was almost musical the way the sounds wove together. One could almost imagine a figment drummer coordinating their movements with a silent timpani only the skeletons could hear.

The undead walked through the open gates of the wooden palisade surrounding the hamlet. Their red glowing gazes were locked forward and there was no reaction to the darkened huts, the quiet homes, and the complete lack of people within the walls. Simply following their issued orders, the skeletons marched with neither passion nor enthusiasm but also without fatigue or distraction. They were told to march to a certain location and so they did.

As such, they were not prepared for the ambush awaiting them.

In the darkening hour and with Incanterra so close, the last thing the attackers wanted to do was draw the attention of sentries on the high battlements, the parapets of the corner towers, or the potential eyes looking out from the elevated vantage point of a sundered Sorceria. In such deep shadows, the glow of a fireball or the flash of a lightning bolt would not just be visible but would attract attention.

As such, when Thade Skystone emerged from the darkness, he struck against the center of the marching column with silence and the enchantments of his twin handaxes unactivated. At the same time, Valos hit the opposite side of the column, slicing through the magical tendons that kept femurs attached to tibias.

Not to be outdone, the two Malinsuli shamans hit other sections of the columns with their tribal melee weapons. Obsidian blades and wooden cudgels made quick work of the skeletal monsters.

Those in the back of the column found themselves skewered from behind by twin short swords as Swayna Snowsong attacked with a speed and silence worthy of her surname. Beside her, Cinder Fireborne struck with her rapier aiming for vulnerable holes in the plate armor. Both knew that none of the skeletons would retreat in fear but this was yet another front along the column to attack and keep the forces of the living from being overwhelmed.

But for all the skill and ferocity with which the Blades and the shamans attacked, none could match the fierceness and the merciless violence of Cavin Jurare. The undead hunting warden was now in his element. Be it the slashes of his silver sword in his right hand or the tumbling and whirling strikes of his quarterstaff in his left, the warrior wizard fought with unbridled savagery. And yet, never once did he let out warcries or screams to strengthen his strikes. He was as cold and emotionless as the skeletons he was cutting down.

As one, the group continued to close ranks, fighting to destroy the skeletal columns but also fighting to get to one another. With Sario's shamanic magic coursing through their souls, there was no need for verbal communication. They could feel when one of their linked spirits was in trouble.

At the rear of the column, Sway and Cinder knew when to feint, pivot, and change targets, tumbling behind or over one another to attack the opposite skeleton. It left skeletal hands swinging swords that sliced only silence.

Valos would parry and drive a skeleton's sword high, leaving its midsection and spine vulnerable to Thade's axes. Valos did not need to call out or direct his attacks. Thade could feel his intent instinctually.

Sario and Amman fought as more than just cousins with years of experience adventuring with one another. They knew when to crash together and hit targets from both flanks with such perfect consort that any skeletal defense against one shaman left it vulnerable to the other.

Despite being vastly outnumbered, with every heartbeat, the squad of seven continued to tip the scales of balance in their favor. Never once did the skeletons show signs of fear or panic. Once the strikes began, they reacted calmly, drawing swords and defending themselves. Whoever had issued orders to the undead soldiers, self-preservation was an obvious caveat.

As more and more skeletons fell to the blades, it began to feel like an inevitability. With each skeletal soldier smashed into piles of lifeless bones, their usual tactics of overwhelming with superior numbers and fodder strategy became less and less possible. But somewhere amongst the column, a sudden dreadful sensation rippled out from one of the skeletons. As it stood amongst its bony brethren, its movements no longer held the same stiff and automated feel. Behind its emotionless mask, there was something about the way it was whipping its head back and forth.

Cavin recognized it. It was surveying the battleground but with eyes that possessed an azure glow instead of crimson. As more and more of the skeletal soldiers began to fall, the sentient skeleton deftly maneuvered to avoid the axes, the sword, the obsidian, the hardened wood, the rapier, and the twin short swords. All around it, more and more skeletons continued to fall. Cavin was even surprised when it pushed one of its skeletal brethren into the undead slayer's path, hoping to delay the inevitable.

Eventually, the single sentient skeleton was all that remained. Amidst the chaos, feeling Cavin's anguish, the group halted. The skeleton stood surrounded by the seven, looking at them with its glowing blue eyes. With fluid beauty and grace, the undead hunter's silver sword slashed skyward in succession. And with each strike, the skeleton's arms shattered at the shoulder socket and fell lifeless to the soil.

Being undead, the monster did not recoil in pain and barely noted the dismemberment. Rushing forward, Cavin clutched the skeletal foe by its vertebrae, holding it strongly in place. The undead hunter pulled the skeleton close so it could look into the glowing pinpricks of light within its hollow eye sockets. While the others could not understand the reason why this particular skeleton was disconcerting to the slayer, they all felt his concern.

"I see you," Cavin hissed.

The skeleton stared back emotionlessly save for the perpetual grin on its face. The monster struggled and strained against Cavin's grip but he was far too strong and vastly outweighed the monster, keeping it firmly in place.

"You think you are safe in that city, behind your shields? You have made it your prison. There's nowhere you can run. There's nowhere you can hide," Cavin warned. "I see you. And I'm coming for you."

With the crossguard of his silver sword planted against the skeleton's sternum, Cavin yanked with all his might on the neckbones he had clutched in his fist. The magical tendons keeping the skeleton knitted together in unlife gave way. The skull spilled backward and plopped onto the soil with a hollow thunk. A heartbeat later, the rest of the bones collapsed into a pile at Cavin's feet.

The six remained silent, watching as Cavin seethed. The slayer sheathed his silver sword. He ran his gloved fingers through his short-cropped hair and took a deep breath in through his nostrils. Coming out of what could only be described as an "anger trance," Cavin tried his best to let his natural smile return to his handsome features as he looked at his compatriots.

"I suppose an explanation is in order," he said.

"Please," Thade said.

"Yeah, even I am curious about this one," Amman added.

"Undead are... undead. Ghouls lurk in graveyards to eat corpses. If you stumble across one and they bite you, you become one. It's how they... reproduce. Skeletons are different. They have to be made. Animated.

"They make great sentries. They don't sleep. No water. No food. All they do is follow simple orders. So you put a pair of them in a treasure chamber and say, 'Kill anyone who comes in here.' A ghost is a lingering spirit. Skeletons are the opposite. They are just animated bones that retain the semblance of intelligence. They follow orders. They think but they can't think. They can't think for themselves."

"I dated a girl like that once," Valos said.

"But that last one, it changed. Its body language changed. It wasn't following orders. It was being controlled. And you could tell because the lights in its eyes changed. This is not an undead horde. I've seen zombies shamble in packs. They absorb others into the collective and that is how they grow. But this... this is different. This is not a horde. It's an *army*."

"So what controls an army of the undead?" Sario asked.

Cavin turned and looked at Cinder. Unlike with so many of their encounters, there were the tinder-smoking hints of fear threatening to swirl into Cavin's features. Cinder shook her head, her long red locks swirling about defiantly. "No," she said. "It's not possible."

"It's the *only* possibility," Cavin countered.

"What is the only possibility?" Sway asked.

Cavin folded his arms across his chest and looked at Cinder, silently daring her to say the word, forcing her to admit the truth to both herself and her brothers and sisters.

Finally, Cinder relented and nodded with solemnity.

"Necromancers."

Chapter 54

Having left behind the meeting of the wizard representatives, Marius Vocazion made his way down the twilight-lit stone pathways of Sorceria. With the recognizable rank of patron, the Necromangian adepts and the occasional Knight of the Imperial Circle were smart enough not to impede his progress. The mage simply squared his shoulders and walked with purpose towards his dynast tower located on the northeast corner of the isle. With such determined strides, the occasional pedestrians out in the late hour were quick to yield the unofficial right of way to the wizard master.

Through the gates of his estate, across the main walk bisecting the lawn, up the steps, and through the foyer doors of his tower, the wizard finally allowed himself to breathe easy once he was back within the friendly confines of his ancestral tower. However, the various halls, chambers, and parlors were uncharacteristically quiet. Even with half the dynasty trapped down in the city, there was a certain pall within the tower.

Up stairways, down passages, and through doors, Marius arrived at a storage area that would have been an armory if the wizards used steel weapons. Rather than racks of swords, daggers, polearms, and other melee weapons, it was shelves, cubbies, and trays filled with collections of the various components needed for the most powerful spells within the dynast's magical arsenal. Marius made his way lazily about the shelves, considering the possibilities and formulating his battle plan.

As he mulled amongst the components, he did not even hear his matron arrive. Arania Vocazion swept into the supply room. "I see you have returned from your meeting. What did the collective decide upon?"

"It wasn't like we conducted a blood ritual or spoke sacred oaths," Marius replied, "but I think it is safe to say a coordinated resistance has begun."

"The group is going to make a stand against Nalazar?" the matron asked. "That is suicide. We are better off biding our time. I hope you did not commit us to their foolish plan."

"So we can be the last lambs slaughtered?" Marius asked while assessing their amount of iron ferrite shavings.

"You would rather jump headfirst into the gaping maw of the dragon?" Arania asked.

"I would rather fight back instead of waiting to die. Thankfully, we are formulating a plan that I believe has a high probability of success."

"I am not going to die alongside a group of foolish martyrs," Arania said as she turned to leave.

"Yes... about that," Marius drawled.

The matron halted her exit and turned slowly to regard her patron. The wisened mage set down a hinged box filled with semiprecious stones that had been smoothed and polished. "I have volunteered your expertise as part of this... *mission*... being put together."

"And what is this role you have volunteered me for?" she asked, anger beginning to simmer under her tone.

"You will be escorting Tanaris Corvalonn. Well, more accurately, he is going to be escorting you. He will be masquerading as our man-at-arms. With the combined efforts of myself and the Ce'Mondere dynasty, we are going to smash through one of the half-gates. Then you and he will ride two of our crystal drakes through. Once outside of the city and away from the eyes of the enemy, Corvalonn will open a portal. You and he will travel to our neighboring kingdoms of Arvaterra and Castratellus where you are going to request the two kings to march the warpath to our capital."

"You are serious?" she scoffed. "I am *not* doing that."

"Very well, then I will go in your place. I figured you could use your beauty and your feminine wiles to entice the kings to action. I will just have to use the timeless art of diplomacy instead."

"Are you suggesting I seduce a child?" the matron questioned hotly.

"Yes, that's *exactly* what I am suggesting," Marius rejoined with a sarcastic roll of his eyes. "What I am saying is a patron and a matron arriving is likely to gain more attention of the courtiers in both Arvaterra and Castratellus. But if you don't want to go, you can fight alongside the demon the Ce'Mondere are summoning for this mission. You might want to bring some nose plugs for all the sulfur. And then you can enjoy being captured, tortured, and inevitably killed by Nalazar. But if you die from the torture, don't worry. Their magic can bring you back from the dead. Have fun with all that. In the meantime, I should pack my bags for my trip. Do you think Castratellus is hot this time of year what with their elevation and all?"

Arania patted the air with her hands and gave a rare submissive nod. Rather than yell or unleash her wand – as she would often do – the matron lowered her voice. "You saw what that monster did to the Jurare when they stood against him."

"I know," Marius whispered.

"If you are part of this... *mission* to get me and Corvalonn out of the city, he could conjure fire from pure *pherein* and rain it down on both our towers."

"Remember, Corvalonn will be in disguise," the patron corrected.

"So only *our* tower will be reduced to rubble? Is that supposed to make me feel better or worse?"

Marius ran his hands through his thinning hair and then rubbed his exhausted eyes. "We have to support this plan. We have to. The threat of Nalazar has left us with no choice."

"Why? Why can we not just ride this out?"

"Because if we do, there won't be a city left underneath us," Marius said, trying to tamp down his anger.

"Commoners," the matron replied with no emotion. "Replaceable commoners."

Marius turned sharply. "I was at the meeting. Representatives were there. Obviously, Jurare wasn't and Lu'Scion has left us in the lurch. But still, Baelannor, Corvalonn, Mutaccio, Ce'Mondere, and even Dinacioun are all contributing to this crusade. I will be damned if the Vocazion dynasty is the one wizard family sitting in the stands while the battle rages in the arena. This is important, Arania."

The matron stood stoically, unconvinced by her patron's words.

"If we are to unseat Nalazar and confront his magical power directly, it will take all of us," Marius explained.

Waves of anger began to silently emanate from the matron but Marius was not about to back down.

"I am committed to this which means we are *all* committed to this," the patron ordered. "You can make your choice. You can either lead the attack on the wall or you can travel with Corvalonn."

"Now you would stand up and be a patron?" Arania seethed. "Now you would command us all and you would be so presumptuous as to speak for me? For *me*?"

The wizardess mage let her hand drop to her magic wand hanging from the cloth sash around her waist. However, Marius turned.

Rather than pivoting sideways to present a smaller target, Marius presented his chest in full view, daring the matron to pull her wand. "You will not," he commanded, letting his hand drop toward his wand. "And if you do, there will be no pulling my spells."

Arania issued a mocking chuckle. "You would kill me over this dispute?"

"That depends on you," Marius countered. "Are you prepared to die over this dispute?"

For the longest time, a cold and pervasive silence lorded over the chamber. Usually, by now, Marius would have relented and cowered away like a mewling pup. But Arania could see there was something different simmering behind his eyes.

Marius spoke calmly and without a hint of fear in his voice. "If we don't take a stand against the Necromangians now… we are all going to end up within their army. I am not going to sit idly by while they convert the entirety of the population of our capital into more soldiers for their horde."

Reluctantly, Arania let her hand slowly retract from her wand. Marius nodded and relaxed his stance as well.

"Now is our best chance to contain this undead threat while it still resides within our walls," the patron said. "If it is allowed to escape, it will run roughshod over the free kingdoms. With every victory, they will only add to their marching army until it grows so large that nothing will be able to stand against it."

Arania let out a defeated sigh. "And is that the argument I am supposed to make in the Castratellan court? Is this my justification to the boy king?"

"Appealing to a person's self-interest – be it a commoner or a king – is often the easiest road to success," the patron replied.

"So when do I leave?"

Marius heaved a sigh of relief and gave her an approving nod, happy with the outcome of their discussion.

"Soon," he warned. "So I suggest gathering whatever components you believe you will need."

Chapter 55

With the sun long past the Pyrewind Peaks and night having fully enveloped the kingdom of Incanterra, Dragan Duskwood walked amongst the once smooth paved pathways of the sundered isle of Sorceria. The Necromangian walked alone, somberly surveying the once glorious isle. Despite his magical gifts and talents – forcibly kept hidden – he had never set foot on the wizardly isle before Nalazar Catabaysi had conquered it.

Still, he could imagine.

He could imagine the cracks healed as he mentally pulled the broken stretches of land back together. In his mind's eye, he could picture the flowers in full bloom, the shrubbery healthy and verdant, the fountains splashing and flowing, and the return of so many species of glowflies, seraphflies, and all the various types of birds nestling amongst the bushes and trees. He could imagine enjoying the calm serenity of the cooling summer air while strolling amongst the pathways. He imagined wizards promenading to and fro, debating magical theories or developing conduits to improve their various spells. And he could imagine walking amongst them, a fellow wizard tipping him a salute or a wizardess offering a polite curtsey. Perhaps in some strange alternate dimension, they would have treated him as a peer.

Instead, the banished Necromangian could feel the stares – imaginary or not – as he swore people were watching him from behind the security of their towers and their stained glass. Passing between the towers of the Ce'Mondere and Corvalonn dynasties, Dragan came to the southern tip of the isle. From his position, he could look down on the great city of Incanterra below and the now-dormant Highstone Harbor.

With the city street lamps all lit with mage-light, the Necromangian could admire the sheer precision of the districts. Everything was a perfect grid. The city was quartered. The quarters were divided into wards. The wards were divided by streets and avenues. The city radiated wizardly precision. And yet, looking at the southern quarters, things were wrong.

In the poorest of the Southwest wards, even with the nightly fog rolling in, there was a gloom about the streets. Down where the former Mutaccio factories once churned out magic potions, the Necromangians like Accursio Twotrees had taken up residence. They now mass-produced his skeletal soldiers from the bodies of the dead.

Meanwhile, in the Southeast District, armorers worked night and day to outfit the skeletons with helms, pauldrons, and chainmail armor. Leatherworkers and cobblers sewed boots and gloves. While certainly not necessary for his undead soldiers, Nalazar Catabaysi was intent on creating a uniformed army. All that came at a cost. Smoke billowed from the southern districts, swirling and melding with the fog. He swore in the poorer section, there was an odd green haze that swirled between the buildings, a runoff and residue from Twotree's boiling cauldrons.

"Master Duskwood?" a voice whispered behind him.

Dragan pivoted. He watched as Demina Summerstone melted out of the shadows. The red-haired wizard was not alone. With her was Zegan Goldheart. The Necromancer was unique amongst the cabal. He was known for being a loner, even in their secret society. The sides of his head were shaved to the scalp but he had an unkempt mane of hair that ran along the top of his head in a stripe. He rarely wore sleeves in his everyday attire, displaying the swirling tribal patterns that coated his arms from his wrists to his shoulders. Gold hoops adorned his earlobes and one nostril. He looked like he would be more at home on the deck of a pirate ship or unloading cargo on the docks than in a library studying magical theories and debating material components.

But despite his fearsome appearance, Zegan was always the first to smile; as it was with this encounter as he approached the second-in-command of the Necromangian cabal. "Demina," Dragan said with a nod. "Zegan, it is good to see you, as always."

"How you living, Dray?" Zegan asked with a familial tone. But before the former professor could answer, Zegan raised a hand to cut him off. "If I am curt, I apologize but only because I know the time is limited."

"I'm not certain what you mean?" Dragan offered.

"Master…" Demina began to whisper but Zegan cut her off as well.

"Yeah, that right there is exactly how you should play it. Deny, deny, deny. What you don't know is cutie patootie here filled me in down below. Now, look. I'm not mad. And I don't want your hackles up which is why I am not burying the important part here with a bunch of flouncy talk. I'm in. But you better be glad I am. You approach the wrong wizard… the wrong servant… the wrong man on the street… and all of us end up in a world of hurt."

"So how do we know who to trust?" Dragan asked.

"That's the question, ain't it?" Zegan responded. "But each one you bring in is another braid in the rope that is going to be used to hang us… after Nal tortures us to death, brings us back to life, heals us, and then tortures us some more. So whoever you try to recruit, you better be damn sure."

"Anyone else who you think might be sympathetic?" Demina asked.

The two watched as Zegan mentally ticked down the members of their cabal. "Nikkala? Maybe. And that is a hard maybe."

"Maybe we would be better off looking to recruit from outside," Dragan offered.

"Potentially but the natural inclination is to go after the wizard class," Zegan said.

"They are the group most capable of engaging his forces directly," Demina added.

Zegan waggled a finger. "The problem is, Nal has the lot of them under his rotting, blackened thumbs. And if the pressure gets too much, they would sell us down the river for leniency. I've heard horror stories down in the city of what our master is doing to the Baelannor dynasty. Do you think they would remain loyal to 'the cause' if Nal started torturing members of their dynasties? And besides, looking out for themselves is what the wizzers do best."

"So if we cannot rely on wizards of the isle as allies, who can we turn to?" Dragan asked.

"Yeah... about that," Demina said. "When I was interviewing victims close to the blight massacre during the Feast of Nas Malador, there were whispers."

Dragan rolled his eyes, "Not these urban legends again. The crime families that control the black market and the kingdoms under the kingdom? Those are tales told around campfires, like the yarns of old to scare children."

"Like the giant monsters in the sewers or the tales of undead lurking in the graveyards or flights of dragons that could burn out a city?" Zegan said with a grin curling up one side of his mouth. He gestured broadly at everything. "All those stories are true, boss. But the idea of a group of thieves banding together in a guild to fleece the city and making coins off peddling illegal spirits and spice and renting out flesh by the hour is too much?"

Dragan tried to counter the argument but reluctantly relented. "And how would we even make contact with these... organizations?"

"You don't," Zegan warned. "At least not directly. That's how they operate. They know someone who knows someone. So we would have to put out a request for an introduction."

"Can you do that?" the master asked. "I mean surely all these operations went further underground during the siege."

"Underground doesn't mean gone. If anything, if they are still operating, it just means they know how to not get caught. Remember, these groups – these families – they aren't the rowdy street toughs that you think they are. These criminals aren't just randomly doing crimes. They are organized.

"Still, I can try to reach out. I think I know a few people that might be connected. But the trick is we have to trade them something they would want. Thankfully, I have that covered already."

Demina snapped her fingers. "Your tunnel," she said.

The roughneck wizard nodded. "She runs all the way out to the city's graveyard and in his power grab, Nalazar failed to seal it."

"Are your mining skeletons still working on the tunnel?" Dragan asked.

"The tunnel is complete. They're still down there. Mainly just shoring it up and making it pretty at this point," Zegan replied.

"We have to get all of the undead out of that tunnel… but softly," Dragan warned. "If Nalazar decides to take over any of their bodies and see through their eyes, this whole operation would be unearthed."

Zegan waggled another finger. "Unearthed. Who said you stuffy professor types don't have a sense of humor?"

Dragan pondered the possibilities. "If worse came to worse, could the tunnel be utilized to smuggle someone out of the city?"

"Sure," Zegan replied. "If we can get them to the tunnel quietly enough."

The second-in-command nodded. "It's a start. At least with the three of us, it is a start. We should break up so as not to invite suspicion."

Zegan nodded but before he turned to leave, he held up a hand. "For the record, I didn't feel comfortable with the direction Nal was taking us. But I still believe in the magic. We deserve a place on this floating isle the same as The Eight. So, I am putting my faith in you, Dray. Don't let me down."

Dragan stood a little taller. "I am proud to have you with us, Zegan Goldheart. You have proven yourself worthy of your surname."

"Yeah, yeah," the wizard said with a flippant wave. "What the hells, huh? We are just taking on a deranged lich that can tap directly into the *pherein*. What could go wrong?"

As the wizard disappeared into the isle, Demina turned to Dragan. "So who is our next recruit?"

Chapter 56

In the dawn of a new day, the collection of seven began to stir from what might have been called sleep from the restless night before. Despite Thade Skystone's suggestion of opening a portal back to his aunt and uncle's farm in the northern end of the kingdom, the crew had decided to stay in Ambershore. If necromancers had commandeered the city, the last thing the rogue wizard wanted to do was give them an additional magical signature to detect.

With the fishing hamlet deserted, there was more than enough space and plenty of beds to be found. Whatever had happened to the residents of the small village occurred recently as linens were still clean, food lined the larders, and the accouterments for living from books, pipeweed, post letters from relatives, and toys were scattered about.

In the only two-story structure in the village, the crew had appropriated the top floor. They had pulled the heavy curtains and even added more cloth to conceal their presence before lighting candles and a few lamps. They ate rations, bread from a pantry, and anything else that did not require heat. The same as with their magical signature, the last thing they wanted was to have smoke leaking from a chimney even in the dead of night.

It was back to skulking in the shadows and moving with stealth between the buildings. Of all the seven, Valos Ironblade was the most in his element. On more than one occasion, he had to reel back his emotions. After all, the city was under siege by an army of undead. And yet… the rogue was almost enjoying himself as he was getting back into a life that he loved.

Valos was the first awake. He was the first out of the mayor's house. While the sun was still low on the horizon and the hamlet was cloaked in the shadows from the tall elms and pine trees growing along the Blue River's shoreline, he was the first to spy on the grand capital from the watchtower amongst the palisade. He heard the ladder creak and turned as Cinder Fireborne joined him on the elevated platform. He offered his sister his spyglass so she could see for herself.

"It is hard to tell from this distance. Well and the fact that all skeletons look the same. *And* the fact they have all their sentries wearing those matchy-matchy armor sets…" the rogue grumbled, "…but I bet those boys are the same ones that were there when we arrived last night."

"I would say you are probably right," she replied.

"I've got to give it to 'em. They make for some damn fine guards. No slipping off to make water. No need for sleep. And I am willing to bet no amount of coins would let us slip through or could be palmed to them so they look the other way."

"Traditional methods aren't going to cut it?"

"I am saying it is not fair. Human guards? I can deal with them. I can't work with this lot. They are no different than those sentinel armor suits the wizards use up on Sorceria. I don't like a game that prohibits me from cheating to win."

"So you are less concerned about the fact they are animating corpses and more concerned about their lack of respect for the game?" Cinder asked trying not to smile.

"We steal stuff. The coppers try to catch us. They put up walls. We find a way over them. They lock their doors. We make lockpicks. They put stuff in vaults. We crack their doors. It's a tale as old as time itself. 'Round and 'round we go. These bone strokers? They don't have honor."

Cinder shook her head and tried not to laugh.

"Any word from the boss?"

Cinder groaned. "I tried. I didn't leave the mirror connected too long just in case they have tendrils out there looking for a magical signature. His mirror is still in the city. As far as I can tell, it is in his apartment. But Gamble is not there to receive the magic."

"Don't mean he's dead," Valos said with a cluck of his tongue. "For all we know, Celesta ordered the family to the Gloom instead of us being out in the open. They could all be held up in the towers making sure we stay safe."

Cinder nodded and Valos continued looking through the spyglass. He saw the energy ripples of the magical shields cutting off the main and half gateways around the city. There were skeletal guards on duty and columns patrolling the tops of the crenelated walls. "Damn, they got that place more secure than a farmer guarding his daughter's silky milkies against the town's boys."

"That seems extremely specific for you to have made that up off the top of your head."

"I had a life before I met you…"

"Nevertheless, I reached out with some very soft detection spells. Not enough to be picked up by another wizard but enough. There is a dome over the city, so even if we could scale the wall, getting over the battlements is still an issue."

"Could we punch through a gate?" he asked.

"Not quietly. And not by myself. Offense is not Cavin's magical discipline. And even with the shaman, there is no way we could force our way in."

"Even if we did, everyone would know we were there. So the sword won't work and the coins won't work," Valos grumbled, referring back to their oath for their initiation into the family.

"So we have to use the dagger in the dark," Cinder nodded. "But how do we sneak past all of that? There has not been a single convoy, caravan, or supply wagon in or out of the city. So nothing we can piggyback on. And even if we went at night, we can't fly through the dome that tents the city."

"Thankfully, I've already got it figured out," Valos said with a cocksure grin.

"How we are getting in?"

"And I know where we are going to eat once we get there," he said as he moved toward the tower ladder.

"When exactly were you going to let me in on this grand master plan?" Cinder asked as Valos slid rakishly down the ladder.

"Where is the fun in telling you when I can show you?" he called back.

Together, the duo made their way through the narrow pathways between the buildings of the fishing hamlet until they arrived at the docks. Flat-bottom fishing boats were still lashed to the piers jutting out into the flowing river.

Standing in the shallows with the river water kissing her ankles, Sario stood silently. Her hands were extended and her eyes were closed. She swayed back and forth in rhythm to a song only she could hear. Slowly, she began kneading and stretching a sphere of magical energy in front of her until it reached a sufficient size. She then floated the sphere into the river where it sunk beneath the currents and held fast. The river water began to swirl into vortexes and eddies and then suddenly, a humanoid form began to emerge.

Cinder watched as she realized it was not a humanoid form emerging from the water. It was a humanoid form made from the river. The water elemental had a thick torso, bulky arms, and a squat head with twin lights that resembled eyes. It had no legs that Cinder could distinguish as its lower half remained connected to the river. Its hue was constantly shifting from a pale green to a colorless clear to a watery blue. But once fully formed, the elemental turned and regarded Sario curiously.

Even with its awkward body language, Cinder could see the creature recognized the shaman. It approached her with genuine joy like a dog separated from its master. It playfully splashed in the river and swam up to Sario, bounding back and forth.

The duo was too far away to hear what Sario said to the water elemental. But whatever she was asking, the creature was more than happy to oblige.

Just then, Amman was making his way down to the shoreline. The same as his cousin, the shaman was accompanied by an elemental of his own but his was comprised of what could only be described as living air. His elemental resembled a swirling torrent like an animated living dust devil or the smallest-scaled tornado in existence. The air elemental swirled out over the water and the two forces danced around each other in a curious display. Cinder swore the two elementals were acknowledging each other with respect.

Then Cinder saw Thade, Sway, and Cavin preparing one of the flat-bottom fishing boats for launch. It was not an overly large vessel but a sufficient size to accommodate their entire crew, provided they did not intend to do any fishing.

"Are you kidding me?" Cinder said.

Valos chuckled.

"How long have you been cooking this hare-brained scheme up?"

Valos clutched his chest melodramatically. "Hare-brained? I will have you know this is a stroke of genius."

"We are all going to *die*," Cinder said.

"Oh absolutely," Valos said with a grin. "But not today... and not because of this plan. This is the story you are going to tell you and Cavin's little *bambos* when you bounce them on your knee decades from now."

With a spring in his step, Valos sauntered towards the river bank.

Chapter 57

To those in the know, summer mornings in Incanterra were always special. Before the sun got too high in the sky and before the heat started baking the stone streets, if the wind was up and the mugginess was down, there was something about walking in the capital before the majority of the population was awake. Normally, the only competition was the early shopkeepers setting up for the morning rush. Café owners wanted to have the *coffea* drinks brewed. Bakers wanted their bread and pastries to have time to cool before being served. There would be very few pedestrians clogging the streets. The mage-light bathing the city would wink off after being touched by the rosy fingers of dawn. And if you walked the right areas, it almost felt like the muted city was yours alone. With her work down below, it was a magic time Kynna'Fyir Lu'Scion loved to take advantage of.

That was before the siege.

Now, the magician had traded her magical robes for commoner clothes. She wore a modest silken cloak with a full hood to try to keep her identity a secret. She even introduced herself now as Kynna Summerwind. Before, her work involved either sedating patients of the sanitariums in the Southwest or creating elaborate sensual illusions for the wealthy residents of the Northwest. Few citizens in the Northeast District would even remotely recognize the magician. So she blended in easily with the people of Shaded Light.

Despite her partnership with Mirawen Autumnlight and her new job helping to distribute Baelannor's conjured rations to the people of the ward, the illusionist wanted to do more. But casting spells of the mind were pointless against the mindless undead. Unwilling to accept her fate, like so many other mornings before, the secret wizardess walked the streets of the ward.

Once dawn had struck, the curfew imposed by Castellan Tallhill was lifted. Although in the current environment and with so many businesses shuttered, most citizens were content to remain in their homes. The isolation on the city streets was no longer restricted to the earliest morning hours. Still, the last thing the wizardess wanted to do was chance upon a Knight of the Imperial Circle. Given how Nalazar's newest enforcers were prone to hero worship of the wizarding class before the siege, she was nervous that a clever knight might recognize her even out of her wizardly attire.

Walking to clear her head, Kynna strolled up the length of First Street, the westernmost road in the ward. It was flanked by the enormous support columns holding up the King's High Way — the elevated thoroughfare bisecting the city and western border of the ward.

As such, Kynna was caught in a tight spot when a squad of Nalazar's living skeletons began approaching from the east. Having spotted them at a distance, the wizardess saw the skeletal columns were led by a pair of Imperial Knights. They were easily recognizable with their white vestments, conical hoods, and alabaster masks. Thankfully, she had spotted them before they had spotted her. Not wanting to risk being questioned and with her options limited, the wizardess retreated to use the buildings as cover and ducked into one of the few infrequent portals that ran underneath the King's High Way.

Hovering in the shadows of the Under Roads entrance, Kynna breathed a sigh of relief as the skeletons and their knights walked passed. "Maybe those masks actually helped me," she whispered to no one.

Before stepping out from the shadows and back out into the streets of the city, Kynna looked back at the vast stretch unofficially named the Under Roads. The area was not labeled as such on any city map. The constables refused to patrol under the High Ways. The various ward archons often repudiated such a location even existed. But the people knew.

The population knew the Under Roads were a no man's land failing to fall into any of the districts. It was the last refuge of the poor, the desperate, and the destitute. It was an combination of hastily hewed hovels, tent shelters, and ramshackle slums erected with whatever materials could be salvaged or stolen. It was also a lawless area ruled by its potentates through strength and steel. The Under Roads were no place for civilized citizens.

Kynna was more than prepared to view the unwashed masses hiding in the shadows of the Ways. But what she saw instead was genuinely more shocking.

The Under Roads had been swept clean.

The penniless population and all of their belongings had been cleansed from the hidden face of the city. From somewhere in the far distance, Kynna swore she detected the hint of sunflowers dancing through the air. The gloom was too much for her eyes to penetrate. Glancing about, the wizardess decided to risk a little more light. Producing a piece of faceted glass gifted to her by Mirawen, the wizard cast her portable mage-light across the hidden face of the shadowed area.

Sure enough, in the distance, there was a perfectly spherical ring left on the smoothly paved stone. Trained all her remembered life in the magical arts, she understood the markings.

It was a burned ring left by a portal to the elemental plane of fire. She knew the stories of the portals to the elemental plane underneath the Southwest District. She knew that was where all of the city's trash, garbage, and sewage were funneled. It was how Incanterra remained so clean.

Such a scouring was not surprising to the magician. If a portal had been opened, even briefly here in the Under Roads, it would not take long for a brigade of living skeletons to push everything into an all-consuming pit of fire. And for all she knew, the very people who lived in the Under Roads might have been the ones forced to cast their belongings into the portal.

The only question was if the population was made part of Nalazar's undead horde before or after the Under Roads were wiped clean.

As she was kneeling to inspect the perfect circle and the soot stains left behind, Kynna suddenly felt a tingle running up her spine and a distinct feeling she was no longer alone.

By the time she heard the scrape against the stone behind her, she knew it was already too late. Still, the magician spun. She was unarmed, not even a dagger on her hip. Stepping into the circle of mage-light provided by her faceted glass piece was an ominous figure.

The creature was no longer living. Its sallow skin was waxy and lifeless. Its irises glowed with an azure hue. However, the dead flesh still looked largely intact. Decay had not set in. Strips and hunks had not been torn away to show exposed bone. And it was even dressed in commoner clothes that were not stained by the grave. While a threat, the ghast was not threatening. It approached with a calm demeanor and eyed Kynna curiously.

"You are in a dangerous area," the beast said. Its voice was harsh and grating, the sound soaked with loose phlegm.

"It was once… before the siege," Kynna replied. "It is hard to label this a dangerous area when I am the only one here."

The creature looked at Kynna curiously. If the young wizardess did not know any better, she would have considered the expression as one of amusement.

"The others might not be able to detect it. Change your clothes all you like. I can still smell it on you," it said.

"Now if that isn't the dagger calling the sword sharp," Kynna quipped.

Half of the ghast's mouth curled into a smile.

"So, I am caught," she said.

"You are."

"And you know."

"I do."

"I guess the question now is can I blast your body to pieces before you can take me down or raise an alarm?"

The ghast looked down at his hands and noted the coal-black weapons at the ends of his fingers resembling claws more than fingernails. The creature then held up his hands and retracted the nails back into his skin.

"Is that to keep me from drawing my wand and blasting your body into a thousand pieces with a lightning bolt?" the magician bluffed.

"I thought it might help establish trust," the creature said.

Kynna eyed the ghast curiously. "Why do I get the impression I am not talking to this walking corpse?"

The ghast offered a very human shrug of its undead shoulders.

Kynna's eyes narrowed. "So you know I am a wizard. You know I am here. And I don't believe you are stalling me until one of your bone squads can arrive. You must want something. Or *need* something."

"I might be looking for someone who cares about the less fortunate and is not happy with the current state of affairs. Do you think that might be you?"

The wizardess's response traveled to the gray and lifeless ears of the ghast. But while the undead monster could not comprehend what was being said, through the magical channels, Kynna's response traveled up to Sorceria itself and deep into the private chamber inside the Baelannor dynasty.

There, wearing one of the Mutaccio-crafted crowns, the Necromangian listened to the response with unmatched clarity, as his consciousness was down in the Under Roads with the secretive wizardess.

And from her response, the wizard knew he had found an ally.

That made Dragan Duskwood smile.

Chapter 58

On the banks of the Blue River, the crew finished preparing the flat-bottom fishing vessel while the Malinsuli shamans continued with what could only be described as a wordless discussion with the water and air elemental summoned into the prime material plane of existence.

"So here is what I don't get," Valos said as he loaded a set of long steering poles into the boat. "We've been gone all of what? Three weeks and some coins? There is no damage to the outer walls. Aside from the wizzer island and the bone squads patrolling the battlements, the city looks the same as it did when we left."

"We haven't seen the southern half," Swayna commented. "Maybe that is where they attacked from?"

"Cav?" Thade asked. "March an undead army up from Highstone Harbor? It would be a good way to be right up against the gates before anyone knew you were under attack."

Cavin bobbed his head back and forth as he considered the strategy. "It would be an advantage," he admitted. "It is not like the skeletons need to breathe. But the sea is pretty unforgiving. How much of your forces are you losing just to the dangers of the seafloor? And it would be slow."

"So that means the only other option would have been to have taken the city from within," Sway postulated. "I mean… there were always rumors. There have been stories told for generations about monsters living in the sewers. Killer plants, giant lizards prowling the waters…"

"Homunculi dragging trash through the tunnel to the eternal burn pits," Thade added.

"Don't joke about that!" Valos spun sharply, waggling a finger. "That's not funny."

"What? The alligators in the sewers?" Sway asked.

"No! The homunculi," he said with an exasperated tone. "Little pixie versions of people. No way. I'd rather fight those lizard people from the sea than an army of pixie people."

"Well, isn't that an interesting piece of the mind puzzle that is Valos Ironblade?" Sway smiled.

With a grunt, Cavin loaded the last of their gear into the flat-bottom boat. Thade turned to acknowledge the undead slayer. "So, with these Necromancers… using the skeletons to guard the gates and patrol the walls. All that sort of stuff. What are we going to find when we get in there?"

Cavin gave a sharp exhale and cocked his head to the side. "Hard to tell. But I imagine it would be the same as any city under siege. A frightened populace. Probably a lot of hungry people. It just depends on what the occupiers want."

"Cind, could you open a portal to the western highlands?" Valos asked. "It could give us at least a slightly elevated view. It would let us look down on the city or see what kind of harbor activity we are looking at."

Cinder shook her head. "I *could* but that still puts us at risk of being detected. If these are Necromancers, they could be looking for any sort of magical signature. It would be like sparking a torch in a darkened arena. It would bring people looking. Right now, we have the element of surprise."

"Speaking of elements," Thade said, "won't they detect the magic of the elementals?"

"Amman explained it to me," Cavin interjected. "The Necros are probably looking for arcane magic. Getting the elementals here into the prime material takes a spark of shamanic magic. It's different from the arcane. But once they are here, they are here. So they don't radiate a detectable signature."

"Maybe that is the reason why Gamble isn't answering his mirror," Sway said, trying to put a hopeful tone in her voice. "Not wanting to give away his position."

"We are ready," Sario called out from the river bank.

The seven proceeded to climb into the riverboat while the elementals waited patiently. Once everyone was aboard and prepared, Thade and Valos used the long poles to propel them out into the deeper waters of the river.

The air elemental proceeded to shrink its form until it was as tight and as small as possible. Meanwhile, the water elemental waded out into the river itself and then disappeared under the gently running water. The flat-bottom boat rocked gently as the moving torrent of water took up position underneath.

Slowly, the elemental began to siphon water from the river itself to expand its physical form. The crew aboard the boat watched as tendrils of water began to swirl up around the sides of the vessel. The water stretched and ran upward in rivulets as if they were coating the outside of a giant glass sphere delicately cradling their boat. Finally, the flows of water began to connect, completing the sphere and encasing the boat and her crew.

With a sprinkling of rain, the air elemental swirled through the water wall and pulled its miniaturized tornado into the center of the water sphere. With the air elemental providing fresh, breathable air for the passengers, the water elemental began to take over.

Slowly, the oversized water bubble began to sink below the surface of the running river water. Gently, the boat and passengers began to descend deeper into the river, the elemental looking to scrape the air sphere against the silt and soil of the river bottom.

The crew looked around at the waters in wonder. Largemouth bass swam in opposite directions from the sphere. Schools of smaller fish darted to and fro. While the light was diffused through the water and the sphere was cast in shadow, the crew could always look up and see the increasing light of the new dawn. Not every member was wowed by the unique journey.

In the center of the riverboat, Sway dug her nails into the webbing between Thade's thumb and index finger. She looked about nervously and her breathing was coming in shallow gasps. From the top of the bubble, the air elemental descended and made it a point to send swirling caresses of air over Sway's hair. The billows were soft enough to calm her but present enough to blow back her blonde sunkissed hair.

"How did you?" Cavin asked Amman.

"We use a similar technique to fish back home," the shaman replied. "The water elementals just make... *holes* in the water. Fish drop in. It is an easy way to collect food for dinner. We've never tried anything of this scale before but I am going to call this a victory."

Freshwater crabs and other crawlers did their best to scuttle out of the way as the bubble continued its path down the river. The closer the ship got to the delta where the river met the sea, the deeper the waters became. The elemental continued to hug the river bottom and the deep shadows. Yet, when Sway continued to breathe sharply or if she clutched Thade's arm too tightly, he simply directed her line of sight up to the sunbeams just out of reach.

"If anything, the deep water shadows will keep us more concealed," Amman said with an approving nod.

The water elemental continued to move slowly, oftentimes letting the current of the water propel them along. On the western banks of the river, the large wooden and stone pillars of the city's river docks began to emerge from out of the greenish-blue depths.

Above them, the great docks cast more concealing shadows down into the water, further cloaking their presence from any watchful eyes. Finally, their destination began to emerge amongst the rocky foundations of Incanterra herself. Valos pointed at the large pipes jutting out from the outcropping of stone. "There," he whispered with a smile. "Back in the days before the Blue Death and the wizards cleaned up the city, there was the original sewer system. It wasn't great. Hence, you know, the Blue Death. But sections of the sewer flowed out of these pipes, into the delta, and then out to sea."

"Today the wizards funnel all the sewage into a permanent portal into the elemental plane of fire," Cavin said.

"And it wasn't like the city mainteneers were going to go in and rip out all the old sewer pipes," Valos replied with a nod. "All these pipes are so far below the current system, most people don't even know they are here."

Under direction from the shaman, the elemental tacked hard and began to approach the submerged sewer pipe. The crew held their breath as the bubble contracted slightly to fit within the pipe but thankfully, they were not met with any sort of magical barrier.

The theory had been proven. The necromancers had not sealed off the entire city. The water elemental took the riverboat deeper into the pipe until it disappeared within the shadows and the darkness beyond.

Chapter 59

In the light of the new day, Devinaya Baelannor went about her usual duties on the island of Sorceria. As a senior member within her dynasty's adept rankings, the wizardess was afforded a variety of tasks set for her house. She was a ground officer charged with making sure the dynasty kept up the levels of food conjuration needed to supply the city during the siege.

The task had not been easy. The entirety of the dynasty's apprentices were working down in the city's kitchens. They used their conjuration magic to summon forth the basic foodstuffs to keep the people fed. Some of the wizards were forced to tap into internal magical essence to bring forth the food for the people. Others were scrambling to create enchanted devices and instruments fueled by magical sources. Regardless of how it was done, the Baelannor dynasty was utilizing all of its critical resources to keep the citizenry fed.

There was always an issue with either a gemstone power source, the proper allocation of material components, or solving problems with the distribution network. Devinaya was one of the more hands-on problem solvers. And her fixes were often so quick and efficient that explaining the task to her chaperones took longer than the fixes. She could swap out a teardrop flame garnet for crystalized titanite, could add more hardened waxwood logs to the cauldron fires to get the temperature hot enough, or could reapply the soaksand moss quicker than explaining why the brown moss was better than the green variety.

Seeing Devinaya dart between tasks and solving so many problems, the majority of the Necromangians and the Knights of the Imperial Circle had learned to give length to her leash. Two weeks prior, one ambitious knight was asking too many questions and having Devinaya walk him through everything she was doing. The resulting delay in the daily rations proved almost catastrophic. The Necromangians knew better than to make the conjurer explain all of her actions, especially to a simpleton who did not cast magic himself.

She was granted leniency to keep the cogs of the machine moving. As a result, she was not stopped or searched when it was time to take a host of material components down into the heart of the city. Even if she had been searched, few would have found the dark black silk kerchief out of place or out of sorts. Like every other normal voyage down to the city, Devinaya boarded the enchanted sloop to take them below.

Their chaperone was one of the lesser-ranking Knights of the Imperial Circle. He wore the ivory vestment, the conical hood, and the alabaster mask. His garments did not sport the flashy accouterments many of his higher-ranking seniors possessed. But from his sharp movements and his attentive presence, he was eager to please his masters and kept a sharp eye on everyone. Unfortunately, he was also young, inexperienced, and not keen on what exactly to look out for.

Precisely on schedule, the boat dropped from Sorceria and made the steady descent to the Northeast District. Devinaya did her best to look calm and relaxed. She took several deep breaths while trying not to draw too much attention to herself.

However, as the ship passed through the permeable magical membrane surrounding the floating isle, Devinaya exhaled a subtle sigh of relief. She could feel the prickling washing over her skin as the sloop took them below. If anything was going to go wrong, it would have happened as the boat pushed through.

Like every other morning, the distributors waited below. They would take the material components and make sure they were distributed where they needed to go within the city. They waited patiently for the boat to arrive and were quick to offer hands to see the cargo off-loaded once the sloop touched down in the ward's central square.

Amongst the distributors and the offloaders, there was a tall girl of Monterran heritage. She had alabaster skin and golden hair braided into pigtails worn high on her head. Her attire could have made her a scullery maid. She could have easily been a tip-earning serving wench had taverns in Incanterra been allowed to sell spirits. Regardless of her profession, her attire was not something worn to the temples, unless involved in the passionate rituals that honored Niverana – the goddess of life and birth. Her skirt was too short. Her bodice was a size too small. And her bosom was so ample it looked as if one soft sneeze would spill her out of it.

The young Knight of the Imperial Circle was very much a man and as such easily distracted by the deepened crevasse nestled between those ivory mounds. As such, his eye once drawn could scarcely look away.

"Oy, knightie," the wench said. "Th' well on th' south lawn has gone dry 'gain. Can your fancy wizzer take a look?"

The knight turned and regarded Devinaya who was patiently waiting to be permitted to leave the sloop. The knight gave a nod. "Be quick about it."

While the conjuror made her way down the gangplank, the wench pinched the hems of her short skirt, flared out the material, and offered a deep curtsey that took her down almost to her knees. "Thank ya, Lord Knight," the lass offered with a smile and a batting of her long eyelashes.

The knight was so distracted he did not notice Drennid Vocazion escorting Devinaya Baelannor to the malfunctioning cobblestone well. Before the sloop's arrival, he had offered her a handful of silvers to ask the knight for help and keep the lad's attention. Then the fugitive mage specifically positioned himself behind the buxom beauty, ensuring he would be perfectly invisible.

Once there was enough distance from the sloop and what should have been the watchful eye of the knight, Devinaya slipped her hand into the inner pocket of her purple and gold-trimmed robe. She pulled the black kerchief out and passed it deftly to the waiting hand of Drennid.

"Sand's almost out of the hourglass," she whispered.

"Then let's not let the clocktower bells toll," he said with a wink as he tucked the kerchief into the pocket of his breeches.

Devinaya walked around the well while she drew out her magic wand. With a large demonstration, the wizardess began casting her conjuration magic. The same as the trim on her robes, Baelannor's magic was tinted with sparkles of glittering gold. The swirling torrent shot skyward and then plunged into the well with a flourish. The spell was teeming with showmanship so if the knight's view could be pulled from Jesca's chasm of cleavage, he would be looking at the conjuration spell and not Drennid Vocazion headed towards a nearby alley without carrying any of the stores to be distributed.

Once off the main streets and having ducked down into one of the narrow alleys crisscrossing the ward, Drennid found a large enough space for his needs. Producing the kerchief, he proceeded to unfold it more times than was physically possible.

By the time he was done, the small square of material had unfolded into a six-foot by six-foot square. Laying flat on the smoothly paved alleyway stone, the magic began to transform the material. The pocket dimension located within was opened.

In a burst, Tanairs Corvalonn, Cedalia Ce'Mondere, Marius Vocazion, and Arania Vocazion jumped from the pocket dimension. In keeping with their narrative, Corvalonn was dressed in traveling clothes instead of his typical robes. His attire was accented with the blue and black colors of the Vocazion dynasty. He subtly matched with Arania Vocazion. Rather than wearing the billowing wizardly robes like her patron, she was attired in blue and black-trimmed traveling clothes. Cedalia was also dressed in attire to match Drennid's commoner disguise.

Inside the extra-dimensional square, there were traveling supplies, food, and even a pair of full beds outfitted with luxurious covers and sheets.

With the wizards extracted out into the alley, Drennid began pulling up the corners of the kerchief. The traveling supplies remained within the pocket dimension as the mage closed up the portal. Once again, the wizard folded the material in on itself over and over again until the kerchief was little more than a pocket square.

The mage gave a nod to Tanairs Corvalonn and passed the kerchief over. The sorcerer tucked the square into his inner pocket. Drennid then turned to his patron and matron. "Masters," he said. "I am glad to see that you all have survived the siege."

"It is good to see you too," Marius replied.

"You have things arranged as we instructed?" Arania asked.

"Of course," the adept replied. "Except I wasn't able to secure a carriage as you all asked. Truth be told, such a conveyance would attract unwanted attention. But I have surveyed the best route to keep us away from prying eyes that might ask questions."

"How far is it?" Arania asked.

"Not far at all. I assume you all have everything you need?"

"We do," Tanairs replied.

"And you are sure you will have sufficient magic to disrupt the shield around the gate?" the mage asked.

"If not, this will be a very short escape attempt," Cedalia said.

Her comment drew several scowls and she deftly tried to pirouette her way out of the situation. Producing a small vial in one hand and holding her summoning scepter in the other, the warlock gave a reassuring smile. "I have all the strength we are going to need."

"Let's hope so," Drennid said as he led the group of wizards down the shadowed alleyway. "If you all will follow me, I'll take you to the half-gate."

Chapter 60

The Southwest District of Incanterra was no stranger to the dingier and dirtier aspects of city life. As one of the most densely populated sections within the city, it was also home to those of the lowest income. Without the monetary clout to influence the city archons, they were not able to structure their wards to keep out the less desirable aspects needed to make such a large city work.

There was a reason why the magical incinerator disposing of the city's waste, garbage, and trash was located in the subterranean levels of the Southwest District. The local archons tried to spin the incinerator as a feature. In the winter, snow never collected on the city streets or sidewalks that the magical apparatus was situated underneath.

While the Northeast District sold and the Southeast District shipped, the Southwest was where the goods were made. Some wards constantly sang with the sound of hammers banging on anvils. All of the city's slaughterhouses were located in the far southwest corner of the district. Many of the city's detention facilities and sanitariums were housed in the Southwest.

It was also the district with the largest real estate holdings of the Mutaccios. It was where the dynasty manufactured almost all of their potions. So the various wards were no strangers to noxious odors and dangerous run-off. The wizards always claimed the waste was disposed of with the ward's safety in mind. These brewing houses were the first civilian targets to be commandeered by the Necromangians.

Easily retrofitted to serve as stations to generate their skeletal army, the Necromangians were processing as many new skeletons as they could manage. The fires under their cauldrons were stoked night and day, day and night. Previously done on small scales – like within the hidden laboratory of one of the city's taxidermy shops – the necromantic pollution was never much of an issue. It was on such a small scale, the citizens of the ward never noticed.

But now, areas closest to the stations felt coated in a greasy green residue that clung to everything. Mixed with and spread about by the city's nightly fog, the buildings, the mage-light streetlamps, and window panes dripped with the thinnest layers of olive-colored slime. Many of the citizens in the Southwest District tried their best to retreat from the confusion and the chaos inundating the ward.

For most, the undead forces of Nalazar Catabaysi were the fuel of nightmares. Armed and armored living skeletons patrolled the streets with only pinpricks of red lights in their shadowed eye sockets and perpetual grins etched on their faces.

The ghasts were even worse. The creatures were more animated corpses with sallow flesh and muscle still attached to the bone. Yet, a ghast was not mindless like a shambling zombie. The terrors possessed sparks of intelligence. They were driven by purpose over instinct. Some could even emote when under the mind control of the Necromangians up on Sorceria.

And yet, as the living dead patrolled the streets and manned the walls, there was a certain reassurance from their lack of emotions. The skeletal warriors operated without passion or prejudice. They were simple tools used to fulfill the orders of their masters.

What was far more terrifying were the flesh and blood men that conducted themselves under the white conical hoods and the alabaster masks. The infamous Knights of the Imperial Circle had quickly elevated from a fictional threat whispered about as the villains of campfire stories to a very real force of malevolence within the city.

While the undead were the foot soldiers and the Knights their lower-ranking commanders, the true leaders of the lich's forces were his Necromangians. To see one of the red-robed wizards walking the street was a rarity but when such a sparse sighting took place, citizens made it a point to cross the street.

Like so many of the Southwest citizens, Novva Mutaccio covered her mouth and nose with a fitted cloth to keep from breathing the noxious fumes directly. Without being dressed in the scarlet and silver trappings of her wizard house and not displaying a prominent wizardly instrument, Novva was just another worker helping the Necromangians to carry out their plans.

While mingling with the commoners, Novva Mutaccio was able to hear the grumbles and the whispers. Almost all were laced with simmering anger for the members of The Eight that allowed this magical incursion to occur. So, while walking amongst the citizens down in the Southwest District, the young alchemist made it a point to keep her hood up and her cloak around her – despite the summer heat – to keep her identity as concealed as possible.

It was the same on this day as the young wizard was making her way to one of the many alchemical stations commandeered by the Necromangians. She was fully prepared to spend her day processing whatever remains were brought in by the skeletons. She would prime their corpses and help transform them into more bone soldiers.

The young but talented alchemist had been working closely with Accursio Twotrees. The Monterran wizard was tall, handsome, and surprisingly comical despite the surroundings and his task laid down by Nalazar Catabaysi. Still, Novva had sensed something off about her new superior and she sensed it was from the pressure being placed upon him by the Necromangian forces stationed up on Sorceria.

As she was entering one of the alchemical stations, Novva noted one of the feared Knights of the Imperial Circle leaving. He had the same conical hood and alabaster mask as his other knights but there was an expense to his priestly vestments along with epaulets and golden braids declaring his superior rank. But as Novva was not outfitted with any wizardly raiment, the knight passed her by without an acknowledgment or a second glance.

Walking up the staircase to the roof-level office that allowed Accursio to view the majority of the production floor, Novva knocked politely and entered. Seeing no one else was in the office save for the Necromangian, Novva granted herself a certain level of familiarity. "Curse?"

"Good morning," the wizard said but his tone was the polar opposite of his words.

"There looked to be a pretty high to-do Circle Knight walking out of here."

"Indeed. It is not every day when you are visited by the Supreme General of the Knights of the Imperial Circle," the Necromangian said.

He nodded towards a modest wooden crate sitting upon his desk. The richly stained container featured a hinged lid with several securing pins. "I was hoping that Dragan could find a way to divert Nalazar from this course of action but apparently not."

"What is in the crate?"

"It is the material components for the master's latest spell casting. It is some newly unearthed piece of arcana from the forbidden chambers up on your island."

"From the Cellarium Vaults?" Novva asked.

"You know them?"

"Every wizard knows them. It is where we house the worst creations of magic so they will not be a blight upon the kingdoms."

Accursio passed over the journal outlined with notations from the lich himself. Novva quickly scanned through the outlines of the spell and reacted with appropriate horror. "He wants you to cast this spell?"

"Thankfully, no. Have you ever heard the term '*subtes*'?"

"I can't say that I have."

"It is an antiquated title of respect from the old tongue. Nowadays, many of the chefs who would be called a *subtes* are often called Second. They are the chefs that prepare everything and get the kitchen ready so the master chef can come in and cook."

"So like an assistant?"

"Yes and no. They are chefs in their own right. But they serve under a talented master."

"So Nalazar wants you to be his Second?"

"Yes and thank goodness for it. There is a reason why this kind of magic is outlawed. To complete the spell, I am afraid that the amount of power necessary would mean tapping into the *pherein*. And I fear that would kill me."

"But Nalazar doesn't have those constraints?" Novva asked, halfway between a question and a statement.

"You can't kill or corrupt flesh that is already dead," the Necromangian said.

"So what did you tell the… the knight… person," Novva asked, "The knight commander? The leader leaving out of here. What did you tell him?"

"I told him I would do as my master commanded me to," Accursio said.

"But how do you feel about it?"

The Necromangian shook his head. "This is a bad idea. This is not going to end well."

"So don't do it," the alchemist said. "Just tell him no."

"You don't understand. You don't tell Master Catabaysi no. I would rather risk unleashing a monster on the city than risk the wrath of disappointing my house's leader."

"Have you considered… you know… sabotaging the casting?"

Accursio winced at the thought. "That is not an option and getting something wrong could result in fierce reprisals. Fierce. Fierce reprisals."

"You think he would kill you if you got something wrong?"

"I think he would. But what this will unleash…" Accursio's voice trailed off. He shook his head and snapped back to reality. "So, I will give you the option. You can walk away now."

Novva nodded reluctantly and began unpacking the various material components within the crate.

Chapter 61

With only the slightest splashing sounds, the flat-bottom riverboat emerged up into the subterranean sewer cistern long left abandoned in Incanterra's underbelly.

Risking the softest of mage-light, Cinder Fireborne held out her piece of faceted glass to give the crew some form of illumination. All around them, there was a network of interconnected waterways and passages made from traditional bricking. The neglected network was silent and empty.

"Welcome to the grand capital of Incanterra," Valos said with a popping slap on Amman's shoulder.

The Malinsuli shaman looked up at the various brick archways and the long, dark tunnels stretching out into the endless shadows. "I love what you all have done with the place," Amman said with a nod. "Yes, this is far superior to our beaches and jungles."

The flat-bottom boat kissed the side of the brick walkway. Thade was the first to hop out and helped everyone onto the landing. With everyone safe, the two shamans turned to their respective air and water elementals. There was a series of exchanges that might have amounted to some form of verbal communication in some far-distant dimension.

Reluctantly, like two scorned canines, the elementals looked genuinely disappointed as they slowly began to dissolve away into nothingness. As they returned to their respective elemental planes of water and air, the natural elements constituting their forms while in the prime material were no longer animated. The winds of the air elemental dispersed into the surrounding tunnels and the fluids of the water elemental collapsed back into the cistern. "It is a fascinating art that you have," Cavin Jurare said to Sario.

"The tunnels, the elementals, a few more of these boats..." Valos inquired. "Could this be a way to smuggle people out of the city?"

"How many are you talking about smuggling?" Amman asked.

"City has... what... four hundred... thousand? Like four hundred thousand people," the rogue replied. "Give or take a few."

"It was hard enough for us to navigate a boat of seven through those pipes," Sario said. "I mean... we could probably do it. It just might take a few decades."

"Not exactly an express solution," he grinned.

"So do we just leave the boat here?" Thade asked.

"You want to take it with us?" Sway retorted.

"No, I don't want to take it with us," the big man hissed hotly. "But it is like leaving a smashed window. People will see it and know we broke in."

"I don't think this area is actively patrolled," Valos replied while inspecting the ancient deposits of nitrate caking the brick walls. "Don't get me wrong, Thade. I am all for covering our tracks. Scuttling the boat is the smarter play. But I think it is better to keep it here in case we need to use it again. I think the odds are better that we will need the boat as a getaway than some random patrol discovering it in a part of the city that has been forgotten."

"That's a good point," Thade said, with a slight dejection in his voice.

"Still top-notch thinking though," Valos said while offering him a pat on the back.

"So now, where do we go from here?" Cinder asked.

Valos continued with his inspection of the architecture. "Given the way the Blue bends around the city, we have to still be in the Southeast District."

"Is that good or bad?" Sario asked.

"It's not..." Valos began and then course corrected. "The city has two major thoroughfares running through it. It divides the city into four districts. The Southeast is not so bad. We know a few of the lords that control the streets. They call themselves the Diamond Order."

"They aren't all great," Sway interjected.

Valos nodded his agreement. "Still, if this is a siege and the necromancers are throwing up walls to keep people in, it makes sense that they would keep the four districts divided too."

"It's what I would do," Thade nodded.

"And they would shield them with the big thoroughfares?" Amman asked.

Valos pointed a finger. "He gets it. So if we made our way straight up right now, we will be in territory controlled by the Diamond Order. That's no good. I want us in an area controlled by the Blades."

"Your people?" Sario asked.

"The best people," Valos smiled.

"So how do we get to Blade territory?" Cavin asked.

Again, Valos looked around. There were no discerning signposts or waymarkers amongst the various tunnels. "We keep it simple. We just head north and maybe slide a little west."

"You are navigating by the stars or the position of the sun?" Sway asked sarcastically while gesturing at the shadows.

Valos tapped the side of his nose and issued a confident smile. "He knows where I need to go."

"He *nose*," Cinder said. "Oh, you are a clever one. When we get out of this, you should really be writing comedic articles for *The Heraldry*. Give up this whole thieving thing. Why deprive the kingdom of your droll wit?"

"He could get a woman. A widower with a couple of ready-made kids," Thade said. "Become a real family man. Go legit."

"And leave you all with all the fun?" Valos replied.

The rogue spun on his heel and proceeded to make his way in a direction the others just assumed was north. The other six followed Valos's lead and began to creep their way through the abandoned sewer tunnels.

"So each of these districts," Sario asked Cinder as they skulked through the shadows, "they each have a 'family' as you like to call it?"

"Yes..." Cinder replied. "...and no. Sort of. The Southeast is controlled by the Diamond Order. The Northwest is controlled by the Crown. The Southwest is a tad unorthodox. It feels like its leadership changes regularly. For now, it is controlled by a group called the Skull Duggers."

"And the Northeast is your district?"

"Technically, our family controls two-thirds of the wards – smaller areas within the district. But one-third is controlled by The Crimson Way."

"I assume there is a story behind all of that?"

"Part of the family legacy. The leader of the family disappeared under some strange circumstances."

"That's terrible," the shaman replied.

"It happens within the guilds more often than anyone will admit," Cinder said. "Still, at the time, the heir apparent was the father's daughter. But the second-in-command of the dynasty who served as the father's hand felt he was deserving of the mantle of leadership."

"And the two could not reconcile?"

"Unfortunately not and the tension was getting out of hand. There was a fight for power. It wasn't pretty. So the guild split. Two-thirds went with Celesta – the daughter – and one-third went with Spyritus."

"The second-in-command."

"Exactly," Cinder nodded. "And to keep the peace, the heads of the other families decided to divide the district. They couldn't have a territorial war. Blood in the streets would bring too much attention from the authorities and hurt all of their business."

"It sounds like they need more mothers in their lives," the shaman replied. "Make them all sit down and talk to one another, figure out a solution that works for all of them."

"Not a lot of them want to take orders from a woman," Cinder whispered. "That was one of the biggest rifts with the family."

"So, did they ever find out what happened to the father?" the shaman asked.

"No one knows. At least not officially. But I have my theories. And I think it had something to do with his secret dealings with the wizard class," Cinder admitted. "It was these theories that got me an introduction to Celesta Darksteel."

"The daughter."

"Technically now… the mother. She is the *caput* of the Shadow Blades."

"*Caput*? I don't know this word."

"It's Ombraterran," Sway said from behind the two. "The old mother tongue. It doesn't have a direct translation. Depends on your dialect. 'Leader' is not quite a one-to-one translation. Too formal. You know? It means… Valos what does it mean?"

"The boss," the Ombraterran called from the front of the line.

"*Da'ranga*?" Sario asked Amman.

"*Da'ranga*," he nodded at the Malinsuli title.

"The problem now is that we have no idea what condition the city is in," Valos said. "We don't know who is alive. We don't know who is dead. The rules could be thrown out the window for all we know. Hells, there might be so few Blades left, Cinder might be the default *caput*."

"Perish *that* thought," Cinder said.

"What you don't want to be the leader of a band of gutter-dwelling vulgarians?" Valos asked with a chuckle.

"We are much nicer than the picture he paints," Sway said with a smile toward Sario.

Chapter 62

In the shadows of the Northeast District's alleyways, Drennid Vocazion led the foursome of fugitive wizards through the elaborate grid of the city. Tanairs Corvalonn stayed close to the young mage, carefully observing the surroundings with a hawk-like gaze. The elder's face twisted into a scowl every time they paused before safely navigating an intersection.

Cedalia Ce'Mondere stayed close behind the sorcerer. She kept her trademark scepter clutched tightly in her hand and had a specific sequence of material components at the ready. If the danger drew too close, the warlock would not hesitate to summon her faithful succubus Libydiss to her side. But for now, she was reserving her strength for the even greater summoning ahead.

The patron and matron duo of Marius and Arania Vocazion brought up the rear. The mages had concealed their wizardly attire under brown cloaks but wands were at the ready. A well-placed lightning bolt or a blast of fire would easily strike down any foe encountered on the city streets. However, they were more concerned with drawing attention to their wayward caravan. For now, secrecy was their greatest weapon.

Of the five wizards, Arania had spent the least amount of time down amongst the boulevards, streets, and avenues that laid the city out in a precision grid. So she was the most oblivious to the sad state of affairs that had fallen block after block of the famed capital.

As they stopped to cross from one ward to another, Corvalonn glanced up and down the avenue. Disgust etched across his face. The city felt deserted. There were very few citizens out and about. Shops were hit-and-miss. Some were dark. Others were boarded up. And the ones that had managed to stay open were operating with only minimal stock. Trash and refuse clogged the alleyways. There was no life, no luster, no joy to be found.

Before they could cross the avenue serving as the unofficial border between the two wards, Drennid halted their advance. He frantically waved the group back into the darkness of the side street. The wizards complied with the mage's silent order. For once, they were thankful for the random trash congesting the alley. They ducked out of sight behind discarded shipping crates and bags of refuse. Looking out from the shadows, they watched as a column marched past.

The leader of the procession was a terrible ghast. It was an undead creature who still had the majority of its undead flesh. In the dark shadows of the night, it might have passed as a human being until one got close enough to see its yellow irises and its long, dangling tongue that had grown three times its regular size.

The ghast was leading two columns of the living skeletons. Uniform in their bones and their armor, the skeletons marched in perfect synchronization, their boots striking the stone-paved roads with symphonic timing. Citizens gave way as the undead horrors marched past and then did their best to go about their daily lives once the column was on its way.

"This is appalling," Corvalonn muttered.

"This is tame," Drennid replied. "You don't want to see the wards south of the Queen's High."

"How bad is it?" Marius asked.

Drennid shook his head. "I know you all aren't going to like to hear this but if it wasn't for the Baelannor dynasty, things would be terrible. The last time I checked, the people haven't resorted to eating the dogs. Or cats if they can catch them. Although, I am not certain how the stable wards are fairing."

"I hope that was a poor attempt at a jest," Arania said.

Drennid could only raise an eyebrow and shrug. "The silver lining is the food is still flowing. If it wasn't for the Baelannor dynasty and their foodstuffs and water, it would be anarchy. Those conjurors need to be protected at all costs."

Corvalonn nodded toward one of the shuttered restaurants in the distance. "How long until the Baelannors can no longer meet the demand of the people though?"

Drennid grumbled. "Once the gates were closed off, the smart people began rationing. Still, there is only so much food to go around. It has been what? Almost a month now? With nothing coming in to replace the stocks. Even with people dying off due to natural causes – and some less than natural – it takes everything the Baelannors have to get the food conjured."

"But if that food runs out or the Baelannor's can't meet that demand...," Cedalia warned, her threat hanging in the air.

Drennid looked back at the group with all the sternness he could muster. "You would not want to be down cityside."

With the marching column of skeletons having turned the corner, Drennid took the group through the intersection and into the next ward. They continued to navigate the alleyways as best they could. "Drennid," Arania called from the back, "how much farther?"

"That was Silver Avenue," he replied. "The next is Steel. Then we will cut up north to Fifth Street. And then down to Titanium. That is where the Half Gate is located. But we have to keep a low profile. All of these wards are run by a street gang called the Crimson Way. They are rough customers."

"Are they allies of the Necromangians?" Corvalonn asked.

"No, they are an ally of coins. And capturing a host of wizard fugitives would net them a tidy profit," the mage replied. "They can be bought by the highest bidder. And even with all the wealth owned by a pair of patrons, down here in the city, right now your wealth doesn't mean a whole lot. The Necros have resources you can't compete with. Food and the like. So be on the lookout for anyone wearing a crimson sash."

Arania groaned. "Watch out for skeletons. Watch out for ghasts. Watch out for Necromangians. Watch out for Imperial Knights. Now we have to watch out for citizens wearing sashes?"

"Technically, I would say look out for *all* the citizens," Drennid replied. "If anyone recognizes you, it probably means triple rations if they assist in your capture. And starving people aren't exactly known to give a shit."

"This time spent amongst them has certainly brought some salt to your language, boy," the matron huffed.

"If this plan of yours gets us back to normal and ousts these tossers from our city, I will be more than happy to return to my sophisticated ways, my matron. But we are wading hip-deep in the tosspot and now's not the best time for me to practice some bitch ass-heeled curtsy."

With several more twists, turns, and crossings, eventually, the group arrived at an alley overlooking the easternmost avenue within the city walls. Like all avenues in the Northeast District, they were named after metals. The easternmost avenue was named in honor of the infamous titan-forged metal. Titanium Avenue ran from the Queen's High in the south to the Northeast Tower serving as part of the city's defensive parapets. In the exact center of that length was one of the city's half-gates.

Smaller than the cardinal gates, the half-gates were a preferred ingress into the city by pedestrians or those riding horses and not hauling wagons. Like all of the other gates, the oaken and iron-banded doors had been shut with their braces fitted in place. But there was also warbling magical energy rippling and radiating as a force shield.

Silently, a squad of eternally vigilant skeletons, armed and armored, stood their posts. Their hollow eyesockets stared out at the east-west running boulevard bisecting the ward. They would then pivot to stare either north or south, up and down Titanium Avenue. With no one needing or getting through the gates, the citizens avoided the whole intersection as if it were soaked with plague. Some would even backtrack to Steel Avenue to avoid the intersection entirely.

Meanwhile, up on the city walls, more skeletons marched on their patrols, observing the city from their elevated vantage point. But before, while the soldiers who manned the walls looked for exterior threats, the skeletons kept their views directed inside and down on the city streets.

From the mouth of the alleyway, Drennid gestured with an open palm toward the half-gate. "I don't know what your plan is," the mage said, "but it better be a good one. You are going to need some serious power to get through there."

"Thankfully, I brought a serious warlock," the sorcerer replied.

Tanaris Corvalonn peeked out from the cover of the corner. He triggered just the slightest amount of passive magic from one of the rings on his fingers. The detection spell washed outward. Seen only through his eyes, he studied the strength of the shielding on the gate and of the membrane arcing upward from the battlements, forming a dome over the city.

As Corvalonn was surveying the situation, Marius Vocazion produced two small crystalline dragon figurines from his pockets. He had not used such a trinket since that fateful day back in the spring on his journey to Malinsula to visit with his daughter. He laughed quietly to himself, thinking if he only knew then how his world would unravel and the shocking truth he would learn later about one Cinder Fireborne.

Passing the figurines to his matron, Marius smiled. "Wait until the last moment to trigger the magic," he warned. "If sniffers are lurking about looking for magical energy, this will lure them in like sharks to blood."

Back deeper in the alley, Cedalia began her summoning.

"Three wands are better than two," Drennid said as he stood beside his father.

Marius shook his head. "No, I am honored by your offer and I would be proud to stand beside you. But I need you down here coordinating the resistance."

Behind them, from Cedalia's summoning, a terrible, wet, disgusting gurgling started to emanate from the alleyway...

Chapter 63

In the shadows of the narrow alleyway, there was not an ear around to hear the soft sound of metal kissing metal as the manhole cover was lifted from out of its position. After being slid to the side on the smooth concrete of the alleyway, silence once more reigned. Below the streets, the group waited for repercussions from the sound. When none came, Thade Skystone gingerly popped his head up out of the hole and quickly glanced around.

Finding the alleyway deserted, the big man hoisted himself up out of the sewer system. Even with garbage in the isolated alley to use as cover, he still moved quickly. He knew the dangers of being out in the open. One by one, he reached down to help each of his friends off the ladder below and out of the sewer.

Valos Ironblade was the first out and he was the quickest to make his way to the mouth of the alleyway. Sway, Cinder, Sario, Amman, and finally Cavin were hoisted out of the underground tunnel. Amman and Thade worked together to fit the manhole cover back in place and cover their tracks.

Out observing the streets, Valos scanned north and south, looking for any potential threat. Hustling back to the group, he did not have to force his smile. "Nestorian Heights," he said. "It could have been worse. The Nest is east of Shaded Light so it is not far to go. If we stick to the back roads, we will be okay. We just need to be mindful of the intersections."

Sway glanced up at the early afternoon sun. "We should have done this at night."

"Finding those intake and outflow pipes in the dark would have been too difficult," Valos replied. "But we'll be okay. Just remember, we are going where we are going. And we are supposed to be where we are. Keep that in mind if we come across someone. Just… walk casually."

Sticking as closely as they could to the less traveled alleyways and side roads bisecting the wards, the group made their way west towards Shaded Light. All the while, Sario stared with an open mouth at the manmade canyons of stone, brick, and wood, spiraling up to dizzying heights. Sidling up beside her, Sway took the shaman by the arm and helped escort her through. "This makes no sense," she whispered. "How did human hands even do all this? I've read stories of course but…"

"Believe me, when this is all said and done," Sway said, "I will take you on a personally guided sightseeing tour. But for now, eyes front."

"Yeah, cousin. At least look like you have been here before. That way you don't look like such a day tripper." Amman said. "Wow, look at that building."

"You aren't the first Malinsuli to grace our city," Thade added. "It is rare but it does happen. Lots of ship captains like to hire your sailors."

"Best in the free kingdoms," Cavin said. "I'd take your kind over an Arvateri admiral any day."

Suddenly, Valos held up a halting hand and gestured for the group to hide. Thankfully, the alleyway was dotted with enough trash receptacles, discarded crates, and other refuse to afford them the necessary cover.

On the street, a patrol of armed and armored skeletons marched past with the same precision as the squad they had dispatched outside the city. Thankfully, none of the skeleton soldiers turned their eyeless gazes down the alley as they went about their patrol.

After the skeletons had turned the corner at the intersection, Valos moved the group along, leading them down the maze. The nimble rogue knew exactly where to cross, which intersections to avoid, when to be stealthy, and when to pour on the speed. Finally, the group crossed Gold Avenue and returned to the friendly confines of Shaded Light.

Each of the Blades began breathing a tad easier, knowing full well that if they chanced across any civilian they would be safe. Or at least safer. Within the ward, the undead horde, the marching skeletons, or the heretofore unseen necromancers were either negligible or easily avoided.

Back in their old stomping grounds, the group made their way toward the center of the ward. At the intersection of Second Street and Copper Avenue, the empty pit where the Shadow's Edge Inn once stood remained untouched. None of the reconstruction had even started.

But across the way, the building secretly housing their cadenta was still intact. The only question remaining was who was still inside. Anxious to find out, Valos looped them around to the back of the building so they could sneak in via the rear entrance.

Valos's steady hands and skeleton key made silent work of the lock. With the hinges on the door aptly greased, the door also made very little noise as it swung open. With a dagger ready to be pulled if necessary, Valos made his way into the main social area just off the foyer. The large room was empty.

"Loredana?" Valos called out, his voice echoing through the hall and up the stairways.

After a heartbeat, the door off the foyer flung open with fury. The tall, blonde madam – still beautiful despite the relentless encroachment of age – strode from her office with purpose. Her exquisite features were twisted into a mix of concern, hope, and disbelief. When she locked eyes with Valos and saw the collection of people within the main parlor, she brought a hand up to cover her agape mouth. Throwing propriety to the winds, she charged forth and wrapped her arms around Valos's neck.

Not satisfied, she reached out to Sway, Thade, and Cinder. The three were not about to disappoint the madam of the house. Hugs were exchanged as well as kisses of both joy and relief.

"I never thought I would see you all again," Loredana said. "We didn't even know if you had made it out of the city before the curtain fell. I just assumed you were… Well, it doesn't matter, you all are here now."

"And with friends," Sway said, gesturing to Cavin, Amman, and Sario.

"You are most welcome to our establishment," Loredana offered with a smile and a bow of respect.

With introductions made, the madam went to the foot of the closest stairway and loudly called for her girls. The cacophony of footfalls became a rumbling waterfall as so many of those employed by the cadenta rushed to the main parlor.

Sario looked at Amman and asked in her native tongue to be polite, *"Ka'rau?"*

Amman shrugged his shoulders but also nodded in affirmation as more of the ladies streamed past him, eager to greet the crew and welcome them back home. As hugs were exchanged and introductions were made, Loredana ordered several of the girls to prepare food for their newly returned champions.

As many went about their tasks, it gave the crew time to settle into the main parlor and sit with the madam. Loredana offered her version of what happened with the attack on Sorceria and the siege of the city.

"You have to understand, the skeletal forces appeared from nowhere and in massive numbers. By the time the sentinels on the walls were able to organize any kind of resistance, they were overwhelmed. Some organizations tried. The *domici dauthis* tried their best but they were cut down quickly."

"What about the Blades?" Valos asked. "We haven't been able to get in contact with Gamble."

"I haven't been outside the ward in weeks," the madam admitted. "We know so little. Ever since the Governance Ward issued the curfew – straight from Castellan Tallhill himself – no one wants to risk running afoul of the skeleton brigades. The Necromangians are scary enough. But it is the Knights of the Imperial Circle that you have to look out for. They are looking for any way possible to impress their wizard masters."

"Necromangians?" Cavin asked.

"The wizards waving the wands and controlling their undead hordes," the madam replied. "Servants of their master, Nalazar Catabaysi."

Both Cavin and Cinder looked at each other after the mention of the wizardly surname.

Thade threw up his hands in disgust. "So the Knights are in on this too? Those tosspots with the hoods are in with the necro-whatevers?"

"They were some of the first to pledge fealty," Loredana said. "The whole of the city is on lockdown. The only time we ever truly feel… well, safe isn't the word. The only time we have a valid excuse to be out is to collect the daily rations distributed by the Baelannor dynasty. If you go out for any other reason, you risk being picked up by any of the evil trio – the skeletons, the knights, or the wizards. So everyone just stays buttoned up."

"But even then you aren't safe," one of the girls said while she was setting up a large table to serve the food. "We hear horror stories of people being dragged away in the middle of the night and never heard from again."

"I heard the jails and the sanitariums are all empty," another of the girls said. "And the Under Roads have been swept clean."

"That is true," Loredana said. "We haven't had issues with the spice-heads since the siege began. If you stay within the confines of the ward, things are quiet. The only time the skeleton forces are prevalent is when they come to collect the bodies of citizens who have passed away."

"Come and eat, please," one of the servers said as she set out another tray.

As the group moved to make the best of the Baelannor conjurations, Cavin and Cinder held back. "There is a reason skeletons would be picking up the dead," the slayer said.

"Adding soldiers to their army," Cinder nodded. "It makes sense to target the jails, the sanitariums, even the Under Roads. Less fuss for the poor and the homeless. But what is their end goal? Assimilate the whole city?"

"Catabaysi?"

Cinder exhaled sharply. "Yeah, I caught that too. We need more information."

Chapter 64

Its true name was utterly unpronounceable in the human tongue but upon its discovery, in the ancient languages, the sojourner wizards called it *deamon infernali terra* – the land of infernal demons. Shortened and later labeled in the trade tongue as Infernali, it was the plane of existence where warlocks summoned forth demons and devils with their unique magic.

The dimensional plane itself resembled a painting on black canvas where the artist was not supplied with enough pigments. Everything felt washed in shadowy blacks and pale grays. Red and the occasional purple were the most dominant hues when they were present.

It was primarily an environment of sharp stone canyons and vast fields where dagger-like columns of stone jutted haphazardly in disheveled directions. The lack of vegetation was unnerving. No grasses grew. There were occasional twisted, gnarled trunks of petrified trees from a forgotten eon. It left one to believe this might have once been a lush and verdant landscape until its hellish occupants twisted the very plane of existence into a nightmare more fitting to their essence. But with the lack of vegetation and, as such, the lack of herbivores, one could correctly wager what the creatures of the dimensional plane ate to sustain themselves.

Several different castes populated Infernali – terrible demons of all different shapes, sizes, and species that would have incited madness if a mortal mind attempted to look directly upon them. There were small, nimble fliers that flittered and darted amongst the stone canyons. Some demons stood at vaguely humanoid shapes and heights. Other colossal titans walked with steps that could clear hills with a single stride. Some were so monstrous they needed to remain in Infernali's boiling seas of crimson liquid to support their bulbous bodies and slithering masses. There was no civilization. There were no structures. There were no signs of an organized society. It was an entire ecology of hiding, hunting, and feeding.

The whole landscape of reds, crimsons, vermillions, purples, grays, browns, and blacks was capped by a perpetual gray of ever-roiling storm clouds, hanging like a curtain of more grays and blacks. Occasionally, the storm clouds would streak with forked bolts of white-cored lightning with bright orange halos.

In this land of perpetual gloom coated with reds, grays, and shadows, when the warlock's convocation magic made its dramatic appearance, the brightly glowing sickly green pools always brought attention. Some demons scampered away, fleeing like frightened field mice. Others were curious and would approach with tentative steps like a cautious hunter. However, some saw the portals as a gleeful opportunity to wreak havoc. They were more than happy to charge forth into the glowing green pool, even if it meant bonded servitude on the prime material plane.

Still, the bondage was never truly existence-threatening. Many of the warlocks wanted to use their demon servants as instruments of war. Fighting on behalf of their wizard masters was enjoyable as nothing squealed quite like a creature from the prime material. The taste of their red blood was sweet and intoxicating.

If the demonic creature did sustain mortal wounds to its corporeal body on the prime material plane, it would simply dissolve away and return to the Infernali plane of existence. To some of the lesser castes of demons, being summoned was almost like a holiday. It was a treat to stroll about in the different dimensions and sow chaos.

Still, higher caste demons saw such servitude as demeaning. They could be drug reluctantly through the bubbling portal if necessary. But sometimes, just sometimes, certain demons could be lured – baited – into crossing over to the prime material.

One of the higher castes of demons was the species labeled by the sojourners as the vaedaemon. Even the smallest of the breed stood over eight feet tall. They were hulking brutes of muscle and sinew. Bipedal but only vaguely humanoid, a poet or a teller of tall tales might have equated it to a muscular bear swirled with a gorilla and a talent to walk upright. Black fur decorated its burnt-red skin. Enormous batwings sprouted from the demon's shoulder blades. The dagger-like claws and its needle teeth were forged straight from nightmares.

The dreaded vaedaemon was the same demonic species that had broken free on the isle of Sorceria and caused the death of two of the highest-ranking members of the Ce'Mondere dynasty. It had taken the combined might of several wizarding houses and the isle's animated armored sentinels to stop its rampage.

Under most circumstances, the vaedaemon would not have even concerned itself with the convocation portal invading its territory but then it smelled what was on the other side. It was not blood. It was not carnage. It was pure holy essence. And the vaedaemon knew what was possible if it could obtain that essence.

Stomping forward, the massive monster swatted away and shoved other demons standing between him and the swirling gateway. The creature began pouring his essence into the glowing, green portal.

Emerging on the other side, the demon had to quickly orient itself and overcome the lack of brimstone and ash within the breathable air. It had to compensate for the lighter gravity. It also had to shield its eyes with an additional membrane to compensate for the sheer brightness of the fiery sun. But once it was prepared to embrace the confounding dimension, its eyes snapped to the warlock who had summoned it.

Like so many humans, she was a soft, puny thing with pale skin. But somehow these feeble wizards had mastered – and in some cases improved – the draconian magic from the days of yore. The one standing before him was one of their females. The vaedaemon knew by the smell of her blood. With another sniff of the air, the demon knew what else she held.

The warlock clutched her magic-channeling scepter with authority. The vaedaemon could feel the tingling and the magical pressure against its burnt-red skin when it tried to move. The unholy creature glared down at the warlock, wondering if she knew it could rend her bonds with a flex. Still, the demon was intrigued. Curious even. And decided to play along… for now.

In the cramped alleyway in the shadows of the Northeast District's eastern half-gate, Cedalia Ce'Mondere held her scepter high. Magical energy pulsed from the instrument's head. Sweat beaded on her forehead and upper lip as she struggled to maintain control of the freshly summoned demon.

The other members of her group stood at what they assumed was a respectful distance. The demon looked upon them with inquisitiveness and some might have interpreted its facial features as twisting into a sign of amusement. But the demon's attention quickly snapped back to Cedalia when she presented a glass vial filled with the essence of a holy amorina.

Cedalia held the vial between two fingers and tantalizingly waggled it for the demon to see. "This is yours," the warlock said, "and I will unleash you from your bindings."

At that statement, Drennid Vocazion looked at the young warlock with a shocked expression. "Cedalia, no!" he hissed.

"I will unleash you from your bindings," Cedalia reiterated. "But you have to smash through *that* gateway."

The warlock gestured toward the half-gate in the distance. The demon eyed the guarded entrance and its magical shielding. But then it looked back at the essence in the glass vial. To prove her sincerity, Cedalia popped the cork stopper from the vial with her thumb.

The smell of the amorina's essence drifted towards the heaving nostrils of the vaedaemon. The creature swooned and then eagerly nodded its agreement to the accord.

Cedalia stepped forward. The demon reached out with its meaty hands and plucked the vial from the wizardess with surprising dexterity. In such proximity, Cedalia was forced to respect the demon's claws that were easily the length of her forearms. The creature snapped up the vial. It brought the essence close to its eyes, admiring it and basking in the moment of finally laying its claws on something so precious. Looking down on the small wizardess with approval, the creature twisted its features into something that possibly resembled a smile. Then it tipped up the vial and poured the contents down its gullet.

With their magical experiments, both Cedalia and Tanairs Corvalonn had seen what occurred when the essences of the holy and the unholy were combined. It was a violent reaction they had been using to power their magical creations instead of using exhaustible material components. The reaction within the demon was not the same.

The vaedaemon's skin grew tighter and its muscles began to swell. The striation became violently pronounced and the monster's veins began to bulge through the taut flesh. Particularly along its arms, shoulders, chest, and the thin membranes between the spines of its bat wings, the crisscrossing network of veins began to glow with an inner white light.

The creature was flooded with energy demanding to be unleashed. Looking into the monster's red irises, Cedalia did her best to recapture the beast's attention as it stood enthralled.

Finally, its eyes snapped to the warlock. "That gate, demon," she said. "Smash through the gate."

The creature roared with an ungodly howl and charged out of the shadows of the alleyway.

Chapter 65

One boat in the small navy afforded to Sorceria came to dock at the main entrance for the floating wizard isle. Stepping off the ferry, Reeve Windwisher was adorned in his full regalia denoting his senior leadership role within the Knights of the Imperial Circle. His ivory attire was neatly pressed and featured not a single blemish as he strode down the pathway between the estates of the Baelannor and Vocazion dynasties.

Windwisher turned sharply and strode through the gates of the Baelannor estate. The Baelannor wizards, the Necromangians, and the servant staff were all smart enough not to impede the knight's progress as he proceeded up the various stairways to approach the private chambers of the house's patron.

Formerly reserved for Asaric Baelannor, the patron's chambers had been commandeered by Nalazar Catabaysi. The undead wizard floated scant inches above the ground. Surrounding him were a series of magical tomes, volumes of lore, and other grimoires of forbidden spells. The books hung with just the slightest thrum of magical energy radiating from them. With waves of his hand and tickling of his fingers, the various books floated into his view and the pages turned to his somatic commands.

The Knight of the Imperial Circle walked through the plushly carpeted narthex where the wizard was studying. Just inside the private chamber, the knight quickly kneeled. His ivory raiment tented around him as he dropped to a knee, placed his hands on the floor, and tucked his chin against his chest.

"You have done as I commanded?" the lich asked, his eerie voice echoing through the parlor.

"The chest has been delivered to Accursio Twotrees, my master."

"Good," Nalazar said as he waggled his fingers and more vellum pages on a black-covered tome turned. "Were there any issues?"

The was a pregnant pause before the knight untucked his chin enough so that his voice would be clear. "No, Master. Twotrees said he would start to work right away."

"Even without your hesitation, I can sense it in your voice, lad," the lich replied. "Rise and speak freely."

The Imperial Knight did as he was commanded and returned to his full height. In a show of respect, Reeve removed his hood and alabaster mask. He turned briefly to look through the narthex and made sure the two of them were alone. "I am concerned with a number within your house, Master. I believe they are questioning the path you are taking them down."

With a wave of his hands, Nalazar parted the circle of tomes surrounding him to give him a clear view of his loyal general. "How do you mean?" the lich asked, as he levitated out of the ring of tomes and approached the loyal knight.

Reeve straightened his tunic and jutted out his chin. "I have always been in awe of magic-users, Lord Master Nalazar. I wish I could harness magic the way you do. Alas, despite my best efforts, my brain cannot grasp the casting concepts. But what you can do, your... *kind* can truly change the kingdoms for the better and elevate all of society. So it is my honor to serve you as best I can."

"Continue," the lich said.

"You have seized a great power, Master. And while your wizards faithful follow you, I feel like they..."

"Yes?"

"I feel like they are reluctant to do what is necessary to enforce your will, even though you and I both know it is for the greater good. I am afraid many within your ranks are too... squeamish."

"And how would you deal with these individuals, lad?" the lich asked. "Put them to the lash? Expel them from the order? Or end them and convert their bodies to join the army?"

"None of these, my liege," Reeve answered with a shake of his head. "Their casting abilities elevate them above the general citizenry of the city. But I am afraid this squeamishness I mention is going to draw reprisals from the people. If they appear weak, it will draw aggression. It could foster resistance."

"So what would you do?" Nalazar asked but he could see the somatic components tumbling in Reeve's eyes before he could speak the words.

"You need a fist. You need a sword. You need a capable enforcer willing to do what must be done to keep the people in line."

Nalazar smiled. "And you believe that you are the person to serve as this... enforcer?"

"I am," Reeve replied confidently. "And I am willing to offer a pledge of loyalty far beyond any that others have."

Nalazar began floating in a slow and lazy circle, taking him behind the Imperial Knight. "A bold claim," he hissed. "To join my inner circle, each member has shown the ultimate faith by dying and trusting in our necromantic magic to return them from the Never. Tell me, boy, did you have to die to join your hooded order of clansmen?"

"I did not," Reeve said after swallowing hard.

The lich floated around to face Reeve once more. "And if I asked you to drink from the glowing green potion that would send you to eternal sleep, would you drink it?"

There was a long pause before Reeve answered. "It depends."

"*Depends*? There are conditions to your loyalty now?"

"Not exactly. The candidates who drank the potion, it was on the condition that they would be accepted into your wizarding house and taught the secrets of your necromantic magic. Correct?"

"It is," the lich hissed spiritedly.

"But we have already established that I am not a magic user. So, if I were to drink the potion... I don't want to be brought back. I don't want resurrection. I want my body to be like *yours*."

The lich's eyes narrowed and he folded his arms across his chest as he eyed Reeve curiously. "Continue," he prompted.

"I have been around wizards enough to know. Just because I cannot cast the magic doesn't mean I don't understand its laws. I know exposure to the *pherein* must be always dealt with cautiously. It is a fear you no longer possess. I want that same freedom from fear."

"You want me to make you undead?"

"Look at your power, Master! Look at what you are now capable of. Why have none of the other wizards come to you and asked you to make them like you?"

Nalazar knew the complications of casting the spell to become a lich even if Reeve did not. Still, even with the knight's flawed understanding of magic, by his logic, it was curious why none of the other wizards had offered to become like him.

Nalazar stretched out his bony hand and summoned forth one of the forbidden black grimoires still hovering in a halo in the center of the parlor. The lich proceeded to flip through the yellowing pages. "What you are asking... it is possible. It might have been dangerous for a living wizard to cast it. I would have to dig deep into my reserves and tap directly into the *pherein*. It would be painful for you."

"But it would be the last pain I would ever experience," Reeve said with a hushed tone. "Correct?"

Nalazar tapped his elongated nail against one of the yellowed pages and then slowly closed the book. "If successful, the spell would kill you. I would hold your soul in place, refusing to let Zaneger take you to the realm beyond. I would then reanimate your slain form. It would not be a resurrection but a reanimation. I would then place your soul within that reanimated body. And in doing so, it would make you immune to pain."

"And in doing so, I would become a version of you, only instead of wielding a wand or a staff, I would swing a sword and wear armor. I would become your death knight."

"How interesting," Nalazar said as he began to return to the halo of books. The undead wizard then gestured towards the private writing desk that used to belong to Asaric Baelannor. "Like all spells from the Necronomicon, such a casting requires certain material components."

Reeve hustled quickly towards the desk, gathering up a few loose pieces of parchment along with a quill and ink.

"But aside from this, if you will be marching down in the city, I believe that my representative will need to be properly outfitted with a suit of armor and bearing weapons appropriate for your position."

"I happen to know the best armorsmiths and weaponsmiths in the city, sire."

"Look in the top right-hand drawer," Nalazar said. "You will find several coin purses filled with gold. Take more than a few of them. We will overpay the workers and compensate them for bringing them here to the isle to do their work."

"Yes, Lord Master Catabaysi."

"Now, as for the reanimation spell, I will need the following ingredients..."

Chapter 66

From the roof of the cadenta, Cavin Jurare was able to look down on the majority of the Northeast District's ward, Shaded Light. The cadenta was one of the tallest buildings in the zone. Looking down below, he could see the small handfuls of citizens scurrying back and forth.

The numbers were far fewer as so many had decided to remain within their homes to not draw the eye or the ire of the siege forces. The undead slayer curled his fingers around the handle of his silver sword and clutched it so tightly that his knuckles turned white.

Seeing the very creatures he had sworn to destroy patrolling and controlling the city he loved so much was mocking his very existence. Years prior, he always felt he had disappointed his matron by choosing not to walk the pure wizard's path. While he would never admit it, Canarr Jurare – Cavin's patron and a former general in the Incanterran military – seemed proud of his son's choice.

Rather than sitting at a desk writing formulas and performing magical experiments or charging the government and trade guilds for their defensive spells, Cavin had chosen to go on the offensive against the terrible undead threats lurking within the free kingdoms.

Remnants of the Great Dragon War, the ageless undead remained an albeit unliving and unbreathing threat to humanity. Yet old age would never claim the ghouls and ghasts hiding within graveyards. Wraiths and wights had to be dispatched with steel and strength. And the dreaded vampires – who fed on human beings – could not be allowed to establish footholds within any society. So, Cavin always assumed Canarr was proud of him for choosing a more heroic path. But seeing living skeletons and the dreaded ghasts walking the city streets mocked his profession.

As much as Cavin wanted to charge down into the city and attack the first skeleton he saw, he knew doing so would only sign his death warrant. The slayer knew he had to be smart and pick his battles properly. And that meant learning exactly what they were dealing with.

Thankfully, the first thing Cinder and her crew did was spread out and start gathering as much information as they could. Unfortunately, Cavin's attempts to find information were as empty as many of the water wells sporadically placed around the city.

Defeated and dejected, the undead slayer stood on the roof of the cadenta, looking down on the city below. Sensing her presence more than hearing her stealthy footsteps and her secretive arrival, Cavin looked over as

Cinder Fireborne walked out from the stairway and onto the roof. "I thought I might find you here," she said with a smile. "How did your reconnoitering go?"

"Not great," he grumbled. "I went to three different *domici dauthis*. Each one was completely vacant."

"I don't suppose they are closed down because there are no dead bodies to prepare for burial?"

"I wish that was true. Judging from the damage to the buildings, they were forcibly cleared out. All of them. I talked to a couple of people over in Brickyard. Apparently, the acolytes of the death god were the first to mount a real coordinated pushback to the occupation. And for their trouble, their whole order was made an example of."

Cinder grumbled and rubbed her chin. "That's terrible. We had business with one of their followers. A good man named Arator Dawnborne. I liked him. He was nice."

"I've had dealings with their kind before. From what I was told, their response didn't surprise me," Cavin said. "Their whole job was to put down those that had escaped their god's grip. All these skeletons... it mocked their whole allegiance to Zaneger."

"Don't you feel the same way?" Cinder asked.

Cavin gave a little shrug. "I do but you have to remove the whole religious zealotry out of the equation. Aside from that, we are not too different. Not all undead slayers are acolytes of Zaneger but all acolytes of Zaneger are undead slayers."

"Say that five times real fast," Cinder replied.

"That. That. That-That-That."

The rogue wizard shook her head but also smiled.

"What about on your end?" Cavin inquired.

"This is not exactly going to come as a shock but *The Heraldry* is no longer publishing and there is not an official historical record but I found a few choice names."

"Do tell..."

"They call themselves Necromangians," Cinder said. "Near as I can tell, they were an underground cabal. Hiding in plain sight, pretending to be normal Incanterran citizens. They were just all hiding a deep dark secret."

"A clandestine group pretending to be something they weren't while hiding in plain sight from the authorities? What a preposterous notion! I have never heard of such folly!"

Cinder raised an eyebrow at Cavin as he smiled. The undead slayer gestured for her to continue. "The leader of this group of hidden wizards was a man named Nalazar Morningflame. Citizens say he was a retired professor over in Academia."

Cavin bobbed his head back and forth. "A wizard pretending to be a sage? It is a pretty convincing cover. It is a good role to hide in."

"Indeed. But it gets worse. Now, he goes by a different surname. Well... technically... Morningflame was not his real surname but now his *real* surname is the name he goes by."

"I understand," Cavin said with a snap of his fingers and a quick waggle of his index finger.

"He now goes by Nalazar... Catabaysi."

The wizarding surname sapped what little mirth and merriment that was trickling from Cavin. "So, it is true."

"It gets worse," the rogue wizard said. "Apparently, a few weeks ago, the wizard cast a terrible spell. I've never heard of anything like it but if I have pieced it together properly, Nalazar died. His soul was then brought back from the Never. But his body remains dead."

"So he is a dead body with a soul?" the slayer surmised. "He is a... reverse zombie?"

"He is a dead body but with a soul and he has all of his memories."

"Which means he knows magic," Cavin said.

Cinder nodded gravely. Cavin paced about nervously and rubbed his hand on the back of his neck as he contemplated the possibilities. He halted his pacing when the realization dawned on him.

"Which would give him complete immunity to the *pherein*."

Cinder let Cavin's statement hang in the air.

"Shit."

"I know," Cinder nodded. "We just did a quick sweep around Shaded Light. All things considered, the ward is surviving. But Valos is adamant about making his way over to one of the other wards. He wants to meet with the upper hierarchy of the Blades. I would be concerned if we had to cross through any of the half-gates under the Ways but I think we can make it."

"Is this a meeting that I can attend?"

Cinder gave a sharp exhale. "Technically... no. You know I trust you. I know you can be trusted. If you were an associate, possibly. They might make you stand outside the meeting room. But at best, you would be considered an asset. I could receive a reprimand for talking about this thing of mine with you. But I trust you."

"So what do I do?" Cavin asked.

"I am hoping you can keep Amman and Sario company."

"I am babysitting?"

Cinder scoffed and clucked her tongue. "What? No. Come on. You are just... well, yes. You are babysitting."

Cavin threw up his hands.

"They don't know the city like you. And it is not like anyone here in the Shade is going to give them a hard time. But I just need you to escort them for a bit. Sario is too eager to help and I want to keep her reined in... just a tad."

Cavin turned and looked out on the city. "I get it. I understand."

"And we will all be working to secure the borders of the ward and take care of our people," Cinder said while rubbing Cavin's back. "Still, I don't think Amman is cut out for city life."

"Are you going to tell me next that Highstone Harbor is wet?"

Cinder allowed herself to laugh. "I know it is a different kingdom than what they are used to. Sario did say a curious thing I cannot refute. She mentioned how everyone has their own apartments and their own rooms within those apartments. So there are a lot of people around but everyone is very alone. She said we are all alone in closed spaces."

Cavin's head snapped up. "Wait. Is that why they call them... *apart*ments? How did I not know this until just now?"

Suddenly, the sound of rumbling thunder echoed across the city. It was an odd noise to be sure as there was not a cloud in the cerulean blue sky. From their vantage point on the tallest building in the ward, the two looked in the direction of the sound somewhere over on the east wall of the district.

"What was that?" Cavin asked.

Another rumbling thunderclap reverberated down the streets. Then another and another.

"Whatever it is," Cinder said, "it can't be good."

Chapter 67

The roar of the vaedaemon echoed off of the stone canyon walls forming the boundaries of the boulevard dividing the Northeast District. Emerging from the shadows of the nearby alley and turning onto the two-lane road, the monster pivoted with grace and agility a creature of its size had no business possessing. It had nightmarish speed. With long, ape-like arms, the demon charged forth on all fours, the knuckles of its massive hands leaving spider web pockmarks on the boulevard's surface. As it closed the distance to the capital gate, the demon roared even louder, an odd intermingling of deep, trumpeting bass and the sound of steel nails raking across slate.

At the half-gate positioned between the eastern cardinal city gate and the corner tower, an assemblage of emotionless skeleton guards was more than enough to dissuade potential rioters. In their jangling plate and chain armor, they walked their patrols and manned their posts with an unsettling, stoic poise. If the swords of the silent sentinels were not sufficient, the thrumming and pulsing energy wall covering the half-gate was more than enough to discourage a potential escape.

The energy wall resembled something similar to the magical shields projected by the Jurare wizards. In the past, their shielding had fended off dragon breath, stones hurled by hill giants, manticore claws, and other terrible monsters. With no battering rams, war engines, or siege equipment at their ready disposal, the citizens of Incanterra had resigned to their fate trapped within the city walls. None dared attack the gates.

The vaedaemon had no such compunctions.

The first of the skeletons that met with the massive clutch of the demon saw its skull completely removed from its spinal column. The attack came with such speed that the rest of its body remained upright for a few heartbeats, waiting to catch up with what the skull had already violently learned. The magical binding of the bones obliterated into nothingness and the disassembled skeleton collapsed into a lifeless pile.

A second skeleton found itself in the unenviable position of being between the unyielding energy shield covering the gate and the irresistible force of the demon's fist. While the armor crumpled and the chains rippled, what was left of the skeleton wearing the armor could only be loosely defined as dust.

After the initial burst attack of the demon, the skeletons did as they were commanded to do. Without fear, they turned their blades against the terrible demon. Of the few skeletons managing to score strikes against the monster's dense skin, such slashes leaked out glowing green fluid for scant instances before the wounds knitted themselves back together.

With such fury and power, the demon charged into the midst. Some skeletons were smashed against the stone like rag dolls. More were caught between the unforgiving magical energy field or the stone of the high walls and the pummeling fists of the demon. Some were trampled under hooves. Others were ripped apart by clawed hands. In what felt like the fluttering of a seraphfly's wings, the entirety of the skeletons stationed at the east wall's half-gate was dispatched.

Wasting no time, the demon began to pound against the energy sealing off the half-gate. Initially, the field held fast but warbled and rippled with each impact strike. Eventually, spider web cracks began to form along the energy field. Pieces of the barrier began to chip, splinter, and fall away.

The voids gave gaps for the demon to insert its claws into. Like a wall of ice or fractured glass, the demon continued to rend pieces from the shattering shield. It would toss the fragments aside where they would melt from existence.

As it continued to smash through, the white energy running through its veins continued to pump with every beat of its massive heart. The demon's skin looked like it was straining to contain the monster's muscles as they wanted to grow beyond the limits of the thick hide.

The creature focused on the locking barriers keeping the gate shut. With each strike, splinters of wood went windmilling through the air. The creature roared with ferocity. Anyone who had not yet fled the scene and was still even remotely close to the carnage had to cover their ears.

Colossal strike after colossal strike threatened to tear the massive gate from its hinges. Masonry began to crack and fracture, sending chips of stone spiraling and plumes of dust into the air. It was a question of if the gate would fall before the demon's strength gave out. But given the monster's ferocity, there was no end in sight.

Finally, with a deafening crack, the large barring brace keeping the door sealed snapped and broke from the hinges. With a massive battering of its shoulder, the doors to the gateway finally flung open. But rather than break out and flee into the hills located on the other side of the river, the demon turned back to regard the occupied city.

It was then that the demon was besieged on both sides by a relentless charge of skeletons from both the north and the south. The skeletons resembled an angry swarm of army ants attacking a much larger predator. The skeletons swarmed and clawed against the demon's thick skin leaving countless bite marks, claw marks, and rakes against the monster's flesh. By themselves, such wounds would have been insignificant. But the swarm of skeletons was so numerous that as they continued to pile on top of the massive demon, the infernal monster could no longer be seen.

As the demon roared and writhed underneath the tidal waves of bones, more than a few of the skeletal warriors were dislodged and thrown free but two more were fearlessly ready to take their place.

More and more glowing pools of the monster's green blood began to leak out onto the boulevard underneath the writhing pile. Still, the monster thrashed and roared. But with too many enemies and too much damage, it was only a matter of time.

A new wave of skeletons began to charge forward brandishing large polearms, looking to skewer demon flesh until a bright flash of white-cored lightning ripped through the air and blasted through the bone lines.

The populace turned to see Marius Vocazion standing in the middle of the boulevard with his wand in hand and proudly displaying his wizard colors of blue. The population glanced about nervously, wanting to cheer the arrival of a protector but not wanting to sympathize with a rebelling wizard.

Looking beyond the demon and the army ants of skeletons, Vocazion saw the magical shield blocking the gateway attempting to regenerate. The wizard reared back with his wand. Snapping the instrument forward, a great forked lightning bolt ripped through the air and simultaneously struck both sides of the open gateway, frying the magical energy before it could solidify.

With lash after snapping lash of blue-haloed lightning, the powerful mage continued to keep the energy from reforming. But with each crackling bolt of lightning, Vocazion drew more and more attention from the army of undead. And with so much of his focus directed on keeping the energy portal open, he did not have enough time to divert to the slowly encroaching skeletons.

As more and more of the skeletons continued to pile on the struggling demon – whose death throes were growing shallower by the heartbeat – Marius knew there would be no help. Still, he cracked off another lightning bolt. He needed to hold the gate open for only a few more moments.

From out of the shadows, two brilliant blue bursts suddenly rocketed overhead. Each drake carried a cloaked rider who each desperately clung to their leather reins and dug their traveling boots into the stirrups of the saddles each was harnessed with. The population ducked out of self-preservation and the sheer power of the wind burst took more than a few citizens off their feet.

A pair of azure crystalline drakes sailed towards the entrance as Vocazion continued to assault the relentless creep of the energy barrier as it attempted to close. Thankfully, the drakes were too fast. The gateway was too tall. And the mounts flew too high for even the tallest of the undead skeletons to impede their escape.

With the pair of drakes through the gateway, Vocazion no longer had to focus on keeping the energy barrier from resealing, much to the dismay of the skeletons attempting to close in around him. Blasts of wind and rippling bolts of chain lightning cracked around the first wave of skeletons attempting to encircle the wizard master.

Unfortunately, even being a patron, Vocazion could only summon so many magical bursts and his enemies were far too many. Thankfully, Arania Vocazion and her "bodyguard" had escaped the city. The plan had succeeded.

But at the foot of the gateway, the last vestiges of the summoned vaedaemon disappeared in clouds of black smoke. Its physical body had sustained too much damage and the demon returned to its infernal plane of existence. That left no more demons for the skeletons to battle.

They turned their eyes to the wizard with the smoking wand. Vocazion's plan had succeeded and now it was time for him to pay the price.

Chapter 68

Valos Ironblade looked over at Cinder Fireborne with shock and disbelief. "What in the cold dark hells was that?" the rogue asked.

Looking at the chaos enveloping the half gate in the far distance, Cinder could only shake her head. Dozens upon dozens of skeletons were leaving their posts and sprinting toward the besieged half-gate on tireless limbs. In the aftermath of the demonic attack and the breaching of the gate, the city was cast into chaos as the necromantic forces moved quickly to regain control and re-establish their authority. "Whatever it is, they have cleared the skeletons off the street," Cinder replied. "For once, let's take the win where we can get it."

"I'm with Red," Sway replied.

"Yeah," Thade added. "Let's haul stones."

As a foursome, the small cadre of thieves hustled with haste down the largely open streets and roads. With so few pedestrians milling about and the skeletons rushing to the half-gate, their path was straight and clear.

Their destination was the ward labeled by locals as Luna Light. Positioned in the northwest section of the district between Seventh and Eighth Street and between Iron and Nickel Avenue, the ward was tucked away off the northwest corner of Trader's Cross, the area bisected by the district's two boulevards.

While not exactly a residential district, the ward was also not a true competition for the hustle and bustle of the district's main markets. There was a nice public park. There were towering tenements for the working class. But the jewel of the district was the massive hotel known as the Moonshine Gloom.

Tall and far more opulent than most other locations within the working-class ward, the Gloom was made up of two towers – a larger main tower and a smaller sister tower that could only be accessed by covered skywalks bridging the two. Being such an establishment, various people from all walks of life were constantly seen coming and going through the hotel's main foyer.

Those that were not in the know had no idea. Some of the locals speculated but could never confirm. But those that were in the know knew. The Moonshine Gloom was the main base of operations for the Shadow Blades. The senior leadership of the secret organized crime family operated out of the large hotel and completely controlled the smaller sister tower.

As made members of the organization, Valos, Sway, Thade, and Cinder had no issues making their way through the hotel and across the lowest level sky bridge that connected the two towers. The crew even breathed a sigh of relief when they saw Galaris Hallowhall walking out of the smaller tower to meet them.

As they crossed the final expanse, Sway even broke decorum and burst into a trot. Their captain spread his arms wide and wrapped Sway up in a paternal embrace. "We were so worried," she said, her voice muffled with her face buried in his chest.

Without breaking his embrace, Gamble was quick to offer an extended hand and arm to the others. "*You* were worried? I was worried!"

Finally slithering out of Sway's grasp, the captain was quick to offer warm embraces to each of his soldiers. "Word got around quick," he warned. "The red robes were targeting the wizards. We felt it best not to use any magic. The last thing we wanted was any of their sniffers snooping about."

Gamble leveled his extended index and pinky finger at Cinder and waggled his hand. "I was especially worried about you," he said with a cock of his head. "Whatever this net is that they threw over the city, you all must have missed it by... heartbeats."

"Has the *Castella Mare* not made it back?" Valos asked.

"If they had, they weren't making it into the harbor."

"So how is everything else?" Thade asked.

"Come and join me in this *sedere* and you will see how bad it is," the captain said.

Entering the smaller tower, the crew began making their way via one of the stairwells toward the upper levels. The *sedere* – a holdover from the Ombraterran tongue – would have been most directly translated into "a sit-down." It was a chance for parties to discuss things, particularly to air grievances. Oftentimes, a senior member would act as an adjudicator. And more often than not, disputes were solved through the single most important thing to the crime family: coins. Transgressions, indiscretions, offenses, and even insults could be smoothed over with a willing exchange of coins.

"So how was Malinsula?"

"You mean except for the fact that Cinder was knocked into next week trying to get us back?"

Gamble halted his ascent and turned to regard the secret wizard. "Are you alright?"

"I guess the necromancers didn't want wizards using portals to get out of or into the city," she offered with a shrug. "I found out the hard way."

"So, other than that?"

Valos recounted the wonderful island of Malinsula along with their ventures and adventures. The promise of quasi-legal and relatively easy coins made their captain smile. He listened intently as the group described their travels up to the Nightwater family farm.

"At least we know this whole fiasco is isolated to the city," he said at the conclusion.

"For now," Valos warned. "We had a tussle with a squad of skellies out at Ambershore."

"I wonder what they were doing out there?" the captain asked.

"That boney bunch isn't exactly talkative fellows," Sway said.

Gamble gave a little shudder. "Ain't that the truth. Those beady little lights for eyes and those permanent smiles. It's too many shades of creep. And don't get me started on those ghasts, they are just…"

"Ghastly?" Valos asked.

"Look who's got jokes all of the sudden," the captain said after rolling his eyes.

"All of a sudden?" Sway scoffed. "Where have you been?"

Gamble chuckled. "Remember, some of us have been in from the jump while others have been sunning and surfing down on some island. Mirth is hard to come by these days."

"Once we get through all this chaos, boss, your fresh-from-the-sea lobster dinner and a tall, cold glass of sangria are going to be on me. Chase that with a shot of their fermented molasses and you will be primed for me to introduce you to one of those brown-skinned, white-haired island girls."

"Now if that isn't motivation to see these undead horrors ousted, I don't know what is."

Emerging from the stairwell, the crew followed Gamble to the parlor he had arranged for the formal meeting. On a well-lit table in the center of the room was a highly detailed map of the city along with small ornaments and tokens to represent various factions.

Valos noted the crimson shading within the Northeast District. The southeastern third had a stair-staggered border indicating the boundaries of territory belonging to the Crimson Way. He noted the obvious erasing to redistrict the map. It denoted control of Shaded Light returning to the Blades and Brickyard serving as a buffer zone between the two families.

"I am sure Mom would love to see you all and I know Armand would fancy a full accounting," Gamble said, referring to Celesta Darksteel – leader of the family – and her *consiliarus*. "But trying to hold things together is a full-time job. Everyone has been scrambling as of late."

"How are we handling the family business?" Valos asked.

"*Atta di'Dios*," Gamble said.

"What?" Valos hissed with an exclaimed hush and wide eyes.

"I don't understand," Cinder said, looking back and forth between the two men. "What does that mean?"

"Act of the gods," Sway said with a small nod.

"Someone knows her Ombraterran," Gamble said proudly. "And she is right. Celesta has suspended all operations. Everything is just being held in a freeze."

"Has the family ever done something like that before?" Valos asked.

"These are unprecedented times," the captain said.

"And those times make for strange bedfellows," a voice behind them called.

The group turned collectively from the map to see Sonnan Silverhelm striding into the parlor. The handsome rogue was dressed in stylish fashions – save for the crimson sash he wore around his waist.

The crew turned and looked at Gamble, waiting to gauge their captain's reaction. Surprisingly, the Blade offered a smile and even approached Silverhelm with open arms. The two exchanged a brotherly embrace.

After, Sonnan turned to address the crew. "You can pick your jaws up off the floor, friends. You keep that up and tongues might start hanging out." He then glanced at Sway. "Not the most terrible of things though."

"Son," Gamble grumbled.

Sonnan patted the air with his hands. "No, no. You are right. My apologies. Old habits and all."

The dashing rogue straightened his sleeveless vest, tugged on the cuffs of his tunic, and straightened the knot on his sash. He then offered a charming smile.

"Relax, everyone. I'm here to help."

Chapter 69

With energy still crackling and a haze of smoke issuing from the wood of his wand, Marius Vocazion stood in the center of the boulevard bisecting the Northeast District. His lightning bolts and evocation magic had cleared the path necessary for their plan to succeed.

Even now, as his fellow conspirators hastened their retreat into the security of the shadows, Vocazion – in his house's full regalia – had all eyes on him. A wizard in his robes standing in the city street assured all eyes – both the living and the undead – were fixed upon him.

With his wand kept down by his side and making no threatening movements, the thrall of undead soldiers closed ranks around Vocazion, standing shoulder to shoulder as they encircled him. As if protected by some invisible field, the skeleton army kept their distance.

Witnesses to the grand display of power stood silently on the sidewalks and on the buildings' various stoops. They watched nervously as the mage was surrounded by more and more undead. Knights of the Imperial Circle began to weave their way through the bony throngs, their conical white hoods and ivory vestments made them hard to miss. But like the mindless soldiers at their command, they too kept a safe distance in case the wizard had one more bolt at the ready within his magic wand.

Finally, members of the Necromangians began to arrive at the battleground. Their red garments – similar and yet starkly different from the Vocazion's blue and black-trimmed robes – were an odd clash as the first of their order began to approach the mage.

Nikkala Whitesnow emerged from the bone circle and approached Marius Vocazion with purpose and confidence yet she was also nonthreatening. Her own wand hung from the sash around her waist but her hands stayed far away from the magical instrument. She was a beautiful creature, tall and lithe, with hair that resembled spun gold.

"Master Vocazion," she said politely, "I was led to believe you were part of the group held above in Sorceria."

"I felt a need to stretch my legs," the patron replied, returning the same level of respect and formality as the Necromangian.

"I am afraid I have to ask for your wand." The gentle command was issued at a whisper, to keep the conversation between the two of them. Yet the Necromangian did not extend a hand.

"And if I were to refuse?"

Nikkala blinked with deliberate slowness. "I *have* to deliver you to Master Catabaysi for your transgressions. I cannot take you before him with you in possession of your wand. I have to humbly ask you to surrender it to me."

"So let me ask you again," the patron said, "if I were to refuse your request?"

"Then I would be forced to take it from you," Nikkala replied. "Do not force me, Master Wizard. *Please.*"

Keeping his feet fixed on the boulevard and remaining as still as possible, Marius elevated his nose to look down upon the acolyte. "I am not some Lu'Scion magician, girl. Nor am I a Jurare warden."

"Of course not, my lord. But I have you surrounded by an army of undead. They would treat you the same as your demon. I have seen the power of your magic. It is impressive. But even you could not fend off my entire horde. It would be… an embarrassment."

"But to hand you over my wand would be—"

"A civility," the Necromangian interjected. "By extending me this courtesy, I will escort you to the floating sloop that has already been summoned. I will return you to Sorceria but I will do so with dignity."

Vocazion's eyes narrowed.

"I will wait until we are aboard the sloop to place you in manacles."

"To preserve my dignity."

"And allow you to return to Sorceria with the respect a man of your stature and station deserves."

Very slowly, Vocazion raised his wand and tumbled the wooden length in his fingers until he held the smoothly-polished business end towards himself and he offered the ornately grooved handle to the Necromangian. "I hereby offer my surrender," the mage said.

Almost on cue, one of the floating sloops completed its descent to the center of the wide boulevard. Riding a cushion of warbling energy, the sloop came to a rest, floating a few scant inches above the stone roadway. A long gangplank was extended.

Nikkala Whitesnow offered her arm to the wizard patron. Marius accepted and the two began the march up the gangplank. The scattering of citizens watched as the wizard was escorted into the boat. The majority of them remained as silent as the grave. Most were uncertain if they should cheer for the capture of one who would defy Nalazar Catabaysi's commands. They did not want to appear disloyal to their new tyrant. But no one had the heart to jeer or heckle someone – even a wizard – that fought to break the chains of their oppression. So, instead, the majority opted for silence.

Once Nikkala Whitesnow and Marius Vocazion were safe aboard the sloop, the skeletal forces began to disperse, returning to their regular patrols and guarding certain stations along the city proper.

As they did, the members of the citizenry began to return to their own various walks of life. Their heads hung a bit lower. Their shoulders drooped a little farther. And their steps did not have the same level of energy. Still, they returned to their meager lives and some form of normalcy.

Riding the energy wave, the sloop began to ascend towards Sorceria, one thousand feet above the city. Away from the prying eyes of the populace, Nikkala outfitted the wizard patron with a pair of elaborate shackles that bound his wrist together as well as placed his fingers within metal sheaths to prevent him from weaving any intricate patterns for his spells.

The shackles were made of a unique alloy, delicate but strong. Marius would not be breaking the chains linking his wrists but these were also not the heavy, clunky manacles one expected of a prisoner. Nikkala then ran a second chain down to a pair of shackles to bind his feet. There was enough slack so that the wizard could walk or shuffle relatively unencumbered but outright running would be impossible.

"I apologize, Master Wizard," the Necromangian offered, "but I have my orders."

Looking out to the east as the vessel continued to rise, Marius watched the skeletons return to a position guarding the half-gate. A pair of acolytes were quick to repair the magical spells shielding the entrance and keeping the population trapped inside the city's walls.

Amongst Catabaysi's assembled skeletons, knights, and wizards, the forces looked more concerned with securing the scene and returning things to normal, which led him to hope his co-conspirators had successfully slunk back into the shadows. If any of the undead horror's bloodhounds were hunting them down, they were doing so covertly.

As the sloop continued its ascent, Marius could only hope Corvalonn and his matron were already within the borders of either Castratellus or Arvaterra. From there, either the boy king to the east or the reclusive defenders to the west would either answer the call or they would not.

The sloop crested the rise and came to a halt at the main landing platform positioned between the two towers of the Baelannor and Vocazion dynasties. There was a muffled jangling of chains as Marius got to his feet. Despite his shackles, the mage walked with confidence and elegance as he returned to the wizard isle.

Nikkala Whitesnow politely steered the wizard patron towards the Baelannor estate. As the duo walked through the main gates of the property, Marius saw him.

Hovering an inch above the threshold of the main entrance to the tower, Nalazar Catabaysi stood – more or less – watching the duo approach. The undead horror was an odd dichotomy. He wore his elegant flowing wizard robes trimmed with black silk hems. He would have been perfectly in place at the finest cotillions or the most sophisticated of parties. Yet his skin was a pallid gray. His eye sockets were sunken deep. And the whispy remains of his hair clung desperately to his scalp.

Yet, as Marius approached and made his way up the steps, there was a brightness to those yellow irises and sharpness to the reds lining those circles. "Master Vocazion," the lich said in his horrible voice.

Still, the undead horror's tone was filled with reverence and what others might call admiration.

"Master Catabaysi," the mage replied.

"Was it worth it?"

Marius looked out to the grand land of Incanterra far below the floating wizardly isle. His eyes narrowed and he offered a grave nod. "She is safe," he said with a convincing tone. "So yes, I would say it was."

The lich's thin lips pulled back just enough to reveal a hint of his yellowing teeth. "You now risk punishment and potential death for your transgressions. Who was it that you helped escape?"

"My matron," Marius said.

The lich hissed a genuine chuckle.

"The things we do for love..."

Chapter 70

"They certainly are clever. I will give them that."

Standing with his hands on his hips, Dragan Duskwood observed the half-gate located on the eastern wall of the Northeast District. Admittedly, the Catabaysi loyal had done their best to repair the damage left behind by the jailbreak. It was a smart strategy. The longer the scars of the battle remained, the more it reminded the common people that Nalazar Catabaysi's authority could be challenged.

He turned and eyed Demina Summerstone and offered the slightest shake of his head. Despite the Dinacioun's news outfit being shuttered and no longer producing the paper news, Demina still wore her leather satchel on her hip and was instinctively clutching her magical writing pen with its endless ink. "Citizens are saying they saw two crystal drakes fly through the half-gate in the middle of the battle. Do we know who it was that got out?"

"I am told Marius Vocazion was apprehended at the battle scene," Dragan replied. "Possibly a son or a daughter? Maybe a son *and* a daughter? Does he have any high-ranking members of his dynasty he would want to see protected?"

"You are assuming they are fleeing the city to keep them safe from us. What if they were escaping to spread the word of the fall of Incanterra?"

Dragan gave a scoff.

"I don't think that is an unrealistic motivation," the reporter said, subconsciously twirling her pen between her fingers.

"Not at all," the Necromangian replied. "But such a fool's errand would be... foolish..."

"That sentence fell apart on you there," Demina interjected with a smile.

"Such a fool's errand would be *pointless*."

"Much more dignified. But why?"

"Where do you go for help?" Dragan asked. "If you head east, Arvaterra has wanted to conquer Incanterra for generations to absorb their magical resources. I suppose on the wings of drakes, they could fly over the Titanspine but you still have to get the Monterran forces down south. That means marching through Arvaterra. The boy king won't allow that. Or he won't allow it cheaply."

"So head west."

Dragan clucked his tongue and winced. "I don't see Castratellus breaking their borders. And even if you venture further west to appeal to the Ombraterrans, it just feels like too much to risk. And even if you could muster forces from either Ombraterra or Monterra, they still have to march here. By then, I would think Nalazar will have drained the city of its resources. There may be nothing left to rescue."

The duo turned and began walking down the sparsely populated boulevard bisecting the district, running from east to west from the half-gate along the eastern wall of the city to the sealed half-gate that ran underneath the King's High Way and into the Northwest District.

The ward where the east-west boulevard intersected with the north-south boulevard was referred to as Trader's Cross. It featured one of the four looming clocktowers within the city and was home to a variety of trade shops and mercantile vendors. Portable kiosks and pushcarts would normally line the streets. Dealers would wheel them in to hawk their wares. At least, that is what it would be under normal circumstances.

These circumstances were the farthest from normal.

At this time of day, the boulevard should have been packed with pedestrians. Wagons should have been hauling textiles into the city. Farmers should have been bringing in foodstuffs on wagons and buckboards. Smaller, specialty farmers would be bringing in delectables by dogcart. But with the city on lockdown, the traffic – foot or wheeled – had trickled to almost nothing. It was an odd sensation to be able to stroll down the practically empty boulevard.

But as such, it was harder for individuals to get lost in the crowd. So when Dragan spotted the white vestment and the conical hood of a Knight of the Imperial Circle, there was little chance the knight could slip away. He was also escorted by a pair of flesh-covered undead ghasts serving as sergeants within the undead army.

As they drew closer, Dragan saw this was not just any Imperial Knight. Given his epaulets, golden braids, and other accouterments, Dragan recognized the Supreme General of the Knights of the Imperial Circle. But what was more concerning was Demina's reaction to the trio the knight leader and his ghastly sergeants were escorting.

Dragan spent far too much time over in the Academia ward in the Northwest District but Demina knew almost every street within the great city, learned by working stories for *The Heraldry*. "Is there an issue?" Dragan asked.

"No," Demina admitted. "It's just... I know him. The man in the lead there with the broad shoulders. That's Noble Ironbound. He is one of the finest armorsmiths in the city. Some would argue he is the best. His shop is by appointment only. He only does custom pieces. The ceremonial armor Castellan Tallhill wore for his inaugural ceremony? Noble crafted that. What business does Windwisher have with him?"

Dragan looked at his apprentice and offered a little smile. "I think you have embraced hiding who we are too well," the wizard said. "Need I remind you? *He* answers to *us*, not the other way around."

Pivoting on his heel, the wizard marched directly towards the Imperial Knight and his assembled entourage. The procession halted before Dragan. Reeve Windwisher offered a curt bow and a flourish of his hand. "Master Duskwood, it is an honor, sir."

"What is this, General? Where are you taking these men?"

"I am escorting them to the nearest port so they can be taken up to Sorceria. Master Catabaysi has a special project. Talking with several people, they all agreed that Ironbound was the best man for the job."

"What job is that?" the Necromangian asked.

Behind his alabaster mask, Dragan couldn't read the man but given the subtle shifts in his shoulders and the sway in his body language, Reeve was not wanting to talk. However, Dragan was not nearly as constricted. His brow furrowed and his eyebrows lowered. All mirth and merriment evaporated from his countenance. It was the same look an ill-prepared student had been given from his lectern while teaching classes in Academia.

Reeve cleared his throat and shifted his gaze. But there was no respite coming, no salvation, and the stern wizard held his ground. With a subtle bob of his head, Reeve relented. "I am working hand in hand with Master Catabaysi. He is having a suit of armor crafted."

"What does Nalazar need with a suit of armor?" Demina Summerstone called from behind Dragan.

"The armor is not for him."

Dragan cocked his chin up. "It's for you."

"Master Catabaysi needs an enforcer – a fist – to see that his wishes are carried out to the letter. He needs a loyal follower – a true acolyte – that will do what must be done."

"And you believe that acolyte is *you*?" Dragan asked.

Reeve gestured back towards the half-gate and the scars of battle that the workers were still trying to spackle and paint over. "Defiance," Windwisher whispered. "These people must be brought to heel. You and I both know tolerance does not keep people in line. Fear does. And after I pledge my loyalty to my master and with my new armor, I will instill fear in the people."

"For peace?"

"No. So Master Catabaysi can unlock the mysteries of magic that have been denied to men by the cursed *pherein*. I believe in Master Catabaysi. I will follow him to the ends of the realms – living or dead. Tell me, Master Duskwood. How strong is your allegiance?"

Reeve pushed past the wizard and it was no accident the way he let his shoulder clip the red-robed wizard.

The ghasts and their newest collection of the armorsmith and his two apprentices continued to make their way to one of the wizard-controlled ports. From there, they could summon down one of the flying sloops.

As Dragan watched them go, Demina kept a sharp eye on her master.

"That one is going to be trouble," he grumbled.

"Do you think he knows?" she whispered.

"That knuckle-dragger?" Dragan scoffed. "I seriously doubt it. But still, that level of boot-licking is a rare thing. Just to please Nalazar, I bet that man would do anything he asked."

"What? Like drink a potion that immobilizes you, stops your heart, and ultimately kills you… so you can be resurrected to prove your loyalty?"

Dragan looked at his young apprentice and allowed himself to laugh. "Your point is taken. But still, a man like that would be willing to go even farther."

"What could be more terrible than letting yourself be resurrected?"

Dragan rubbed his chin and thought back to the legends and the myths of the old ways.

"I would say… returning from the Never as something… worse."

Chapter 71

"How desperate have we become if this is who we are turning to for help?" Valos Ironblade asked with a chuckle as he spread his arms out wide.

"Me?" Sonnan Silverhelm pointed to his chest. "I was wondering when you were going to show up for work."

In a rare display of affection, a Blade and a member of the Crimson Way shared a back-slapping embrace. Neither of the two felt a need to point out this was not the first time they had seen each other since the schism between the crime families. Gamble eyed the exchange closely until more and more members of both the Blades and the Crimson Way filtered their way into the parlor for their meeting.

Members of the family were happy to see the stewards of Shaded Light in attendance. Many were quick to offer hugs, slaps on the back, and kisses on the cheeks. "Alright, down to business," Gamble called out, settling the soldiers and bringing the room to order. "As you can all see, Valos and his crew have joined us. Better late than never I always say. And we are lucky to have them back in the embrace. If you all will indulge me just to get them caught up."

The attending soldiers all made the same hand gesture and clutched the neckline of their tunics and jerkins with their right hand, tucking their fingers inside the collar. Gamble gave them all an acknowledgment of respect.

"When the wizard war first popped off, it caught us all flat-footed," the captain began. "The curtains came down and trapped us all in. Aside from the curfews mandated by the dead wizard and pushed through by Castellan Tallhill and his archons, we were pretty much left alone. It was a wizard thing between wizards and we felt it best not to get involved. But then their little agenda started to creep towards the common man."

There was an uneasy ripple amongst the soldiers.

"How are the other families handling things?" Valos asked.

"I wish I could tell you," Gamble replied. "When the tents went down and sealed off the gates, they also sealed off the pass-throughs under the High Ways. Moving between districts is not exactly easy. So we just have to handle what we can handle."

"And how have we been handling things?" Cinder asked.

"We stay in the shadows as much as we can but if an opportunity to present itself is offered, we make members of this unholy alliance... disappear."

There was a muddled smattering of laughter amongst those in attendance regardless if they wore black sheaths or crimson sashes.

"So give me reports," Gamble said.

Bouncing around from soldier to soldier, each gave recountings of various happenings within their respective wards. Some were happy to offer techniques for making the skeletons vanish from the city after they were dispatched. Patrol schedules were corroborated. They discussed guerilla tactics slowly chipping away at the forces of the Necromangians. Once all was said that needed to be said, Gamble dismissed the soldiers until the same time next week.

As the various ground-level crews were breaking up to leave, Sway and Thade made it a point to say hello and offer embraces to Vinson Blackshield. A contemporary of Valos, the tall, handsome rogue was the leader of the crew that ran Nestorian Heights, the ward positioned east of Shaded Light and north of Brickyard. Vinson was a capable thief and he was happy to see the return of his neighbors. "I will come by the cadenta," he said after offering Thade a back-slapping embrace. "I will get you caught up on all the particulars and how we are doing this thing."

"We would appreciate that very much," Sway said.

"Are you kidding?" the rogue replied while kissing her on the cheek. "I am happy to have your weapons in the fight. We are going to make a lot more of those boners disappear now."

As the majority of the soldiers dispersed and made their way out of the various exits of the hotel itself, Gamble, the Shaded Light crew, and Sonnan Silverhelm were the last in the salon. Thade, Sway, and Cinder stayed closer to the doorway while the trio was talking. "Ain't this a bitch," Sonnan said with a laugh and a smile.

Valos looked about nervously. It was an uncharacteristic trait for the seasoned veteran. Gamble could see that his crew leader wanted to say something. "We have suspended monetary operations but rule number five is still in effect, Val. Spill it."

"I still remember the rules," Sonnan said with a hint of pride in his voice.

"Feel free to remind Master Valos here."

"'When asked for information, the answer must be the truth.' Some of our guys need to get that tattooed across their backs as a reminder. It is a rule I respect. Lie to the constables all day long. But you never lie to the boss."

"The sasher is right, Val. So out with it. Tell me what's going on in that big brain of yours."

"I am loyal to the family. I am loyal to Celesta. I am loyal to this thing of ours," Valos said.

"No one has ever doubted that," Gamble said confidently. "Is there a 'but' coming on?"

"But..." Valos said, looking at Sonnan, "it is good to see you, brother."

Sonnan was quick to extend his arms and offered Valos a warm embrace. The two patted each other on the back more than a few times. Gamble allowed the display and remained silent while the two worked things out.

Sonnan broke the embrace and gave them both a nod. "Strange times. Strange alliances. Look, just between us, I don't exactly see Celesta and Spyritus sitting down and breaking bread together. They can be cordial in public. I don't know how they would do one on one. But like I said, strange times."

Gamble nodded. "Before, I was happy with things. It was a thing I understood. Coppers can be bought. Puppet archons can be elected and put in place to serve our needs. Magistrates that can't be bought can be... removed if necessary. But this lot? Zealots. They are zealots loyal to a mad tyrant. There is no negotiating with their types. No appealing to a greater interest."

"Meaning they can't be bribed?" Valos asked.

Gamble squeezed his fists. "How crazy is that? I could be offering stacks of coins, stacks of spice, stacks of women... Nothing. I can't deal with those types."

"This is the bigger threat," Sonnan said. "So we have to work together. If only to run these guys out of town on the tip of a sword."

"The initiation," Valos said proudly. "Cinder and I had a similar conversation earlier. I am glad to hear we are reading the same scroll."

Gamble wagged his fingers approvingly at his subordinate soldier.

"We use coins when we can. We use a dagger in the dark if coins don't work..." Valos stated.

"And you use a sword if both of those fail," Sonnan finished the thought with a nod. "Well, trust me, boys. The only way we run these types out of town is with a sword."

"Or a few wands," Valos added while glancing in Cinder's direction.

"Still, at what point do we start nailing skulls to the clocktower in the center of the district to send a message?" Valos asked.

Gamble was quick to waggle a finger. "Not yet. Secrecy is the real key here. Mom was crystal clear on that one. If you snag a boner, no witnesses. The bones get ground up into powder and dumped in the sewer. That's why we target them primarily. They aren't exactly talking if things go wrong. So you only snag one of those pointy hoods or a red rober if you can *guarantee* they go away forever."

"The game changes when they can cast their death magic and bring people back to life," Sonnan added.

"So no bodies," Gamble stressed. "At the very least – I mean the very least – a head and a body need to be in separate wards."

"I understand," Valos said.

"Not just you," Gamble added and then wagged his finger at the crew. "All of you. When you strike, no witnesses."

"You got it, boss," Thade called back.

"Any of their order sees us attacking and this is all over," the captain said. "And if I am being honest—"

"There is rule number five again," Sonnan interjected.

"I wouldn't even trust most citizens," he continued. "Soldiers? Definitely. Associates? For the most part. Assets? That is starting to stretch it. But anyone not part of this thing of ours, I would not trust. Things are bad now. But they aren't terrible. They aren't as bad as it can go. Once the food starts running out and people start panicking, they will sell their mothers to those red robers for a sack of potatoes."

Valos nodded. "So we thrive in the uncertainty. Make them wonder why their patrols are coming back light or not at all. But nobody can know nothing."

"Let 'em *think*. Let 'em *speculate*. But they can't *know*."

Valos set his mind whirling as he pondered the possibility. "We're happy to be in the fight with you."

"And we're happy to have you back," the captain said.

Gamble took his leave, giving assuring hugs to each of the four members of the crew and a nod of mutual respect to Sonnan.

The crimson sasher smiled at his friend. "What do you say you all start policing Shaded Light? Do what you can. And then for old time's sake, we work together to crack a few skulls over in Brickyard."

"You're on," Valos said and offered another embrace.

Chapter 72

The sitting salon within the Baelannor dynasty was everything Marius Vocazion expected it to be. Based on the ledgers and the vaults, the Baelannor dynasty was the highest in stature amongst The Eight. They were the wealthiest and Asaric never had qualms about displaying their fortune. It was evident in the décor of the room. Be it objet d'art, crystalline sculptures, oil paintings, or the soft, supple leather on the sitting couches, the entire salon dripped with opulence.

This was on the ground floor of the tower.

Marius could not imagine what the upper levels were like. Despite the two plots of their respective estates sharing a border, this was the first time the Vocazion mage had been inside the private tower of the Baelannor dynasty. Such a fact would not be surprising to a Sorcerian native. Neighbors were not known for popping over to borrow a cup of sugar or break bread within the inner sanctums.

Standing at the window within the salon, Marius could look out to the east and see the Vocazion estate. Secretly, he wondered if he would ever step foot on his dynast grounds again. He wondered if he was going to even leave the salon alive.

The silence of the room was disturbed by a faint, muted warbling. Marius turned and watched as Nalazar Catabaysi floated in. The undead horror was dressed in flowing robes worthy of the highest-ranked patron but there was an addition to his attire. The lich was thankfully wearing a hood complete with a black ceramic mask concealing his withering undead features.

The undead wizard extended a gloved hand towards one of the two sitting couches positioned opposite one another. "Would you care for a seat?" the lich asked.

Marius issued a huffing exhale and crossed the span between the window and the couch. Tenting his robes, the mage took the offered seat. The undead wizard presented all of the courtesies and waited for his guest to sit before he took his place on the opposite couch. "So, Marius... Tell me. May I call you Marius?"

"Shall I call you Nalazar?"

The undead lich leaned forward and pantomimed an exhalation even though the wizard no longer needed to breathe. "Honestly, I wish you would. We are simply two wizards talking."

"Is that how you see this playing out? A conversation?"

"It is part of the reason why I chose this regalia," the lich said with a gesture toward his hood and mask. "I understand that my physical appearance might be considered... unsettling. But I hope that you will see me as a colleague. A contemporary."

"If only there was a magical discipline that could conceal your identity... in a... what do they call that?" Marius snapped his fingers a few times. "An illusion. Yes, if only there were some magicians available that could help."

"Is this the sardonic Vocazion wit I hear so much about?"

Marius shrugged. "I have my moments."

"Alas, the Lu'Scions could not comprehend the magnificence of my magic."

"Nor could the Jurare."

There was a long, uncomfortable pause. Nalazar Catabaysi suddenly clapped his hands together and clucked his tongue. "My manners!" he proclaimed. "I should have offered you something to eat. Something to drink in the least! My most humble of apologies."

Marius considered his response carefully. So much so that the pregnant pause elongated into another uncomfortable silence. The lich sighed. "I bet you have made your fair share of trips down to Stonelyn. Am I right? The theater district? I bet you are a regular at all of those various venues and you watch the actors play their roles in their fantastical stories."

Marius cocked an eyebrow. "What would make you say that?"

"Because you are assuming I will offer you food. You will enjoy it despite yourself. And then I will say, 'Did you enjoy the meal?' And you will say you did. And then I say something witty like, 'I hope so because it was your last.' And then I strike you down with my magic. How am I doing so far?"

Marius tried to not let his nervous swallow bounce his throat apple too much. "The thought... had crossed my mind."

"I am not a monster, my friend."

"Says the person hiding behind a mask."

"If it helps soothe your mind, consider my physical appearance as... an affliction. Consider it like the disease that turns men's flesh to scales if that helps. Consider it a physical deformity."

"It is not just your appearance," Marius argued. "We have all heard the screams of Asaric Baelannor."

Nalazar nodded. "A deserved punishment, I am afraid."

"And what was his sin to warrant such egregious and sustained punishment?"

"You don't know?"

The mage remained silent.

"Baelannor knew of a secret entrance to the Cellarium Vaults. Did you even know there was a back door to the repository of dangerous realm-ending magic? Hmmm? And once a month, he, his *maggior*, and a 'volunteer' would make a secret pilgrimage into the vault. There, he would use magic from our Necronomicons – magic outlawed by your dynasties. He would leech the life essence from his volunteer and add it to his own to unnaturally extend his own life."

Marius sat silently as he considered the revelation.

"You dwell too much on the undead creatures, my friend. Necromancy's true power lies within the transfer of life force from one creature to another. Tell me. Have you ever benefited from any of the magical spells your dynasties outlawed?"

Vocazion straightened his blue robes. "No," he answered confidently.

"Then you have nothing to fear from me," the lich replied. He clucked his tongue and then snapped a finger. "Well, that is not *entirely* true. I would say that before *today*, you had nothing to fear from me. But then you went and defied my authority. For that transgression, punishment *must* be meted out."

"Like the punishment you delivered to Jurare?"

"They did attack me first."

"They responded after you cracked Sorceria in half," the mage said, his tone turning hostile. "You destroyed the sentinels that protect the island. And you threatened all of us."

The lich contemplated the words for a moment and then threw his hands exhaustively into the air. "Guilty as charged. Still, I want to know who you helped escape from the city."

"It was my matron and our house man-at-arms," the patron said.

While tough to read behind his mask, the lich let his shoulders drop with an anticlimactic gesture. "No game of cat and mouse where I attempt to extract the truth and you resist me?"

"Wouldn't such a gesture be pointless?"

The undead wizard considered his options and then nodded in agreement.

"I see what you are doing here, Nalazar. Maybe you halt your progress as you have claimed once you have the army you desire. Maybe you don't. But freeing Arania from this city ensured her survival."

"At least for a while," the lich replied. "Still, the matron is an... odd choice. Isn't it? I could see a father risking everything for his children but to send your wife away?"

"I understand you have been living down in the city for a while," the mage stated. "Let me be clear. I did not send away my wife. I sent away my matron. And if I feel that way about her, perhaps you can understand what little sentimental attachment I have to my adepts, my apprentices, and my tyros."

"For your insolence and defiance of my law, there must be consequences. I hope you understand that."

"I do."

"Right now, I am leaning towards sentencing you to tower arrest. You would not be allowed to leave your dynast grounds. I would see to it that your needs are tended to. Food, water, the lot. With your matron gone, I could even see have carnal entertainment provided for you."

"Respectfully, the punishment does not fit the crime."

The lich cocked his head to the side with curiosity. "You would prefer a dank cell, deep underground, and be fed gruel and crusts of molding bread? Because I have all of that available at the snap of a finger. However, doing so would not help bring about my ultimate goal."

"And what is your ultimate goal, Master Catabaysi?"

"Oh, now. Things were going so swimmingly. I am back to being 'Master Catabaysi' now?"

"Then what is your ultimate goal, Nalazar?"

"Is it not obvious? Recruitment," the lich said with a laugh. "No longer being a victim of the *pherein*, I am free to explore the mysteries of magic that the dragons either did not want us to know or sought to keep from us. You are a patron, a master wizard. I could use a talent like you beside me, not opposing me."

Marius looked at the black mask, the silk gloves, and the concealing robes that covered the undead wizard from head to toe.

"Maybe there is a reason why such mysteries were kept from us. Maybe it is a warning that certain spheres were not meant to be explored or harnessed."

"Spoken like a mortal," Nalazar replied.

Chapter 73

There was a sigh of relief from many when the rear entrance to the cadenta opened and the crew returned home. Cavin Jurare was the first to greet the group, quickly giving Cinder an affectionate embrace. Both Sario and Amman offered greetings. Loredana Summerbrook was happy to see her business partners return as were many of the ladies working within the nameless cadenta.

But joy turned to outright excitement when they saw the dogcart parked in the rear alleyway. It was loaded down with gifted stores from the private reserve of the Moonshine Gloom. It was not magically conjured food cursed with half flavors. It was real food dating from before the occupation.

With hushed whispers, Loredana ordered the girls to help bring the food inside before Shader citizens could catch a glimpse. As the last of the crates and bags were hauled inside, Valos Ironblade looked over at the madam. "The family provides," he said confidently.

"I have never doubted you," she said with an affectionate pat on the shoulder.

Once inside, there was a palpable crackling of excitement within the cadenta. Back into her role as house mother, Loredana was quickly issuing orders and directing traffic within the halls. Popping her head inside the kitchen, she noted Thade Skystone was separating the foodstuffs from The Gloom and talking about his time spent aboard the *Castella Mare*. The ship's mother told him how armies march on their bellies. Sailors sailed on theirs. The ladies of the cadenta deserved the same.

Waiting for a break in his commentary, the madam called out with authority. "Thade, I know too many chefs spoil the soup but many hands make light work. Whatever girls you need to prepare the meal are at your disposal."

"Thank you, Lady Summerbrook."

The madam and Valos continued their walk through the cadenta. "What did your masters have to say about the other situations?" she asked.

"I don't know if I like that term," the rogue replied. "The family is not too different than what you have built here. I doubt any of your girls call you 'master' or 'mistress.' 'Mother' is probably a more appropriate term."

"That usually costs extra," she said with a grin.

"Luckily, I've got some extra coins," he said with a chuckle. "But no. It is the damnedest thing. Lady Darksteel has suspended tribute."

"That is *unprecedented*," the madam replied. "These truly are desperate times. Still, it wasn't like men were coming in droves to fulfill their urges anyway."

"But especially now, you think this would be the ultimate time for a person to want to get lost in the garden of earthly delights."

"Not a lot of disposable coins circulating. Especially when you don't know where your next meal is coming from."

The duo watched as several of the girls and the male shaman were busy hauling furniture out of the main parlor to make as much space as possible. Sario was busy issuing orders and directing girls.

In another of the parlors, Sway, Cinder, and a small collection of the ladies were busy setting up a large communal table to allow everyone to eat together. "I wonder how Anslo and Theobold are," Sway said. "They were always doing jobs for me but it sounds like running the streets is too risky nowadays. I hope they are well."

"Those are those two runners you use, right?" Cinder asked.

"Yes, they are too young to be considered proper assets but when they get older…" Sway's voice trailed off as she glanced around at the various place settings. "You know, we would have a lot more room on the roof."

Cinder halted her preparation. "That's true. But would it put undo attention on us? We've got enough food for us here. I don't want to necessarily rub it in the noses of other Shaders."

"We would be on the roof. Who is going to see us? Ain't no building tall enough around us. And we are in the blind spot of the big floaty island."

"That is true. Make sure the sun is past the mountains. Eat in the shade?"

The two turned as the duo of Loredana and Valos stood in the entryway. "Lady Summerbrook," Cinder said. "Shall we dine in the fresh air of the evening?"

"It is better if we stay inside," the madam said. "If the wind is wrong and the fog rolls in from the south, it is… not good to be outside. South of the High is not a good place right now."

The rogue wizard nodded. "We will make it work."

And make it work they did. Using the underground passage joining the cadenta with the bathhouse next door, the entire group had made it a point to bathe or shower and get dressed in nice attire. Then, as a collective, the members of the unnamed cadenta sat and enjoyed a simple but hearty evening meal as a family.

Cinder had brought forth a handful of her air-chilling pots to keep the room cool. There were sporadically placed faceted glass pieces emitting mage-light. It was just enough to banish the darkness but not so much as to attract attention.

Crocks of vegetables, mashed potatoes, and pan-seared chicken were passed around. A few bottles from Valos's private reserve were made available along with ice-chilled water and sugared lemon drinks.

As they ate and passed bowls back and forth, far too many eyes lingered on Amman's broad, bronze shoulders and the long braids of white hair he kept lashed back out of his face. Seeing a Malinsuli in the flesh was a rarity and Amman's natural handsomeness and size were something to be admired. But rather than shirk or shrink from the attention, the shaman leaned in and was happy to carry on conversations with any of the young women.

After dinner, everyone either chipped in to clean or joined Sario for her latest experiment in the cadenta's main hall. The furniture had all been removed and the mage-light glasses placed within the dormant fireplace. The many ladies of the cadenta had retired to their rooms but, as per the shaman's instructions, had returned in their sleepwear, carrying pillows and blankets.

Sario had arranged a whole host of mattresses brought from the upstairs rooms and had them arranged around the main hall. Several of the girls heard the shaman referring to it as "the Malinsuli way."

Full from the rich and abundant meal, a scattered dashing of wine, and their eyes heavy, many of the girls were quick to find places to sleep, often pairing or even tripling up on a mattress. Some laid down to sleep and stretched a hand out to hold another on the next mattress over.

Amongst the group, Cinder found herself beside Sario. The shaman wore a look of satisfaction on her lovely features. "Together," she said proudly. "Not apart."

From behind the two, Valos sidled out of the shadows. "I am not going to lie. I have dreamed about walking into rooms like this."

Cinder shook her head. "I would say you've got competition. Did you see the way all the ladies were ogling Amman?"

"Rat bastard," Valos replied. "What with all his tallness, good looks, that mane of white hair, and that dumb accent of his."

"You know I have that dumb accent too."

Valos pretended to be startled and jumped at Sario's voice. "In the darkness, I thought you were Sway."

"I wish I had her hips," the shaman said. "Amman is just getting the same attention you did down in Malinsula, what with you all being the foreigners down there."

"Still, all that being said, this is a good idea," Valos said, gesturing toward the room.

"Not just because this is your fantasy?" Cinder asked.

"Even though this *is* my fantasy," Valos corrected. "No, this is the bonding that we need. For the girls, for us, for the crew... for the family. For now, we are safe behind our locked doors. Sario is right. There is no sense in us locking ourselves away from each other in even smaller rooms. We've suspended tribute. Everyone is fed. They have a safe bed. Gestures like this build loyalty."

Sario hunched her shoulders and attempted her best Ombraterran accent. "What do you do?"

Valos shook his head. "Between you and your cousin, neither one of you can figure out the right way to use that expression. You'll get it though."

From out of the throngs of attendance for the communal sleeping arrangement, one of the girls approached the trio. Cinder had seen the young lady before. She was a pretty, young thing, short in stature but well known and highly ranked amongst the workers within the cadenta. If the madam was the family *caput*, then she had earned the title of captain amongst her fellow girls. Cinder struggled to place her name. Sway would have recognized her first name, family name, knew the young lady's backstory, and could probably tell the trio how many siblings she had.

"Abella," Valos acknowledged the woman with a nod.

Abella Rosesworn's family name finally triggered Cinder's memory.

"Time for bed," Abella said.

Taking Valos by the hand, she guided him to a comfortable mattress with an assortment of pillows and soft blankets.

Chapter 74

Beyond the walls of the Incanterran capital, over the Blue River running along the city's eastern border and into Highstone Harbor, up along the gently rolling hills hosting the city's grand arena and a thick deciduous forest, the pair of crystalline drakes touched softly down against the forest floor. From their location up on the hills and looking down into the capital itself, Arania Vocazion and Tanairs Corvalonn took a moment to glance backward at the besieged capital and the sundered wizarding isle hanging above.

The matron mage's breath caught in her throat as she saw the totality of the city and the scarred isle of Sorceria. It was one thing to see the isle from the top of her tower or the lush lawns of the wizard grounds. But to see the once proud and majestic island shattered and hanging ominously above the city was a whole new perspective.

Standing behind her, Corvalonn wasted no time, stripping out of his masquerade. The sorcerer then began donning the crimson and cream-trimmed robes of his noble wizarding dynasty. Once he was properly attired, he took a moment to share Arania's view of his beloved island and her capital.

"Tragic, is it not?" the mage asked.

From their position in the east, they were unable to see the rubble of what was once the Jurare tower, yet, even at a distance and with so much time removed, small tufts of smoke continued to swirl and curl up into the late afternoon sky.

Casting his gaze down into the city proper, Corvalonn noted the districts and wards south of the Queen's High Way. The summer temperatures were baking the city and heat mirages rippled in waves. But included within those shimmering waves were the noxious green pollution clouds that even the strongest southern winds could not cast out.

"This will be a dark part of our history," Corvalonn said as he began to rummage through a leather satchel on his hip.

"I take it the drakes will no longer be needed?" Arania asked.

"No," he replied curtly as he continued searching for a specific keystone.

Producing her magic wand, Arania began to cast a quick dispelling. In a swirling torrent, the crystalline drakes began to dissolve. The tornado of blue sparkles and azure shimmers coalesced into twin figurines landing softly on the forest floor and ended so small that Arania could place them both in the palm of her hand. She tucked the crystal figures into one of the padded and reinforced pouches on her traveling belt.

Corvalonn continued to meticulously sort through the various material components in his small array of pouches. "Now then," he said confidently, "I figure it is best not to open a portal in the middle of the king's throne room."

"I thought time was of the essence."

"Completely bypassing their kingdom's army and the sovereign's royal security is probably not the best way to instill trust in the young man."

Arania rolled her eyes and gently paced as Corvalonn prepared the material components for his spell. "I suppose you are right," she begrudgingly admitted. "All those corn-fed Arvateri probably wouldn't know how to respond to a proper wizard within their presence anyway."

"I do believe the Arvateri have their own wizards," Corvalonn quipped.

"And I am sure they rank right up there with those hoodoo shamans of Malinsula or the entrail-reading witch doctors of Selvaterra."

Corvalonn tried to restrain his chuckle. "Nevertheless, I believe the boy king will be an easier sell than the king of Castratellus. Still, if I had my choice, I would go visit, Crown Lucerria first. But if we can have secured Arvateri support, it will certainly be a bargaining chip we can use to bring the Castratellans into the fight."

"I hear the Castratellans have sun magic?"

"Their wizards divine their magic from both solar and lunar energies," the sorcerer said. "It is the reason why I would rather travel there first. I am curious to see how they spin up their magic as opposed to our arcane style."

"Well then, get us to Arvaterra, we will do what we have to and then you can hop, skip, and jump the two of us over to the Land of Castles."

Corvalonn arched an eyebrow. "Do not look to the second task before we have secured the first. We must tread lightly into Messis and the king's castle. We were both hinted witnesses to the quiet chaos that befell Ce'Mondere with the unexpected death of their patron. That was one wizarding house. Now, amplify that with the magnitude of a king."

"Poor planning on their part," Arania replied coldly.

"In King Ceres's defense, I don't think any sovereign *plans* on losing both his princely heirs to a war with Monterra."

"And in the name of the gods, it would be sacrilegious to let his mother reign until the boy came of age."

Corvalonn halted his preparations and turned abruptly and with authority. He glared silently for several heartbeats before properly enunciating his carefully crafted thoughts. "Arvaterra is not Incanterra and you would be well advised to keep that in mind when we go before the king. He has stewards. He has advisors. He has his courtesans. But he is also young. Even though we refer to him as the boy king in jest, the lad certainly has his first sprouts of fuzz on his stones. And to be frank, as I understand it, the boy is a bit of a prick – as would any ill-raised child who is now granted his every whim and never told no.

"So let me reiterate, strongly and again, we must tread lightly.

"We cannot afford a single misstep or insult. During our meeting, Marius suggested you should be the envoy to counterbalance my… sternness. So I am expecting you to be charming… accommodating… nice."

"Maybe you should have brought a plethora of the most curvaceous ladies Incanterra has to offer or that air-brained Acelendra Mutaccio," Arania suggested.

"What I need is a second voice – a feminine counterpart – to smile and make nice who is not a dullard or a nitwit. We are trying to convince this king to send his armies to war when the last conflict killed his older siblings."

"A tragedy to be sure," Arania replied smoothly, "but a tragedy that put the boy on the throne."

Corvalonn raised his chin and then let a smile slowly creep across his face. "And it is insight like *that* which proves Marius was correct. That is the persuasive voice that I need. Anyone can tickle the boy's nethers. I need someone to slither into his brain and convince him it is in his best interest to send his soldiers to war against an undead foe."

"I will do my best to assist you," the mage matron replied.

Continuing his search through his keystones, Corvalonn scanned the various stones he had acquired over his wizarding career. There was the ingot of Monterran ore that always felt cold. There was the sandstone of Agavinsula. He touched the soft tufts of mossy flocking on a piece of wood from the tall slither root trees of Selvaterra.

Finally, Corvalonn produced a small hexagonal piece of granite marked with a variety of runes. Touching the smooth stone with his bare fingertips, the wizard was able to sense the connection with the neighboring kingdom of Arvaterra to the east. Sealing the flap on his belt pouch, the wizard prepared to summon his incantation.

Before he could begin casting, he shook his head and took a deep breath. "Arvaterra," he grumbled.

"Are they that bad?"

Corvalonn issued a growl from deep in his chest. "It is not an easy answer. They are not bad people. They are just unenlightened. One might say they are behind the times."

Thinking back to the assemblage of the wizarding patrons within the confines of Sorceria's basilica or the male leadership amongst Incanterra's castellan and her archons, Arania thought it best not to point out the hypocrisy of the patron's statement.

"Castratellus will be a different matter," Corvalonn said. "They are more progressive with their views. They are more forward-thinking and willing to embrace new ideas. I feel like the citizens of Arvaterra cling to this fog-viewed belief of the glory of a wonderous age from the past."

"While they are shitting in buckets and dumping it in alleys," Arania replied abruptly.

Corvalonn dipped his chin, waved his hands, and tried not to laugh. "I have often said if we could bring the Arvateri people to Incanterra and show them what we have to offer, they would embrace us as brothers. Instead, the boy king wants all our magic while keeping to their traditions. Still, these are arguments for another day."

"What if that is the price to march his army? What if the boy king wants some sort of wizard exchange program to send his troops to war?"

Corvalonn pondered the question for a moment and then said, "We'll send them Acelendra Mutaccio."

With that, the wizard whipped his wand to the ready and began opening a portal. The circle of red magic tinged with flowing black circles crackled and expanded. Reality shimmered and distorted and when it snapped clear, the gentle, wheat-covered hills of Arvaterra and her kingly capital of Messis warbled into view.

The patron and matron stepped through from Incanterra to Arvaterra. With a collapsing whoosh, the magical portal devoured into itself and then sizzled out of reality, leaving the Incanterran wind to rustle the forest trees.

Chapter 75

The last thing Reeve Windwisher remembered before the world went dark was clutching the spherical glass bottle filled with an unnaturally glowing, sickly green concoction. He remembered downing the liquid in big, forceful gulps but for the life of him, he couldn't remember what the glowing ooze tasted like. What he remembered was his body becoming completely limp. His muscles pooled like soup in a bowl.

It was for the best because, with the fire that came next, Reeve felt for certain his skin and clothes were going to burst into flame. He wanted to scream and writhe in pain but he could not even blink. Eventually, he could not even take a breath. Slowly, darkness began to creep into the edges of his vision.

He tumbled further and further down the tunnel until his vision was little more than a single pinprick of light. Finally, that single dot of light warbled, then wavered, and then blinked out of existence.

And then there was nothing.

It could have been but a twinkling. It could have been a century. For Reeve Windwisher, there was only darkness. Then, like an opaque pane of glass shattered by a titan's hammer, the darkness was smashed away. Reeve gasped the deepest breath and sat up abruptly from the cold onyx slab.

And yet, with that sharp intake of breath, there was something different. Something was off. He quickly realized it was instinct alone and the once precious air was no longer a necessity.

Reeve looked down at his hands and his forearms peeking out from under the wide-hemmed ceremonial robes he wore. His flesh was oddly tinted as if a painter had dabbed the smallest dollops of blue and mixed them with a flat gray. His tongue had no taste. And as he rubbed his fingertips together, it was like his flesh had been coated in velvet.

The sound of steel clattering against stone rang out from behind him. Reeve turned abruptly, swiveling on the altar, and saw Nalazar Catabaysi floating beside him. The ring of steel continued to echo as the long sword finally settled from its clanging drop.

Reaching out with a sense Reeve could barely process, he could feel the presence of Nalazar writ large before him. But beyond the necro-lord, beyond the walls of the chamber, and outward, Reeve could also sense the other undead milling about or standing guard. Instinctively, he felt a bond. It was hard to describe as a mental connection as the undead did not have traditional minds. And yet, Reeve understood he could telepathically command them to tasks of his choosing.

Rising from the altar, Reeve knelt to pick up the sword left on the floor by his lich master. The hilt felt odd in his hands. While it was bare skin connecting with the weapon, Reeve would have sworn he was wearing gloves.

One of the doors to the altar room grated open on squeaking hinges. Reeve turned and saw three prisoners paraded inside, lashed together in chains. An apprentice Necromangian quickly released them from their shackles while a second stood by. Once the prisoners were freed, each was handed a modest longsword. Gathering up the chains, the necromancers hustled quickly from the room.

Nalazar began to gently float toward the balcony positioned high on the room's walls for an elevated view of the festivities. His eerie voice reverberated off the stone. "Before you is the path to your freedom," the lich said. "Slay the one in front of you and any that survive will be granted a pardon and released."

Reeve settled his gaze on the three prisoners. All of the men were desperate and afraid but, with swords held at the ready, they were invited to take their destiny into their own hands. They looked upon their single undead opponent like jackals eyeing a wounded predator.

Little did they know, Reeve had trained more than a few of the Knights of the Imperial Circle. He was no stranger to the blade. He brought the heavy weapon up to bear in a battle stance.

Despite not knowing each other, the prisoners coordinated their maneuvers and did their best to encircle the enforcer before moving to attack. Reeve easily parried the first lunging strike, pivoted, ducked a cut aimed for his neck, and then fended off another advance.

The foursome danced around the arena. The ring of steel against steel echoed off the walls and the high ceiling. As the fight wore on, Reeve was amazed at how fatigue refused to set in. The strength of his sword swings and the speed of his steps never slowed. If anything, he felt he was faster than he was before. It was not like he had swigged one of Mutaccio's famed speed potions. He was not superhuman but still faster than he should have been. It was just enough of an uptick to make his timing difficult to anticipate.

One of the prisoners learned this the hard way when he predicted a blocking parry from Reeve. Instead, the knight pulled back at the last second. The lunge left the man overextended and stumbling to regain his balance. That small mistake was all it took.

Reeve's massive blade swung like a clock wheel. The blade descended with incredible speed and relieved the man's neck of the burden of his head. The body dropped lifelessly and the decapitated head bounced several times against the stone floor.

Enraged by the death of his comrade, the second prisoner charged forward. Scooping up the abandoned blade of the dead prisoner, he attacked Reeve with twin weapons. With Reeve fighting two-handed and the prisoner fighting with two weapons, the man was finally able to work his way through Reeve's defenses.

Sword slashes connected. Slicing through his ceremonial attire, cuts began to mar Reeve's undead flesh, connecting with his shoulder, across his chest, and a deep slash across his midsection. Yet, not once did the undead knight cry out or even register the pain. Even when the desperate prisoner skewered the knight through the belly, Reeve glared at the man for the briefest of moments...

And proceeded to run him through with his two-handed blade.

The third prisoner dropped his sword to the floor, a loud clang reverberating through the chamber. As the prisoner turned to run, Reeve reversed his grip on his longsword and hurled the weapon like a javelin. The sword sliced through the man's back and erupted from the prisoner's chest along with a vomit of blood. The man stumbled, staggered, and then collapsed to the stone, his blood pooling underneath him.

Taking a deep, instinctive, but wholly unnecessary breath, Reeve looked at the bodies lying scattered about the makeshift arena and then down at the sword slashes across his body refusing to leak any sort of fluid or ichor.

From the balcony above, Nalazar used his magical powers to float to the floor. He looked upon his newest apprentice – his newest weapon – with pride and admiration. "How do you feel?"

Reeve gave a little scoff and then a smile. "Ironically, I feel... alive."

Nalazar nodded knowingly. "It is as if a veil has been lifted. For the first time, you are now free from the weight of fear."

Reeve's eyes went wide. "That is it, Master. That is it exactly."

"And once we are truly free from the confines and weakness of the flesh, we can explore the true mysteries of the world. But you also need to heal."

Reeve was following Nalazar as the wizard master walked over to the closest slain prisoner. "But I was under the impression healing spells do not work on dead flesh."

"That is true. Thankfully, we have other means."

Instinctively, Reeve understood what he meant. Kneeling, the death knight leaned over and sank his yellowing teeth into the prisoner's bicep. Tearing away the muscle in large hunks, he continued to chew and swallow. Slowly, Reeve could feel his undead flesh begin to knit and bind itself back together.

If he could have seen himself from outside of his body, he would have noted the blue tinges in his ashen flesh receding slightly and his pallid color regaining more of its natural hue. Over a long enough time, his wounds would seal up and even disappear.

Having eaten his fill, the dead knight returned to his feet and spun to gaze upon Nalazar. "Thank you, Master. Thank you for this amazing gift you have bestowed upon me. How can I repay you?"

"I have the armorsmiths you brought me preparing something special for you. They are modifying a suit of the sentinel armor the wizards used to patrol and defend Sorceria. The alloy it is made from will provide additional defense against the wizards... and believe me, they will be targeting you."

"I am not afraid," the knight replied.

"And that is why you will become my best weapon. You will become the weapon I need to discourage those who would stand against us."

"Who would you have me target, Master?"

Chapter 76

Concealed in the dark of the night, from the rooftop of the building in the Shaded Light ward, Cavin Jurare was holding court. Alongside him were Valos, Sway, Thade, Cinder, and their newest friends Sario and Amman. With his spyglass in hand, Cavin was looking carefully down into the city streets below. Finally seeing what he was looking for, he collapsed the spyglass with a snap and then pointed down the avenue.

"There," he whispered. "Look there."

In the mage-light still prominent along the streets and avenues, there were two marching columns of skeleton soldiers. They were equipped with modest armor and short swords with little to no ornamentation. These were the bargain basement soldiers within the undead ranks patrolling a normally quiet ward. They marched in such unison that the stomp of their hard-soled heels made an almost musical rhythm echoing out into the night.

"So, I've been watching these skellies for more than a few days now. Zombies are undead that run on basic instinct. And the most basic instinct is to feed."

Valos started to object with a lascivious comment but Sway glared at him before he could.

Cavin continued. "Once a zombie is created and loosed upon the world, they know no master. They just shamble about biting and eating anything that they can. Skeletons are different. I wouldn't go so far as to call them smart. You can't hand them a slate and some chalk and expect them to do arithmetic. But they follow orders. Now, look at that skeleton patrol there."

The skeletons marched with a methodical and relentless pace but they also marched in lockstep with one another. Even the swinging of their arms was in unison. It was synchronicity only seen outside of a group of artistic performers or a dancing troop.

"Think of them as sharing a singular mind and that unison is reinforced once you get more than a few of these things together," the undead slayer explained. "But that is the key to this whole thing. If all of those skellies are in lockstep, it means they are not being directly controlled by a Necromangian up there on Sorceria."

"What does it look like when a Necromangian is controlling one of the skeletons?" Amman asked.

"They don't move in unison because you can tell they are being controlled albeit remotely. They move differently. They move under the command of a master. This lot here, they are not under direct control."

Valos understood the stakes. "So no witnesses."

"If we are fast enough," Cavin replied. "We slay 'em quick. Haul the bones away. They're just a random patrol that never came back."

"So we test the theory," Thade said. "We take them out. Wait for reprisals. If there are none, we feed this out to the other captains."

"And the sashers," Valos noted. He paused briefly and then sharply exhaled through his nostrils. "That still feels strange to say."

"Those columns there," Sway said. "What is that? A dozen? Don't get me wrong. Putting a dozen skeletons in a locker is not a bad thing. But how many skellies do they have at their disposal?"

Thade pulled one of his hand axes from the leather thong on his belt. "After tonight? Twelve less."

The collection was quick to follow Thade's lead. The group of seven silently sidled down the stairs to get down to the ground floor. "I don't know if we are dressed properly for this kind of thing. Shouldn't we all be outfitted in black with deep cloaks with hoods and what not?" Sway asked.

"Which is more conspicuous out on the street?" Valos answered. "A group of seven citizens working late at night? Or a group of seven assassins skulking through the darkness?"

Exiting out into the alleyway and running along the rear of the building, Thade noted a plethora of empty sundry bags. Trash removal had been spotty at best since the siege began and the alleys were as good a place as any for people to dump their refuse. Snatching up several handfuls of the burlap bags, he passed them out to his cohorts. "No evidence," he said.

Moving quickly through the alleys, the seven set upon the entrance out into the street and silently waited for the patrol of skeletons to make their way past. Sway hunkered close to Cinder. "So, if you wizards can cast mage-light, can you summon darkness?" Sway asked. "Because that would be really helpful right now."

"There is a darkness spell. But aside from my wand and the somatic components, I need a thimble full of coal dust and a pinch of bat fur. The coal dust is not too hard to come by. But with all the apothecary shops either closed up or Necromangian spots to trap wayward wizards, I don't have the components I need to cast the spell."

"We will just have to settle for speed then," Sario replied, producing her wooden cudgel.

"Seven against twelve," Valos said.

"I like our chances," Amman replied.

The skeletons sustained their ceaseless synchronized stomping as they continued their patrol down the street. It was a curious display as the skeletons kept what passed as their eyes pointed straight ahead. The small pinpricks of glowing red lights in their eye sockets were not scanning up and down the side streets or the alleyways. The marching felt more like a display of force to remind the citizens of Incanterra who were truly in charge.

As such, when the skeletons marched past a certain alleyway, they met with a predator of opportunity. The charge hit the pair of columns in the center and with such swiftness, the skeletons at the front of the procession continued their methodical march even after a lightning-lined axe took one skull from its exposed spinal column. An obsidian weapon cleaved mystical tendons at elbows and knees. A silver longsword slashed, stabbed, and swatted its way through defenses.

Skeletons were clacking to the paved road in calcified piles, accompanied by the sounds of rattling chainmail and armor plates. Swords clanged against stone. The skeleton patrol leaders turned at the sound of the commotion and they were met with swift blades and unlife-ending slashes.

Thankfully, without voices, there were no screams of pain. There were no cries of anguish. There were no whimpers for mercy as a shadowed Blade mounted on top of a hobbled and amputated skeleton. And there was no death rattle as spinal columns were smashed and skulls were left decapitated.

As quickly as the attack began, it was over.

The coalition of the seven glanced up and down the quiet streets. Thankfully, they were dark and empty. There were no witnesses and the group breathed a collective sigh of relief. Now, there was the issue of the dozen slain skeletons lying in the street.

While the lights in the front of the shop positioned next to the street never flickered to life and the apartments above remained dark, the main door of the shuttered mercantile opened up. Several of the group spun with an initial flash of weapons but they quickly saw they were not needed.

The frame around the top of the door was decorated with a black piece of metal shaped in the form of a dagger. Valos was quick to approach the family who paid protection money. Seeing all that had occurred, the members of different families sheltering in the apartments were quickly coming outside. Each member carried the same style of sundry bag Thade had snatched from the alleyway.

Working together, the Incanterrans began stuffing the inanimate bones into the bags. The armor and weapons were quickly confiscated. They scrambled to pick up every wayward piece of the now inanimate skeletons.

Valos pulled aside the apparent senior leader of the citizens, "I want you to do me a favor," the rogue said while trying to palm the man some coins.

The citizen politely refused. "I can't take that, Master Ironblade. We are here to help."

"Good man," he replied with a nod. "Have everyone gather up the armor and weapons. Stash them. But make them available to any citizen who can swing a sword when the time comes. Man, woman, lad, lass, I don't care who."

"We can do that."

"Good. After that, I need you to make these bones disappear however you have to. Smash 'em. Grind 'em up. Dump them piece by piece in different sewer grates. I don't care how you do it as long as it gets done. But do me a favor. Keep the skulls."

The citizen nodded his understanding.

"The back alley behind the bathhouse. You know the one I mean?"

"Yes sir."

"Good. You will find some empty crates there. Put the skulls in bags and as quietly as you can, get them over there. Leave the skulls in the crates. Be careful now. Don't get caught. But I want them to send those tossers a message."

"This is the start of it?" the man asked hopefully.

"Strikes like this are," Valos assured him. "And once we have enough, you better believe we are going to be making a clear and loud statement."

"Whatever we need?" the man asked.

Valos nodded and smiled. "Whatever you need."

Chapter 77

With so many businesses shuttered, with so many people released from their daily duties, and with so many children left at home during the academic shutdown, the streets of Incanterra had transformed into ghost walks. What used to be a vibrant and bustling city had been reduced to a shell of its former self. But it was not just the districts and the wards suffering such a cruel fate.

Even before the undead siege, the wizardly isle of Sorceria would never have been described as congested. The dynasties of The Eight were larger than any traditional family with many branches of the relative tree living within the dynasty towers. There was the isle's support staff tending to the chores and tasks a wizard would never sully their hands with. Yet, the word "crowded" would never be used amongst descriptions used by the bards or the poets.

Still, like many of the citizens living down below, most of the wizards chose to remain inside their towers as much as possible. Scullery maids, cooks, and other staff were minimal at best. With Catabaysi banning travel down to the city except for closely monitored and regulated traffic, the support staff was forced to live in the basement quarters of most towers. And even then, only the most necessary, loyal, and tolerable staffers were allowed to remain within the estate grounds.

With so many remaining within their towers and with no support staff milling about tending to shrubbery, the lawns, or cleaning the communal structures, when a wizard did venture out, they were easily spotted. Easily scrutinized. Easily targeted.

Standing on one of the balconies of the Baelannor tower and looking down on the empty Sorcerian paths, it was all too easy for Devinaya Baelannor to see. Instead of seeing the bright and outstanding colors of the various dynasties milling about, the isle was populated with the red robes of the Necromangians.

Unfortunately, it was not just their wizard cabal. The Knights of the Imperial Order had been granted access to the floating isle with far greater privileges than anyone else. While their initial sojourns had fostered an attitude of reverence and wonder, now, the knights were growing comfortable. And with that comfort grew entitlement. While their ivory vestments and their conical hoods made them stand out even more, there were still far too many knights walking amongst the pathways.

Unfortunately, more than a few of the Imperial Knights were happy to take excessive advantage of the magical amenities offered on the isle, including the legal loophole allowing the consumption of spirits. After pledging and proving their loyalty to Master Catabaysi, then fueled with intoxicants, many of the knights considered themselves privileged. With that privilege, they felt entitled to become handsy with any servant they chose. And what was more, believing the Catabaysi to now be the "superior", they took liberties with wizardesses from "lesser" houses that no knight in his right mind would have attempted down in the city.

Looking down on the empty winding pathways curling between the eight wizarding towers and the communal structures in the center of the isle, Devinaya exhaled sharply out of her nose. The sundering of the isle, the overtaking of the Catabaysi, the open flaunting from the Knights of the Imperial Circle... It was all too much.

The wizardess could not decide if it was better to walk alone or in pairs when traversing the isle. Was it better to attract less attention or was it better to have witnesses if confronted? She was angered by both scenarios. This was Sorceria, not the Southwest District. But she did not know how to reverse the course.

After the initial crippling wave of the isle siege, Devinaya had done her best to memorize the names and faces of the various Necromangians that had overtaken her ancestral tower. Still, between the elite hierarchy, the adepts, the tyros, and the apprentices, it was hard to keep so many names and faces straight in her head.

The last thing she wanted to do was write things down in a scroll or a ledger to help her keep the individuals straight and the Necromangian numbers properly tallied. There could be no scroll trail. She did not want evidence that could be brought before Nalazar Catabaysi... especially after how she heard the lich made her stoic master scream.

"Mistress Devinaya?" a pipsqueak came from behind her.

The conjurer turned to see one of her apprentices – a sweet girl named Villea – standing in her doorway. The youngling was not even into double digits but she was quickly ascending the ranks of the apprentices with her innate magical talent. Her long, blonde hair was braided into twin plaits and pulled back out of her face. Devinaya thought the lass would be better off concealing her ears which were just a size too big and stuck out too far. The young wizardess clutched a tome to her chest so oversized that she had to wrap both arms around it to keep a hold of it.

"Villea," Devinaya said while beckoning her into the private sanctum with a wave of her arm.

"There will be no lessons today?" the lass asked, unable to hide her disappointment.

Devinaya heaved a sigh and gestured for the young conjurer to join her out on one of the padded benches on her balcony. "I think of all The Eight, we Baelannors might use material components the most," she said as she took a seat.

The young pupil plopped down on the bench beside her, putting the heavy spellcasting tome in her lap.

"Well... maybe. I am not certain," Devinaya continued. "The Lu'Scions might have us beat if you tabulate all the strange material components they need because their magic is so diverse. And all the potion brewing means the Mutaccios are no slouches. But theirs are mostly the things like the xanthorr extract that makes up the stock of most of their drinkable potions."

Devinaya shook her head to clear her thoughts and looked down at little Villea. "My point is," she said with a smile, "we don't have enough spare materials to allow you to practice. We need to save them in case we need them."

Villea protruded her bottom lip. In a rare show of affection, Devinaya reached over and rubbed the little girl's back. "It's not fair," Villea pouted.

"I know, my little *wysard*," she said sympathetically.

The two sat in silence for a short while.

"I envy you, Vee," Devinaya said.

"Truly? Why?"

"For you, it is just about the magic. You just want to learn how to cast spells."

"I think it is fun!" she said with resolve. "I like not knowing how to do things and then learning how to do them."

"I wish I could remember how fun it is to just cast. Not for coins. Not for the people. Not for the city. Just for the joy of casting magic."

"What's stopping you?" the lass asked.

Devinaya gestured towards the sundered isle, the darkened wizarding tower of Lu'Scion in the distance, and the pile of rubble where the Jurare tower once stood. "And let's not forget," the wizardess said.

She curled her face up in a snarl, stuck out her tongue, and gestured towards the girl with gnarled, curled hands.

"I don't like them," Villea admitted. "The skeletons are scary but not as scary as those ghasts with all the dead meat on them."

"I am not a fan of any of them either."

"But I especially don't like that Nalazar."

"Don't say that too loudly," Devinaya warned. "You never know who might be listening to us."

Villea nervously drummed her fingers on the cover of the spell tome.

"We will get things back to how they were before," Devinaya assured her. "But when we do, you must promise me something."

"Of course," the little girl said with a smile.

"I see your brothers and sisters — the older ones — and I have my concerns. I am afraid they don't appreciate the wizarding life we have provided them. I often wonder if we have treated them too softly. I feel like they are out living the good life without appreciating what it took to get here and what it takes to maintain it.

"But I see the spark in your eyes. I see the excitement when you are trying over and over again to master a spell. I don't want you to lose that excitement. I want you to remember why we do what we do. It is not exclusively about the coins and the vaults. Those are important but they aren't the *only* reasons. We do this for the good of the people and for the good of Incanterra…"

Devinaya's words trailed off as her attention was pulled down into the front courtyard. Striding along the paving stones was a warrior dressed in coal-black plate armor.

The wizardess got to her feet and went to the railing. She watched as the armored enforcer strode through the gates, pivoted hard, and began making his way to the marble landing to take one of the sloops down to the city.

She noted the massive two-handed sword strapped at an angle on his back, the scabbard running underneath the tenting and billowing cape he wore. There was an aura of fear permeating and surrounding the figure that Devinaya had only experienced when she was alone in a room with Nalazar Catabaysi.

If Nalazar was an undead wizard, Devinaya wanted to assume whoever was wearing the demonic plate armor…

Could he have been an undead… warrior?

Chapter 78

When word was sent down for the Crimson Way to hand over control of Shaded Light to the Shadow Blades, like everything within the organizations, it was done so quietly. There was no fanfare. There were no formal declarations. The people who needed to know knew.

As for the citizenry, it was subtle. It took a while for them to notice the crimson sashes were no longer prominent within the oversized ward encompassing four full city blocks. Those kicking their protection coins over to the sashers were the first to notice the absence but for those who did not know the workings of the underground, life continued as normal.

After Valos, Sway, Thade, and Cinder quietly established themselves, whispers began to circulate, radiating outward from beyond those in the know. If you needed something, the quartet known to hang around the Shadow's Edge Inn could not get it for you... but they knew someone who could.

If you needed a temporary loan, if you needed something found, if you needed something wrongfully taken returned, or if you wanted keys to certain outlawed vices, people knew who to point to. Few knew how they did it but when you needed something off the books, people did not ask how. But, unlike when the Crimson Way was in control, things changed dramatically once magic was introduced to the ward.

It was simple things. Mage-light eliminated the need for candles and oil lamps. The Blades had access to affordable cooling pots to condition the air in the summer. They had heating stones to ward off the cold in the winter. They had even hotter stones used to heat skillets and ovens. But most importantly, it was offered at a price the common folk could finally afford.

As such, the infamous four – signified by the black daggers and black sheathes – were quickly spreading a reputation. Before the tragic fire, the people of the Shaded Light ward knew the four held a stake in the Shadow's Edge Inn. Shaders knew about the bathhouse, the affordable laundry services, the shop selling the iced cream, and other businesses backed by the four. There were also the whispers of the private social club where special companionship could be rented for an hour.

With all of these amenities offered to the people as well as a strong hand keeping the people safe, discouraging incursions from the Under Roads, restricting petty thefts, and keeping the poison spice off the street, the four had become folk heroes within the ward.

When the magical curtains descended on the gateways and the dead walked the streets, Shaders immediately looked to the foursome who repelled the Unbound to keep their people safe. But the heroes were not to be found.

Gone? Lost. Vanished? Taken. Dead?

Rumors were rampant.

But upon their return, word spread through the ward like streams of sunshine after a tragic tornado. So it was of little surprise that heads turned, wrists begged to be clasped, and appreciative nods were offered when Valos Ironblade walked the streets of Shaded Light.

"They treat you like King Muera," Amman said with a smile as he walked down the sidewalk beside Valos.

"Oh, I think they are paying more attention to you," Valos replied. "Don't take it personally. It is not an everyday thing to see a Malinsuli shaman walking Shaded Light. If I would have known it was going to be like this, I would have started a kiosk selling drool rags to all the ladies. I would have made a killing. Any chance you want to take your shirt off or swap out that sarong for something that displays your coins and prizes a little more prominently?"

"You sound like Swayna," Amman laughed. "She told me of her plans to start a house that offers the services of something her and Cinder were going to call... what was it?"

"Their 'Dandy Lions'?"

"That's it," Amman said with a snap of his fingers.

"Yeah, they have had that on a slow burn for a while now. Male belowsies. They are welcome to try but I don't see women paying for it."

"Maybe they wouldn't just cater to female clientele," Amman postulated.

"Hey, they can put it wherever they want as long as they are paying coin. That's all I care about."

Amman smiled and chose to hold his tongue. It was a brave display the rogue put out to the world. But given how the Incanterran citizens looked at Valos with such respect and even admiration, it was clear the man was not the vicious crime lord one expected him to be.

Rounding the corner, the two approached a large warehouse with big, sliding barn doors. Crowares Trade served as a waystation for importers who were waiting for customs inspectors to authorize their imports into the city. Normally, the business was stocked to the exposed rafters with items to keep a city flourishing. But with all trade now halted, the only remaining inventory was harder to move items or specialties that lacked demand.

Normally, at this time of day, Agrimiro Titanhand – the owner – would be barking orders to his dockhands and the men loading or unloading the wagons.

Instead, the floor was quiet. The retired soldier turned as the shadows of Valos and Amman darkened his doorway. "Valos!" he happily exclaimed.

The burly man stomped over to the doorway and was happy to embrace the Blade with his one good arm. "It is good to see you again. How is Cinder?"

"We are doing well," Valos said as he slapped Agrimiro on the back several times.

"I'd kill for a shipment from her right about now," the merchant said. "Although with my current stock, it would be hard to move items she likes to bring me."

"Agrimiro, I want you to meet a friend of *mine*," Valos said, gesturing toward his Malinsuli companion. "This is Amman. He is visiting from way down south."

"I would say so," Agrimiro said, offering up his wrist for a clasping.

"So with the stockpiles so low, is it even worth keeping the doors open?" Valos inquired.

Agrimiro shrugged. "After about probably two weeks in, I sent all my workers home. Nothing was coming in. I didn't have much else to go out. Still, I can't just shuffle around in my apartment. There is always a corner that needs sweeping. At least if I am here, the doors are open. Strangely, I think it gives people... I am not sure... Hope? Or at least a sense of normalcy."

Valos nodded as the merchant continued. "Although, there have been quiet whispers—"

"As opposed to loud ones?"

"Well, there are whispers and then there are whispers. But the people are talking about some sort of resistance? You wouldn't know anything about that, would you? Talk about missing skeletons squads?"

"Nope," Valos said with a hard inflection. "I wouldn't know."

"But would you know someone who knows someone?" Agrimiro pressed.

"Not only do I not know anyone, but even if I did, I wouldn't speak about it."

In their time together, Amman had never heard Valos issue such a serious tone.

"These red robers, the knights with their stupid hoods, and their boner squads, they don't play by straight rules," Valos continued. "The coppers? I had some respect for them. They had rules. Even if a copper knew, if he couldn't prove it, there was nothing he could do. You couldn't just trot a man up before the magistrate on suspicion. Hells, they even passed laws that said you had to have a barrister working for you.

"But these tossers? They are rounding up people for the smallest of infractions. It's not like the coppers had a solid presence in Shaded Light before but when was the last time you saw one of their shiny badges out on the street?"

Agrimiro nodded solemnly and looked to offer an apology but Valos waved him off. "If I sound serious, it is only because this is as serious as it gets. You have seen how they are rounding people up. They are looking for any sort of infraction. Our names cannot slip past anyone's lips. No light can be shined on us. None. Me, Cinder, that whole group? We are just normal citizens. If anyone asks, Amman is just a normal foreigner. So let's not give them an invitation."

"An invitation for what?" Agrimiro asked with a grin.

"My man," Valos said.

As a show of good faith, Valos opened his arms wide and gave the veteran a heartfelt hug.

Off in the distance, the clock tower in the center of the district rang her bells to signify the top of the hour. A few moments later, without even turning around to look out onto the city street, Valos gestured behind him, noting the methodical and synchronized stomping of skeletal feet wearing hard-soled leather boots as they marched past.

"The top of the hour," Valos noted to Amman. "Boners march past Crowares Trade."

Amman had risked a subtle look backward. "A dozen."

The former soldier nodded. "Scouting mission?"

"Tracking for patterns."

With the skeletons marched past and now down the street, Valos and Amman walked out of Crowares Trade and moved to their next target with a purpose without looking like they had a purpose.

"Happy hunting," Agrimiro whispered.

Chapter 79

"Kynna'Fyir!" the excited voice hissed with a whisper so as not to attract attention but was loud enough to cut across the din and through the modest mid-day crowd of Trader's Cross.

Despite not being dressed in the grass-green and copper-trimmed robes identifying her as a member of the Lu'Scion dynasty, the wizard-in-hiding turned abruptly.

Thyra Bellflower emerged from the crowd filling the square where the Northeast District's twin boulevards bisected. Frustrated shoppers did their best to scrounge through sundries and rummage over the dwindling stockpiles. Carrying a small bundle of scarce supplies and a bag of recently received rations, the young lady approached with a quickness steeped with relief and excitement.

Thyra was as short as some primary school students and looked as squat as she was tall. She had a cute, cherubic face and long brown hair she kept in a tightly braided plait. The young lady was as nice as could be and was known for her chipmunk laugh. But someone who knew Kynna's true identity was the last person the magician wanted to see on the city streets.

The young woman approached and was conflicted. She knew about the wizardly aversion for physical contact but, given the wizardess's commoner disguise, the last thing she wanted to do was out the magician to any suspicious eyes. Trader's Cross was crowded compared to some of the other streets – perhaps the most populated since the siege began – and Thyra was afraid of who would be lurking.

Having spent time with Mirawen Autumnlight and grown comfortable over in Shaded Light, Kynna leaned down to offer the Sorcerian attendant a hug. "Kynna," she whispered in her ear. "Kynna Summerwind."

Breaking their embrace, the lass nodded knowingly and flashed a quick wink. "What're you doing down here? Well... no. I mean... I know why you're down here but what are you doing down here?"

"I am over in Shaded Light," Kynna said. "I am working with one of the girls to hand out rations to the locals."

Thyra clapped her hands, "I'm doing the same thing over in Nestorian Heights. I cannot believe this. We've been neighbors all this time and didn't even know it."

For the slightest of moments, Kynna thought she detected the sudden smell of sunflowers but she passed it off as Thyra's perfume. Before she could comment on it, amongst the citizens, an uneasy wave of noise began to echo and rattle about the shopping areas of Trader's Cross. Turning in time, Kynna saw what had the populace on edge.

Reeve Windwisher walked the streets of Trader's Cross. He was adorned from head to toe in coal-black chainmail and dark plates of armor the color of the deepest cave. His helmet featured a T-shaped visor that revealed only the smallest strip of his eyes with their now yellow corneas and a sliver of the gray-blue skin of his nose and mouth. The undead knight wore a long, flowing cape that tented and billowed behind him, draped over the two-handed sword and scabbard strapped diagonally across his back.

As he walked, there was an ominous rattling and rustling of his plates and chain armor. His greaves sported a pair of terribly spiked spurs that jangled as he strode down the smoothly-paved boulevard.

The citizens of Incanterra moved with Reeve, hustling to stay out of arms and sword reach. They almost resembled a school of small fish, all moving in unspoken unison and just looking to stay out of striking distance of the large, lurking predator swimming amongst the sea of people. They would part and then fill back in after his wake had moved past.

As he approached the clock tower in the center of the square, the undead warrior performed the somatic components of the spell exactly as his master had taught him. He ran his thumb and index finger down the inner seams of the T-visor from the top of his nose down to his chin. The enchantment infused in his helmet came to life and his voice echoed with amplification far greater than normally possible.

"Citizens of Incanterra," the undead knight said, his voice reverberating off the walls of the nearby buildings. "I am the Sword of Lord Master Nalazar Catabaysi and I bring to you a formal declaration from my master."

The citizenry stopped their shopping and stood still as statues as all eyes fell upon the death knight.

"Wizards are hiding amongst you. Let it be known. Harboring them – directly or indirectly – is a formal crime. These wizards have absconded with certain relics and artifacts taken from the secure vaults within Sorceria. These terrible weapons were never meant to be amongst the people because they are so dangerous. I have been tasked with keeping you safe and I have been charged with retrieving these terrible weapons of war."

Kynna took a brief moment and glanced down at Thyra. She shook her head ever so slightly and whispered as quietly as she could. "That's a lie."

"If a citizen comes forward with information that leads to the capture of any wayward wizard, rewards will be offered in the form of coins, rations, and other sundries. Even greater rewards will be offered if the arrests of these wizard fugitives lead to the retrieval of these dangerous items.

"Because these items are so dangerous, Lord Master Nalazar has declared that if a wizard is caught within your ranks, all those within the building they are found in will be punished. The punishment will be meted out by his loyal Necromangians. The punishment depends on the severity of the offense. You could be fined. It could be corporal punishment. It could be death."

Reeve let his words hang ominously in the air to reinforce the gravity of the situation.

"If this seems unfair, it is proportionate to the danger involved. It needs to be known how dangerous harboring them is. Not only do I encourage you to come forward if you know something but I expect the citizenry to begin actively seeking them out.

"However, Lord Master Nalazar is merciful. He does not expect anyone to attempt to apprehend a wizard. Bring us information and we will handle the situation accordingly. Once Lord Master Nalazar has the stolen items, he will begin his crusade and Incanterra will be returned to you. If you want a return to normalcy, then help us."

Kynna looked at Thyra again and cocked her head to the side. "This one needs to break out a rod, a line, and some bait he's fishing so hard."

"Even if it is all a ruse, you have certainly perfected the Shaded Light attitude," Thyra smiled. "Still, it is an aggressive policy. It will certainly make people think twice about not saying something if they see something."

Kynna scoffed. "Any smart wizard ditched their robes a long time ago. It makes you wonder. Will constables start stopping and frisking citizens looking for wands, scepters, or other magical instruments?"

"What if the citizenry started feeding the Necros information that strangely turned out to be… you know… *false*?" Thyra asked.

"Now who is sounding like a Shader?"

Still, as Reeve continued his slow circling of the clock tower, looking out at the assembled citizens, he noted that amongst some, there was not the typical cowering and the averting of their gazes. As the undead knight approached the southwest corner of the clock tower circle, there were more than a few that refused to look away. Some glared right back at the knight. Others folded their arms defiantly over their chests. And a select few, including a small handful wearing crimson sashes around their waists, actually chortled as the knight came closer.

The strangeness of their response caught Reeve's attention. As the undead knight approached, the sea of humanity parted and several of the red sashers retreated amongst the crowd. As they did, they revealed their inside joke.

On the sidewalk, there was a pyramid stack of skulls. Some were whole. Others were cracked. Some featured terrible damage. But others were fitted inside the helmets worn by the undead patrols tirelessly walking the streets of Incanterra. Stacked level upon level atop one another, the pyramid reached up to Reeve's waist as he approached.

The undead knight remained stoic behind his helmet as he looked into the empty eyesockets that once held the glowing red pinpricks of light signifying their infusion of undead magic. The silent skulls stared back at the knight, a hint of mockery in their lifeless eye sockets.

Closing his lids over his yellow eyes, the undead knight issued a silent call to his master far above. The telepathic message sprang at the speed of thought up to Sorceria and the knight awaited his master's response.

What that response would be was hard to say but Reeve Windwisher knew it would not bode well for the citizens of Incanterra.

Chapter 80

Of all the magical signatures of The Eight, the Corvalonn sorcerers might have been the most widely recognized amongst the wizard dynasties. Their swirling rings of red were pocked and scattered with dark circles of black energy. The signature sound of the Corvalonn portals was a hissing resembling embers in a campfire mixed with the fluttering of hummingbird wings.

The portal opened with angry authority in the center of Trader's Cross. In the middle of the circle, the wizarding isle of Sorceria could be seen, along with the Corvalonn apprentice who had opened the portal. He was a young student but such a portal being close to Sorceria was an easy enough spell to produce. Still, odd electric fluctuations rippled within the flowing hoop of energy as the magic spell breached the energy barrier the undead wizard had cast around the floating isle. One was curious about what might have happened had this spell been cast without a specific wizard's permission.

The Incanterran citizens populating Trader's Cross took several pensive steps back as Nalazar Catabaysi himself floated effortlessly through the portal. The undead wizard was dressed in all of his wizardly fineries and even wore his onyx mask to hide his features.

On each side, the master was flanked by a pair of flesh-covered undead ghouls adorned in modest leathers. The armor was less about protection to keep the ghouls free from wounds or pain. Rather it was so their undead limbs would last as long as possible since creating a replacement was exhausting.

The ghouls did not walk with a mindless shamble or a rigorous march like the skeleton patrols. Instead, the ghouls gazed about, taking in the sights and sounds of the ward. What the citizens could not know was inside one of the receptive minds of the ghouls was the second-in-command of the Necromangians. However, in a curious display for those living in Sorceria above but unbeknownst to the people below, the second ghoul was controlled by Devinaya Baelannor.

Safely back up on Sorceria, the two mortals – the necromancer and the conjuror – were using the enchanted crowns provided by the Mutaccio dynasty to place their consciousness within the undead bodies of the ghouls.

Awaiting their arrival was Reeve Windwisher in all the glory of his coal-black plate and chain armor suit. The undead knight stood stoically with his two-handed sword drawn from its scabbard, the razor-sharp blade eager to be brought to bear at a moment's notice.

Positioned beside the undead enforcer was the neatly stacked pyramid of skulls left behind by unknown citizens. Nalazar looked at the arrangement and placed his gloved hands inside the opposite sleeves of his robes.

"How interesting," the lich said.

"Interesting?" Reeve scoffed. "Lord Master, they have defied you. Someone must pay for this transgression."

"Honestly, I am amazed it has taken them this long," Nalazar replied.

"Are you not mad?" Reeve asked.

"Inevitably there was going to be some pushback. The two most important questions are who is responsible and how are we going to respond?"

Dragan cleared his throat which made an odd, sick gurgling within the ghast he was inhabiting, "Perhaps this is a conversation best conducted in private."

Looking around at the crowd, Devinaya opted to remain silent. She scanned the various eyes of what should have been frightened citizens. The fear was still present, still palpable. Yet, there was a collection looking back at her. Some looked positively amused by the situation. Others glared back with a certain lifeless menace in their eyes. There was a coldness hiding a simmering desire for revenge.

If Nalazar saw the same thing, he did not show it. The lich remained too focused on the lightless eye sockets of the decapitated skulls. "You are right, Dragan," the lich conceded. "We will return to Sorceria for a proper discussion. Reeve, why don't you question some of the locals? Surely they have to know something. Someone knows who is responsible. Find out for me."

Reeve snapped to attention, causing his chain armor to jangle, and even knelt before his master, the poleyn covering his knee clacking against the stone street. "Yes, Lord Master," he said eagerly. "And what would you have me do with the skulls?"

Nalazar finally looked out at the crowd who was eyeing him nervously. Behind his mask, the undead wizard allowed himself to smile. "Leave them."

"Is that the best move, Master?" Dragan whispered.

"Yes, let them have their show of defiance. Let them all see. When we retaliate, I want them to know why. That way they will know, they brought this upon themselves."

The wizard then turned and began a lackadaisical drift toward the portal held open by the Corvalonn apprentice. The wizard eyed the people closely, watching for their response. But none of the mortals were brave enough to offer a challenge. Nalazar floated through, followed closely by his two ghouls.

The portal closed behind them as the trio returned to Sorceria. Up in the highest levels of the Baelannor tower, both Dragan and Devinaya severed the mental connection with their respective ghouls. Removing their enchanted crowns, both took more than a few heartbeats and several breaths to reorient themselves to the real world.

Dragan knew Nalazar would come floating into the parlor at any moment. He eyed Devinaya curiously. The woman wore an unreadable mask over her emotions as she blinked away the unsettling feeling and a mild bout of queasiness from the magical mental travel.

Regardless, Dragan could not stop his mind from tumbling. Somewhere in the city, there was a resistance that could share his ultimate goal. There was a potential ally down below. But there was no time to ponder or allow such treasonous thoughts to enter his mind as Nalazar calmly floated into the parlor where both Dragan and Devinaya Baelannor were sitting.

"At the very least, it is a question answered," the lich said. "We wondered how long it would take for the masses to push back. Now we know."

Nalazar floated behind the plush couch Devinaya was sitting on. "I am certain the pushback would have occurred much sooner if not for your capable dynasty, my dear," the lich said to the conjuror. "Were they not fed, the uprising would have proved inevitable. Or perhaps they are frustrated life has not returned to normal in a timely fashion. Perhaps we should note the date. There is only so long of an occupation a people will tolerate."

"Why do you appear in such good humor?" Dragan asked bluntly.

"A force is rising in opposition. Games of strategy require opponents, my boy. I cannot play a game of Scachi without someone sitting on the other side of the board. Do we have any likely suspects?"

"There is a group..." Devinaya said reluctantly. "There is a group that calls themselves the Swords of Honor. Their guild hall is located over in the Burkshire ward. It is not too far from Trader's Cross. They have a man there. Zaccario Whitestone. He leads the band of mercenaries. We used them a few seasons back to help us resolve a sorcerite mining dispute in Agavinsula. If he and his mercenaries are trapped behind the walls, they aren't earning any coins. They could be responsible."

"It can't just be a group of concerned citizens?" Dragan asked. "They could have attacked a patrol in any of the various wards that run up and down the district."

"Stronglash," the lich hissed.

Dragan could only hope he concealed his wince of pain as the lich began down a mental path the second hoped his leader had forgotten about. "Gurnoth Stronglash is working for a secretive band of thieves operating in the shadows."

"Like a thieves' guild?" Devinaya asked. "You all don't believe in that? Do you? That there is some secret shadowy society organizing all the crime in the city? Those are all just street whispers. Folk tales told to children."

"We know a thing or two that you all didn't about hidden societies," the lich said smugly.

"Rogues in the shadows attacking skeleton patrols," Dragan said. "Wouldn't that be counter to them hiding under everyone's nose?"

"If their society is predicated on earning coins, I would think that a siege of the city would be against their best interest," Nalazar hissed.

"Or they are making more money than ever before selling merchandise."

The lich waved off any more discussion. He had made up his mind, much to Dragan's silent chagrin.

"Summon Gurnoth. Bring him before me. I would learn more of these rogues and thieves."

Chapter 81

It was an odd sound rippling across Incanterra. It was the distorted pitter-patter of rain striking against the semi-permeable magical bubble doming the city. With the heat of the summer in full bloom, such rainstorms were a rarity. Yet on this night, the rain was falling in fat drops. It would strike against the dome of energy and, eventually, drip down onto the city below.

It was a cleansing rain the city – especially the southern districts – so desperately needed. The Northeast District was not immune to the wafting pollution creeping its way north. But as the rain fell, puddles tinted with a green haze could be seen in the back alleys and the side streets. Some lazy rivers – also tinted green – made their way down the sluice grates into the sewers below.

A collection of shadows was clustered under the covered loading dock of the Northeast District ward labeled as Brickyard. So named for most of its tall building exteriors being made of kiln-baked bricks, the ward was quiet. With the rain falling, the late hour, and the mandated curfew by the Necromangian oppressors, no citizens were milling out and about. It was the quietest anyone could remember.

Mingling within the darkness of the alleyway were seven figures in long, black, concealing cloaks. Underneath, black attire was the fashion for the evening. Their soft boots, breeches, tunics, gloves, and even kerchiefs tied over the lower halves of their faces were as dark as midnight. Blades were coated in a tar-like weapon black to keep them from glinting in the mage-light radiating from the street lamps. Soaked with rainwater, the seven waited silently.

They waited for the next skeleton patrol to make their rounds. Valos, Sway, Thade, Cinder, Cavin, Sario, and Amman all stood poised and waiting. As the water ran down the bricks of the adjacent building, Thade noted the eerie green tint amongst the puddles. "I am not the only one seeing this, right?" the big man said, pointing the blackened head of one of his hand axes at the closest puddle. "That's what? Pollution from all the necro spells?"

"They have those spell cooker cauldrons running night and day. Sounds right to me," Sway replied.

"But I mean look at it. What are we half stupid or something to just ignore all this?" Thade asked hotly.

"I mean breathing the clouds is one thing," Valos offered. "What I would be more concerned about is all this polluted water down in the sewers. No telling what kind of twisted monsters it is going to turn all the rats into. Or the crocodiles."

"Maybe the giant crocodiles will eat the mutant rats," Thade said.

"There are no crocodiles in the sewers," Cinder chimed in. "That's just one of those stories."

Valos scoffed. "So the Dark Destroyer had a tryst with the Mother, spawning their child Death. Dragons fly over the city, a city that is walled off to fend off twisted amalgams from the Great Dragon War. And undead walk the streets. But you draw the line at crocodiles in the sewer? That is the legend that finally makes you say 'That's a little too far'?"

"A girl has to have a code," Cinder quipped back.

The core four broke out into laughter. Near the mouth of the alley, Cavin banged the pommel of his sword against the closest rain pipe.

"Great. You got us in trouble," Sway shooshed.

"You're an idiot," Valos said to Cinder, his eyes wrinkling from the smile hidden behind his mask.

"This coming from the person that believed taking a slowing potion would improve his bedroom activities."

"Time will prove me right on that one," the rogue whispered back with a hiss and a pointing finger.

From her position deeper within the alley, Sario risked the sparkles of light to summon forth the elemental energy she and her fellow Malinsuli shaman were famous for. However, the water elemental was forced to pull tainted rainwater runoff out of the sewer grates to formulate its body. As a result, the water elemental was wracked with pollution.

Sario shook her head. Normally, she would allow her hand to slip into the flowing appendages of her summoned elementals to reinforce their bond. Instead, Sario whispered words in her native tongue and let the elemental return to its natural plane of existence. The shaman stomped her foot in protest and returned to the group.

"I know," Amman said, offering his cousin a reassuring squeeze of her shoulder.

"There is no soil for me to summon an earth elemental. The water elemental was so polluted I could not keep it here," Sario sobbed. "A fire elemental would attract too much attention. I don't see how an air elemental would fend against bones. I want to *help*."

"You *are* helping," Valos responded both quickly and earnestly. "We aren't here without you."

"I want to help in the fight," Sario replied.

"What if we used your air elementals?" Cavin asked as he looked up at the high roofs of the Brickyard buildings. "If they are strong enough, could the elementals lift Sway to the rooftops to let her rain crossbow bolts? Or lift us all to the roofs to escape?"

Before the tactics could be discussed, the rhythmic march of skeletal feet adorned in leather boots began to echo down the city streets. The shadows moved into their attack positions. With their practice, the strikes were starting to become routine. But as they moved into their places, Cinder could feel a radiance coming from Cavin that was not normal. "Bigger," he hissed back to the crew.

Indeed, the march of the footsteps was louder than the typical squads they had been dispatching as of late. Walking down the street were twin columns with a dozen skeletons marching in each. But Cavin Jurare was not about to let so many prime targets last a heartbeat longer than necessary.

Using the tried and true tactic of hitting the column in the center, the group descended as shadows in the night, slashing, hammering, crashing, crushing, and bashing their way through the arms, armor, and bones of the skeletal lines. Luck and surprise gave the shadows an early advantage but the superior numbers eventually began to tip the scales towards balance.

The far greater threat was the flesh-covered undead ghast marching at the rear of the columns. The undead sergeant froze as the attack began. Rather than engaging in direct combat, the ghast's milky white eyes and its discolored pupils rolled back into its head as it issued an unheard, voiceless call.

Once completed, the pupils of its eyes descended, this time colored with a glowing, azure tint radiating out like candlelight from behind its irises and pupils. The ghast's movements then shifted as well, morphing into something more organic. It was now directly controlled.

But more than being controlled, it had issued a psychic command to all within range. As the shadowy seven continued to combat and strike down more and more skeletal soldiers, they were ill-prepared to hear more booted columns hustling with haste toward the battle zone. Rounding corners and running at breakneck speeds, more sword-swinging skeletons charged to join the fight.

With stealth and secrecy now off the table, both Cinder and Cavin drew forth their magical instruments. Sario and Amman readied their spells, tapping into the elemental planes for their energy. Thade's axe heads flared to life as well as Valos's blades. The bolt locked into Sway's crossbow hissed angrily.

But before the skeletal reinforcements could close the distance, they found themselves hit from out of other alleyways. These defenders were adorned in crimson sashes worn around their waists.

As the battle raged around them, Thade closed another gap and found himself squared off with the ghast and its glowing blue eyes. However, the monster was being controlled from elsewhere by a wizard who was not nearly skilled enough in proper battle tactics. The ghast's leather armor did not stand a chance against the magical sharpness of the axe heads and Thade's impossible strength.

The undead monster could not be felled by traditional strikes that would have taken human pieces off the Scachi board. However, the ghost quickly became dramatically less effective when Thade's powerful strike severed one arm off at the shoulder and a second cut took the other.

All around the amputated ghast, the last of his skeletal forces were collapsing to the rain-soaked streets into piles of still and lifeless bones. Following their *caput's* direct commands, the members of the Crimson Way began gathering up the lifeless skulls and placing them into unfurled burlap bags.

"You think this is a victory?" the wizard asked through the voice of the ghost. "Our numbers are legion. This city is ours. March yourself to the nearest constabulary hall and face your consequences. Perhaps Master Nalazar will be merciful."

"Yeah, we are not going to be doing that," Sway said from behind the anonymity of her mask.

"Then the people will be punished for your transgressions," the monster said ominously.

Finally, the ghast reacted as a dagger slipped into the back of its neck. The eerie light within its rotting eyes slowly winked away to darkness and the monster collapsed to the rain-soaked streets between the standing forms of Thade Skystone and Sonnan Silverhelm.

The member of the Crimson Way cleaned off his weapon before tucking it back into the sash around his waist. Looking about, the criminal crew had gathered their tokens and their trophies. Valos found Sonnan Silverhelm and offered the quickest of embraces. "Strange bedfellows," Valos whispered.

"Stay safe," Sonnan whispered back.

As the groups retreated into their separate alleyways, Sway swore she smelled the scent of sunflowers mixed in with the rains...

Chapter 82

The chefs, waitrons, cooks, hosts, and cleaning staff had long since left the Silver Lighthouse abandoned after the lockdown. Before, the rooftop dining establishment was known to host wizards, dignitaries, archons, and prominent guild masters, presenting meals that were as much works of art as they were nutritional flair. But after the siege began, such decadent ingredients became impossible to procure and the wealthy were content to hide behind the walls of their posh, upscale estates.

As such, there was nary a witness to be found when Kynna'Fyir Lu'Scion walked through the doors of the closed restaurant. Using her hidden illusory magic, Kynna had transformed herself from the persona of Kynna Summerstone, a Northeast District scullery maid and distributor of rations, into more of an upscale façade that would not draw the attention of Necromangians walking in the Northwest District. It was better to be slightly overdressed and appear as if she belonged than to attempt to hide by dressing down. The stratagem had proven successful as she had navigated through the Under Roads, across the Northwest District, and up into the rooftop restaurant for a secret meeting.

He was already waiting when she arrived. But like Kynna, her companion had eschewed his wizardly robes in exchange for sage attire that he was known for wearing while teaching history in Academia. Ever the elder statesman, Dragan Duskwood was well-kempt, freshly shaven, perfumed, and powdered for his meeting. "If I had proffered a gentlemen's wager, I would have just lost," he said with a smile.

"Betting if I would have shown up?" Kynna asked.

"I gave it's odds as one in three."

"I am happy to disappoint."

Dragan clapped his hands together and rubbed his palms vigorously. "Can we dispense with the pretense? Can we both agree right off the bat that neither of us is here to kill the other so we can transition right to business?"

"I can agree to your terms. As long as you tell me what I am doing here."

The wizardly sage smiled. He took a deep breath, having to force the traitorous words passed his lips. "The leader of my dynasty has to be removed from power."

Kynna stood for a moment and then made her way over to one of the dining room chairs covered in a white sheet. She took a seat on top of the dust cover and gestured toward the chair across from her. Dragan obliged.

"Now, I want it known. I am not condemning necromancy. The magic of the dead is just as viable and important as anything cast by the Baelannors, the

Corvalonns, or any other of The Eight. It is a pretty slim gap between us and the magic cast by the Ce'Mondere. But that is an argument for another time. The pressing issue is the leader of our dynasty has tapped into forces that have twisted him. He needs to be removed from power... and I cannot do it alone."

"So what are you asking?" Kynna inquired. "Do you want me to return to Sorceria and round up wizards to help you?"

"That is exactly what I am asking. Coming from me, who is going to believe me? But if you bring them the idea..."

"You are asking them to take on a terrible risk," Kynna shook her head.

"I have access to a tunnel. I could get members of their dynasty out of the city. I could afford them safe passage."

"In exchange."

"In exchange for their help. We get the younger generation out of the city. The patrons rally to me. And together, we take down Nalazar."

"And then what?"

"Sorceria is returned to the wizards. Incanterra is returned to the people."

"And what of your death cult? What of your Necromangians?" the magician asked.

Dragan thought about the question for a long time. "I would hope my actions in dethroning Nalazar would be taken into account by the magistrates. But if there are further consequences, I will face them."

"What about Nalazar's other devotees?"

Dragan pondered but then swallowed hard and nodded his head. "Once the battle lines are drawn, if they stand with Nalazar, they can face their consequences. For those who stand with me, I would hope the same leniency would be extended. But if someone must serve time in Irongate for this... I would do so."

"You are a better person than I am, Dragan— Is it Dragan Catabaysi?"

"Dragan Duskwood," he corrected.

A sliver of pain knifed through Kynna's head. She instinctively brought her hand up to massage under her left eye.

"An issue?" Dragan asked.

"I've been having headaches. It started after the siege."

Dragan's bone wand slid easily into his hand. "May I? It is just a simple spell. A detection. You won't feel a thing."

The magician nodded.

While spells of intense detection – clairvoyance, far-seeing, and the like – were the purview of the Dinaciouns, all magical dynasties had their versions of a spell to detect magical signatures.

The Necromangian cast his spell over Kynna. To his credit, the magical wash was undetectable to her. But in his eyes, he could see the glowing auras of light that swirled around and permeated through the young wizardess... including a unique concentration within her skull.

"Interesting..." the wizard mused.

"What is interesting?" she asked.

"Believe it or not, history was not the only topic I studied in Academia. When you have a high status, you can research topics in restricted sections."

"What kind of topics?"

"Magic topics," he answered as he continued his scan. "But rather than bore you with fancy terminology and magical theory... if I may?"

"Please."

"So someone – I am going to guess your patron – has placed a spell within your head. If you think of this spell as sand in an hourglass, the sand wants to leak out. In this case, let's imagine it leaking out through your nose."

"You do paint a picture," Kynna said.

"The 'stopper' keeping this magical spell from draining out of your nose is failing and the magical sand is releasing out into the aether. Much the same as your arrival today, if I were placing a gentlemen's wager, I would say someone in your dynasty keeps replacing that stopper to keep the sand in."

"But with me being down in the city..."

"And you being cut off from your dynasty's hierarchy that has fled..."

"The stopper is breaking down."

"And so the sand is running out," Dragan said with a nod and a smile. "Thus, the headaches."

"So what does the sand do?" Kynna asked with a hint of nervousness in her tone.

"Given the nature of the magic and the signature of its energy, and again if I am betting..." Dragan rubbed his chin. "What can you tell me about your time before you became a magician?"

Kynna's brow furrowed as she reached back into her memories. Her eyes darted back and forth. Her breath quickened and she shifted uncomfortably in her seat. "It is fine," Dragan said. The Necromangian even reached out and patted the top of her hand for reassurance. "How about just any childhood memory?"

"I... I... I can't," she whispered. "I remember my training. I remember my induction into the dynasty. But I cannot recall anything before that. Is that odd?"

"Not if you are in your sixties. Then the stories of youth tend to fade. But I still remember my childhood. I am guessing you are... Early twenties?"

"I'm twenty-one. Or at least I think I am. I was born in '35. Or at least I was *told* I was born in '35. Now I don't know what to think!"

"Hang on, I am still doing that math. 1756 minus 1735." The wizard closed his eyes and pretended to do calculations while counting tallies on his fingers. "Yes. Twenty-one. That would be right."

He squeezed his eyes open and looked at Kynna. "Not a time for jokes?"

"Not particularly," she harumphed.

"So, you are telling me you don't remember hardly anything about when you were a child?"

"I mean... a few... feelings... maybe?"

"Something tells me that the longer this goes on, the more memories are going to return."

"Memories of my childhood?"

"I would assume so," the sage replied. "And memories of who you were before you were recruited to the Lu'Scion dynasty."

"But why would they do such a thing?"

"You might have been found late," Dragan speculated. "Attachment is a bane of proper training. That is why children are often taken when they are young. Some are given up willingly. Others are traded for coins. If they do sell them, the parents willingly sign a contract that jinxes them to where they cannot talk about the sale or their children. Then they slowly forget them entirely. It keeps everything off the record. But the dynasties continue to swell their ranks."

"I had no idea," Kynna whispered.

"I am guessing most of you don't. The Eight? They all have dark secrets."

"Like how necromancy was outlawed?"

"And how my dynasty was banished. But my master is now seeking revenge because one of the patrons was using the same magic we were outlawed for using. That desire for revenge has corrupted him, twisted him. So I have to end him."

Kynna took a deep breath and looked deep into Dragan's eyes. "Then you are going to need help to do it."

Chapter 83

It was late in the summer day and the sun was finally creeping behind the Pyrewind Peaks along Incanterra's western border. Rain clouds still filled the sky and fat drops continued to cascade down and through the magical dome tenting the capital city. With the long day coming to a close and with the curfew looming, so many of the populace had retreated to their homes.

Be it cool white mage-light or the flickering glow of candles or lanterns, lights filled the myriad of windows along the tall apartments looming over the city streets. The cleansing rain had thankfully washed the city and provided a slight respite from the oppressive heat of the season.

The unnamed building unofficially housing the Blades' cadenta in Shaded Light was one of the tallest buildings in the ward. The rooftop was the first structure to feel the cleansing rain so it was the perfect place for Sario. The Malinsuli shaman stood at the edge of the building with her arms outstretched towards the heavens and the life-giving rain.

The water kissed her bronze skin and wetted her long, flowing white hair as she stood silently, eyes closed, basking in the glory of nature. Sensing the other presence on the roof, Sario squeezed one eye open and glanced behind her to acknowledge Swayna Snowsong's arrival.

With her arms still cast skyward, the shaman flicked her fingers and motioned for Sway to join her. "You know most people have sense enough to get *out* of the rain," the rogue said as she stepped out onto the rooftop.

"And most never know the pleasure of communing with the Mother and all of her glory!" Sario called back.

Almost on cue, a flash of lightning splayed across the clouds and the rumble of thunder shook windows in their panes.

"Glory?" Sway asked.

"Feel her power. Feel her strength. Feel her gentle kiss upon your skin," the shaman replied with a broad smile. "Hers is a power eternal. Against the mother of nature, none can stand."

"If this is so great, how come Amman is not out here with you?" Sway asked as she walked out amongst the falling rain.

"Last I checked, he was being preyed upon by more than a few of the ladies in your establishment."

Sway cocked her head to the side, "I guess he is interested in different kinds of snow hills and valleys."

"Aren't they all?" Sario asked with a laugh.

Standing with the shaman, Sway turned her gaze upward. It did not take long for her cotton tunic and breeches to become waterlogged. The material clung to her skin and soon her rain-slicked hair was flat against her head. But strangely, Sway found herself smiling.

Sario was correct. The rain was cool. Power and energy were lingering in the air, left behind by the bolts of lightning. She could feel the deep rumbles of thunder. Sario grasped Sway's hand and placed her palm against her chest. Sway could feel the hammering heartbeat of the shaman. "She speaks to each of us. We just have to learn how to listen."

Together, the two stood in the pouring rain. Sario reached out and wrapped Sway in her arms, holding her in a sisterly embrace. "Your world is strange, *tahine*," Sario said in Sway's ear. "The farm that we went to. That place made sense to me. This city does not. Too many strangers all crammed together. It doesn't make sense."

Sway broke the tight embrace but still held onto Sario's arms. She wanted to be able to look her in the eyes. "I am glad to hear you say that. It makes what I am about to say easier."

Sario looked at her quizzically.

"This isn't what you signed up for. You or Amman. The saving grace is none of us knew this was happening. But if we did, I know there is no way we would have let you come here."

"What are you saying?" Sario asked.

"The boat we left down in the sewer. It has to still be there. We should go back there, even if it is just you, Amman, me, and Cinder. You summon another water elemental. We get you two out of the city. Once we are beyond the barrier, Cinder opens up one of her portals and sends you home."

Sario shook her head but before she could speak, Sway held up her hand. "Look, me and my crew. We have been through some stuff. We have. But this thing. It feels different. I don't think all of us are making it out of this one. Fending off an invasion of an undead horde, you all didn't sign up for this.

"It is not that I don't want you here or that I don't want your help. But I don't know if I could face it if something happened to either you or Amman. So, I am giving you the out. No loss of honor. No hard feelings."

Sario smiled and gave Sway another sisterly embrace. Taking her by the hand, Sario walked to the edge of the building to look out at all the various apartments and buildings. "Generations ago – almost a century past – a terrible pox infested one of the villages on Malinsula. It swept across the island. Many were sick. Many died. It ravaged the island and it took generations to recover.

"When my mother was a child, one of the villages started to display the same type of pox. Thankfully, the witch doctors had the teachings from those who suffered through the first illness. The king made a declaration. The village was sealed off. They were not allowed to travel out and we were not allowed to travel in. The pox killed many people. It was very sad. Their bodies were burned. Huts were burned. But it was contained to one village. Had we allowed the pox to spread across the island, the devastation would have been tenfold."

"Is Incanterra the village?" Sway asked.

"She is. I could go home. I could take Amman with me. But we have to stop this wildfire before it can spread. If you catch it early, you win. Right now, this undead horde is thankfully restricted within your capital's borders. If this horde or swarm is allowed to escape, it will sweep across your kingdom. How much harder will it be to contain then? If they convert the populace, how easy will it be for them to overrun the farming villages like the one you brought us to?"

Sway's eyebrow twitched nervously as she considered the implications.

"The little villages dotting the northern end of your kingdom? They will fall one by one. Each conquering will only add more soldiers to this Nalazar Catabaysi's legion. How far can any of us run? Be it tomorrow or a year from now, this swarm will come for us all. We should stand here now and fight."

Sharing the view, Sway reached out and wrapped an arm around Sario's waist. "You know what the really funny thing is? A month ago, neither of us knew the other existed. And here you are ready to lay down your life beside a stranger. You Malinsuli are either a proud culture or a special breed of dumb."

Sario laughed at the jest. "It is the right thing to do," she said proudly.

"Yeah but you could slide out of here. And if the tables were turned and this event was happening in Malinsula, I don't know if Incanterra would be mounting up a navy to sail to your defense."

"Would your Blades sail to our aid?" the shaman asked.

Sway held far too long of a pregnant pause. "I don't know," she finally admitted. "For them, it all depends on if coins can be made from the endeavor. When the sun sets behind the mountains, that is all they care about."

"And what do *you* care about?" Sario asked.

Sway took a deep breath as she considered the answer. "You know when we first got started, all of us agreed that we were going to do this thing with honor. It's a tough row to hoe. You have to project enough strength so people don't think you are a sucker. But I don't want to be so heavy-handed that people hate us. You know? Fair is fair. I'm not gonna lie. We've done some bad things." Sway jutted out her jaw and did her best imitation of Valos, "But not to nobody that didn't deserve it. We did things the Ombraterran way."

Sario laughed and tried her best imitation as well as including Valos's signature hand gestures. "What do you do?"

"Right?" Sway said with a smile. "But look. It is not like we are running deep here. This is not some blood feud. You two don't have to do this. So why help us specifically?"

"Aside from the aforementioned pox story?"

"Yeah, I mean... why us? Why the Blades?"

"Because you are in trouble."

"Freakin' idealists."

Sario laughed again and wiped away some raindrops from her eyes. "If it makes you feel better, I will say it is because I am looking forward to the trade route we will establish when this is all said and done. Get us some beef and milk cows down on the island."

Sway waggled a finger. "Now, you are making sense. A little self... uh... what's the word I am looking for? Self-interest finally reveals itself. I trust that far more than some random altruism."

Sway cinched her grip around Sario's waist and the shaman draped her arm across the rogue's shoulders. "If I am being completely honest, I am glad you didn't take the offer... even though I *did* make the effort to get us some water-breathing potions for the swim back up the sewer pipes."

"Then we have to make sure nothing happens to Amman or me."

"I'll protect you with my life," Sway smiled.

"And I will protect you with mine," the shaman replied.

She then leaned in, offered a comforting embrace, and placed her lips gently against Sway's own.

Once more, thunder rumbled across the skies.

Chapter 84

With the hard soles of leather boots clacking against the rain-slicked stone of the sidewalk, the pair of merchants walked with a purpose down the street in the Northwest District. With the night finally setting in and the rain still falling, there were few citizens out and about on the streets. Each carried a bundle over their shoulders filled with proper sundries.

Essential workers helping keep the city functioning had been granted special permission papers to conduct business but these were often people like clerics who healed the sick, people distributing rations, or mainteneers keeping the essential services of the city flowing.

Workers kept these permissions close at all times as the undead patrols had increased substantially. The patrols featured twin marching columns populated by skeletons with heavy arms and heavier armor. They were greater in numbers. And now, the pairs of marching columns were led. It was either a ghast, a Knight of the Imperial Circle, or even a Necromangian draped in red robes.

These were no longer patrols keeping the streets clear and the people tucked away inside. These patrols were searching. Random pedestrians were stopped, asked for their permissions, questioned, and even sometimes searched. If they issued any sort of resistance, often they were taken into custody and hauled away to places that citizens could only imagine.

So the merchants had their papers at the ready just in case they came across one of these wayward patrols. "I think given the circumstances, we don't have much of a choice," the first merchant was saying.

"That is the last person I want to accept help from—"

The duo stopped short as they rounded the corner and almost ran into a pair of marching skeletal columns. The undead troop was led by a ghast with glowing blue eyes and was adorned in flowing black robes.

"Papers," the ghast hissed with a guttural tone that bubbled from deep down in its diaphragm. The ghast snapped out a gnarled claw of a hand at the two. Both men averted their gazes but complied as quickly as possible. "Where are you going?" the creature asked.

"Delivering sundries," one of the two replied.

"To?"

The two glanced nervously at one another. But one nodded and the other spoke up. "The Goldcrests are paying top dollar for essentials. They are trying to keep their estate stocked."

"So many of the mercantile shoppes are running low on supplies," the ghast said as it examined the papers. "Where did you acquire these sundries?"

"You have to know where to look," the second merchant explained.

"Elaborate..." the ghast hissed. "Please."

The merchants nodded at each other. "There's a lot of vacant apartments now. If you know where to look. Some of the former residents left... abruptly. Left supplies in the cupboards. We are just... redistributing the goods."

"Thievery?" the ghast inquired, looking up from the papers and glaring at the two from under what was left of its eyebrows.

"If the apartment is abandoned and their things were left behind, does that constitute thieving?" the first merchant asked.

"Your legal defense you would have your barrister argue is... 'finders keepers'?" the ghast asked.

The second merchant shrugged and nodded. The ghast snapped his fingers and pointed toward the merchants. "Search them," the undead commander ordered his skeletons.

As the skeletons advanced, it happened in the fluttering of a seraphfly's wings. The first merchant snapped daggers into both hands from nowhere. At the same time, the second merchant slid out of his tunic sleeve a wooden wand that flared angrily.

Grayson Rathorrian quickly showed why he was given the street name of Graver as he plunged his first dagger in between the neckbones of the nearest skeleton. A twist of the blade severed the magical bonds keeping the animated bones together and the skull popped from the spinal column like a cork in a carbonated bottle of wine.

But the looming danger was the long whip of lightning dangling like a cat o' nine tails from Drennid Vocazion's wand. With the snap of his wrist like an oar master keeping his slave rowers in line, the mage cracked the lightning into the closest assembly of skeletons. It sent their de-animated bones clattering to the stone street.

As Drennid continued to whip-crack his way through the skeletal forces, Graver turned in the direction of their ghastly leader. Through a mental command, a swirling of transmutation magic, and the sound of steel scraping against a whetstone, Graver's blades elongated from daggers to short swords and then out to a length to be considered longswords.

The ghast found himself quickly isolated from his crumbling skeletal forces because of Drennid and his lightning whip. There was nowhere to run from the deadly assassin and his midnight black, razor-sharp blades. Strike after strike took pieces from the ghast as it attempted to defend itself. Its hands went first. Arms were cut at the elbow. Then again at the shoulder, leaving withered limbs lying on the sidewalk.

A pommel strike to the ghast's head left it staggering and a front snap kick pushed the undead creature's body against the wall of the nearby shop. Graver plunged his sword through the unbeating heart of the creature. The soft body gave way and the sword sank up to the crossguard. Pushing forward with all his strength, Graver sunk the tip of the weapon into the soft pine wood of the nearby building, leaving the armless ghast impaled and stranded.

Thankfully, the assassin had his second blade which was more than enough to help Drennid cut down the remaining skeletal forces. As the last of the skeletons collapsed to either the sidewalk or the street, Drennid turned and glared at the skewered ghast. He approached with a gait both purposeful and an intentional saunter.

Clutching the jaw of the ghast, Drennid leaned in close, wanting to not just look into the monster's eyes but what lay within them. "I know you're in there," the wizard hissed. "And I know what you are going to say next. You will demand that I turn myself in or you are going to start torturing the civilian populace until I surrender."

The ghast glared back and produced only silence.

Drennid nodded. "You can threaten that all you want. But I just want you to know that your little plan won't work. You think killing innocent civilians will weaken my resolve. And if that is your plan, it might be time for some restructuring because you have sorely underestimated me and – more importantly – how much I love myself."

Drennid leaned in even closer and his countenance turned to stone. "Understand this. I don't give a bucket of piss for these people. I am a wizard. I am worth a thousand – ten thousand – of these pathetic non-magicals. Your dog death knight can threaten all you want. You can march your undead commanders, your pathetic ass-kissing knights, or even bring your Necromangians to duel against me directly. Your tactic will not work. And I am not some 'sroom-popping magician. I don't need a cauldron to brew my magic. I am a *mage*. I am the worst enemy you could have standing in your way. So go all the way up to your necro-lord and let him know. I am going to destroy patrol after patrol until you open up the gates and let me out of this prison. I await your response."

With that, Drennid slashed his lightning whip across the throat of the impaled ghast. The lightning cut clean through the neck of the impaled undead and left a searing scorch mark on the wall behind it. The head toppled from the skewered body and plopped onto the sidewalk.

"So, that was a thing," Graver said as he grabbed his sword hilt and placed a boot against the torso of the decapitated ghast.

With a mighty tug, the blade pulled free. The body collapsed. And Graver's weapons returned to their concealing size. The duo looked about, scanning for any witnesses or potential reinforcements before gathering their things and moving off into the shadows of the night.

"So, as I was saying," Graver said nonchalantly, "I think given the circumstances, we don't have much of a choice. If there is any group that we need to align with, it is hers. Smuggling, hiding from constables, underworld activities, if anyone can survive or break a siege, it is going to be them."

"Me going to *her* for help," Drennid shook his head, "she will never let me live it down."

"But at least you will be living to live it down..."

The conversation drifted off into the wind. Meanwhile, the last vestiges of consciousness began to evaporate from the skull of the ghast. That consciousness swam quickly up into the private parlor in the Baelannor tower. Sitting in the comfortable high-backed chair, the Necromangian opened his eyes.

"Now, that is interesting," Dragan Duskwood said.

Chapter 85

Except for the living skeletons and undead ghasts, few individuals parted citizens of Sorceria like Gurnoth Stronglash. On this day, in particular, the big man was covered in grime and soot from a hard day's work down in the Southwest District. He did not look like a typical scholarly wizard. He was far more muscled, sported a scraggly beard, and his hair was unkempt. He radiated a rough-and-tumble aura. Under normal circumstances, the wizard would have bathed and adorned himself in proper attire.

But when Nalazar Catabaysi called, Gurnoth Stronglash came running.

The lich was located in the commandeered study of the Baelannor patron perusing through the various banned grimoires taken from the Cellarium Vaults. He was telekinetically turning another page, studying another forbidden spell when Gurnoth arrived. The wizard apprentice knelt low inside the narthex of the study and waited for Nalazar to summon him in.

It took several moments for the lich to notice his follower as the big man was both silent and patient. "Gurnoth," the lich said with what would pass as a smile. "Please, enter."

"I did not want to interrupt, Lord Master."

"Not at all. You should have said something. Cleared your throat. Anything."

Gurnoth rose and strode confidently into the study. In a far alcove of the private chambers, the roughneck wizard noted the still but breathing form of Asaric Baelannor laid out on a cold stone slab. The wizard failed to summon even a droplet of sympathy for the broken patron and focused his gaze on his lich lord.

Nalazar continued to float about the room in his wizard robes. He was not wearing his coal-black mask but of all his followers, Gurnoth was the least phased by his master's undead appearance.

"How may I be of service, Master?"

"How are things down in the city?"

"Twotrees and I are perfecting the spell you have ordered. Things will be ready very soon."

"Ah yes, the amalgamation," the lich said. "That is going to be interesting."

The lich gestured towards one of the sitting couches but Gurnoth held still. "Master, I came as quickly as I could. I wouldn't want to soil your furniture."

The lich snickered. "Decorum as always. As you wish. I want information about the before times. I want you to tell me about this criminal organization you infiltrated."

"The Skull Duggers? I am afraid they want me dead more than anyone these days."

"How so?"

"My allegiance has always been to you, Master. Always. But when they induct you into a family, they expect that family to come first. It doesn't matter if your sainted mother is laying on her deathbed. If they call, you answer."

"And your failure to answer their call constitutes a death warrant?"

Gurnoth cocked his head to the side. "They are big on loyalty. It's not the not answering. It is putting another organization before the family. Nothing comes before the family. Or as they call it 'this thing of ours.'"

"So, every quarter within the city has a different family?"

"Yes, my lord. In the Southwest, before everything, the Skull Duggers ran things. But that district was... volatile. It was run through strength and steel. So control changed hands regularly. But we own the ward now. Hells, I could walk you through the front door of the place's clubhouse right now."

As Gurnoth spoke, his diction became less sharp and he unconsciously slipped back into his street accent. "Southeast's a little more civil. Lots of coins running through there what with the warehouses and the piers. Lots of skimming. Lots of stuff disappearin' off ships. Thing like that needs to be a little more reliable. People gotta know. So, the Diamond Order runs things. Talamezzo Hardstone runs the dee. And he lives up to his surname. I know he runs the show out of a moneychanger's shop down near the east docks.

"The Northeast? That place is a mess. They appear all middle-class like they are better than those south of the High. But that place was a glass sphere of lamp oil just looking for a spark. Two different families were constantly vying for control, wrestling wards away from each other."

"And the Northwest?" Nalazar asked with rapt attention.

"Eh, a bunch of snoots catering to the sins of the financial elite. Most probably don't even oil their swords. But then again, they don't have to. Look, all these families, that's all they do. They cater to the sins and the vices. You want something you can't get on the street, you go to them. Spirits, spice, some willing flesh, gambling, bloodsports; that is what they provide. If a constable won't help you out and you need someone roughed up, you see them. Some dirtbag knocks up your little girl and won't pay for the child's shoes, you send them. You need coins and the banks won't loan to you, you see them."

"And how do they do all this without getting caught?"

"Coppers are clueless. They're so far behind. But they ain't too different from us before. Everyone's got a job. Or they got businesses as fronts. You know. We sell — whatever — we sell honey in the front but we move hooch out the back. We don't care if the honey even moves because the hooch does. So they wear convincing masks. But just by telling you this, I would be executed. There is a strict code of silence. If you get picked up by the coppers, you keep your mouth shut. If they pinch you, we got good barristers and more than a few magistrates in our pockets. But if you do get sent for a stretch in the 'Gate, you do your time and the family will take care of you both on the inside and when you get out. There is no family and nobody knows nothin'."

Gurnoth had to shake his head. It was as if he was a stage actor stepping out of his role. Like the snuffing of a candle, Gurnoth's street performance disappeared and the loyal servant of Catabaysi returned. "That is how they operate, Lord Master."

"So operating in this shadow arena requires stealth and subterfuge. It requires an ability to keep secrets and to move in the darkness."

"If not, you end up in Irongate."

Nalazar nodded. "Someone has been quietly assassinating our skeletal squads. They vanish off the streets without a trace. And a large contingent of those that have gone missing is located in the Northeast District."

Gurnoth clucked his tongue and shook his head. "I don't know a lot about things north of the High. The Northwest District is solid. Their leadership doesn't change. The Warcrowns run that show. But the Northeast? There was a civil war in the family here not too long ago. That I know. But my master — my former master — Malath Armorworn was part of a council. You can't have two families openly at war for the coppers and the people to see. It is bad for business. So they split the ward. But as far as who controls which ward, I cannot tell you. As far as who is taking out the skeletal patrols, it could be the Shadow Blades or it could be the Crimson Way."

"All of these gangs of thieves have cute little names?" the lich laughed.

"I am afraid so, Master."

"So where do these Shadow Blades and Crimson Wayers reside?"

"That's the thing. You don't know. Anyone could be a Blade. These members are the opposite of the Knights of the Imperial Circle. They don't broadcast their allegiance. In fact, I heard a story of some people trading on the name, pretending to be a member so they could shake people down for coins. Needless to say, that did not go over well."

"So how do they know who is a true member?"

"They have codes, secret cants, and signals they can give to one another. But what those signals are, I don't know. And for all I know, they changed them all up once the siege began. They might be criminals but they aren't stupid."

"So there are the Shadow Blades and the Crimson Way."

"I know the Crimson Way is smaller. They might be easier to spot because they wear crimson sashes. But there are rankings in all the organizations. Just because we snag a man wearing a sash doesn't mean he is going to know what you need to know."

Nalazar drummed his bony fingers on his chin in contemplation. "How far along is Twotrees?"

"Far."

The lich nodded and turned to look out the window and down on Sorceria. He paused for a good long while as he contemplated his next Scachi board move. "Very well. I am going to take you off his detail. You have a new mission. I want a representative of both these organizations brought before me for questioning."

The lich turned to look at his faithful follower. Mercy had washed from Nalazar's face and his voice was even colder than normal.

"We will learn what we need to know."

Chapter 86

The echoes of skeleton boots marching on the stone streets had become so regular the citizens of Incanterra had almost become accustomed to the rhythmic, synchronized sound. In the ward christened Shaded Light, the skeletons made more rounds than the constables did before the siege. But the street-wise citizens living within the ward knew how to avoid the undead gaze of the skeletons. They did not tarry in their errands. Entire apartment buildings were banding together to make sure people were staying safe and doing supply runs to keep as many people off the streets as possible.

The skeletons were easy enough to avoid. Most citizens had even figured out that the undead show of force was exactly that: strictly a show of force. They were projections of strength to keep the people in line. However, with classes in the city's academies canceled, many of the ward's children had nothing to do.

In Shaded Light, the children had learned to avoid the patrols even better than their parents. They had done their best to reclaim their run of the alleys and the side streets, as they had before the siege. Anything was better than staying cooped up inside. So they leaned on clever schemes to let them sneak out and meet up for small games of sport and play. Two of the ringleaders were the pair Theobold and Anslo.

The duo had gained a reputation with the other kids. There were whispers about them running errands for certain notorious figures living within the ward. They were earning coins. Before the siege, they made it a habit of buying up baked confections and sweet treats that they handed out to other kids. No one knew or questioned if it was the discounted stock the baker had left over before closing up shop for the day. They were just happy for the treats. That made both Theobold and Anslo neighborhood favorites.

During the siege, the young duo was not exactly known for asking parental permission to gather up a gaggle of kids to play games in the alleys. As long as they weren't seen or did not challenge the patrols directly, the skeletons would march on. The pair was smart enough to rotate lookouts on the corners. Everyone knew the signals. The children learned quickly. Hide for five minutes and then they could play for an hour before it was time for the next stomping and jangling patrol to march by. It left them plenty of time to play a round of Stickball, Hooper-Looper, Snake in the Gully, or Sovereign in the Circle. Even the younger kids were allowed to join if they could successfully win a game of Sneak'n Seek, proving they were good enough to hide from the boners. Hiding well earned the right to play outside with the group.

On this particular day, the gaggle had taken up playing in the alley behind Stonehill's barber shop. Old Man Sovino's place was not even open to the public so there was no one to chase them off as they played another round of their games. All of the kids heard the light tinkling of the silver bell held by the lookout on the corner.

Under the wizarding Eight, piles of trash were a scarcity as refuse was gathered weekly and taken to the magical incinerator located below the Southwest District. The Necromangians did not run the city with such skill as the previous bureaucratic regime. As such, there were now plenty of places to easily hide within the alleys. At the sound of the bell, the children quickly scampered to their predetermined hiding places.

Even the lookouts fell back to their makeshift hiding spots, concealing themselves with paperboard boxes, ration bags, or burlap trash sacks. In the space of a few heartbeats, they all disappeared. In their different hidey holes, several of the younglings even sat quietly with their hands over their mouths to muffle their breathing.

When the sound of the booted footfalls receded far enough, the designated watchers emerged. They would make sure the patrols were gone and then signal when it was safe to come back out. Both Theobold and Anslo waited for the signal of the silver bell.

Once it sounded, the children all cautiously started to reappear. There was no whooping or hollering. The kids were way too smart for that. Instead, Anslo reminded everyone of the standing score of Sovereign in the Circle and whose turn it was. "I got next," a voice called behind them.

Both Theobold and Anslo recognized the voice and swung with excitement.

"Lady Sway!" the two said in unison.

Rushing forward, the two were quick to offer an embrace to the legendary Shader. Swayna Snowsong happily hugged the two in return.

Many of the other younger kids were excited to look up at the towering tree that was Thade Skystone. The big man knelt and was quick to pass out generous helpings of the honey rolls he carried in a paperboard box. All of the youngsters were eager to accept the fresh and hand-prepared food.

"So what's the word, boys?" Sway asked. "What do you hear?"

"Some bad stuff going down, my lady," Theobold said, eyeing Thade and trying to keep focus.

The big man happily tossed Theobold one of his honey rolls. Sway swore he had a hunk torn from the roll and in his mouth before he even caught it. "Patrols getting worse?" Sway asked.

"Depends," the lad replied with rampant chewing and one side of his mouth full. "Boners are easy enough to slip. They don't get tired. But they're also dumb. They just walk in the same pattern. So we can time 'em pretty close. But these last few days, it ain't just them. They got them leaders. Like them tossers in the white hoods? They ain't just patrolling. They're looking. I mean *actively* looking."

"What are they looking for?" Thade asked as he handed out more rolls. He smiled at one of the blonde boys and touseled his straw locks.

"They're looking for *you*," Anslo said too quickly, drawing a pop on the arm from Theobold.

"What he means is," Theobold grumbled, "they're looking for people that know how to get things."

Thade and Sway exchanged concerned looks.

"*Unfortunately*," Theobold said, stretching out the emphasis on his words, "after the Shadow's Edge Inn went up in flames, the crew that could get you things had to move out. It was not just their work. It was where they lived."

Sway nodded. "And where did they move to?"

"I heard they moved back to Ombraterra," Anslo said.

"Nah, they jumped over to one of the river towns on the border with Arvaterra," Theobold added. "My cousin told me they moved to the Southeast District. Some say they went up-kingdom and are in the northern farmlands."

"My papa said they died in the fire," one of the other kids chimed in. "Was the wizzers that kilt 'em."

"Aye," another boy said. "Wizzers killed 'em. My parents say that too."

Sway gave Anslo an affirming pat on his shoulder. "I know this won't do you a lot of good right now," she said as she palmed over a few flashes of silver, "but Thade and I are going to get this straightened out. You keep that under your mattress and when things are back to normal, everyone's iced cream is on us. Heard?"

Quick hugs were handed out to those closest to Sway and Thade and then the two disappeared back down into the deeper sections of the alley. Once they were safely away and out of earshot, the two could freely talk.

"I am more than just a little impressed," Thade said. "None of the citizens giving us up?"

Sway nodded. "Not only not giving us up but handing out lies to send the Necros on a wild faerie hunt? Means we've still got some pull. Maybe we are doing something right."

"But why are they hunting us?" Thade asked. "I thought they were targeting wizzers. Do you think they are looking for Cee and Cav specifically?"

Sway clucked her tongue. "Too hard to say… unless we can snag one of those knights in the silly hoods and make 'em talk. But it doesn't add up. We know Cee has been dealing in magic but the people don't know where it comes from. My greater fear is that they are targeting the family. And the captains of the other wards might not have fostered the same level of loyalty as we have. Someone is going to talk."

The two continued on their way down the alleys. Sway rubbed her chin and shook her head back and forth. "Remember branding cows up on the farm?"

"Only thing I hated more was the banding," Thade grumbled with a hint of nausea in his tone and an instinctive soft grip on his groin. "Still, you had to mark the cattle somehow to prove they were yours."

"I think it is safe to say the Blades have a brand," Sway contemplated. "It might be time for a new brand, a rebranding. I think too many people outside our thing know too much. Might be time for some new slang. New disguises."

"Like eye patches or faking a limp?"

"Fool, I will snatch your soul out of your body."

Halting at the mouth of the alley, the duo watched as a Knight of the Imperial Circle stood flanked by his columns of skeletal soldiers. The knight was questioning a pair of citizens just trying to deliver the conjured food rations provided by the Baelannor dynasty.

Sway turned to Thade. "What can we do?"

The big man shook his head.

"Too many of 'em. Not enough of us. Nothing we can do… for now."

Chapter 87

Like so many of the wards within the city of Incanterra, the Northwest District had her streets. There were the avenues. Then there were the smaller side streets. And there were even smaller alleyways. In the Northwest, the alleyways often served as residential borders and were reserved for things like refuse disposal and deliveries for the various estates. While no one would admit it, more than a few secret paramours were quietly escorted to and from the estates by way of the seldom-used pathways.

Some of the wealthy living within the various estates had never even walked the cobblestone paths. Most of the entrances were concealed behind ivy, trellises, or some other secreting method so as not to mar the beautiful facings of the Northwest District.

But the same as any other ward within the city, the alleyways held entrances to places refusing to advertise their activities. A turn down the right alleyway would lead you to a private club where one could witness live carnal acts for a fee. Another alleyway granted access to a secluded shop where the purest and most refined spices could be procured. Other small businesses would sell bootlegged items off their rear docks that they could never sell in the front of the house. But you had to know who to ask for and whose palms to grease.

However, there was one incredibly secretive organization even quieter than the criminal families that pretended they did not exist. Unlike the mercenary companies like the Swords of Honor or the Black House openly advertising their guild halls, this group's headquarters had no placard or signage above the door.

Grayson Rathorrian knew he was potentially violating a commandment by bringing Drennid Vocazion with him but these were difficult and dangerous times. After a series of twists, turns, secret knocks, and unlocked doors later, Graver stood in one of the antechambers of his assassin's guildhall.

Illuminated by candlelight, the room was elegant. The accouterments and the art hanging on the wall were tasteful and expensive. The seats were comfortable. And the silence within the hall rivaled the libraries in Academia.

As a second door opened on silent, oiled hinges, the woman walking through was the antithesis of a woman currently outlasting a siege. She was bathed, perfumed, and wearing a fashionable but functional dress. She walked without sound and carried with her a small, tightly wound scroll. Grayson snapped to attention as she entered and gave her a respectful nod.

"This was not an easy ask," the woman said as she passed over the thin scroll to Graver's waiting hand.

"It is appreciated," Graver said with solemnity. "I could not think of another organization to get me the information while exercising the discretion needed."

"Some of those names were provided by the grandfather himself," she replied.

"That is…" Graver stammered.

"Indeed but he understands how important this is."

Graver unfurled the scroll and began reading the elegant penmanship within. He stood completely silent as his eyes ran down the scroll. He scanned it a second time and then a third. With everything sufficiently committed to memory, he held the scroll over the open flame of one of the candles positioned on the table. He then placed the burning scroll in the wide and flat ritual metal tray positioned between the two candlesticks. As the scroll burned away to nothingness, Graver looked at the woman and offered a smile. "You have given us a path forward. Where it goes from there is up to destiny to decide. But I thank you for your help."

"You are attempting to arrange a meeting?" the woman asked.

"We are," Graver replied.

The side of the woman's mouth curled up in a grin. "You are playing a dangerous game."

Graver nodded. "These are dangerous times."

"Come back to us whole."

The mysterious woman glanced at Drennid sitting in the chair wearing his convincing merchant disguise and nodded at him respectfully. "It is an honor, Master Vocazion."

Drennid remained silent, following Graver's instructions to keep the lowest of profiles. He nodded back with equal respect.

Graver reached out and offered the woman a comforting hug. The two men then took their leave without another word. The heavy oaken door closed behind them with barely a whisper. The two continued out of the alleys that had brought them to the secluded spot.

"You care to enlighten me?" Drennid asked.

"This might be one of those scenarios where the less you know the better," Graver admitted.

"No, I want to know."

"The wizards keep me on retainer to help them track down their acquisitions. They keep me employed and they keep me paid. But sometimes, people need to disappear. When that happens, they go to my guild."

"Isn't that what these secret crime families do?" Drennid asked.

"Those families don't kill unless it is a last resort. It is tough to get money out of a dead man. My organization doesn't deal in the black market and all of those vices. We just make people go away."

"So you are assassins for hire."

"I guess I should have led with that and called it a day."

"And the crime families?"

"In both our lines of work, our circles can intersect. Call it a professional courtesy but the grandfather likes to reach out to the heads of the families from time to time. We would rather know before if a target is protected."

"Don't want to step on any toes?"

"We don't want to pay the toll. Say what you will about the families but coins fix everything. There is no problem you cannot buy your way out of. Everyone has a price... especially people like the Blades and the Crown. It is often cheaper to reject a job than have to pay off a begrudged family."

"So... wait. How many 'jobs' have you done as an assassin?" Drennid asked. "And who do you target?"

"Thankfully, I only target the people who reject having their children recruited. Most sign the contract. But not all of them. That's where I come in. And it happens enough for the wizard dynasties to keep me employed and living comfortably. So I cater exclusively to them."

As they made their way through the alleys, Graver stole a look at Drennid. The young man's face was ashen.

"I am guessing you didn't know the *full* extent of how the sausage was made," Graver commented.

"Not the full full extent."

"Yeah, all kinds of cards are getting laid out on the table these days."

"Well, like you told the girl. Dangerous times. What was her name again?"

"Nope," Graver said flatly.

"Is that some sort of clever nickname? Like how they call you 'Graver'? If she comes for you, you have nope chance?"

"Nope as is no I am not even telling you her name. That crew is one societal circle you would be best not to try to dip your wick into."

"I would remind you I am a wizard," the mage scoffed.

"A junior wizard, maybe. On a good day," Graver said.

Drennid clutched his hands melodramatically to his heart. "That is hurtful, Uncle. I know I am not ready for the role of patron or even a senior position. But *junior*? You make it sound like I am some runny-nosed apprentice."

"Again, and let me stress this once more, the members of that guild are not targeting two-bit drunks or corrupt coppers. Our assassinations change the course of history. I am talking about foreign dignitaries and those in high positions of government power."

"I don't recall any significant political assassinations in the news..." Drennid scoffed.

"That's because the best assassinations don't *look* like assassinations."

"Indeed. Still, these crime families, the cabal of Necromangians hiding under our noses, now a secret order of assassins... how many covert operations are lurking in this damn city? Does every butcher, baker, and candlestick maker have a secret uniform in the back of their closets?"

"You can't blame society," Graver replied. "You wizards chose to isolate yourselves up on your floating isle. From the second they plucked that isle out of Highstone Harbor and floated it above the city all those generations ago, you literally decided to look down your nose at the people. That arrogance and haughtiness only begat more arrogance."

The two halted at an intersection and carefully surveyed the streets. Poised in the mouth of the alley, Graver turned to Drennid with a somber tone and whispered. "Not all wizards are elitist. Ombraterra isn't like that. Castratellus isn't like that. But this path is the destiny the wizards of Incanterra chose to walk and now it is coming back to bite them. They cast their aspersions from on high telling people how they should morally live their lives.

"You have to *listen* to the people. The king of Monterra didn't heed that advice and look at what happened to him. It is why my sister and I came to Incanterra in the first place. If you want to know what is going on with the people, you can't isolate yourself in an ivory tower. You have to be down amongst them. Then the wizards started backing political movements to take away things like spirits. Of course, black markets and underground organizations were going to spring up."

The two quickly crossed the street and into another set of alleyways. "Love them or hate them, these thieves' guilds are for the people. Yet the law would brand them as criminals," Graver said. "So I find it deliciously ironic that this same group is going to help save the city."

Chapter 88

The southwest corner of the Northeast District was dominated by the Shaded Light ward. Running from First Street up to Third Street and spanning from Bronze to Copper and over to Gold Avenue, the ward took up four square blocks of the district. East of Shaded Light was the ward of Brickyard, a section that had been declared a neutral ground to act as a buffer between the Shadow Blades and the Crimson Way until the dust had finally settled between the two crime families. North of Brickyard and east of Shaded Light was Nestorian Heights.

Also controlled by the Shadow Blades, on the social ladder, the ward was a rung above Shaded Light because it was not bordered by the busy and noisy High Ways. However, the apartments, the shops, and the businesses could have easily been plucked from their foundations by the hands of a titan and swapped with each other without anyone noting the difference.

Mostly populated with Ombraterran immigrants, the sound of their accents and dialects, the smells from the cookpots and ovens, and the music of the people saturated the streets. Arvateri families were welcome. Selvaterrans held more than a few apartments. These were the people who had finally saved enough coins to graduate north of the Queen's High but still commuted to the Southeast District to work.

Within the ward was the business of Cezame Travel. If you needed to journey from the city to anywhere in the free kingdoms, people knew Cezame was the place to go. While they did not possess boats, wagons, carriages, or other modes of transportation, they knew people who did. They could get you the best rates and the most comfortable voyages. It was not a business that looked like it would make coins hand over fist.

But for the owner of the business and his silent partner, Vinson Blackshield, the business was a passport to wealth. If you needed freight quietly delivered from a neighboring or faraway kingdom, Vinson knew the right deckhands, quartermasters, and captains to talk to. Cezame Travel was the reason why Vinson rarely had to hustle to kick his coins up to his captain. Gamble Hallowhall knew Vinson was a good earner and mostly left him alone to do his earning.

Like so many sworn Shadow Blades soldiers, Vinson and his Nestorian crew had heard about the coins earned over in Shaded Light. There was even a modicum of professional jealousy as they saw the bargain basement ward suddenly putting up stacks of coins under Valos Ironblade's leadership. While Vinson and his crew had worked hard to foster the goodwill of the citizens with protection, money loaning, and catering to illegal thirsts, their loyalties were not above reproach... or purchase.

News of the betrayal had spread quickly.

When it reached the cadenta in the heart of Shaded Light, Valos snatched his sword and was still buckling it around his waist by the time he was through the front door. Six pairs of footfalls chased after Valos as he ran down the streets and cut back across the avenues. Sway, Thade, Cinder, Cavin, Sario, and Amman all moved with speed, racing to keep up.

Crossing Gold Avenue took them across the border of Shaded Light and into Nestorian Heights. Unfortunately, Cezame Travel was located too deep into the ward itself. Navigating through the streets and avenues, Cinder had closed the gap between her and Valos. Thankfully, she was there to hold him back and keep him from crossing the intersection.

There was a ring of people standing outside of Cezame Travel, far many more citizens than there should have been. Inside the business and up into the offices above the shop itself, there were the angry sounds of fighting. Clashes of steel, roars of pain, and defiant shouts echoed out onto the street. But slowly, the sounds began to recede until they echoed no more. Then, the chaos of combat was replaced by the jangling of chain links and the rattling of armor plates. Emotionless, more and more armored skeletons began to file out of the building. They assembled out on the street.

Lifeless bodies were drug from the building and neatly laid out on the sidewalk in a disturbing line. From across the street, Valos could see the fallen. Sprinkled amongst the corpses, some of the victims had black sheaths and black daggers clipped to their belts. From the distance, Valos could not easily identify any of the slain individuals but then he did not know every associate on Vinson's scrolls.

But then a large and heavily armored darkness emerged from the front of the business. Armored from head to toe and sporting a large, demonic sword, the deadly, undead enforcer carried the lifeless body of Vinson Blackshield across the wide and thick pauldrons protecting his shoulders. Amman and Cinder had to struggle to hold Valos back.

"Val, stop," Cinder hissed. "You'll draw their eye."

Knowing she was right, Valos halted almost immediately. The rogue knew the importance of blending in. Still, anger radiated from him like white-hot energy. The crew watched as a Necromangian, adorned in their dynasty's signature red robes, emerged from the building.

"The hells?" Thade Skystone grumbled.

"What?" Sway asked.

"I know that one," he replied. "The doofer in the red robes. I mean I don't know his name. It's… Stronglash. Something Stronglash. Gurroth? Gurroth Stronglash. Maybe. He's a Dugger."

Valos turned sharply. "He's a Skull Dugger?"

"I mean…" Thade shrugged and gestured toward the man. "Maybe being a Dugger was his cover. Being a Necro was his role within a role. But that one was connected. I remember his ink."

Sway's eyes began darting back and forth. Cezame Travel was located in the center of the block of businesses. "This isn't random. This isn't sweeping up and down the block looking for someone," she hissed. "They were targeted."

"Why are the Necros targeting the Blades?" Cavin asked the group.

Thade grumbled from deep in his chest. "Because they couldn't find us in Shaded Light."

"He's right," Sway said. "They have been searching for us but no one was giving us up. Even better, they were feeding them false information."

"Brickyard is a no man's land," Cinder said.

"So, Nestorian Heights was just the next block on the list," Thade said.

"Why are they targeting the family?" Valos whispered.

"Because of the threat we represent," Cinder said.

The group then watched as one of the sloops descended and landed in the middle of the street. The tall, armored warrior and the red-robed Necromangian quickly moved to board the boat. They were taking the slain body of Vinson Blackshield with them. Conversely, a commandeered wagon arrived and the skeletons were carelessly loading the bodies of the other slain soldiers inside.

Valos spat. He wanted to engage but Cinder kept him reined in. "You know what they are going to do to him."

"I don't know what they are going to do with him," Sario said. "What are they going to do with him?"

Cinder pointed to the flying sloop. "They are taking him up to Sorceria. It is where Nalazar Catabaysi is held up. The necromancer will bring our brother back to life and question him about the family."

"No one stands up to that level of torture," Valos grumbled.

"We have to get to the Gloom," Sway said.

Thade looked about, noting the ever-increasing number of skeleton soldiers. "You want us to get north of the boulevard?" Thade asked while jutting his chin towards several marching columns of the undead. "At this point, I am not even certain we can safely get west of Gold and back into the Shade."

Cinder's eyes continued to dart back and forth as she silently weighed her options. With a groan of frustration, she finally said, "I could open a portal."

"Absolutely not," Valos replied quickly. "Things are too hot for you to be unconscious for two days."

"And we don't have the grandmothers here to take care of you," Sario said while rubbing Cinder on the small of her back.

"Maybe that is because we were trying to portal in through the shield doming the city," Cinder argued.

"There is a whole family of portal casters, right?" Amman asked. "If you were the dead magickers, wouldn't you set up traps for them?"

Cavin pointed an approving finger at Amman. "Brains and brawn," the slayer said. "If I was in their position, I would have portal wells set up all over this city."

"The magic mirrors?" Sway asked.

"Gamble said he shut them down to reduce their magical signature," Cinder replied. "They didn't want to give the sniffers a scent to follow."

Valos nodded grimly. "So we head uptown the old-fashioned way. Take the long route to avoid the patrols. Who's up for a stroll to Luna Light?"

Chapter 89

Despite the earlier summer shower's best attempts, the ward within the Southwest District still felt permeated with a coating of grime. The various commandeered factories still spewed their noxious vapors into the sky.

Even though the preparing floor was baked by the summer heat, workers still dressed in as many coverings as they could stomach. They wore water-soaked kerchiefs tied around the bottom half of their faces. They kept their hair pulled back and bundled under bonnets. They wore long sleeves and gloves. No one wanted anything splashing on exposed skin.

On and on the citizens worked, hoping their compliance would somehow buy them some sort of favoritism for either themselves or their families. Admittedly, Accursio Twotrees could have easily remained in the office positioned high above the factory floor. Instead, the Necromangian was known for walking amongst the staff and pitching in to make sure everything ran at peak efficiency. He knew the importance of the skeleton army he and his workers were manufacturing.

Unlike the haughty wizards of The Eight, particularly those of the Mutaccio dynasty, Accursio chipped in and lifted the heavy loads alongside them. As such, when special orders were sent down from Nalazar Catabaysi himself, Twotrees knew exactly which workers to pick for his new assignment.

He was creating a concoction and he wanted the right assistant chefs to help him create a banquet. He knew the ones with attention to detail. He knew the ones who worked tirelessly without complaint. And he knew the ones smart enough to assist without getting in the way.

But what he was about to do, even Accursio – who previously worked as a taxidermist to hide his affiliation with the Necromangians – was not certain he could do what was next.

Looking up at the large windows of the elevated supervisor's office, Twotrees was surprised to see the purple and gold-trimmed robes of the Baelannor dynasty. It was rare that such a high-profile wizard would sully themselves by traveling down to the Southwest District. Twotrees certainly never thought to see someone as respected as the wizardess Devinaya Baelannor.

Leaving his cauldrons to simmer, the Necromangian made his way up the flight of stairs, trying his best to make himself look presentable to the ravishing young woman. Striding through the doorway into the office, the wizard allowed himself a broad smile. He even gave a dramatic flourish with his arms and bowed at the waist. "Lady Baelannor, to what do I owe the honor?"

"I come bearing a message from Lord Master Catabaysi."

"Well, this certainly sounds serious," the Necromangian replied.

"He has been detained up on Sorceria. His new death knight has brought him a lead to interrogate. There have been whispers of some underground group posing a threat of insurrection and he is looking to root them out."

Twotrees arched his eyebrows and gave a little frown. "That is a shame. He should have come to me."

"Why is that?"

"I had a group of people that used to sell me bodies back before... What should we call it? The Emergence? Are we like some debutant being presented at her formal presentation? What are those called?"

"I have no idea, nor do I care."

"I certainly would. I bet the catering at those affairs is amazing. But I wouldn't know, what with being south of the Way most of my time. I figured that would be something you Sorcerian wizards would know all about."

"Sounds more like a Northwest District sort of thing."

Twotrees waved his hands. "Ah, you are probably right. Still, I had a couple of lads from back before. They brought me bodies and accepted coins. Most importantly, they didn't ask questions."

"Where did they get the bodies?" Devinaya asked skeptically.

"I returned the same courtesy they extended to me. No questions." The Necromangian then gestured down toward the processing floor. "But it allowed me to perfect my process for creating the animated skeletons. Which made me valuable. I am not much good as a wand-waving wizard. My skills are more in the creation."

"I am guessing the Mutaccios would have snatched you up to be part of their dynasty."

Twotrees put both hands on his chest and clutched his heart. "Oh, to learn at the foot of Aldor Mutaccio? That is the dream. Especially when I see how he organized his production. I mean... before us. But still!"

The two wizards looked down on the production floor. Before, this would have been one of the many facilities churning out the various potions created by the Mutaccio dynasty. Whether they sold to the government, the military, or private citizens, the Mutaccios knew how to market their products. Before, it was potions granting the imbibed magical speed, protection from injury, the ability to breathe water, or any host of other transmutational properties.

Now, the massive cauldrons bubbled with glowing, sickly green concoctions that converted the bodies of the slain into living undead marching the city streets.

"The new spell Nalazar is developing?" Devinaya asked.

"It is a direct response to the demonic servants the Ce'Mondere summon. It is a weapon to keep them in check."

Devinaya craned her neck skeptically. "It sounds like something to fuel the nightmares of children."

"And a few adults too... I admit I am not a big supporter of it."

Devinaya stepped closer to the Necromangian. Despite the two of them being alone in the office, she cut her voice to just above a whisper. "Then don't cast the spell!"

"I am not the one casting it. I don't have the skill to do it. I am just getting everything prepared so Nalazar can step in, cast away, and then be done."

"But you have said the monster it will create will be terrifying. Don't facilitate the casting of the spell."

Accursio scoffed and then turned to look at Devinaya so he could look deep into her eyes. For the first time, the Baelannor wizardess saw it. His eyes were tinged with fear. "I will tell you the same thing I told one of my workers. You don't tell Nalazar Catabaysi no."

"Accursio... May I call you Accursio?"

"Of course."

"Accursio, your master is not... Something is wrong with him. Whoever he was before his... whatever you would call it... his transition, it didn't make it through with him. Whatever humanity he possessed when he died, when his soul got put back in his body, his humanity did not come back with it."

He nodded reluctantly. "I understand. I do. But Nalazar is a... he is a... he is a... a means to an end. What Nalazar has done is not just a 'once-in-a-generation' thing. This is like when Nas Ravalon gave humanity fire. This is like when the dragons gifted humanity magic. Only what the dragons gifted us was a curse. It turned us into weapons to fight against the Red Tyrant and his chromatic legions. Nalazar is now free of that curse. Imagine what magic he will be able to unlock now that he has been untethered and immune to the *pherein*."

The young wizardess took a moment to absorb the Necromangian's words. Finally, she relented and nodded her head. "I understand," she said.

Her tone was both relenting and almost sympathetic.

"And... who knows?" Twotrees said with a little laugh. "Maybe Nalazar can help delay my judgment."

"It is tough to be prosecuted by the authorities when your master has had the authorities disbanded."

Twotrees waved his hand. "You think I care about what some magistrates decree in a court of mortal law? No, I am more afraid of the acolytes of Zaneger. I am sure more than a few of them want to get their scythes and swords in me.

And then once I am finished, I worry about how I will stand in judgment before Zaneger himself. I can't imagine the god of death is very happy with me."

"What with all the undead skeletons and all?"

Twotrees pointed his palms to the ceiling and shrugged his shoulders. "Maybe the skeletons are not so bad. The eternal souls have been properly sent on to wherever they go. The meat and the flesh are all stripped away. It is just animated bones. It is not like I am imprisoning souls and keeping them from their eternal reward."

Devinaya gave a little grumble. "Remember a few years back? There was that scandal at one of the *domici dauthis*. There was one of the assistants. He was the one who cleaned up the bodies and prepared them for either Zaneger's Breath or a proper burial?"

"Oh, that one sick fellow!"

"Yes. Families were *not* happy. And the soul had long left the body. I could see if they were being kept in a sanitarium and they were swimming in the milk. At least then the body is..."

"Warm?"

"I was going to say alive."

Twotrees visibly shuddered.

"Yeah, people weren't happy. Call me crazy but people don't like granny's corpse being violated. I have to imagine that extends to reanimating her bones to round up undesirables."

The wizard then gestured toward the glowing cauldrons below. "And then there is this? Trust me. If he pulls this one off, Nalazar is not going to be winning the hearts and minds of anyone anytime soon."

"No," Accursio Twotrees said flatly. "But the fear will keep them in line."

Chapter 90

The magical flying sloops traversing the expanse between Sorceria and the Incanterran capital usually did so with elegant grace. So it was incredibly jarring when the wooden boat came crashing down onto the street. Planks of wood cracked and splintered. Deck pieces were sent pinwheeling through the air. The metal mooring cleats rang and sang as they bounced and skittered against the stone street.

Finally, the wreckage shifted to a halt and settled into a twisted morass of broken timber. Previously clinging to the heavily padded cushions in the well of the vessel, a lone figure managed to emerge.

Vinson Blackshield shook the splinters out of his hair and dusted off his shoulders. On wobbly legs, the rogue did his best to climb and clamor his way free of the wreckage. Looking around, he recognized the architecture of the Northeast District. But the streets were completely abandoned.

Looking north and south up the avenues, peering east and west down the streets, there was not a single soul to be found. In the light of the high sun, candlelight would have barely stood out but every business looked dark and empty.

The ominous silence was deafening. Voices, the footfalls of pedestrians, the click-clack of horse hooves, and the rumble of wagon wheels had completely vanished. The entire metropolis was a ghost town. Against his better judgment, Vinson brought his hands up to his mouth.

"Hello???"

His voice echoed down the stone and wood canyons made of looming apartment complexes. After the echoes receded into the void, silence was the only reply.

Leaving the wreckage of the sloop behind, Vinson stumbled his way west. With each step, more of his equilibrium returned. He started heading toward the boulevard bisecting the ward. As he emerged from Third Street onto Salvatorian Boulevard, he looked north and could see Trader's Cross. Looking south, the half-gate running underneath the Queen's High Way was there in the distance. But again, there was not a soul to be found.

However, the shadows within the half-gate were far deeper and darker than they had any right to be. Slowly, from out of the darkness, a pair of sharply glowing green eyes opened. Wreathed in flame and emanating an infernal glow, the sinister orbs locked onto Vinson. A guttural, feral growl echoed from out of the shadows. What emerged with slow measured steps could only be described as some sort of undead monster.

The beast looked like a massive canine. Its shoulders stood easily as tall as a man's. But the undead monster was completely skinned. All of the gray-tinted muscle and yellowish sinew were now on full display. Its horrible maw was filled with terrible, jagged fangs.

Vinson, unarmed and unarmored, scrambled backward, turned, and sprinted north as fast as his legs could carry him. He raced as rapidly as he could in the direction of the abandoned Trader's Cross.

The hellhound began at a slow but steady, methodical pace as it gave chase. The pads of its feet scraped and grated against the stone streets. It issued growls and howls as it loped forward at a leisurely pace. There was no way the pesky human was going to outrun it. And the hellhound knew the flesh was more savory when it was soaked with fear. So the chase began.

As Vinson ran, he could only think of one place where he could be safe. Despite the distance he needed to cover, from somewhere down deep that he could not explain, his lungs never burned. Despite his frantic sprinting, his legs never ached. It had to be the adrenaline of being chased. It had to be. The rogue refused to question his good fortune.

On he sprinted. Through the empty boulevards intersecting to make Trader's Cross, Vinson broke to the west and started making his way up Nickel Avenue, skirting Burkshire and the half ward making up the mercantile businesses on the northwest corner of Trader's Cross.

Risking a look back, Vinson saw the hellhound continuing its lazy lope as it continued to give chase, howling and growling all the way. The beast stayed close behind him, yet never accelerated in hopes of finally dragging down its prey.

On he sprinted. Passing Seventh Street, the ward of Luna Light loomed largely. Vinson ducked and wove his way toward the center of the ward. Positioned within the ward's heart was the traveler's inn known as the Moonshine Gloom. He was happy to see the tall structure and the sister tower. It was not for the building itself but the secret the building held. The Moonshine Gloom was the secret headquarters of the Shadow Blades and if anyone could protect Vinson from the hellhound it was his fellow brothers and sisters.

Being a hotel for the public, the doors to the inn were never closed unless it was particularly cold in the winter months. Grasping the brass handles of the twin entrance doors, Vinson had to heave mightily, as if the entrance was mired in molasses. Behind him, the hellhound gave another roar and began frantically charging. Whatever was inside the Moonshine Gloom, the undead canine did not want Vinson to reach it. Chancing a look behind him, the rogue saw the monster moving with all speed. He pulled harder and harder. Finally, the doors reluctantly gave way and began to swing open.

Seeing inside the building, there was only swirling perpetual darkness but anything was better than facing the jaws of the closing beast. Plunging inside, Vinson found himself swimming in a sea of shadows.

He was suspended in a limitless void. His feet no longer held purchase on the ground. His hands flailed wildly searching for anything to make contact with. In the absolute darkness, he could not even tell which way was up or if he was moving at all. He screamed at the top of his lungs yet there was not an echo or a single reverberation. The sound wafted out into the void, drifting endlessly and never to return.

Time held no meaning. Vinson could no longer tell how long he hung suspended within the infinite darkness.

But then, a single pinprick of white light formed in the distance. He could not tell if the light was approaching him or if he was being dragged toward it. Either way, the speck was growing larger and brighter until it was barreling toward him with the speed and fury of a rampaging chimera.

Vinson gasped as he was plunged from the great void and returned to the land of the living. Disoriented and flailing about to find anything tangible and real, he gasped as a pair of armored hands clutched him and hauled him back to his feet. As he tried to regain his senses, he looked out and saw the terrible form of Nalazar Catabaysi approaching him.

The lich was banishing the last of the mind link he had established with the rogue. Vinson's body still reeled and swooned, an aftereffect of the ingestion of the Lu'Scion's bioluminescent mushrooms.

"Thank you," the lich said, issuing what might have been considered a smile. The undead wizard then pivoted his gaze to Reeve Windwisher, who held Vinson in his armored clutches. "The Moonshine Gloom."

The death knight nodded. "I know it."

"Then you know what I want done."

Reeve rattled the rogue by his shoulders. "And this one?"

Nalazar raised his chin and glared down what was left of his nose at Vinson. His yellow eyes narrowed. "He has given us all the information we need," the wizard said coldly. "To the vats."

There was a long and dramatic ring of steel behind Vinson as the death knight drew forth his terrible two-handed sword. The wizard stared at the shaky rogue as his psyche began to fall apart. "You have given me all I need," the lich said. "On this, you have my word. No more resurrections. Five is more than most can handle. You have earned the darkness awaiting you. I promise. Your body on the other hand... well, what will you care? The Never awaits."

So broken and mangled by the torture at the bony hands of the uncaring lich, the last scraps of his sanity flittering away, Vinson barely felt the piercing sting and the terrible heat as the death knight's blade stabbed into his back and cleaved his heart in two.

Vinson Blackshield's corpse collapsed to the carpet in the parlor. Nalazar looked up with no expression on his twisted, undead features. He looked at his loyal death knight who stood at attention.

"The people need to know. Any opposition will be met with a... *disproportionate* response."

"Yes, Lord Master," Reeve replied, snapping a closed fist against his heart.

Nalazar nodded his approval.

"Send the message immediately," the lich ordered.

Chapter 91

In the light of the high sun, making their way from the wards of Shaded Light and Nestorian Heights, crossing the bisecting boulevard dividing the district, and then crossing into Luna Light was not going to be the easiest of street treks. Still, the squad of seven moved with a sense of purpose.

Valos, Sway, Thade, Cinder, Cavin, Sario, and Amman moved as quickly as they could without fear of drawing attention to themselves. After retreating from the altercation in Nestorian Heights, the crew had returned to Shaded Light and their hidden cadenta. Leather armor was adorned. Swords were clacked into sheathes. Concealed cloaks were pulled onto shoulders.

During the preparation, Thade was circulating food amongst the group, forcing them to chew chicken breasts and down water as they prepared for what was to happen next.

As silent as shadows, the group left through the back alleys and proceeded to make their way north through the city's Northeast District. As much as the shamans from Malinsula wanted to stop and marvel at the architectural wonders dominating the city, there were far too many threats potentially lurking around the next corner.

Still, as the cavalcade continued to make its way north, Sway glanced up and down the streets as they shifted from alleyway to alleyway. She made it a point to catch Thade's attention as she motioned toward one of the emptier streets. "I am not trying to look at the unicorn's teeth here but shouldn't this be a little... I don't know. Harder maybe?"

At the front of the column, Valos held up before looking to cross the east-west running main street. As much as he was happy at what he saw, the experienced rogue knew Sway was correct. In most other instances, the skeleton patrols were always prominent. It always felt as if there was a column prepared to march by at any moment. Even if they were not led by the disgusting ghouls, a Knight of the Imperial Circle, or the rare Necromangian, that skeletal presence was always looming large.

And yet now, at a moment where their presence was the least wanted, a djinn had granted their wish. "The one time we need the streets empty and they are?" Sway said. "We are never this lucky."

"I know," Thade grimaced. "For some strange reason, this turn of good fortune feels... worse?"

With the way clear, Valos led them across the street and the crew continued to navigate up more of the alleyways. Traversing the trash-strewn corridors was slower but the tall buildings and the narrow alleys provided the essential cover they needed. Seven armed men and women moving at speed in a group down a city street were certain to draw unwanted attention.

The group paused at the next intersection. Valos stuck his head out to see if the way was clear. Again, to an almost unnerving extent, the street was free of skeletal patrols. The pause did give the group time to cluster together and catch their collective breaths.

"The *Nagaru'tai*," Amman said from behind Thade and Sway.

Sway looked back and patted her rump. "Thank you, I have been doing these lunges to help sculpt it. It is so nice of you to notice."

Amman laughed and rolled his eyes. "The *Nagaru'tai*. I am trying to think of the correct translation from the Malinsuli tongue."

The shaman cast a glance at Sario. She contemplated it for a moment. "Big swell?"

"It has been called worse," Sway said. "No, wait. What I should have said was 'well, it has that effect on some men.' That's it. That's the one. Nailed it."

"A... tidal... wave?" Amman half-asked and half-stated.

"What is a *nah-garr-oo-tai*?" Thade asked.

"Sometimes deep in the ocean, there is an earthquake. The energy released from that quake produces a massive wave, a tidal wave. It is not exactly the right word because it has nothing to do with the tides but... before it hits, the water from the beaches recedes. It pulls the water off the beach to feed the coming wave. And when it hits, it wipes out everything along the shore. It is a terrible event. Nothing spreads fear like the *Nagaru'tai*."

"So they are pulling back their forces so they can attack in one massive wave?" Thade asked.

The group all shared nervous glances at one another. "It's the tactic I would use," Cavin Jurare said calmly. "This leader of theirs – this Nalazar Catabaysi – he may be a powerful wizard. He is a threat. But he is a wizard doing wizardly things. He was probably a book reader before his transformation. Not saying that is a bad thing. But there is a difference between reading about battle strategy and *understanding* it. It is not enough to know when to perform a pincer maneuver—"

"You've been talking to Valos's girl," Sway quipped.

"—it is important to know *why* to do a pincer maneuver. This wizard's battle strategy is just throwing massive amounts of brute force at an enemy."

"It is not a bad strategy when your soldiers are already dead," Valos replied.

"You don't have to care about the lives of the people who have pledged devotion to you," Sario added.

"You can literally look at them like pieces on the Scachi board," Cinder said with a shake of her head. "Who cares if dead soldiers get taken out of the game?"

There was a long uncomfortable pause between the group. Finally, Sway relented. "Val, you know this Blade. You know Vinson better than the rest of us. Is he going to talk?"

Valos winced as he considered what his brother might be going through at this very moment. "Vinson is as loyal as they come. I know he got caught up a couple of times. The Blades have some top-shelf barristers. He got pinched for charging some *vinna* on some friendly loans. It wasn't enough of a sentence to send him up to the 'Gate. So he just did the time here in the jails. The man never made a peep. Never ratted."

"But this isn't exactly avoiding a prison sentence," Cavin warned. "Necromancy is a... it is a dangerous magic. Imagine putting someone in so much pain that you die. I mean die. And then you get brought back from the Never? I think at some point, even the most stalwart among us would be begging to give Catabaysi the information he wants just to stop the pain."

As much as the assembled wanted to disagree with the undead slayer, deep down, they were terribly afraid he was correct.

Valos gathered himself and even spit onto the stone of the alleyway. "I think we should risk a portal," he said. "We need to get to the Gloom now. They have to be warned. I will even volunteer to go through it first so we don't risk losing Cinder or Cavin."

"Val, no," Sway protested. "You are just as valuable—"

"I am one blade at best. If I am knocked unconscious for a few days, the fight lives on. It is worth the risk."

"We've come this far already," Thade said, cutting off the discussion. "I say we sack up and just press on. The streets are clear for now. Let's use the safe advantage we have in front of us."

Valos looked into the stern eyes of the big man. Thade offered a reassuring nod. "Lead on, Valos."

Spinning on his heel, Valos took them up the northern path toward Luna Light. Pausing only at intersections to make sure the streets were clear, the crew of seven continued to slip and slither their way through the clogged alleys and the empty side streets.

Soon – but not soon enough for Valos's liking – the ward of Luna Light began to draw closer and closer. But with each street navigated and the nearer they came to the ward, a terrible cacophony continued to grow.

It was an unmistakable noise because nothing in the natural world sounded quite like the waging of war.

Slipping down another alleyway, the crew was navigating between the storefronts of a mapmaker and an Agavinsula spicer merchant. Neither business had been swarming with customers since the siege began so there was no one close by to see them emerge from the mouth of the alleyway.

Valos initially wanted to glance left and right to make sure the street was clear but his eye was immediately drawn to the looming towers of the Moonshine Gloom.

Valos's breath caught in his throat.

"No..."

Chapter 92

Exhausted from her effort of delivering rations to the people of Shaded Light, Mirawen Autumnlight walked the quiet streets of the ward. The summer sun was out in full force but a stiff wind was blowing in from the north, a harbinger of heavy storms. It was very much summer but the heat was unseasonably tolerable. Still, the young woman had to billow out her blouse to get a fresh flow going and hopefully air out. She also had to cinch her belt to keep her breeches up.

While technically nutritious, the conjured food presented by the Baelannor dynasty offered the required nutrients to survive but "tasty" was not going to make it into the menu description. The protein wedges and other staple commodities were bland building blocks at best.

Making her way around the streets, hauling the hand-pulled wagon filled with supplies, climbing stairs, and the constant movement had caused Mirawen to shed more than a pound. She never thought she would miss the days of being a scullery maid in the Shadow's Edge Inn.

But even then, that was less about the work. It was about her relationship with the dearly departed Runso Longbush who she saw as a caring uncle. It was also about her relationship with Cinder Fireborne. And it helped that the Shadow Blades who ran the inn as silent partners paid her a salary considered exorbitant for a woman to change sheets and clean rooms. But then, those coin stacks also bought loyalty and silence.

As she rounded the corner and came to the intersection in the center of the ward, she saw the empty lot where the Shadow's Edge Inn once stood. It caused the memory of Runso to come rushing back to her with far more intensity than she was prepared for. His laugh. That crease of teeth when he smiled, parting his enormous bushy beard from his thick mustache. She missed him terribly. Thankfully, her benefactors had survived the attack.

Still, when the Shadow's Edge Inn went up in flames, the last thing Mirawen wanted to do was work in the secretive cadenta. As much as she loved Valos, Sway, Thade, and Cinder, she just could not support it.

She fully understood that no woman working under their roof was there against her will. She had heard stories of women, a smattering of men, certain lady-boys, lad-girls, and, unfortunately, sometimes even youngsters pressganged into serving in the flesh trade. She had heard both Sway and Cinder joking about wanting to start a sister business with male employees that they flippantly called their "dandy lions." It did not sit well with Mirawen how the two looked at people as commodities but she was never brave enough to voice her complaints.

Still, she had heard stories from the Southwest. Some had signed terrible deals transforming themselves into slaves working against a rigged system that would never allow them to earn enough to repay the debt to their pimpers.

The saving grace was she knew the shadow crew was not like that. Their workers were free to come and go as they pleased. But it was still an obstacle she could not climb over. She felt a person could always do better than trading an intimate embrace for coins even if both participants were consenting. It was a special gift not to be cheapened to a business transaction.

Mirawen found purpose distributing the rations to the people of Shaded Light. Still, as she stood at the safety railing surrounding the open basement where the Shadow's Edge once stood, she could not help but reminisce about the before times. She thought back to the days even before the mysterious redheaded stranger arrived on their doorstep wanting to become a silent partner. The bond formed with her, Runso, and Cinder Fireborne grew strong as they struggled to keep the doors of the inn open. Still, given everything happening now in Incanterra, Mirawen desperately wished she could go back to the days of scrounging for profits and juggling coins to keep the lamp wicks burning.

So lost in her reverie, Mirawen almost did not even sense the shadow falling over her until it was almost too late. He was already within striking distance when Mirawen turned. Thankfully, he was living, breathing, not holding a blade, and dressed in commoner attire. But as the former scullery maid turned and could examine him more closely, Mirawen noted his cloak might have been shabby but the clothes worn underneath it were something more akin to the Northwest District. "Well met, young lady," the dark-haired, handsome man said with a smile. "A friend of mine directed me to you and given his description, I believe you are exactly who I am looking for. You are Mirawen Autumnlight, correct?"

Her eyes narrowed and she began to speak "Depends on—"

"—who is asking? Yes, I have heard that more than my fair share of times. But if we may. Can we bypass the whole preamble? I am not here to hurt you or cause any trouble but we need an introduction."

Looking past the handsome man's shabby cloak, Mirawen noted a second cloaked man lurking. As her eyes fell upon him, the cloaker turned away from her. "He's with you?"

"He is. I am told you know everyone in the neighborhood. What with the delivering of rations and your profession before."

"Profession before? I was a maid. That's a job. No one ever in the history of employment has referred to being a maid as their 'profession.'"

"Be that as it may, you worked for a group. The silent partners of your inn. I need an introduction. After the fire there, they scattered to the winds. I need to speak with them."

"What makes you think I know where they are?"

"Because you are a smart girl and the lives of every single person trapped in this city are hanging in the balance. I need to speak with Cinder Fireborne."

Looking over the man's shoulder, Mirawen's eyes were drawn in the direction of the second stranger. At a distance, it was hard to be sure but there was a distinct recognition. There was something about his movements.

"I don't know where she is at this *exact* moment," Mirawen said, keeping an eye on the second man. "But I can get you in touch with her. You looking for some kind of wizzer reunion?"

The man smiled. "Something like that."

"So who are you?"

"My name is Grayson Rathorrian."

"Rathorrian? That sounds like a wizard surname. But not one of The Eight."

"No. Well, yes. But no."

"That makes it infinitely clearer."

"Yes, it is a wizard surname. It is from a Monterran dynasty. But I am not a wizard, I promise you. If you mention that name, she will know who I am."

Mirawen cast a skeptical glance Graver's way. "You family?"

"Something like that."

"I am guessing more the first family than the second?"

"Her first."

"From up there?" Mirawen asked but she purposefully kept focused on Graver with not even an eye gesture up towards Sorceria.

"Not me personally but yes."

Mirawen shifted her gaze once more back to the second man in the distance in his threadbare cloak. From underneath the hood, the man finally returned her gaze.

"I remember that one," Mirawen whispered.

Despite the summer heat, a chilling shiver of fear rippled up Mirawen's spine and her flesh began to crawl. Behind her, over the void of the open basement, was where the floor planks of the Shadow's Edge Inn once stood. It was on those planks that Mirawen sat tied to a chair watching. She watched as the man standing across the street tortured and eventually killed Runso Longbush. Her lower lip began to tremble and tears threatened to leak from her eyes.

Graver looked at the girl curiously and then glanced back at Drennid Vocazion. Like many Incanterrans, he had heard the whispers. Back last spring, everyone was talking. The wizards had burned down an inn. Given the scullery maid's reaction and seeing Drennid, the tumblers began clicking into place.

Graver groaned and shifted his position to block Drennid from the woman's view. "Please, Lady Autumnlight," he whispered in the most soothing of tones. "Please, Mirawen. Whatever happened between the two of you... whatever it was... I apologize. But we have to put that aside."

Mirawen had to push her words through gritted teeth. "He murdered my friend."

Graver held up a hand and exhaled a deep breath. "Please believe me when I tell you. This is bigger than any single one of us. This is a matter... of life and death."

There would only be a handful of reasons why the wizards would want to meet with members of the family. "For real?" she asked.

"As real as it gets. Life *versus* death."

Somewhere in the distance, the synchronous marching boots of skeletons could be heard echoing down the streets.

Graver silently noted the sound and then gave a subtle nod. "Life versus death. And regardless of who we are or what we do, all of us are on the side of life. I don't care if I am fighting alongside a copper or criminal as long as I am fighting on the side of the living. How about you?"

"If I do this for you," Mirawen said, "is there any chance you take a stray pup off my hands?"

Chapter 93

The sheer number of skeletons surrounding the Moonshine Gloom was a baffling sight to behold. From their position across the alleyway, Valos Ironblade was convinced he could have leaped up onto the head and shoulders of the assembled bone masses and walked from the alley to the front door of the inn and never touch the street.

Naturally, the calamity had drawn citizens from their homes and surrounding buildings, adding to the mass of humanity. As Valos took in the scene, he noted the exterior sky bridges. On even-numbered floors, the sky bridges connected the main building with her smaller sister tower. That second tower was completely controlled by the Blades. The bridges were fiercely damaged. In some sections, it looked as if a titan's axe had sliced completely through the bridge. It left a wide enough open-air void that jumping across would be impossible.

"The bridges," Sway said.

"Yeah," Valos replied with a grim nod. "That's intentional. One of the last lines of defense."

"But they could have got out through the basement, right?"

Valos winced and clucked his tongue. Silently stewing, he went to pull his sword blade. Thankfully, Sway was close and was able to stop him before too much of the glinting blade made it into the daylight.

"What are you doing?" she hissed.

"We have to do something," he protested.

"Have you looked out there? We wouldn't even make it to the Gloom, even with Cinder and Cavin cutting paths for us."

"But we have to—"

Sway cut him off. "Vee, it's already too late. If we throw in, we will just be captured."

"We stood down with Vinson. Not again. Gamble is in there. We have to try."

"Gamble would agree with me!" Sway said as she clacked Valos's blade back into its scabbard. "Now, take a breath. Breathe. Come on. You know I'm right. This isn't the time for some legendary maneuver."

"Our boy is back," Thade said, drawing the attention of the group.

He gestured towards the elites milling about the step-up entrance to the main foyer of the Gloom. There in the distance was the recognizable Gurnoth Stronglash of the Necromangians.

Past the mouth of the alley, there was a smattering of the nightly renters and the day trippers trapped in the city when the magic shield came down. Women were sobbing. There was quiet weeping. Cinder studied them all. She swore she caught Arvateri accents, some choice Castratellus dialects, and other foreign brogues and twangs. Yet, amongst those escaping the horrors, there were no porters, no scullery maids, and no employees of any kind. And the group had yet to see a single person with a black sheath on their belt.

From within the sprawling inn itself with its multiple floors, sounds began to grow quieter and quieter. The angry shouts of combat grew ever softer. And then, only silence remained. Amongst the rings and columns of skeletal soldiers, many did not even have to draw their blades. They simply stood, silent and obedient, waiting for their masters to send them next into the sin den of the corrupt. But the order was not needed.

More and more red-robed wizards eventually made their way out of the front entrance to the Moonshine Gloom, confident there was not a single member of resistance left alive within the building.

Valos stood, defiant and closed-lipped. The left side of his mouth twitched along with his cheek. As he stood, even his left eye blinked slower than his right. Finally, he managed a grumble. "If they light the place on fire..."

Cinder found herself next to her friend and wrapped a comforting arm around his waist. "I don't think they operate that way."

"I swear to the gods, I am going to sprout Nas wings out of my back, fly up to Sorceria, and cut that monster's rotting head off his withered shoulders," the rogue cursed.

"We don't know..." Cinder tried to say but Valos cut her off.

"Where else would they be? Celesta, Armand, Thorn... the entire senior hierarchy would all be up in there. Where else would they be? Hells, is Gamble up in there?"

Thade turned back to look at Sario and Amman. All he could do was shake his head. The two Malinsuli stayed back, not wanting to interfere or be in the way. As the crew retreated into the darkness of the alley, Amman reached out and placed a reassuring hand on Thade's shoulder. Sario made it a point to hold the hands of both Thade and Sway.

Cavin wanted to unleash his silver sword but the slayer knew it would draw too much attention from the undead army. Instead, he gave a tug on Cinder's cloak to pull her back further out of view.

But Valos Ironblade stood firm. He stood glaring at the once great façade of the Moonshine Gloom. His father had sworn his blood oath on the top floor in the ballroom, back when it was still safe to unfurl the scrolls within the main tower and induct members. It had been one of the last crowning achievements of Varazze Darksteel – before the fever took him – to purchase the Moonshine Gloom and transform it into the family's main bastion.

Seeing it desecrated by the Necromangian's undead horde, it was all Valos could do to remain in control.

From back deep in the alley, Thade broke from the group and strode towards his friend. The big man took a moment to share the gaze into the abyss. The two stood, their eyes locked on the building, ignoring those scuttling past the alley entrance.

"We don't know," Thade said, a hint of mournfulness in his tone. "The basement. That is where Celesta took command of the Blades. Right?"

"It is."

"So there is a chance that some – if not all of them – made it out. Sorrowsword is resourceful. And all of them are fighters to the last. But if they didn't, I promise you. I am going to stand beside you and we are going to grind every single one of these skeletons into powder. Not one of those red-robed-wearing pusillanimous villains is making it out of this city alive. And that Stronglash traitor, he is going to get it worse than any of them. He may not be a Blade but he is still betraying a family."

Valos turned. The rogue was processing a series of emotions until he finally settled on what might have passed as stuttering laughter. Thade smiled in return. "I don't know if I have *ever* heard you talk like that," Valos said.

"These are strange times."

"Hey, I am not complaining. Pusillanimous? Talk about a gold coin word. I just didn't know you had it in you. Good to know it is there if we need it. And all it took was a besieging of the city and a marching army of undead ghoulies to bring it out."

Popping Thade in the chest with the back of his hand, Valos finally turned and made his way back into the darker recesses of the alleyway where the other five were waiting.

"Do we risk a portal to get us back to the cadenta?" Sway asked.

"I say no," Cavin said. "It is too large a contingent out there. If they have their sniffers out and close, it might draw their attention."

"We fall back to Seventh Street and then head west," Sway said, taking charge. "We make our way over to Bronze, yeah? Then just go straight south. Keep the King's High on the right-hand side. Act as if we belong there. Let's go."

Wasting no time and inviting no debate, Sway headed south and the crew went with her. Soon enough, they were out of the alleyway maze and heading west on Seventh Street.

Thankfully, with so many of the Necromangian forces congregating at the attack of the Moonshine Gloom, once the group was out of the Luna Light ward, there were very few obstacles, granting them passage on the city's main thoroughfares.

The group continued west to the intersection of Seventh and Bronze. Bronze was the westernmost avenue of the Northeast District and ran parallel to the King's High Way. Heading south, the crew would eventually be within the safe confines of the Shaded Light ward and run into the intersection of the King and the Queen's High Way.

With enough distance between them and the Gloom, Valos finally threw up his arms in exasperation. "Is there something in the water I don't know about? Aside from the atrocity of what happened back there, are the wizards doing something to mess with our minds? Look at us. We are following Sway like she is a general. Thade is speaking like a scholar. A Jurare wizard is helping the family. We gave two Malinsulis a free pass to avoid certain death... and they turned it down?"

He then turned and looked Cinder up and down. "I've never understood your whole deal so I don't even pretend to know what you are going to do next. I am just pointing out that nothing about any of this is right. What is next? Am I going to forego caring about coins? Find women unappealing?"

"Don't forget. We are in a tentative alliance with the Crimson Way," Thade said.

"Yeah, normally that would be a banner headline in *The Heraldry*," Valos said with a flummoxed tone. "Now, even that is relegated to the back of the paper because of all this insanity."

"Meanwhile, here I was concerned more about the marching undead, the ghosts, and the secret necromancer cult," Cavin said.

"Plus there is all that!" Valos roared. "Tadorin's stones, even the goody two-booter gets a dig in on me. What are things coming to? I am getting close to my limit. I cannot take another thing that is going to turn this whole situation upside down again."

Chapter 94

As the sun began its descent behind the Pyrewind Peaks, thick, dark storm clouds rolled in once more, obliterating the stars, and quickly began drenching the city in still much-needed rain. Fat drops splattered and smattered against the sun-baked stone, cooling the city and the air. As the evening continued to deepen, the Knights of the Imperial Circle retreated to their strongholds to stay dry. The Necromangians returned to Sorceria or their upscale commandeered accommodations within the Northwest District. It left only the predictable marching columns of skeletons to patrol the wards.

Even the citizens of Incanterra were buttoning up to survive the heavy downpours. Some children sat beside their apartment windows, looking wistfully out at the rain. Some would extend their hands out into the downpour. But no mother was about to let them go frolic and play in the rain and the night air. It was far too close to their bedtimes and many of the citizens were content to let the music of the rain soothe them to sleep with one of the Mother's most beautiful lullabies.

Meanwhile, the closed businesses on the street level of the buildings remained dark and vacant. Since the magic shield descended upon Incanterra, there was no shortage of businesses forced to shutter. Throughout the four districts, inside every ward, and on every street, a business had either locked its doors, been boarded up, or had just been left open for any squatter to lay claim to. Whether the owners could no longer purchase stock to keep their doors open or if they had been rounded up by the skeletal squads, many of the businesses were left abandoned.

The only saving grace was with skeletons constantly on patrol, none of the abandoned businesses were openly ransacked. Glass windows were not busted out. Trash was piling up in the alleyways but was still largely contained. It was as if the businesses had quietly gone dormant, waiting for their masters to return and breathe life back into them.

One of these cornerstone businesses was Stonehill's Barbershop. It was a popular destination for the men of Shaded Light. Sovino Stonehill and his prentices offered haircuts and shaves at reasonable prices. But the Ombraterran immigrant had closed his shop to keep his employees safe and citizens off the street. It was easy enough to pull the curtains along the windows at the front of the shop and along the glass windows within the main entrance.

With only the softest lighting provided by a few of the mage-light stones stashed within the shop itself, the citizens and the roving patrols were ignorant of the clandestine meeting happening behind closed doors.

Grayson Rathorrian and Drennid Vocazion sat patiently in the empty barbershop. Grayson was utilizing the time and the shop's resources to shave clean while Drennid was haphazardly reading through old editions of *The Heraldry*.

"You realize this could all be a ruse," Drennid said as he tossed one of the papers onto the counter in front of him. "She could be having a good laugh right now at our expense. Meanwhile, we are sitting around waiting whilst we clutch our manhoods."

"I certainly hope you mean you will be holding your own," Graver said as he deftly shaved underneath his bottom lip with one of Sovino's straight razors.

"You know what I mean," the lad said irritably. "How long do we wait for her to arrange this meeting?"

"Do you need to rush off and imbibe a tonic? Do you have a pressing social engagement? Some cotillion I am unaware of? Don't forget, we are coming to them for help."

Drennid waved off the comment and harrumphed his derision. "I think it is safe to say we are the dragon's share of power within this little arrangement."

"Spoken like a true wizard," Graver said. "And yet, these secretive lads are sleeping in their beds and probably still living a somewhat comfortable life. Whereas you... and Sorceria... and your wizarding kind... not nearly as much. I hope you can find a way to recline that chair to make it comfortable enough for you to sleep in. We might be staying here."

Drennid waved off Graver's comments.

"I would be careful how you assign power, Nephew. Not all power can be quantified as strength of arms or how you wield your wand. Look at how much power someone has right now if they have a warm bed and cupboards full of food that is *not* wartime rations."

"I think you have been living down amongst them for too long," the mage replied.

"Say what you will. The so-called crime families are particularly adept at fostering loyalty amongst their people. The citizens *love* them. Whereas, I am afraid the citizens *fear* you."

"You say that like it is a bad thing."

"Fear motivates in the short term. But true loyalty to an organization? People will die for it. People will kill for it. And say what you will but people haven't rolled over on these families. There has to be something to that."

The rear entrance to the barber shop opened with the slightest whisper of noise followed by the sound of rain. From the darkness of the rear alley, two cloaked forms emerged and removed their hoods. The two men expected Mirawen Autumnlight but Drennid was surprised to see Kynna'Fyir Lu'Scion.

"Well, Lady Lu'Scion. Isn't this a development?" the mage said as the magician stepped into the light.

"Hello, Drennid," Kynna said with a respectful nod.

"And here I thought the entirety of the Lu'Scions had fled to safer environs. Did your patron leave you behind or just forget that you were trapped down in the city when everything happened?"

Graver glared at Drennid. "Must every comment you make be condescending? Is it your nature to be so combative? Or can you just not help yourself?"

Drennid clapped his hands together and spun haphazardly in the rotating barber's chair. Graver turned and offered a respectful bow to the young magician. "My lady, it is a pleasure to see you again. I am glad to see that you have survived all of the recent hostilities. You are a testament to your dynasty." The assassin then turned abruptly to face Drennid. "See? See how much better that is than your snipes and slights?"

Drennid rolled his eyes and took another lackadaisical spin in his chair. Graver turned to address Mirawen. "I hope you are here to provide us with good news."

"Word is circulating around the city," Mirawen said. "Apparently, the boner forces have been targeting the families. It is a lot of speculation. But stories are the Blades have been hit. So have the Diamond Way in the Southeast and the Skull Duggers in the Southwest. No word yet about the Crown in the Northwest but if they were hit, it might have been so covert that the fancy pants in their estates might not even have noticed."

"What does that mean for us?" Graver asked.

"Nothing," Drennid called out. "Our meeting was never going to be with their leadership anyway. We need a meeting with… *her*."

"I am told they have returned to their base of operations but I am afraid of blindsiding them," Mirawen said. "So I will go and get permission to bring you to them."

"That sounds like a lot of back tracking," Drennid said, causing Graver to glare in his direction. "What happens if you get snagged by the boner patrols?"

"It sounds like she is being cautious," the assassin said. "Still, I understand. Do however you see fit, young lady. But if things truly are getting desperate out there, time is of the essence."

"I will return as soon as I can," Mirawen said. "But it is important to note that the rules of a sitdown are fiercely enforced by their group. There can be no aggression displayed. It is a rule. All of this is just to talk."

As she gathered up her cloak and prepared to leave through the rear entrance, Drennid called out, "And maybe bring some food back with you?"

The door to the alley closed behind Mirawen.

"You heard her," Kynna said. "At this sit down, there can be no aggression to everyone that is involved?"

"Those are the rules," Graver said.

"And a den of thieves is always going to abide by the law," Drennid laughed.

"He can say what he wants," Graver said, directing his reply to Kynna. "The group we are negotiating with consider themselves to be men of honor. Laws are one thing. Rules are another."

Kynna began gathering up her cloak.

"Where are you going?" Graver gently demanded.

"There is another recruit that should be a part of this meeting. I will vouch for them," she said, "and I will meet you there."

Graver started to protest but the back door was already closing behind Kynna as she made her way out into the pouring rain.

Chapter 95

The portal to the Southwest District opened with an energy best described as angry. The magical signature on the production floor of the Southwest District warehouse flared with wrath and urgency. The dark red swirls of sparks clumped together in slow-moving clusters almost resembling tendrils. It was utilitarian and to the point. There were no frills or artistry with the casting. The center of the ring rippled as the spell locked into place, revealing the wizarding isle of Sorceria on the other side.

Dressed in his blood-red robes and wearing his concealing onyx mask, Nalazar Catabaysi floated from Sorceria, through the portal, and then onto the production floor of the warehouse. His feet glided above the smooth concrete floor of the facility.

In the late hour, the warehouse was awash in mage-light. Many of the large, rolling doors had been flung open on their tracks. Windows were propped open. A cool breeze wafted through the warehouse, bringing with it the smell and mist of the heavy rain falling in buckets outside the building.

While many of the cauldrons lining the production floor still bubbled and simmered, the working class of the Southwest manning the facility had been sent home to sleep. There were the occasional sounds of calcified clackings up on the catwalks.

Looking up at the high ceilings, the undead wizard witnessed a few scatterings of skeletons performing menial tasks. More than a few of the bone servants were stirring bubbling cauldrons with what could have passed for boat oars. Others were washing and rinsing out some of the iron pots. But they did so silently, casting the large warehouse with a calmness only disturbed by the sound of the pouring rain and the occasional metal rattling from the skeletons' cleaning.

Walking from around one of the rows of the cauldrons, Accursio Twotrees was surprised to see his master down within his humble abode. The Necromangian stopped short and offered a respectful bow. "Lord Master Catabaysi," he said, face pointed towards the floor. "It is an honor."

The undead horror slowly glanced around at the facility but behind his featureless mask, it was impossible to tell what reaction was being garnered as his eyes scanned the various cauldrons, the catwalks, the pulley systems, and the dumbwaiters used to deliver the various ingredients.

"The *impreca'caro* spell," the lich hissed. "The accursed flesh. Are we ready?"

"I have prepared the cauldron exactly as you requested, Lord Master. And I have arranged a certain number of *volunteers* for the skeletal support."

The loyal Necromangian bade his master follow him. He then escorted the lich to a far corner of the warehouse. It was secluded away and specifically prepared for this new spell that could only be cast by someone such as Nalazar.

A large copper cauldron with a ballooned rounded bottom was positioned in the corner, surrounded by an elevated wooden catwalk. Suspended on squat legs, the cauldron was poised over a ring of protective concrete blocks. Within those blocks were a variety of dormant heater stones. These were the same types of stones sold by the Vocazion dynasty to the people of the city to fuel their ovens and cookstoves. But these particular igneous cubes were infused with tremendous magic to burn both hotter and longer. There were whispers of special negotiations between the patrons of both the Mutaccio and Vocazion dynasties. Some said the stones were crafted by Marius Vocazion himself.

Next to the large copper cauldron was a series of vats filled with purified water. Within those water-filled vats was fuel for nightmares. Accursio Twotrees was charged with sloughing the muscle, organs, and skin off of the dead bodies brought to him. His technique created a pristine skeleton. Once the magic was infused into the ligaments, the bones came out of his cauldron as obedient undead servants.

But with the discovery of outlawed magic within the Cellarium Vaults, the lich had called for a change to how the skeletal soldiers were processed. Now, instead of the muscle and flesh dissolving away into a disgusting slurry, Twotrees was preserving the material. After a few issues involving vomiting from his workers, the reclamation process was relegated to the skeletal servants.

And now, with the material properly prepared, Nalazar Catabaysi had arrived to cast the critical element of the spell to bring forth a new and terrible weapon into his arsenal.

Not needing a magic wand or any other type of wizardly instrument, Nalazar simply flung his hands outward with his fingers outstretched. The paper-thin lids over his yellow eyes slid shut and he disappeared into a casting trance. The sound of sloshing water rang out. Having tapped into his transmutation magic, Nalazar reached out into the vats and began levitating the contents.

As he directed them into the copper cauldron, the stones underneath roared to magical life and quickly began infusing the concoction with incredible heat. The conglomeration of muscle and flesh slipped into the vat. Then, following Nalazar's telepathic commands, the assembled skeletons marched up the stairs of the scaffolding surrounding the cauldron.

Without a single drop of hesitation or fear, the silent skeletons toppled head-first into the bubbling liquid. Slowly, within the lathering green sludge, the bones began to infuse with the muscle and flesh circulating within.

Slowly, the lich lowered his hands and his eyelids slid open. Behind his mask, the undead horror smiled. "Now we wait," Nalazar hissed. "Once the amalgamation has formed, I will need to cast one last component into the spell. Then we will have the first of our terribly wonderful weapons."

Twotrees stood an obedient step behind and off the flank of his master, listening to the cauldron froth and roil. "Master," he said tentatively, "this is a response to the demons summoned by Ce'Mondere. Correct? They used one to perform the jailbreak at the city gate. So this is to fight back against their infernal weapons?"

"It is…" the lich said. "It is not the *only* reason but it is a good enough one. While this creation will surely be able to go against any infernal claw or fang, it is also a deterrent. It is a reminder. I have had enough. The insubordination by the escaping wizard was one thing. These criminal families pose a threat. I have decided to elevate my plan in response. When I do, the people will not be happy. This will be my deterrent to keep them in line."

Accursio stood for a moment. He looked about the warehouse with a mask of confusion etched on his face. "Master, I thought the plan was to unlock the forbidden secrets of magic. How does the population of Incanterra fit in?"

Nalazar turned with a slowness one would expect of a melodramatic stage actor. "Unlocking the magic *is* part of the plan but it is not the *entire* plan. It is also to make the wizards pay for their treachery. It is also to make their accomplices pay. Once I have dispatched them, I will use their bodies, bring them back through unlife, and assemble an army that will march across the face of Incanterra. We will recruit all that we find within every town, every village, and every hamlet. The only question is do I march first on Castratellus to the west or Arvaterra to the east?"

As Nalazar completed his turn, Accursio Twotrees had taken a pensive step back and one more off to the side. The lich glanced back over his shoulder in the direction of the copper cauldron and the shimmering heat mirage radiating from underneath.

Behind the lich's mask, Accursio could see his master's eyes close once more. "I can feel it," the lich said. "I can feel its essence pulling the very fibers apart and restructuring them. I can sense the bones sinking into the flesh and the muscles accepting them. It is creating something… beautiful. And it is all thanks to you, my loyal servant."

Nalazar's eyes opened and settled on Accursio. "All that remains is the final infusion and the first of my new weapons will be ready to rise."

The lich began to unleash more transmutation energy only this time, it was directed at Accursio. The Necromangian struggled against the magical energy, trying to slough off the effects. He floated up into the air, his feet dangling inches above the warehouse floor.

With a flick of his wrist, the lich dragged Accursio towards him until he caught his follower by his throat. Thankfully, it was over quickly. The life essence drained from Accursio, aging him impossibly fast and withering his body so much that when Nalazar finally released his corpse, it sounded like a pile of dried leaves smacking against the warehouse floor.

Wasting no time, the lich then transferred the life energy into his new grotesque creation. It took several heartbeats for the monster within the copper cauldron to stir. The noxious fluid within sloshed, slopped, and splattered its way up and over the rim of the cauldron followed by a hideously formed fist of flesh. The mammoth creature then pulled itself up out of its disgusting bath.

Behind his mask, Nalazar Catabaysi smiled and prepared to welcome his newest creation into the land of the living. He smiled knowing this would help transform Incanterra into the city of the dead.

Chapter 96

In the late evening, the rain continued to fall, drenching the Northeast District and the ward of Shaded Light. As much as the people inside the secret cadenta wished to fling open the windows and throw back the curtains to let the rain-cooled air swirl inside, the last thing they wanted was the light in their windows radiating out onto the street. They preferred the entire multi-story structure to appear as an abandoned building to keep from attracting the attention of any roving skeletal patrols.

Instead, within the main parlor, the assembled crew risked a few small hints of magic. An illusory fire lit the fireplace, radiating all sorts of flickering light but not a single bit of heat. There were also a few cooling pots scattered about to condition the air, making the heat of the summer almost a memory.

Freshly bathed and having adorned clean attire, the group of Valos, Sway, Thade, Cinder, Cavin, Sario, and Amman had gathered in the building's main ground floor parlor. Most of the building's employees had retired to the security of their respective rooms for the night. So many of the cadenta's girls felt safer under Loredana Summerbrook's roof and had opted to remain in the cadenta for the duration of the siege.

The ladies were smart enough to leave the gathered seven to their commiserating in the main hall. It was typically reserved for entertaining clientele until they were ready to head up to the upper floors for some companionship. But tonight, Loredana had smartened the girls up and ensured the group would have their privacy.

Cavin Jurare took a moment to refill his sweet lemonwater, rattling around the square cubes of ice in his glass. He took a drink and cleared his throat. "I am going to say some things now," the undead slayer declared. "It is not going to be popular but it is going to be practical. Now, look. I know there is honor in going down with the ship. I know loyalty is big with your family. I get that. But if the sails are on fire, the rigging is burning, and you are taking on water… at some point, you have to go for the longboats."

"What are you suggesting?" Valos asked. Strangely, there was minimal inflection in his tone. He was simply asking.

"I think it is time to abandon the city," Jurare replied. "People are saying there are abandoned ships in the harbor. We commandeer one of those and we get out of here."

"We have to take Loredana with us," Sway said without hesitation. "And all of the girls."

The two Malinsuli shamans looked at each other, silently assessing. "That is a lot of people to smuggle out," Sario said. "A lot of people to smuggle out in a single trip."

"We would have to get to the boats extremely quietly," Amman added.

"What about the rest of the ward?" Thade asked. "A substantial number of people pay us to protect them."

"Errmmm..." Valos grumbled, drawing eyes to him. "It is one thing to protect them from getting ripped off. Your son-in-law is beating your daughter? We can handle that. You need some funds and can't get a coin from the bank? Sure. A copper does you wrong? We can help. Those are the things we protect against. This whole thing... this thing is an act of the gods. This is a natural disaster. No one would expect protection from a— Amman, what did you call it? The big wave?"

"The *Nagaru'tai*," the shaman replied.

"The *Naga*— The *Nagar*— What he said. The big wave. It's a natural disaster."

"So we leave them to die?" Sway asked.

Valos frustratedly rubbed his forehead and then ran his fingers through his hair. "Yeah, I don't like the sound of it either. But even if we had some giant tunnel to get them out of the city, where do we move them to once we get them out?"

Amman and Sario looked at each other, again sharing knowing looks. They mumbled back and forth as well as shrugging their shoulders and shaking their heads. Sway looked at them both. "Hey, you two are a part of this group. Everyone's opinion is important. No bad ideas."

Sario cleared her throat. "Moving people through the water with an elemental is possible but it would be slow. And truthfully, you could only do it at night. The problem is that in this city there is no soil. There is no connection to the earth. If we could get that connection, maybe we could summon earth elementals to create a tunnel to get people out of the city. It would be faster than trying to get them out through the water."

"We still have the issue of where to take them once they are beyond the curtain," Thade said. "Something tells me neither Castratellus nor Arvaterra would be tremendously accepting of refugees."

"We have to finance all this somehow," Valos said, wagging his finger. "How is that going to look when we start charging people to take them out of the city?"

"Better than being dead in it," Thade said. "Still, people on our ledgers should get preferential treatment."

"One of the bigger issues is how do we make it look like Shaded Light is still populated?" Cinder said, finally chiming in. "Once they notice an entire ward empty, the boners are going to start asking questions. If people stop showing up to collect their rations, it is going to be a warning flag."

"And we still have to figure out where we are taking them," Valos grumbled. "I doubt Aunt Erayllia is prepared to make food for a few thousand."

"I don't think any of those frontier or aggie towns could handle the flow," Thade said.

"What about the border forts?" Sway asked. "Remember back when we 'found' those crates of magical supplies? They were shipping them somewhere. They were going to that fort on the border with Arvaterra. Why not send them all there?"

"If the fort is still standing," Valos said. "Remember that skeletal force marching on Ambershore? For all we know, they are overrun with undead too."

From out of the foyer, Loredana Summerbrook entered the chamber at a brisk pace. "My friends," she said. "You have a visitor."

The group all turned together as a rain-soaked, cloaked figure entered the room. As the man pulled back his black hood, Valos gasped in excitement. "Arator," he proclaimed.

The rogue was up like he had been shot from a crossbow. He crossed the expanse quickly with his arms spread wide. The two friends shared a heartfelt embrace and slapped each other on the back more times than could be quickly counted. "You've survived," Valos said, relief saturating his voice.

"And you," Arator Dawnborne replied.

As they broke their embrace, the tall Monterran scanned the parlor. "You have added some new faces to your menagerie," he said with a smile.

"Indeed. New faces, this is Arator Dawnborne. We go way back. Way back. He is an acolyte of Zaneger, a member of the *domici dauthis*, and a sworn enemy of the undead. So this is someone we want on our side.

"Arator, that is Sario and Amman – shamans from Malinsula."

"You two are a long way from home."

"Indeed," Amman replied with a nod of respect.

"And this is Cavin Ju—"

"Cavin Jurare!" Arator said excitedly. "I did not recognize you out of your slayer uniform."

The big man strode forward and happily extended his hand in greeting. "It is a pleasure to meet a fellow slayer," Cavin smiled. "Good to meet you."

"And you, fine sir," Arator said. He then turned back to address the collection of Blades assembled within the room. "I assume you are planning to take back the city. How can I help?"

The group all exchanged nervous glances.

"You *are* planning on taking back the city?"

Valos uneasily tugged on his collar. "We were talking about how to get the hells out of here."

"What? We cannot abandon Incanterra in its time of need."

Valos offered Arator a seat but the big man was more inclined to pace in front of the heatless fire. "It is not that simple," Valos said. "They have been targeting your houses of the dead. They struck at the heart of the Blades."

"If the Blades existed," Sway interrupted.

"If the Blades existed," Valos parroted, holding up his hands. "The wizarding dynasties have been brought to heel. The coppers were dismissed. The army was slaughtered. Cavin had a powerful sinking ship metaphor before you got here. It was a whole thing."

Arator turned towards Cavin with a crestfallen look on his handsome features. The undead slayer held firm for a few heartbeats but then gave a rejected nod. "It's true. Incanterra is lost. This small little band – even adding you to the list – would be eight against an army of undead and a walking nightmare wizard rose from the grave?"

Before the argument could escalate, Loredana returned to the main parlor. "Not another visitor?" Thade said with a light laugh.

Sway threw up her hands. "You know for a secret hideout, a lot of people know where to find us."

"This one is... different," Loredana replied. "They are officially requesting a *sedere*. And they are asking for the rules of such a meeting to be enforced."

"They specifically asked for a *sedere*?" Valos asked.

"They did."

"So, who is it? The Crimson Way? Of course. Show them in."

"That's a problem," Loredana said. "They are not members of the Crimson Way..."

Chapter 97

With the late night hour and the pouring rain, there were no citizens out and about to notice the arrival of the magical sloop from Sorceria. The torrential rain masked the soft warbling hum accompanying the flight of the magical boat. The lone occupant had doused the mage-light glass serving as the vessel's running lights.

The boat navigated its way down to the city and into the open central courtyard of the square building. The vessel landed lightly within the perfectly sized, recessed wooden cradle allowing the occupant to step directly onto the cool, rain-slicked marble floor of the courtyard.

After disembarking and the vessel being free and clear, the sloop began its silent ascent so it could return to Sorceria. He watched the boat levitate out of the courtyard. "No going back," he whispered to the void.

Rather than being dressed in his traditional blood-red robes, the Necromangian had opted for a black cloak to help keep his identity concealed. The last thing the second-in-command of the death cult wanted to be was recognized. With a flourish, a turn, and a snap of his increasingly waterlogged cloak, Dragan Duskwood headed into the covered sections of the empty landing station.

Once out of the rain, he pulled up short as a cloaked figure was in the shadows waiting for him. The magical dweomer would have kept a regular citizen from stumbling into the building so the Necromangian felt no need to draw out his magic wand. Stepping into the interior's soft blend of evocation light and illusory images to make it resemble the flickering of candles, Dragan offered a heartfelt smile. "Hello, Kynna'Fyir Lu'Scion. It is a pleasure to finally meet you in the flesh."

Kynna offered a quick but respectful curtsey. The young wizard was also in disguise, wearing the expected attire of a scullery maid and a traveling cloak to help shield her from the rain. "It is a pleasure to meet you as well."

Stepping deeper into the covered areas of the landing, Dragan tried his best to shake off the excess water from his cloak. From somewhere within the landing, Dragan noted the smell of sunflowers. It was good to know that even with the siege locking down the city, the small amenities – like the wafting of magically conjured pleasant smells – were still in working order.

"So you said there is a summit meeting?" the Necromangian asked.

"Indeed and if there was a time to add yourself to the collective, this is going to be it," Kynna said. "I have a friend on the inside who will vouch for me and I will vouch for you. That should keep their blades out of your back long enough to state your case. Of course, it will all depend on how well you sell yourself. I can guarantee your safety going in. Maybe not getting back out."

"Thank the pantheon there is no pressure," Dragan said. "Where is this meeting taking place?"

"I can get you there," Kynna said.

"Finally!" a new voice called from the shadows.

The smell of sunflowers wafted through again and from out of both the darkness and the light, a figure melted into existence. Unlike so many of the wizards in hiding, she had not eschewed her wizardly wardrobe. In the candlelight, the copper trim on her grass-green robes glinted and gleamed. Tall and strong, the young woman had blonde locks that spilled down her back. Her shoulders were rounded and her arms toned, putting her more at ease in a lineup with the professional soldiers manning the city walls as opposed to the spindly wizards roaming a library.

As she stepped into reality, the magician looked at the two sternly. "I have been waiting for you all to *finally* get your act together."

Kynna breathed a sigh of relief. "Mirage!"

Having spent too much time down with the citizens, Kynna ignored the wizardly protocols and threw her arms around Mirage Lu'Scion's neck. The wizarding superior accepted the breach of etiquette and returned the embrace.

"Do you know how hard it is prowling about the city, cloaked in invisibility, gathering information, and trying to avert calamity after calamity?" the magician asked as the two broke their embrace. "How are you?"

"This has not been easy," Kynna admitted.

"I can tell that based on your clothes alone. You bring a whole new description to the term 'slumming it.'"

"I had to hide somewhere when the curtain came down. The Northeast was the last place I thought they would look while still being tolerable."

Mirage nodded her agreement but then looked at the young lady critically. "What else?" she asked.

Kynna started to wave off the concerns but Mirage stepped closer. Kynna stiffened and knew better than to lie. "I've been hurting," she admitted. "Headaches. And not from reading too much or studying too hard. It is something different."

Mirage stepped close and placed her thumb between Kynna's eyebrows. She closed her eyes and reached out with a basic magic detection cantrip. "We will see what we can do to get you right," the magician promised. "But for now, we have a summit to crash."

Mirage reached into one of the pouches and proceeded to retrieve a glowing gemstone. She pointed in the direction of the stable of horseless carriages lining the far wall of the landing. She stopped and pivoted. "Wherever we are going, we weren't walking in the rain. Were we?"

"Well..." Kynna stammered.

Mirage rolled her eyes and moved towards the closest carriage; a surrey wagon with seating for four and a canopy top. There should have been harness struts and other equipment to hitch up horses but thanks to magical engineering, it would not be necessary.

Climbing into the front seat, Mirage placed the power gem in the metal receptacle positioned on the floorboard between her and the passenger side of the bench seats. The stone would power the telekinesis propulsion magic infused into the wagon itself. But then Mirage gave out a grumble.

"Problem?" Dragan asked as he climbed into the passenger seat.

"Those damn Mutaccios," she replied. "Always wanting to keep their special toys to themselves. I bet those big ugly wagons don't have locking mechanisms on them. But old Aldor likes to keep the fun things for himself. Mustachioed swine."

Sure enough, the shaft connecting the magic receptacle to the wheels underneath the carriage featured an ornate padlock fixed in place.

"I am guessing you don't have a key?" Kynna asked from the rear bench seat.

Mirage issued a scoffing exhale. In her left hand, the magician produced a rather short-shafted magic wand equipped with a spherical head. As she brought the wand to bear, on her right hand, an ornate titan metal ring inset with a variety of jewels flared with magical energy. With both the gemstones and the sphere glowing, Mirage closed her eyes. From the ring, light began to stack upon itself over and over until it formed a cylindrical shaft.

Placing the shaft inside the lock, Mirage used her extrasensory perception to feel out the specific configuration of the tumblers housed within. Through her mental command, the cylinder then expanded to fit the lock. A turn of her wrist was all it took. Extracting the cylinder, Mirage dispelled the magic. The key returned to nothingness.

Dragan looked at the mid-tier illusionist with a degree of respect. In many ways, the resourceful wizardess reminded him of Demina Summerstone. She was too far advanced to be considered an apprentice but not so old as to have become entangled in the quagmire that was the leadership echelon of her dynasty.

"That is impressive," Dragan said. "I've never seen anything like that. What is that magic—?"

"I call it 'hard light.' It is a... construction. It is similar to the same way my dynasty craft their illusions only these are physically tangible," the magician explained.

"Something new then?"

"We have been working on it in secret."

"Looking to climb the rungs of the ladder?"

"Except your kind destroyed the ladder," Mirage said as she began throwing the driving levers. The wagon's telekinesis magic began propelling the conveyance without the need for beasts of burden.

Following programmed magical commands, as the surrey approached the large gateway leading out to the city street, the landing's wooden gates were pushed open by invisible hands.

Mirage threw more levers and banked the surrey out onto the city street. The gates closed back behind them and the security dweomer sealed the wizard-owned building away from the common citizens who had no business using the floating sloops on their own.

The pelting rain felt like needles on their skin but the harsh storm also cleared the streets of pedestrians as the surrey rolled down the way. "This is not the least conspicuous mode of transportation," Dragan called out as the wind blew through his hair.

"Yeah but I don't see any of those boners keeping up if they try to give chase," Mirage said. "So where are we going?"

"Southwest corner," Kynna called from the back. "The Shaded Light ward."

"Oh, the garden spot of the district," Mirage said.

She cranked the lever forward and threw even more speed to the carriage as it sped away into the night.

Chapter 98

"Uncle."

"Niece."

"Sister."

"Brother…"

Mirawen Autumnlight, Graver Rathorrian, and Drennid Vocazion had walked into the central parlor on the main floor of the cadenta operated by the Shadow Blades.

Sario, Amman, and Arator Dawnborne were ill-informed of the volatile history between the two factions. Cavin Jurare had heard the story. But Valos, Sway, Thade, and Cinder all had deeply seared memories from their last encounter with the Vocazion mage.

The rogue wizard was happy to see her old friend in Mirawen. She was happy to see her uncle on her mother's side of the dynasty. But when Drennid joined the assembly, the Blades were quick to their feet.

Relaxed and comfortable, none of the Blades had thought to keep their weapons close at hand. Thankfully, Drennid did not brandish his wizardly instrument. Wet from the rain, the wizard took to removing his waterlogged cloak, causing the rogues to react with suspicion. The mage simply walked to the coat rack in the corner and hung up his soaked attire. He even glanced out of the side of his eye at the standing rogues and curled the side of his lip up in a closed-mouth grin. "I promise to keep my wand tucked away if you promise to do the same, sweet sister."

"The stones on you," Sway spat.

"She is right," Thade said. "You have a lot of nerve walking in here. Does anyone want to take the odds that he walks out?"

"Ladies… lords…" Drennid said with a long drawl. "I was told by your representative we are meeting under a banner of parlay. I can't be touched."

"That's the pirate code," Valos said. "It doesn't float here on land."

Drennid snapped his fingers at Mirawen. "Tell them, darling. Please. What is this bargain parlance that you touted?"

"A *sedere*," Mirawen replied.

"Parlay, a sit-down, a *sedere*, these all still fall under our code," Valos said. "But you aren't part of our code. And the last time we saw each other, you tried to burn us all alive."

"So what stops us from serving up your rotting corpse to the Necromangians?" Sway huffed. "Let them transform your body into one of those undead ghoulies running about."

Drennid folded his arms across his chest and looked down his nose – literally and figuratively – at the smaller Sway. "You could," he replied. "But I believe you have just answered your own question. I am here because of those Necromangians."

"If I may?" the older and calmer Grayson stepped forward and gestured for Drennid to take a seat in the high-backed upholstered chair in the salon's corner.

Drennid rolled his eyes and reluctantly did as he was bid. He sat in the corner and crossed his legs, putting an ankle up on his opposite knee. Graver turned to address the rogues, offering them a return to their seats. With similar reservations, the group sat but everyone looked more perched than sitting comfortably.

"So…" Graver began. "Earlier, you might have heard about the pair of wizards that escaped the city."

The crew all sat silently in response.

"Alright then. Tough room. So, earlier, a pair of wizards escaped the city. They powered their way through the northeastern half-gate. The two wizards were Arania Vocazion and a wizard masquerading as a master-at-arms serving as her bodyguard. But in truth, it was Tanaris Corvalonn."

Both Cinder and Cavin did their best to keep their reactions in check.

"That's the leader of the portal wizards, right?" Valos asked.

"Sorcerer, yes," Graver nodded in the affirmative. "They hid his inclusion because they didn't want Nalazar to catch wind of the plan. Corvalonn is trying to use his diplomatic skills to bring the armies of Arvaterra and Castratellus to bear against the city."

"Well, that is something," Cavin replied.

"But to get those wizards out, it resulted in the capture of Marius Vocazion."

Cinder blanched at Graver's statement. "The Ce'Mondere were impotent before the siege. The Lu'Scions have vanished. The Jurare are gone. The wizards don't have the resources to mount another assault. So we need to rally the people. We have some time. Not a lot but some. But when those armies start marching down the Blossom Fields and the Mercari Road, we need to be sowing chaos inside the city. I've heard about the attacks on the crime families – including yours. Neither one of our factions can do this on our own."

"So you want… an *alliance*?" Cinder asked.

"Ain't that a bitch?" Drennid replied with a light laugh.

Eyes shifted to the mage in the corner. Drennid recoiled into the back of his seat and placed a hand on his chest. "I was told that was an expression of yours down here. Did I not use it correctly?"

"Oh no, it's a bitch," Sway said. She then changed her accent to something more of a highfalutin flair and rolled r-sounds. "It is just r-r-r-rare to hear such uncouth r-r-r-ribaldry from a man of your stature, good sir." She then switched back to her cityside accent. "You frigger tosspot."

Graver looked back and forth between Drennid and the faction. "This tension between you all – no matter how warranted – what is happening out there is bigger than all of us. Once we have reclaimed the city and ousted this necromancer and his nightmare brigades, you all can go back to threatening each other all the live long day. But for now..."

"Handsome Jack is right," Valos said.

"Grayson," Rathorrian corrected.

"The Graver," Jurare added.

"People seriously call you that?" Sway asked. "I mean without laughing at you behind your back?"

"Oh, no one laughs at the Graver," Cavin replied. "He does some pretty unspeakable things for The Eight and they pay him handsomely for it."

"Well, some of my actions may not be acceptable to the common man," Graver said.

"But he is not funding a house of ill-repute trafficking young women in the flesh trade," Drennid laughed.

"Oh," Sway exclaimed. "Ain't no one here against their will. We took them off the streets. They are safe. And we take care of our girls a lot better than the pimpers they were with before."

"Yes, I am sure people are lining up to impart you with humanitarian awards," Drennid said with a scoff.

From the corner of the room, Amman rose to his feet and slammed his open palms together. "This does nothing for the cause," the shaman proclaimed. "There is obviously a long history between you all. But you do not see the other side fighting amongst themselves. The skeletons are not bickering with the ghouls and such. So all of you need to put this... this... *ma'ahara*—"

"Animosity," Sario added.

"You need to put this animosity behind you if you are to defeat this enemy," Amman continued. "The undead do not fight amongst themselves. We should not either."

"The Malinsuli is right," Graver said as he waved his hands with his fingers widespread. He then turned to face both Amman and Sario. *"Rang'mare kia koe."*

Sario smiled at his pronunciation and his attempt at an accent. "And peace to you," she repeated in reply using the trader's tongue.

"We need each other," Graver said to the group. "So, yes, I am proposing an alliance. We can bring magical power. Your group knows how to navigate the city without getting caught. If we partner together, perhaps we can cut off the head of the snake and in doing so, his undead army will fall."

Cinder turned to look at Cavin and also garnered the attention of Sario. "The magic from Ignaterra," she said. "The private vault and the magic it contained."

Cavin began to nod. "If magic is his only weapon and we neutralize his magic, the necromancer would be... *vulnerable*."

Sario smiled. "Looks like we are going back to my island after all."

Cinder turned back to the group. "We might have something to help fell the undead wizard but it would be helpful if we knew more of his inner workings."

At the front of the house, there was a forceful knock on the door. The crew turned as one.

"Coppers?" Sway asked.

"Coppers don't knock like that," Valos countered.

"Boners?" Amman posited.

"Something tells me they don't knock like that either."

Sway shrugged at Valos's comment. "Either way, we are going to need a new hideout when this is all said and done."

Mirawen held up a hand and an extended finger. "That *might* be one of mine. A little more magical backup to help us with our assassination plot. A Lu'Scion that got caught when the curtain came down."

The sound of rain poured into the room as Loredana Summerbrook opened the door and found three cloaked individuals on her porch steps.

Chapter 99

When the group of wizarding refugees approached the multistory building rising into the stormy night, it looked positively unassuming. Lost in the shadows and sparsely illuminated by the street lamps, when it was lit up by the occasional flash of lightning, the architecture did not stand out from the other buildings.

After cloaking their self-driving surrey with invisibility, the trio of Mirage Lu'Scion, Kynna Lu'Scion, and Dragan Duskwood made their way up the concrete steps forming the building's stoop. There were no welcoming lights. Running up her many stories, every window was dark. One might even doubt if a single soul resided within.

Yet, after Mirage's forceful knock, the door swung open on silent, well-oiled hinges. Inside was a completely different story. While the furnishings were not as ornate as something found in Sorceria or the estates within the Northwest District, it was clear that pride and care had been taken with the interior decoration of the social club.

With the furniture, the art on the walls, and an array of curtains, the owners had spun coppers into gold. It was both spacious and cozy. It had more than enough room yet also felt intimate. It felt exclusive and at the same time inviting.

The woman who welcomed them inside was a vision. Given the late-night hour, Kynna had half expected someone to answer in a dressing gown and a sleeping cap holding a candle in a shaky hand. Yet, this senior woman in her sixties – despite living in a city under siege and the hour – had her long, blonde hair freshly brushed, her maquillage was subtle but flattering, and even her dress was becoming.

The refined woman escorted them through the foyer, between the pair of curved staircases that led to the floors above, and then into the main parlor lit with mage-light. The illusionist was quick to spot spells of her dynasty, the flames offering soft, flickering, flattering light while producing no heat. Assembled in the parlor was an uncanny collection of individuals, most of which held various reactions to their arrival showcased in a variety of emotions.

But before Kynna could even process everything that was happening, everyone's attention was drawn to Drennid Vocazion. As an evocation mage, all knew the terrible bursts of magic the wizard could produce, so each one took it deadly seriously when he brought his wand to bear.

Having anticipated the reaction, Dragan Duskwood raised his hands, palms toward the mage. Using the same tone he often used to settle the students in his classroom back in his other life, Dragan spoke with commanding authority.

"Wait!"

Slowly and deliberately, Dragan parted his traveling cloak and produced his hidden magical instrument. The bone wand featured a carved handle and a long shaft that tapered down to a blunt point. Holding the wand perpendicular to Drennid, the Necromangian then swiveled the wand and presented its handle towards the mage.

The gesture gave Cinder, Cavin, Graver, and Drennid pause.

"What is going on?" Valos asked.

"He is one of *them*," Drennid hissed.

"One of them who?" Sway asked.

"I am a Necromangian," Dragan offered with a knowing nod and the smallest of sympathetic grins. "And young master Drennid Vocazion is afraid I have brought death to your doorstep. I appreciate your caution and your skepticism, lad. I truly do. This is not a ruse. This is not a ploy. I am here to join this... this... I am here to join your alliance."

"Mirage, Kynna," Drennid asked. "Is this true?"

"Yes, Drennid," Kynna said. "I will vouch for him."

With her words, amongst the group of thieves, the biggest of the four turned almost in shock. He was tall. He was far more muscular than any man had any business being. At first, he looked upon her like one imagined a hunter might. He stared at her as if he was looking down the length of a crossbow bolt. But then his visage changed. It was a look of recognition.

Whatever aura he was radiating, the far shorter woman with the ample curves noted it first. She turned and looked with curiosity. She could see the big man's pulse throbbing in his neck. His lower lip started to tremble and he subtly shook his head in disbelief as his mind continued to click the tumblers into place. Then slowly, the hunter's gaze started to melt away, replaced by an infinite softness mixed with both disbelief and hope.

As the two locked eyes, Kynna suddenly felt a wave ripple through her head. There was a stark stab of pain that receded quickly and was replaced by a sensation she could only describe as a release of pressure. It was as if for the first time in a decade, she smelled a far-too-familiar dish cooking on the stove, sparking ephemeral memories she could not scoop into her hands. The more she tried to cling to them, the more flittering they became. And yet, she was able to hold on to a single tangible thing. It was a name she knew but she had no idea why she knew it.

The young woman looked at the big man, struggling to wrap her mind around what was happening until she finally whispered – but knowing not why.

"Thade?"

Abandoning subtlety and decorum, Thade Skystone stormed forward. Even if the entire room had stood before him, there would not have been a single person, single army, or single titan that could have stopped him. He shoved chairs to the side and moved with more speed than a man of his size should have been capable. Approaching Kynna Lu'Scion, Thade wrapped the woman up in his massive arms and clutched Gwelin Skystone to his chest.

"Oh my gods, Gwelin," he panted unable to hold back his tears.

"Thade! I can't... I can't... What is this? What is happening?"

The room stood silent. Finally, Swayna Snowsong spoke. "Thade?"

The big man turned to his best friend with tears in his eyes and nodded. He managed to croak out his words. "It is," he gasped. "I don't know how but it is."

Sway addressed the group while crossing the distance. "She's his sister."

The rogue closed the gap and moved to share their embrace. Graver, Drennid, Cavin, and Cinder all shared knowing looks. More than any of them, Grayson Rathorrian understood the significance of what was occurring. He turned to the group. "Family reunion."

"I certainly don't mean to undercut the moment," Drennid Vocazion said, "but let's not sweep the fact under the rug that the infamous hand of Nalazar Catabaysi is standing before us."

"If he is of your enemy..." Amman began.

"Our enemy," Sario corrected.

"If he is of our enemy," the shaman said, "it seems foolish he would so easily surrender his wizard wand and leave himself vulnerable to us."

"How about it, Gentleman Wiz?" Valos said. "You playing a long con or are you legit here to toss in?"

Dragan Duskwood looked at the bone wand he clutched in his hand. "I practice necromancy. I practice it with the same love and passion Drennid practices his evocation and Mirage practices her illusions. I love my art. I feel like it is misunderstood and it was outlawed out of fear and... probably a touch of jealousy. But I still love my art. I will never renounce it.

"Lord Master Nalazar has corrupted this art. Either that or the art has corrupted him because he dug into depths he never should have. Regardless, he has taken something beautiful and perverted it. So, Lord Master Nalazar has to be destroyed. I helped create him so I am duty-bound to help end him. Unfortunately, I cannot do it on my own. These clandestine families cannot do it on their own. And neither can the wizarding dynasties. But together, united, allied, and working towards a singular goal... we might stand a chance."

"And what happens after?" Cinder asked.

Dragan offered a smile. "I like your optimism, young lady. But that is assuming we even make it to 'after.' What I do know is if Nalazar is not stopped, he will turn all of Incanterra into a city of the dead. He will not be satisfied there. Once he consumes the city, he will march across the face of the free kingdoms, adding to his eternal army. So we have to stop him... together."

In the parlor of a cadenta – a house of wanton carnality – a collection of a dozen individuals aligned with criminal organizations, wizardly dynasties, assassin guilds, undead slaying forces, elementalist brotherhoods, and even representatives of the common civilians all stood looking at one another.

Valos gave a grin. "We might not be diverse enough," the rogue said. "If we could wait a little bit, I could get this copper I know just to round out the group. Knock some corners off the edges. But I don't know any of those military types that used to man the walls. Jurare, your dynasty is chummy with that group. Got anyone you can call? Just so we can be all-inclusive."

Standing in front of the illusory flames in the fireplace, Cinder Fireborne folded her arms across her chest as she contemplated the path forward. She nodded and took a deep breath.

"So..." she said. "An alliance."

Chapter 100

Despite the late hour, the collection of individuals sat around the large dining table. Certain reserves of both food and beverage had been called up to feed the group as they contemplated their plans.

Direct assaults, skulking subterfuge, recruitments, overwhelming tactics... all possibilities were thrown about, batted back and forth, discussed, argued, debated, and rehashed. Somewhere amidst it all, Cinder Fireborne took a moment and excused herself from the strategy session.

Absent from the discussion – albeit acceptably so – was the brother and sister of Thade and Gwelin Skystone. There were so many questions to ask. There was so much time to make up for. It was understandable the duo might not have offered the most enlightened of contributions to the plan as the group tried to move forward and hammer out their strategies.

Cinder left the reunited duo to their isolation. She wandered into the main parlor and found herself gazing into the illusory flames within the fireplace. She did not snap from her reverie until she heard the rattle of ice.

Valos Ironblade stood beside her, the last splashes of a brown-tinted spirit sloshing in his glass. He shared her view of the magical fire and basked in the heat that was not there.

From out of the strategy session in the dining hall, Swayna Snowsong entered the parlor. She walked over to the duo. One glance between the three was all that was needed.

From the gloom of the rear parlor, Thade Skystone emerged and made his way over to the fireplace where the trio stood to become a foursome. Valos looked at all of them, gave a nod, and then turned to look back into the illusory fire as he was unable to look them in the eye.

"It is a curious thing," the rogue began. "Growing up in the Northeast. It wasn't the worst. My mother... She did her best to raise me on her own. Dad would come by now and again to check on us. Check on her. And me too I guess. I often thought it was less about checking on us. I think he had more than a few ladies stashed around the city. And if one was being uppity or they were having a spat, he could always count on my mother to be nice. She'd throw him a tussle. Make him happy. Maybe squeeze a little more coin out of 'em. I don't fault him. He was married to the life. And the life comes first. Even above your other family."

Valos took the smallest sip of his spirit and continued to stare at the magical flames. "I suppose after that my mother was pretty bow-shy about having more children. Can't blame her either. So I never had a brother or a sister. Had the uncles. Had the aunts. More than a few cousins but most of them were idiots. If we were picking teams, they would be at the bottom of the pecking order.

"It wasn't like my father came along, threw his arm around my shoulder, and sat me down. 'Alright now son, this is how the Shadow Blades work.' He was a soldier at most. Never a captain. He was a low rung on the ladder. But growing up in the neighborhood, you hear things. And people know you. So... I *might* have traded on his name to get an introduction. And I get in with Thorn Sorrowsword. He was just a captain back then. I think he saw something in me. Ambition or whatnot. I was hungry. I always wanted to be better than my old man. More elevated. I wanted to make more coins. Chip on my shoulder. Whatever."

Valos clucked his tongue and gave a little wince as he thought back to a painful memory. The trio stood silently, letting him find his way. "My first run... before I got pinched and went up to do my stretch? It was nothing like what we had. Have. Nothing. I was content to be on my own. I didn't want to rely on *anyone*. I'd been disappointed by my old man over and over. So I said, 'Nope. Never again.' Of course, then my seraph came into the picture. Wedged her way into my heart."

"I remember you talking about her on the *Castella Mare*..." Cinder said softly.

"Yeah. That one... that one hurt. But before all that, I was still wolfing it. And I get pinched for the hooch. I'm doing my stretch. Thorn comes up to visit me in the 'Gate. Gives me the bad news about her. He knew about my lone wolf streak. And I think he knew that if I devolved, I would've ended up dead. And he just asked me, point blank, 'How has that worked out for you?' He made me rethink things. The locked-up life became easier after that. Easier doesn't always mean easy though. The hole left by my seraph... so I just decided to wall it all off again."

Valos stopped, paused, and smiled at a memory.

"After my stretch, Thorn shows up at the 'Gate and he's got a proposition for me. He's got a new place in the family. He wants me to be a part of it. I can't say why but I felt like this was a real chance to elevate. So I say, sure. And the next thing I know, the three of you, me, and shark bait are taking a ride on a ship out into the ocean."

Valos turned and looked through the archway into the dining parlor beyond where the unique collection of new allies had assembled and was hashing out the strategy.

"Some families you get born into. We've got no choice in that. You have your assets, your associates, and your allies. Those are all well and good. But your friends? They are a whole different level of family.

"Friends are the family you choose. And this family... this group... this chosen blood, I love you all. With all my heart, I love you all. And after everything that happened with my seraph, I never thought I would come to say that again."

With the lightest and softest of shifts, Cinder reached out and ran her hand between Valos's shoulder blades. The rogue took a deep breath in through his nostrils and exhaled through his mouth.

"We were just getting started. Things were going good. We were on the right path. The money was set to flow. And then these tosspots come along and upend *everything*."

Valos turned and looked Cinder hard in her eyes. She gave him a silent nod of recognition.

"I love all of you," he said. "I am sorry if I have not said that enough or not been vocal enough with my feelings. But I love all of you. I love what we do. I love our lives together. And I am *furious* over what this city – our city – has become." Valos's voice deepened and a gravity infected his tone. "I want my city back."

Sway nodded her agreement. "I want my city back."

Thade grimaced and ground the knuckles of his right hand into his left palm. "I want my city back."

Cinder Fireborne looked at the chosen blood and spoke with a determination that would not be denied.

"Then we take it back."

The Shadow Blades Will Return.

The Shadow Blades
The Incanterran War

COMING IN 2024

Appendix

Crime Families of Incanterra

The Crown: The Crown is the criminal organization that controls illegal activities in the wealthy Northwest District of Incanterra. They quietly cater to the outlawed vices of their upscale clientele where discretion is paramount. Of all the crime families, theirs is the one most hidden. Exposure within such an upscale district could prompt scrutiny from powerful and influential forces. The number of members is the smallest of all the criminal families but they generate incredible income. The Crown is led by Sondossa Warcrown.

The Shadow Blades: Founded in 1679 by Varazze "The Wraith" Darksteel, the Darksteel bloodline has ruled the criminal family. Operating in the "common man's" district of Incanterra, the Blades currently control two-thirds of the Northeast District. In 1754, Celesta Darksteel attempted to take the mantle of leadership but she was challenged by the family's *infracaput*, Spyritus Swiftwind. Losing in combat with Celesta, Spyritus relinquished his claim to the title. The *infracaput* left the family and one-third of the Blades left with him. The heads of the other three families decreed the Northeast District would be divided rather than allowing things to escalate to open war.

The Crimson Way: In the summer of 1754, Spyritus Swiftwind left his position in the Shadow Blades to start his own family. During his departure, one-third of the Blades went with the former *infracaput*. Swiftwind and his crew were granted one-third of the Northeast District that they control today. The two families have maintained a tentative truce for the last two years.

The Diamond Order: The Southwest District is often labeled the "working man's" district, dominated by harbor docks, warehouses, and people who work for a living. The Diamond Order crime family reflects that attitude. Their caskers serve stout drinks and malty beer. They know the value of a woman's embrace and the joy of gambling. It is these outlawed rights that the Order gives back to the people. The Diamond Order is led by Talamezzo Hardstone.

The Skull Duggers: The Skull Duggers are the latest in a long line of crime families to control the Southwest District. The least affluent of all the districts, the poorer wards do not stand on tradition and family heritage. Strength and violence command the ward. Challengers to the throne have to be fended off with strength. Malath Armorworn and the Skull Duggers have kept the district in line through their brutal tactics but peace has resulted in the last few years.

<u>Wizarding Families of Incanterra</u>

Baelannor: (*Bail-uh-norr*) The highest-ranking wizard dynasty of Sorceria. They practice conjuration magic – summoning essence from nothingness. Their leader is Asaric Baelannor.

Corvalonn: (*Core-vuh-lon*) The second-ranked wizard dynasty of Sorceria. The sorcerors practice dimensionation magic, opening portals. Their leaders are Tanairs and Lilura Corvalonn.

Mutaccio: (*Moo-tay-see-oh*) The third-ranked wizard dynasty of Sorceria. The alchemists practice transmutation – changing properties – and brew potions. Their leaders are Aldor and Acelendra Mutaccio.

Ce'Mondere: (*See Mon-dee-airy*) The disputed fourth-ranked wizard dynasty of Sorceria. The warlocks practice convocation – the summoning of demonic minions. After the murder of Matron Qaava, the house is leaderless.

Vocazion: (*Voh-kay-zee-in*) The disputed fifth-ranked wizard dynasty of Sorceria. The mages practice evocation – the creation of burst energy like fire and lightning. Their leaders are Marius and Arania Vocazion.

Jurare: (*Zhoo-rare*) The sixth-ranked wizard dynasty of Sorceria. The wardens practice abjuration – defensive and shielding magic. Their leaders are Canarr and Jillayna Jurare.

Dinacioun: (*Din-ay-see-ohn*) The seventh-ranked wizard dynasty of Sorceria. The magi practice divination – using magic to acquire information. After the murder of Patron Gaviel by Nalazar Catabaysi, Matron Clarion Dinacioun is the current steward.

Lu'Scion: (*Lew-Sigh-on*) The eighth-ranked wizard dynasty of Sorceria. The magicians practice illusions, phantasms, and magic that confounds the mind. Their leaders are Kerryn and Mirare Lu'Scion.

Lesser Factions of Incanterra

Knights of the Imperial Circle: A former military arm that served as enforcers of wizarding doctrine in Incanterra. They are known for their white vestments, alabaster masks, and conical hoods.

The Necromangians: A secret cabal of underground wizards who practice the forbidden magic of necromancy. They keep their wizarding talents secret by masquerading as ordinary Incanterran citizens.

The Silent: A covert squad of warriors that operate out of the *domici dauthis*. Their mission is to destroy any undead that has escaped the scythe of Zaneger. Some agents are acolytes of the death god. Others are nondenominational.

The Unbound: A grassroots, unstructured political protest group that opposes magical forces within Incanterra. They believe magic is a perversion of nature and should be forbidden.

The Pantheon

Tadorin: (*Tah-door-in*) The All-Father. Ruler, protector, and father of all things. Master of the Nas Legions. Husband of Aurorien. Brother of Tu'Dagoth. Father of Niverana.

Aurorien: (*Uh-roar-ee-in*) The Mother. Lady of nature, weather. Wife of Tadorin. Mother of Niverana and Zaneger.

Tu'Dagoth: (*Too-day-goth*) The Dark Destroyer. He who would undo. Master of the infernal and controller of the demonic. Brother of Tadorin. Father of Zaneger.

Niverana: (*Niv-err-ah-na*) Giver of Life. The patron of life and its creation. Daughter of Tadorin and Aurorien. Sister of Zaneger.

Zaneger: (*Zah-nay-gur*) The Taker of Life. The patron of death and life's ending. Son of Aurorien and Tu'Dagoth. Brother of Niverana.

Atlas of the Free Kingdoms

Agavinsula: (*Uh-GAH-vin-soo-luh*) The island of fire. An archipelago located east of Selvaterra in the Grand Gulf, the island features a desert climate with unique flora, peppers, and spices that are only found within the island chain.

Arvaterra: (*AHRR-vuh-tehr-uh*) The land of fields. The easternmost isle within the free realms, located south of Monterra and east of Incanterra. Arvaterra has the largest livable land mass and biggest population in the alliance of realms. It is known for its farmland, standing army, and powerful navy.

Castratellus: (*Cast-ruh-tell-us*) The land of the fortress. A landlocked kingdom west of Incanterra and east of Ombraterra. It is known for its impenetrable defenses and the priests' mastery of solar and lunar magical practices.

Ignaterra: (*Igg-nuh-tehr-uh*) The land of lava. A vast wasteland that dominates the southern landmass. It was made uninhabitable as a result of the Great Dragon War. No organized society lives in the former kingdom.

Incanterra: (*In-CAN-tehr-uh*) The land of magic. Positioned between Arvaterra and Castratellus with a southern border on the Great Gulf. Founded after the Great Dragon Wars, it is the home to eight wizarding dynasties.

Malinsula: (*Mah-lynn-soo-luh*) The island of the shark. The southernmost isle within the free realms. Her natives are known for their bronze skin and white hair. They worship the sea powers.

Mnama'tellus: (*Nah-ma-tell-us*) The land of beasts. A landlocked kingdom in the southern landmass positioned west of Ignaterra and south of Selvaterra. Bisected by the planet's equator, it is known for its massive thunder lizards.

Monterra: (*MON-tehr-uh*) The land of mountains. The northernmost kingdom amongst the alliance of realms. The northern part of the kingdom resides within the planet's Arctic Circle. It is known for its timber and mineral resources.

Ombraterra: (*Ohm-bruh-tehr-uh*) The land of shadows. The westernmost kingdom amongst the alliance of realms. The kingdom lies in the shadows of the tallest mountains. It is known for its cuisine, marble, and idyllic coastline.

Selvaterra: (*Sell-vuh-tehr-uh*) The land of jungles. The kingdom forms the western edge of the Great Gulf and bridges the northern and southern realms. It is known for its dense jungles, tropical foliage, and tall western mountains.

The Shadow Blades Family

Celesta Darksteel: Leader of the Shadow Blades. Celesta Varazzia Darksteel is the *caput famiglia*. She is the daughter of Varazzen Darksteel and the granddaughter of Varazze "The Wraith" Darksteel – the founder of the family.

Armand: An Ombraterran sage, Armand is the *consiliarus* to the *caput*. He is her wartime counsel.

Thorn Sorrowsword: Sorrowsword is the family's *infracaput*. He is the second-in-command of the family and manages day-to-day operations.

Kivale Sundawn: The family's adjudicator.

Ithisar Highwall: The manager of finances.

Elren Stoutbrew: House doctor for the family.

Temper Honorsworn: Weapons master of the family.

Kedigo Mournsword: Bodyguard of the *Caput Famiglia*.

Captains of the Shadow Blades
Vinson Blackshield: Blackshield oversees the Nestorian Heights ward.
Turiano Emberwood: Emberwood oversees the Deckshire ward.
Galaris "Gamble" Hallowhall: Hallowhall oversees Reiner Park, Nestorian Heights, and Shaded Light wards.
Lavinia Loneriver: Loneriver oversees the Shalan ward.
Surrano Netherdream: Netherdream oversees the High Stable ward.
Cozen Sunfall: Sunfall oversees the Stonelyn ward.
Alviero Thunderman: Thunderman oversees the Tower Hold ward.

Soldiers Serving Under Gamble Hallowhall:
- Valos Ironblade
- Swayna Snowsong
- Thade Skystone
- Cinder Fireborne

About the Author

Ryan Foley was born in Toms River, New Jersey in 1974 to Phil and Diane Foley. The family moved to Adair, Oklahoma when Ryan was in his teens. He considers the small, rural town his home. He attended Adair High School and nearby Rogers State University, where a love of graphic novels, comic books, fantasy novels, and role-playing games fueled his passion for storytelling.

Previously published with works at Image Comics, MVCreations, Arcana Comics, Yali Dream Creations, and Campfire Graphic Novels, *The Shadow Blades* was Ryan's first published prose novel. *The Unbound Curse* and *The Chosen Blood* are his proud sequels.

Ryan cites the works of R.A. Salvatore and Stan Lee as his greatest influences. He still resides in Adair with his three children, Alex, Jason, and Lauren, whom he loves very deeply and credits as motivation for him to chase his creative dreams.

Other Works by the Author

The Shadow Blades (2021)
The Shadow Blades: The Unbound Curse (2022)
The Shadow Blades: The Chosen Blood (2023)

Clown Zero (2022)

Published by Image Comics
Masters of the Universe: Vol. 3, Issue #8

Published by Campfire Graphic Novels
Stolen Hearts: The Love of Eros & Psyche
Legend: The Labours of Heracles
Zeus & The Rise of the Olympians
Perseus: Destiny's Call

Published by Arcana Comics
Dragon's Lair
Space Ace
The Praetorian
Midnight to Daylight

Acknowledgments

The Shadow Blades took me seven years of research, developing, writing, and editing to put together. If you will indulge a metaphor, I couldn't just serve you a meal. I had to build the home and the kitchen, construct the table, make the plates, forge the silverware, and cook the food before I could serve you up a story. So, it made complete sense to cook another meal because I could reuse the house, the cookware, and the cutlery.

Thankfully, *The Unbound Curse* came together a lot faster.

Now, the same can be said for *The Chosen Blood*.

The Shadow Blades set the table. *The Unbound Curse* and *The Chosen Blood* are the first and second novels in the Necromangian trilogy. If you are reading this, it makes your third helping of what I am serving. So, I must be doing something right.

I've said it before but I will say it again. In a metaphysical sense, this book doesn't exist... until you read it. Valos, Sway, Thade, and Cinder have to wait for you to bring them to life in your imagination. So, I want to use this space to thank you, the reader. There are all sorts of intellectual properties vying for your attention and you have sat down and let me tell you three different tales! You have now had three sittings in my little magical world of Incanterra with my band of loveable misfit thieves and snooty wizards. For you to take the time to absorb all this hard work means more to me than you will ever know.

Most importantly, I hope you enjoyed it! I hope you loved the characters, the story, and the realm as much as I loved creating it. A third act – the conclusion of the Necromangian trilogy – is being developed. I promise. I have found the best advertisement is a word of recommendation from you. So, if you did enjoy this, tell a friend or post a review.

This book doesn't exist without you. So, thank you, dear reader, for bringing my creations to life with your imagination. You're the best. As the Blades would say, "Whatever you need."

Copyright